# FATE OF THE LOST

## BOOK 3 OF THE CHOSEN OF THE SPEARS

SANAN KOLVA

*To Temple, for many afternoons pretending to be X-Men or TMNT, for letting me drag you along to watch Star Trek TNG, for playing that terrible RPG I created in high school (yeah, it was bad), and for all the encouragement and inspiration. You might not have managed the mutant turtle (yet), and got a few years past teenage, but you are the awesome ninja cousin.*

1

———

KITHR

*"For all you have done to further my release, Spearbearer, I give you the gift of knowledge… and the curse of despair."*

K ithr cast a look at his companion, trying to read Lyan's face for any clue as to his silence. The closer they drew to home, the more withdrawn Lyan became. His silence had grown pronounced since they entered Eilidh Wood late the previous day. Kithr was accustomed to quiet, and usually welcomed it, but to ride for this long beside Lyan without so much as a comment on the sky or forest from his friend grew unsettling.

"What's wrong, Lyan?" Kithr finally asked, breaking the silence when Lyan did not.

Lyan gave no indication of surprise when he answered. "Nothing."

"Horse turds. You've said barely two sentences all morning. We rode past three of your favorite stargazing spots on this end of the forest, and you didn't say a word. You haven't looked at the sky since last night, and just a glance then. What's wrong?"

A thin smile touched Lyan's mouth, but didn't reach his eyes. "How many seasons have you been telling me to pull my head out of the clouds and watch my feet? And now you're worried because I've finally done so?"

Kithr fumbled for an answer, but couldn't put his unease into words. He'd always been one for action rather than talk, and Lyan made his worry sound foolish. "I just… It feels like you're hiding something. Something you saw, or something that happened."

"How could I hide something I saw, when the things I see are the signs written in the stars for anyone to read?" Lyan countered.

*Because you're the one who knows how to read the stars. I'm no astrologer. All I see are glittering lights. I don't know what they mean.* "All right…," Kithr said aloud. "Then what does my fortune say?"

Lyan did tilt his head back and look to the sky, brushing loose locks of red hair from his face. "You'll have to wait until night to know. I can't see the stars during the day."

Kithr couldn't shake the sense that the clear sky overhead relieved Lyan. As if, for the first time in his life, Lyan didn't *want* to see the stars. As if, with the clearing of the clouds that had obscured the night sky for so many moons, Lyan's love of stargazing had been stripped from him.

"Tonight, then. I'll hold you to that."

"Why the sudden interest, Kithr?" Lyan asked. "You've shown little concern for your fortune before."

Kithr gave the first excuse he could think of. "If I'm going to be taking any more unexpected trips trying to watch a friend's back, I'd like a little warning." Warning Lyan had *not* given him before. Although, if Kithr was being honest, Lyan hadn't exactly invited him along.

Lyan gave him another thin smile. "Any trips you take in the near future will be ones you plan first."

"So you *do* know something of my fortune without looking at the stars."

"I know *you*, Kithr, stars or not."

*Are you telling me that something is going to happen that will make me plan to leave Heartshrine Village again? What could possibly make me want to do that?*

Lyan drew his black stallion, Shadowstar, to a stop and combed his fingers through the horse's dark brown mane. "Kithr, when you returned to Eilidh Wood after the war, did you ever feel like everything had changed?"

That, finally, gave him some idea about what troubled Lyan, even if the comparison stirred up unpleasant memories. "Yes. But Eilidh Wood hadn't changed. I had." Kithr looked at Lyan.

At a glance, his friend looked little different than he had when he left Eilidh Wood in the company of Cailean and the Tathren lord's followers. Lyan's red hair hung in a short tail. He might be a little more lean and toned than when he left. No obvious scars. And yet, anyone who knew Lyan would see something had changed. The way he held himself. The shadows in his gaze.

And, of course, the Spear.

Lyan shifted under Kithr's scrutiny, and his hand moved to rest on Equinox. The only visible memento Lyan carried of their travels was strapped onto Shadowstar's saddle, though Lyan sometimes wore it at his back: a spear taller than Lyan. At a glance, it appeared to be a beautiful, deadly weapon forged of a silvery metal and etched with runes inlaid with gold. Even the wicked barbs on the spearhead added to its beauty rather than detracting.

The sight of Equinox, one of the two Spears of the Stars, legendary weapons powerful enough to defeat gods with the right wielder, being borne by Lyan, astrologer of Heartshrine Village, never failed to jolt Kithr. Not that Lyan hadn't earned the right to bear it—he had. But for so long, Kithr had unconsciously thought his friend weak for his love of stargazing and avoidance of battle, and he knew Lyan had been more aware, and more bothered, by the dismissal of his skills than he'd let anyone know.

*But he faced the Spear's Trials and earned the right to carry Equinox. I know he can use its powers, but even I'm still uncomfortable seeing him with the Spear of the Stars. Is that what's bothering Lyan? Is he thinking about the reception he'll get in our village when others learn that he bears one of the most powerful weapons known to us? The Spear is a burden he chose, but he didn't leave home planning to become Spearbearer. And he can't just give it up again now that we've stopped the Mad God's minions in Tather. Equinox is his for the rest of his life.*

Lyan turned Shadowstar off the main road and onto the narrow trail to Heartshrine Village. Kithr followed. No one challenged them, but Kithr heard whispers of movement as someone slipped away ahead of them to tell the village of their return. The elves who served as sentries were skilled in stealth, much as Kithr himself was, and he heard the watcher only because he knew what to listen for.

When they reached the shrine, Kithr untensed. *Home.* Five stones, each taller than an elf, stood in a half-circle around a low, flat altar. Intricate images of Soldarr, Feyra, and Tesseia, the three gods worshiped by the elves of Eilidh Wood, were inscribed into the stones. This shrine was older than the village itself—Heartshrine Village had taken its name from the presence of this shrine.

Both Kithr and Lyan dismounted and knelt. Stiff muscles protested as Kithr bowed his head and prayed. *Thank you for guiding us on this journey, and for protecting us.* Kithr paused. *And… thank you for everything we encountered on this journey, and for opening my eyes and showing me that I was Lost, and for guiding me back onto the path an elf of Eilidh Wood should follow. Thank you even for the Tathrens.*

A few months ago, Kithr would have scoffed at anyone who said he would be grateful for Tathrens. Only sixty years ago, Kithr answered the call to war against the human nation of Tather, as had most young men of his generation. The elves of Eilidh Wood invaded Tather, seeking to claim Solstice, the second Spear of the Stars. Though they failed to capture Solstice, the war had left deep scars on both lands, and on those who fought. Most humans who'd fought were dead or old men, but for the elves, it remained a fresh memory. Kithr had held to his hate of them, nursing his grievances like old, familiar companions. If he allowed himself, he could readily summon the litany of sins he'd laid at Tathren feet, foremost among them his father's death. Kithr cut the thought short before he followed it further.

Though only a few years separated Lyan and Kithr, Lyan was not called to war, too important to Heartshrine Village as the astrologer's sole apprentice. He never fought and killed Tathrens, never saw the war directly. And when a chance encounter with a group of Tathrens introduced Lyan to Cailean Dev'gilla, Lyan had been fascinated.

*No,* Kithr amended. *That's not fair to Lyan. He was eluding a pooka, fell into a ravine, sprained his ankle, and was rescued by the Tathrens. Inviting them to our village was the hospitable thing to do. The fact that he then left the village again with them... that was motivated by responsibility, not curiosity, no matter what I thought at the time. But thank the gods I did not know back then that Cailean bore Solstice. Whether or not I would have succeeded, I know I would have tried to kill him.*

Kithr waited for Lyan. His friend remained still and silent, head bowed, for so long that Kithr wondered if he'd dozed off. Just as Kithr was considering shaking his shoulder to rouse him, Lyan stood.

"I'm ready."

Kithr rose and dusted off his pants—not that dirt showed on his brown clothing. "We're almost home."

"Yes. Almost there." Lyan climbed into Shadowstar's saddle.

Kithr heard strained notes in Lyan's voice and hesitated. The way Lyan spoke, it sounded like a man preparing to say his final farewells. "Lyan…"

"We shouldn't keep the Elder waiting." Lyan didn't look at him, gaze instead fixed ahead, though Heartshrine Village couldn't be seen through the trees yet.

"Ash and rot Lyan, what is it? Do you not want to go back? Is something happening at home that you don't want to deal with?" Kithr struggled for words. "We don't have to return if you're not ready. Is there something else, some other place we should be?"

Lyan sighed. "You're kind to ask, Kithr. But I know you want to be home, and I'm not going to take that from you. It wouldn't make a difference, here or somewhere else. So we might as well go where one of us wants to be."

"Where do *you* want to be, Lyan?"

"I don't know." Lyan still didn't turn to face him. "The Elder is waiting for us."

"Why in Soldarr's name won't you tell me what is *wrong*, Lyan?" Kithr burst in frustration.

Lyan's whispered answer was almost too soft to hear. "Because it won't help."

Kithr opened his mouth, then closed it again. He didn't know if Lyan meant him to hear that, but suspected not. He swung into the saddle and urged his horse after Shadowstar.

The horses rounded the last turn, and weight lifted from Kithr's spirit. The stiffness in his spine eased. He drew a slow, deep breath. *Home.* The sense had been growing since they entered Eilidh Wood, and now, finally seeing his village again, his worries seemed distant and unfounded. *We're home.*

Elves gathered in the village common and ran toward them. "Lyan! You've returned! Where have you been?"

Kithr smiled wryly. A few people called out greetings and welcomes to him, but he knew Lyan's absence had been noticed long before his own.

*I've been lost to our people even though I came back from the war, and I didn't see it. Much as I hate to think it, I owe that Tathren lord Cailean Dev'gilla for making me see the truth.*

Lyan smiled and laughed—a sharp contrast from his foreboding air not so long ago—but didn't answer the question as he slid from Shadowstar's back and let himself be enveloped in jubilant hugs. Kithr couldn't convince himself to trust that light-hearted voice as Lyan greeted everyone, but at the same time, it was difficult to focus on his fears. For the first time in far too long, he was *home*. Eilidh Wood surrounded him, the spirit of the forest greeting its missing children. He drew a deep breath, smelling the familiar, welcome scents of fresh apple bread wafting from more than one house.

Kithr dismounted and scratched his horse's ears, then turned the animal over to one of the village youth. He trusted that his bags would reach his door and the horse would receive proper care. Shadowstar stayed close to Lyan, but the stallion stepped aside to allow a pack of children to run up and grab Lyan's legs, tugging to get his attention.

"Lyan! Lyan! Tell us a story!" Their voices rose in a chorus around him, and Kithr chuckled softly.

His amusement faltered when he looked at Lyan, and saw his friend's expression tighten—a forced smile as Lyan shooed them back. "Not right now. Maybe later."

"But where have you *been*, Lyan? You have to tell us!" protested one boy.

Lyan only shook his head. "Not yet." He slipped closer to Shadowstar, and finally pulled Equinox from the saddle. Kithr waited for the questions he knew would come, waited for the first person to ask where Lyan had gotten such a weapon. Yet the question never came. Kithr watched eyes slide over Equinox without settling on it, as if they didn't see or didn't notice the Spear in Lyan's hand.

*What are you doing, Lyan? Why?*

Tearing his thoughts from the unsettling questions, Kithr gazed around the village, seeing it with fresh eyes. Houses stood in the shadows of ancient trees, sheltered and shaded by the spreading branches. Kithr found his own home waiting for his return. At least his absence had been noticed *somewhere* in the village. Suddenly wanting nothing more than to be in his house with his feet up, he moved toward it.

Lyan seized his arm, stopping him. Kithr gave him a startled look, feeling tension in Lyan's tight grip. He followed his friend's gaze. The crowd parted, and Elder Brenhan walked toward them.

The elder still stood tall and healthy, despite the six centuries he carried. His silver hair was cut short, and green stains on his robe said he'd been among plants recently. Elder Brenhan's keen brown eyes studied Lyan sharply. Lyan stiffened slightly, standing straighter and meeting the elder's gaze.

"Welcome home, Lyan. Your absence caused much distress among us," Elder Brenhan said.

Lyan bowed, releasing Kithr's arm. "With the stars hidden behind the clouds every night, my presence was an unnecessary burden on our village, Elder. I did tell you that I would guide Cailean and his men."

*But the implication when you said it was that you would see them to the edge of Eilidh Wood, not go with them.*

Elder Brenhan's eyes narrowed, but his tone didn't change. "I trust that the Tathrens have returned to their own land?"

"Yes, Elder."

"And good riddance," Kithr muttered.

Elder Brenhan looked at him as if he hadn't noticed

Kithr's presence before. His lips curled in a smile at Kithr's words, but he said, mildly chastising, "We are at war with them no longer, Kithr."

"I know, Elder," he said. *I don't even know why I said that. Habit?*

Elder Brenhan just nodded and looked at Lyan again. Kithr was left feeling out of place, as if even the Elder hadn't noticed his absence. But that sense was relieved when Elder Brenhan spoke. "Tomorrow, once you both have rested from your journey, I would hear the tale of what drove you from Eilidh Wood and into this long absence. Tonight, however, we celebrate your return!"

Villagers cheered enthusiastically, and Kithr grinned. Elder Brenhan smiled, pleased with the response. Lyan, too, smiled, but the tension in his shoulders stood at odds with his expression.

"We're honored," Lyan said.

The Elder made a shooing motion. "Go, wash away the dust of your journey."

Lyan and Kithr both bowed. The crowd allowed them through, people dispersing back to their own homes to prepare for the celebration. Some preparations had undoubtedly already begun. Eilidh Wood had ways of letting its inhabitants know when their own had returned. While the two of them had been surrounded by the rest of the villagers, someone had tended the horses and taken the saddlebags to the proper doorsteps. Shadowstar nuzzled Lyan's hair, then trotted toward the path out of the village. Kithr's horse followed him.

"Take care, Shadowstar," Lyan said softly, raising one hand in a brief farewell.

Kithr made for his house. A bundle of fresh basil and thyme hung from the handle. As he untied it, Kithr realized that Lyan had followed him rather than turning to his own.

Picking up his bags from the doorstep, Kithr turned to Lyan. "You want to come in?"

Lyan silently accepted the invitation. Kithr shut the door after him, dropped his bags on the floor, and looked around self-consciously. He crushed the bundle of herbs in his hand, releasing the fragrance of the herbs to chase away the musty odor of absence. Weapons hung on his walls, many of them Tathren in origin—the less grisly of the trophies he'd brought home from the war.

Lyan gave them no mind, looking intently at Kithr. He started to say something, paused, then spoke. "Kithr, tonight, please don't say anything about where we went or why. If anyone presses, tell them it isn't right to tell the story before the Elder hears it."

"As much attention as anyone gave me when we arrived, I'll be surprised if they even think to ask me," Kithr said with a slight laugh that hid stung feelings.

Lyan didn't smile, only looked worried. "Please, don't look for attention, Kithr. Not right now. I can't explain. Please don't ask me."

A chill ran down his spine. *Something is wrong. Something is very, very wrong.* Kithr looked into Lyan's anxious eyes. "If I do as you ask, will you read my fortune tonight?"

"I said I would."

"Then I'll do as you've asked."

Lyan closed his eyes a moment and nodded, his shoulders slumping in relief. "Thank you, Kithr." He turned to leave, but Kithr caught his arm, stopping him.

"Lyan, I need to ask you something."

Lyan took a deep breath, then turned back to face Kithr. "What is it?"

"I'm not going to ask why, just, will you tell me, yes or no, are you using Equinox to direct attention away from the Spear... and away from me?"

Lyan bit his lip, then quickly, silently, nodded.

"All right. I'll trust that you have a good reason for doing so, and that sometime, you'll explain it to me."

"You'll understand," Lyan answered quietly. He retreated out Kithr's door, closing it behind him.

Kithr debated following Lyan. He let out a long breath. *Lyan knows what he's doing, and it's long past time I started trusting him.*

Someone had thoughtfully left him a bucket of clean water. He washed some of the dust away before changing into a fresh set of his typical brown shirt and trousers. The only real difference between the clothes he shed and the new ones was the smell and the wear.

Kithr unpacked his bags, laying out his bedroll to wash with his clothes. He started when someone knocked on his door. Thinking Lyan might have returned, he opened it.

A black-haired elf, slightly taller than Kithr, stood on his stoop carrying a covered basket. He greeted Kithr with an easy smile. "I have no idea how in the First Seeds it escaped me to welcome you earlier, Kithr!" He offered the basket. "You probably think no one noticed your absence."

The words bore an uncanny resemblance to Kithr's earlier thoughts. He chuckled softly, accepting the basket. Perhaps all former soldiers thought alike. "Don't worry, Declan. One bad-tempered hunter's departure, compared to that of the village astrologer? I know which of us is more important."

"Not just a hunter, Kithr," Declan said, growing serious. "One of our own. A fellow warrior." Like so many elven men around Kithr's age, Declan had fought in Tather, though he and Kithr had not fought together. Declan leaned against the doorframe. "Wish you'd told us you were going. We debated whether to follow you, but the Elder didn't seem worried, and by the time we realized you and Lyan weren't going to be returning soon, it was too late to pick up your trail."

"We?" Kithr asked. "You and Seine?" Declan's wife wasn't a warrior, but she was the best tracker in Heartshrine Village.

"Us and the rest of my company in the village—Pyrn, Fitch, and Ihm," Declan told him. "And if you'd *told* us, I could have called in a few more from nearby villages."

"I didn't intend to be gone this long," Kithr admitted. "I just meant to drag Lyan straight back to Eilidh Wood."

"And we all want to know why you didn't!" Declan said, chuckling. "I want the full story after you and Lyan have told Elder Brenhan. I *know* it has something to do with those Tathrens."

"I'm out of practice telling tales," Kithr hedged.

"Hah! You would have been the next Keeper of Tales if not for the war, Kithr. I know you can spin a good one from this." Declan looked over his shoulder. "Well, Seine's gotten through the line bringing food to Lyan. I'll talk to you later, Kithr."

"Thanks." Kithr nodded to the basket.

"Can't have either of you starving after your long absence!" Declan grinned. "If you need any help, let us know, Kithr. Especially with your winter stores."

"I will," Kithr promised.

After Declan left, Kithr uncovered the basket. Inside, he found bundles of dried meat, bunches of garlic, some plums, and several small loaves of fresh bread. Kithr smiled. Elven tradition called for travelers to be welcomed home with gifts of food so they could recover before worrying about finding sustenance. Lyan was undoubtedly overwhelmed with gifts.

Kithr had just finished unloading Declan's basket when his next visitor knocked. Pyrn had packed herbs and nuts in his basket, with packets of smoked river trout. "Good to have you and Lyan back, Kithr. The village hasn't been quite the same without you."

"That might or might not be a bad thing," Kithr told him. "But thanks. It's good to be home."

"I wouldn't call the change good," Pyrn responded quietly, running a hand through his chestnut hair. "Hopefully, it'll all settle back to normal now that you're back. And…" He stopped, then shook his head. "Never mind. Glad you're back."

"Declan's already said he wants the tale," Kithr said, taking a guess at what Pyrn had been about to say. "Don't worry, if I tell it, I'll let you all know."

"Do. I want to hear it," Pyrn agreed.

After him, Ihm and Fitch arrived within moments of each other, nearly racing to Kithr's door. Kithr gave them both dubious looks. "Does the last one here owe the rest drinks?"

Both flushed. "Something like that," Fitch admitted. "Welcome back, Kithr."

With his typical lack of tact, Ihm asked, "Where *were* you, Kithr? What have you and Lyan been doing these last months?"

"No one gets to hear the tale before the Elder," Kithr said.

"Kithr! You were gone for *months*! Is that all you're going to say?" Ihm protested.

Kithr gazed at him, a smile creeping onto his face. "Yes."

Fitch laughed. "Nope, Kithr hasn't changed. Come on, Ihm. He can out-stubborn you any day. If he's going to tell us, it'll be when he wants to."

"I won't tell anyone else," Ihm promised Kithr, a promise he undoubtedly meant in all sincerity, and would break within twenty paces of leaving. "A hint? Something?"

"Thanks for the supplies," Kithr said. "I appreciate them."

Ihm sighed, but accepted defeat. "Glad to have you and Lyan back."

After they left, Kithr stepped outside. His gaze drifted over the village, pausing on various trees. Among the healthy growth, the dry skeletons of brittle wood marked younger trees dead before their time. He could put names to many, but not, he realized uncomfortably, to all. A tree sprouted at the birth of every elf of Eilidh Wood, dying when the elf did. Elder Brenhan's walnut tree, by far the oldest and largest in the village, spread its branches far and wide, offering shade and shelter to those who walked in its shadow. Kithr looked up at his own tree—a pine. He picked a handful of needles off the ground, smiling slightly.

"Stiff, unbending, and prickly. So fitting."

As evening drew close, Kithr heard pipes. He looked outside to see youths running about, hanging lanterns on tree branches while musicians practiced. The flameless lanterns were a jealously guarded craft of the elves, rarely given to outsiders, but here as common as oil lamps in a human city. Benches held the growing bounty of food, and the smell of meat, bread, and fruits filled the village.

Noticing him, one woman waved him over. "Kithr! What are you waiting for? You're one of the guests of honor! Come on! Start the festivities."

He laughed and crossed the village common. "I wouldn't dream of risking your wrath by sampling before everything's ready, Iola."

She gave him a curious, studying look. Kithr paused. "What?"

"Something's changed. You seem more at peace than you have in a long time, Kithr."

"A lot happened," he said simply. Without Lyan beside him, directing attention away from Kithr, he found reassurance that he had been missed, and that people were genuinely glad to have him home again.

"It's a good change," Iola told him.

"Thank you. It's good to finally be home."

"So…" She waved at the platters.

"Let me see if Lyan's ready," Kithr said.

He walked to his friend's house, nestled under a tall ash, and knocked. "Lyan?"

Lyan opened the door and gestured Kithr inside. The

interior of Lyan's house had always been a vision of disorder, crammed with books and scrolls in no order Kithr could discern, but now the situation was exacerbated. Baskets piled with food and other gifts covered the table, the chairs, and overflowed onto the floor. Kithr stepped over several baskets and pushed the door closed behind him with a chuckle.

"Welcome home. I think people missed you."

Lyan's smile was genuine. "It seems so. I wasn't sure anyone actually would."

Kithr looked at his friend, startled. "What are you talking about, Lyan? Of course they did!"

Lyan made a vague gesture toward the ceiling, covered by a mural of the night sky filled with stars. "I kept telling everyone that there was a problem, and that the clouds covering the stars were unnatural. My fears were dismissed, over and over again. No one listened to me. I began to question whether they listened to what I said when I *could* see the stars."

Kithr shifted uncomfortably. "I'm sorry, Lyan."

Lyan precariously balanced a basket on the table's edge, clearing the path to the door a little more. "You weren't the only one doing it, Kithr."

"I know." That knowledge didn't make it any better. He looked at the baskets and tried to steer the conversation back to safer ground. "More people missed you than did me, certainly."

Lyan smiled faintly. "People feel obligated to bring me gifts. They don't think I'll be able to forage for myself. And they might be right. The ones who came to see you did so because they have been genuinely concerned by your absence, and not because they feel duty-bound to feed and clothe you."

Kithr chuckled wryly. "All right, but it's going to make gathering stores for autumn and winter a strain."

Something flickered across Lyan's face, and Kithr tried to

identify it. Guilt? It vanished as Lyan softly said, "I wouldn't worry about that, Kithr."

Kithr considered pressing, then changed his mind. Whatever bothered Lyan, he didn't want to talk about it yet, and trying to force the issue would only make him more stubborn. Kithr made himself smile instead. "Then I won't! Now come on. Everyone's waiting for us, and I've been smelling the food all afternoon."

"Thank you, Kithr." Lyan stepped over a basket overflowing with fresh sweet rolls, carefully avoiding crushing the berries that had spilled onto the floor.

Kithr caught Lyan's arm to steady him. "Are you ready?"

Lyan nodded.

"You're not bringing Equinox?" The Spear had been constantly with Lyan, and Kithr knew his friend grew anxious and uneasy without it in immediate reach.

But Lyan shook his head quickly. "No. Not here, not tonight. I don't want someone to notice, and ask…"

Kithr nodded in understanding. "All right. I know you can call it if you need it. There will be plenty of time to deal with the rest of the village knowing about the Spear after we talk to Elder Brenhan." He opened the door and stepped outside, followed by Lyan.

Fresh-cut branches and late summer flowers ornamented the benches, and the lanterns cast glows around the village common. Twilight spread as the sun sank low. Lyan walked beside Kithr, and he smiled warmly as elves called out welcomes. Elder Brenhan awaited them beside the first bench, and he smiled.

"Tonight, we celebrate the return of those who have journeyed far, and who the gods have brought safely back to us."

Kithr remembered the same words being spoken when he and other warriors returned from the war in Tather. At that time, he had silently mocked them and derided the gods. This time, he whispered the words with the Elder. The gods had indeed brought them through this journey—and not the elven gods alone. The Tathren gods, as well, had played a part. So had the unpredictable god of monsters, Nachyne, though Nachyne's reasons for doing so were more personal than those of the other gods. The god of monsters was bound to Equinox, and the bearer of the Spear could summon him at will—a fact known to very few.

Lyan bowed. "Thank you, Elder Brenhan. We give thanks to the gods for guiding our steps and bringing us home once more."

Formalities before elven feasts were blessedly brief. The Elder smiled, nodding in acknowledgment of Lyan's words. "Then let our guests of honor begin."

People cheered, throwing a shower of flowers and leaves over Lyan and Kithr. Kithr laughed and twisted aside as he glimpsed movement from the corner of his eye, narrowly avoiding Declan's attempt to shove a handful of slimy, wet river weeds down the back of his shirt. Lyan managed to escape the enthusiastic greeting and piled a plate with food. Kithr wrestled the slimy plants out of Declan's grasp and tossed them aside.

"If you make me miss getting Auna's candied plums, you'll regret it," Kithr promised, seeing others already moving toward the food.

Declan laughed. "I'm not that brave! Go on, since some seem to forget that you're a guest of honor as well."

When Kithr took a plate, the elves around him quickly apologized and offered to step aside, though he waved them back.

"Sorry, Kithr! I thought you'd already gone," the man in front of him said.

"Don't worry about it," Kithr said. He reminded himself of Lyan's admission that he was turning attention away from Kithr. *It doesn't mean I've been forgotten.*

He took wine for himself and Lyan and settled cross-legged on the ground beside his friend. They both attacked their food ravenously. Kithr was relieved to see Lyan devouring his meal—the astrologer's appetite had been lackluster.

*Not that I'd blame him for growing tired of my cooking. I certainly did.*

Roasted boar, fresh breads, and a wealth of late summer fruits accompanied assortments of grains and legumes from the Appret Plains. The nomadic horse-herders who lived on the plains traded with the elves during summer, when the heat of the open land grew too oppressive and water too scarce, driving them to the edges of Eilidh Wood. The largest clan, the Na'Khahra, led by Ohrlan, particularly favored the elves of Heartshrine Village. Whether or not Lyan realized it, the stargazer was the main reason for that. Kithr knew Lyan had read the stars for birth of Ohrlan's father, Ohrlan, and all Ohrlan's brood of children, but hadn't realized what deep respect they felt for Lyan until he'd encountered the tribe while following after Lyan and the Tathrens. Ohrlan had gifted Kithr with one of the finest horses of his herd—a gift worthy of a prince. Not only that, but he had already given six horses to Lyan's Tathren companions, so that they could ride, despite his concerns over Lyan's safety in the company of strangers.

*And now, strange as it feels to admit it, I'd trust those Tathrens almost as much as I would any elf who I fought alongside and who came home from the war. I would trust them with Lyan's life.*

Somber thoughts for a celebration. Kithr put them aside and bit into a plum. "Oh gods, I've missed these," he mumbled around a mouthful, juice dribbling down his chin as the rich, sweet flavor filled his mouth. The fruit trees around Heartshrine Village produced varieties superior to any he'd found elsewhere in Eilidh Wood, much less outside the forest.

"It's good," Lyan agreed around his own food.

"Lyan! Now that you're back, will you read my son's fortune?" One villager ran up and set a small basket of bread beside Lyan.

Lyan hesitated, but only for a moment. "Of course. I'm sorry… I know you've been waiting for me to return."

The man shook his head. "When you left, we knew there had to be a reason. But gods know, it's good to have you back!"

"Thank you." Lyan smiled.

He managed to get another bite of food, but more villagers were gathering close, eager to ask Lyan to read the stars. Kithr set aside his plate and stood, planting his hands on his hips. "Let Lyan eat! Has he *ever* told *anyone* that he wouldn't read their fortunes? Do you think he's going to start now?"

Ripples of laughter ran through the crowd. To Kithr's relief, his words also served the desired purpose, and gave Lyan an opportunity to finish his meal. He shot Kithr a look of thanks.

Elder Brenhan spoke over the sounds of the crowd. "I would ask you to wait before reading any fortunes, Lyan."

Lyan started and looked up. He tensed when the Elder addressed him. "To wait, Elder?"

"Until tomorrow, at least. I would like to hear of your journeys."

Lyan's tone was polite, but firm. "Elder, I have a responsibility as the astrologer of Heartshrine Village. My doing my duty will not change what has happened already. And I will say nothing of my travels until you have heard the tale first."

Elder Brenhan's brow wrinkled in a small frown. Kithr frowned as well, surprised that Lyan would insist on reading the stars when he seemed averse to the idea earlier. Lyan held the Elder's gaze, challenging him to argue over the matter. The rest of the village watched elder and astrologer uncertainly. Even the music started to trail away. Neither Lyan nor Elder Brenhan blinked, but before the tension grew too strong, Elder Brenhan laughed.

"I shouldn't be surprised—of course you wish to return to stargazing, Lyan. I'm glad you've returned, and your skill can serve your home once again. I will not keep you from it."

"Thank you, Elder." Lyan's voice remained polite, but that was all Kithr heard in it—no sense of Lyan's thoughts.

*Something just happened, and I don't know what it was. The Elder laughs it off, but he isn't pleased.* Kithr glanced at Lyan but, for once, he could read nothing from his friend.

Lyan looked around the crowd. "I can't promise to read everyone's stars tonight, but I will do what I can."

Someone chuckled. "Don't worry—we know you need some sleep too, Lyan."

"You're not giving yourself much chance to enjoy the homecoming celebration in your honor," Kithr told him as Elder Brenhan moved away.

Lyan swallowed the last gulp of wine and set aside his empty plate. "Enjoy it for me. Dance, celebrate—enjoy being home, Kithr. You should."

"While you go on brooding and not telling me what the problem is. Sure, that sounds *so* enjoyable," Kithr said under his breath.

Lyan heard him. "I'm fine, Kithr. A lot on my mind, that's all. I'm not brooding."

"You're brooding," Kithr told him.

"And you're worrying like a mother hen!" Lyan countered. He stood. "I'll keep my promise, Kithr. Please, enjoy the celebration. I'll be reading the stars at my usual spot. I need a little air anyway."

Lyan was moving before Kithr had a chance to respond. Kithr sighed, then finished his food. As he stood, a young woman with raven hair caught his arm.

"Kithr! Come dance!"

"Uh..." He'd meant to grab another handful of fruit and

follow Lyan, but found himself drawn toward the circle of dancers instead. The musicians played a lively tune, and the celebrants readily welcomed Kithr among them. He was soon caught up in the dancing, laughing and trying not to trip over his feet. In Lyan's absence, attention turned to him, and few, if any, were aware they had been ignoring him before.

Late in the night, as the celebration began to disperse, Kithr made his escape. He knew he would be stiff and sore in the morning—he couldn't remember the last time he'd danced so long. He started automatically toward his house, then stopped and instead walked to the edge of the village. Lyan's favorite place in the village for stargazing was near the stream, where the trees parted and offered an unobstructed view of the sky.

Kithr paused, letting his eyes adjust to the darkness. The sounds of the celebration gradually faded behind him, like the last flickers of a dying fire. Ahead, the stream trickled in its bed, accompanied by the chirps and hums of insects.

"Lyan?" he asked quietly.

"I'm here." Lyan sounded weary.

Kithr found his friend seated on a broad, flat rock, his knees drawn up and his chin resting on them as he looked down at the water glittering in the light of the waxing moon. He was alone, but a collection of dark shapes around the base of the rock indicated the many gifts brought by those who had come to hear their fortunes. Kithr sank down in the grass near Lyan.

"Did you have fun?" Lyan asked.

"I did," Kithr told him. "You would have too."

Lyan shrugged in silent answer.

Kithr waited a moment. When Lyan said nothing, Kithr spoke. "I know you don't need me to tell you the signs I was named under, Lyan, any more than you need me here to read my fortune."

"Kithr, do you trust me?" Lyan asked softly.

"Of course I do!"

"Do you trust me enough to do something for me without understanding why?" Lyan continued gazing into the water.

Kithr blinked. "What is it you want me to do, Lyan?"

"Do you, Kithr? Do you trust me enough to do that?"

"Yes." He didn't know what he was agreeing to, but he heard anxiety in Lyan's voice.

"Tomorrow... tomorrow, you'll have your first introduction to... things I can't tell you." Lyan finally looked up at the sky. "You'll be confused and angry, but... if you will do one thing, you'll be safe."

"Safe?" Kithr repeated. "Safe from *what*, Lyan?"

Lyan turned and met Kithr's eyes. "If I tell you that, Kithr, you won't be able to restrain your anger, and then..." He shook his head sharply and shivered. "I'm not going to say."

"You won't tell me." Kithr's eyes narrowed.

"Kithr, you've protected me. You've been my friend for as long as I remember, and I trust you with my life. I *need* your help." Lyan spoke quickly, his gaze intent and urgent. "You would do anything to keep me safe—I know it, and you do too. If something I know something will protect you, I will use that knowledge however I must. Do you understand that? I would not forgive myself if I knew something terrible would happen to you, and I chose to do nothing when I could have prevented it." He leaned forward, not blinking. "I *need* your help, Kithr, but if you don't trust me, you won't be able to when I need it."

Kithr opened his mouth, but didn't speak. *We're home. We're in Eilidh Wood, for the gods' sake! What could happen that's so terrible Lyan can't tell me?* He took a deep breath, then asked, "What do you need me to do, Lyan?"

Lyan shivered, but not with cold. "Tomorrow, Kithr, I need..." He stopped, taking a deep breath. His fingers twisted stalks of grass into braids. "I need you not to say a word. Not a single word to anyone. Not even to me, or to the Elder, until I tell you that you can. No matter *what* happens, you must not say *anything*."

Of all the things Lyan could have asked of him, that caught Kithr by surprise. "That's it?" he asked. "Me not saying anything will protect me from whatever unnamable disaster you're reading in the stars?"

Lyan closed his eyes and nodded. "That's all. It won't be as easy as you think, Kithr."

"You have my word, Lyan, I won't say a word tomorrow until you tell me I can."

Lyan's shoulders slumped in relief. "Thank you, Kithr. You have no idea how much I thank you."

"Lyan, what's wrong? Why won't you *tell* me?"

"Please trust me, Kithr."

"I do. But if some danger is coming, how can I prepare if I don't know what it is?"

"You *can't* prepare, Kithr. You shouldn't prepare," Lyan said.

Kithr's brow winkled in confusion. "Why not?"

Lyan twisted his hands in his lap. "It's hard to explain. But all the pieces that lead to these events are bound together, like threads in a tapestry." He raised his hand, fingers spread. "Pulling too hard on one could distort and change the whole image." He wrapped one finger around the next, and folded the other two down. "And every action tugs on one thread or another."

Kithr frowned. "You can read all this from the stars?"

Lyan glanced away, looking into the stream. "Not just the stars. There's something else that gives me a larger view of the tapestry. And please, *please* don't ask me to tell you more about that, Kithr. It is a delicate thread."

"But my silence tomorrow keeps these threads intact?" Kithr asked.

Lyan nodded.

"All right. But you'll explain things when you can, right?"

"If I can, when I can." Lyan's shoulders slumped. "I'm sorry, Kithr. I don't *want* to keep these secrets, but please, just trust me that revealing them makes everything so much worse."

"I believe you, Lyan. Even if I don't understand yet."

"Thank you," Lyan whispered.

## 2

## CAILEAN

*"Ewart might have promised to restore titles and lands, but he could never restore the honor of my family if I turned against you, my lord."*

The Great Hall of Kalisna, home of the Dev'gilla family, earls of the Tathren province of Ihvako, teemed with vassals, supplicants, guards, servants, and heads of towns and villages gathered to hear the results of their lord's trip to the royal court. Cailean passed through the preliminary matters quickly—news from the court, decrees and pronouncements that would affect his lands. Even King Hakon's confirmation of Cailean's victory over the usurper Ewart Col'renn required only a brief announcement, though afterwards, he had to wait for the cheering to die down.

Aside from a privileged few, his people knew only fragments of the full tale. They knew that Ewart, cousin to Cailean's father, had laid siege to the keep and forced Cailean to flee. Accompanied by a handful of loyal men, he'd set out in search of aid, and returned with Lyan, elven Spearbearer of Equinox, and his friend Kithr. Together, they defeated Ewart and Porephyn, a priest of Murdo, the Mad God.

Minstrels already composed tales of adventure and battle to fill in the gaps of the months Cailean had been gone. He'd heard a few. None came anywhere near the truth. They certainly didn't include the detail that Cailean had been cursed, preventing him from calling on Solstice's powers. Nor did they reveal that at their first meeting, Lyan had not been the bearer of Equinox—he only gained that role after completing the Trials and proving himself to the Spear. They said nothing of the tension and distrust between the elves and the humans.

He supposed it was better that way. Pretty lies rather than unflattering truth. But still, he could repair one rift, heal one wound opened during their journey.

"Aikan Unne, come forward," Cailean called.

Aikan bowed, stepping from the front of the gathering. "My lord."

Cailean rose and held a scroll toward his gray-haired steward, the man who had served his father, then him, all fifty-four years of his life. With all the formality befitting his words, he said, "Aikan Unne, by my right as lord of these lands, and with the blessing of His Majesty, King Hakon, I hereby grant you and your family all the lands and holdings formerly belonging to the traitor Ewart Col'renn."

Aikan stared at his lord, stunned into silence. At a nudge from his daughter, he stepped forward and accepted the scroll. His calloused hands shook as he broke the seal. "My lord…"

Aikan's wife had died nearly fifteen years ago, but his daughter, Haidee, stepped to her father's side and curtsied deeply. "Lord Cailean, no words can express the honor you do us."

No more than six people in the entire hall knew of the attempt Ewart had made to incite Aikan to betray Cailean. He had promised to restore the Unne family to nobility in exchange for Aikan's loyalty. To that handful who knew, Cailean's proclamation was the ultimate statement of forgiveness. When Aikan raised his head and met Cailean's eyes, he needed no words to express his understanding or his gratitude.

Cailean rose, resting a hand on Aikan's shoulder. "I know that I fulfill the wishes of my grandfather by this act, Aikan. And I know of no one more deserving of this honor than you."

A cheer rose from the assembly of servants, soldiers, and supplicants who had gathered to hear the news their lord brought from the royal court. Others took up the applause, and Cailean smiled. He'd recognized the first voice, and wasn't surprised. Shiolto Rona, horse tender, now chief of Cailean's stables, had been part of Cailean's small band that searched for Equinox. He and his older brother Dalrian knew all that had happened during their journey—the suspicions against Aikan, the hints and blatant accusations meant to give Aikan the appearance of a traitor. And they knew who had really betrayed Cailean and walked according to the will of the Mad God.

With the cheers nearly drowning his voice, Aikan bowed his head and quietly spoke. "My lord, thank you."

Cailean nodded. He didn't have to say anything more. Messengers from the king's court had been dispatched to carry the news to Ewart's holdings. Cailean doubted it would be greeted as warmly there, and he knew Aikan might not be welcomed in his new holdings. But he believed his steward was equal to the responsibility.

Once the cheering died down, Cailean passed on minor news from the court, and mediated a dispute between two villagers over a pig that had gotten into a garden. As he'd expected, most of the issues that had arisen in his absence had been dealt with already. Aikan was a skilled administrator, and Cailean knew he would desperately miss him when he left to attend his new home. But there were others who could take over Aikan's duties, and the opportunity had been one Cailean couldn't allow to pass.

With audiences concluded and immediate business resolved, Cailean escaped the hall to walk along the walls of his keep. Repairs to the buildings continued. Ewart's siege had inflicted heavy damage on some parts of the keep. He hoped to have the majority of it complete before he had to release the workers for harvest. The outer wall stood whole and strong again, and Cailean's men patrolled. He found the captain of his guard, Ralston.

Ralston saluted him. "Lord Cailean. Nothing to report, sir."

"Thank you." Cailean scanned the wall and the ground below. "No new bodies found, I hope?"

"No sir, and no signs of where the one we did find came from. It seems most likely he was one of Ewart's. No guess as to whether he fell or was pushed." Ralston made a vague gesture toward the back of the keep. During the repairs, a decomposing corpse had been discovered on the rocks outside the wall. The animals had been at work, and the decay had been advanced enough that no one could hazard a good guess as to when he had died, except that it had been recent enough for flesh to remain on the corpse, and rain hadn't washed the blood from the jagged stones. The stranger's remains had been buried in the graveyard with a plain marker.

Cailean nodded. "Where's Yion?"

A brief scowl flashed across Ralston's face. He didn't particularly like the mercenary. "He went hunting with Dalrian, milord."

*Hunting? That's unusual for Yion. Hunting game, or hunting men?* Cailean didn't voice his thoughts. "Send him to me once he returns."

"Yes sir."

He returned to his study after making his rounds. While he

sorted through the missives Aikan had lain out for him, someone rapped on the door. He looked up. "Enter."

The door swung open, and Yion ghosted inside on nearly silent feet. Shorter than Cailean, with deeply tanned skin and a compact body, Yion wore Cailean's colors, though today he wore plain leathers rather than a uniform. Slick black hair was pulled up in a topknot. A pair of short swords hung from his belt, but Cailean couldn't guess how many other weapons he had secreted about his person. Yion's face was flatter than that of a Tathren, and the corners of his narrow brown eyes slanted upward. In the center of his forehead lay an odd divot, as if something had once been embedded in his skin, but was now absent without leaving a scar. Yion's expression was, as ever, serene and at ease.

"Lord Cailean, welcome home." Yion spoke with a noticeable accent, though Cailean couldn't identify its origins. "Captain Ralston said that you wished to speak with me."

"Thank you, Yion. It's good to be home. You've been hunting?"

"Indeed. Dalrian wished my company as he tested his new bow. We took the opportunity also to practice our stealth and tracking, trailing a wildcat to her lair without alerting her, then hunted deer."

"Any signs of trouble in the woodlands?"

"No, Lord Cailean—all appears well." Yion waited patiently for Cailean to move on to his reason for calling him.

"Has your lord told you anything to indicate more trouble coming our way?" Cailean asked.

Yion was far more than just a mercenary who had left Ewart's forces to help Cailean and his men escape, far more than a man with training in stealth and weapons. He was a champion of Saiboti, Tathren god of warriors, and that was the lord who Yion called his own—none other. He didn't even call Cailean his lord, though he never lacked respect in his address.

"My lord knows that the Mad God will not be dissuaded from his goals so easily as to give up with the failure of Ewart and Porephyn, Lord Cailean. But if he knows specifics, he has not yet imparted that knowledge to me."

"I went to the astrologer in the king's court to ask for a reading of the stars. He heard my name and refused to speak to me. He did warn me that I would receive a visitor soon who I would not refuse, even though I should, whatever that means." He tried to sound annoyed rather than concerned, but the astrologer's warning nagged at his thoughts.

Yion considered, brow furrowing a moment before smoothing again. "I do not know what visitor he might refer to, I fear. The workings of the heavens are not known to me. When my lord chose me for his own, he severed my fate's bond to divination, that none may read it. To the stars, I do not exist."

Cailean blinked. "So not even Lyan could read your fortune?"

Yion shook his head. "I fear not. There is nothing of me in the heavens for him to read." The mercenary paused. "Lord Cailean, Lyan is no doubt home once again, under the watch of the gods of his people, and under Kithr's guard. You should not fear for him."

Cailean smiled. He shouldn't be surprised Yion knew the direction his thoughts turned. "I know. Still, it would be nice to know he's safe."

"Is there no means for the Spears to pass word one to another?" Yion asked. "If not, I shall ask my lord if he might discretely make inquiry into Lyan's well-being."

Saiboti didn't hold the same grudge against elves that his brother Ahebban did, but he tended not to openly address the elven gods. Cailean didn't pretend to understand divine politics or its inner workings. "Thank you, Yion."

*"Solstice, can you reach Equinox and find out if Lyan is all right?"*

He couldn't describe the Spear's response as words,

exactly. Rather, a rush of sensations came—impressions for his mind to interpret. Solstice told him that it could send a message to Equinox, and had, when Cailean asked. Whether or not an answer came depended on Lyan—the Spearbearer controlled the Spear's powers.

Cailean caught a hint of something he hadn't considered before. *"You need a Spearbearer in order to use your powers. Neither you nor Equinox can act alone or on your own?"*

Agreement from Solstice, then an attempt to expound. Some places in the world had ties to the Spears, and they could employ some portion of their power there even without a bearer.

*"Places like Equinox's shrine—Equinox can do some things there that it can't do outside the Shrine."*

Agreement again.

*"If Equinox's place of power is its shrine, do you have one as well? Is there a Shrine of Solstice?"*

Silence from the Spear. Cailean waited several long moments before deciding Solstice wasn't going to answer him. He wondered why not, but pressing for an explanation wouldn't do any good. *So, we have to wait for Lyan to decide to answer?*

Agreement from Solstice, with a faint echo of concern that a response hadn't come immediately.

*"Both he and I are new to being Spearbearers,"* Cailean told Solstice. *"Maybe he needs a little time to understand what he's sensing from Equinox."*

Turning his attention back to the study, Cailean found Yion still waiting patiently. He had yet to see Yion look impatient, ever. Cailean spoke. "Solstice is waiting for Lyan to answer. That might take a little while, if Lyan's distracted."

Yion smiled. "I should never wish to imply that the stargazer is easily caught up in those things that he enjoys, but I shall ask my lord if he might listen for word of Lyan and Kithr as well."

"Thank you, Yion."

Yion bowed. "I call them friends as well, Lord Cailean." He withdrew, leaving Cailean to his paperwork once again.

Aikan waited until evening to find Cailean. Cailean recognized him by the knock on the study door, before he even saw his steward. "Come in, Aikan."

He knew Aikan's hair hadn't always been gray, but Cailean was hard-pressed to remember it being any other color, though it had once held more streaks of dark brown. Aikan's beard was neatly trimmed, and his gaze keen and sharp as he faced his lord. He closed the door and walked to Cailean's desk. "Good evening, milord." He cast a look over the piles on Cailean's desk.

"Yes, I've been reviewing everything you set out for me, Aikan," Cailean said with a wry smile, knowing Aikan would be ready to chide him for any appearance of avoiding his duties.

"That's not why I wanted to speak to you, Lord Cailean." Aikan's tone and expression were serious.

Cailean pushed aside the last few documents he needed to read, and leaned back in his chair, waving Aikan to sit. "What is it?"

"Why did you put Ewart's lands in my hands?" Aikan asked plainly, settling in a chair. "After I…"

"Because you didn't betray me, Aikan. I can't restore your family to the place it once held, but I can return you to the ranks of nobility."

"By taking it from another?" Aikan asked.

"Who?" Cailean countered. "Ewart is dead with no heir. His only offspring is a bastard who he disavowed."

"He disavowed Vynzent?" Aikan straightened. "And what did you do?"

Cailean's jaw tightened. "When both he and I were boys, I pitied Vynzent. I have no more sympathy for him. He chose his path, and he can walk it alone. He has no place in the Dev'gilla family."

Aikan nodded, unsurprised. "He deserves none."

Like Cailean, Vynzent had sought Equinox. In his efforts to find the Spear before Cailean, Vynzent and his ragged band of hired men had abducted and tortured Lyan.

"Have you sent anyone to find out the state of Ew… your holdings?" Cailean asked.

"Not yet," Aikan said. "Tomorrow morning, I have a man set to leave. I'm not sure I want to know what state Ewart left his own lands in when he came to attack yours. I know for certain that we must cleanse the profane shrine hidden in that place, and requested that a priest of Ahebban make all possible haste to the site." He paused. "I've talked with Haidee. Once she and her betrothed wed, they will make Ewart's keep their home."

Cailean raised an eyebrow in surprise.

Aikan stood straighter. "I will join them initially and see what affairs must be put in order, but it will be their home. I'm too old to be starting such a new life. And without me, who will keep your house in order, Lord Cailean?"

"Aikan…"

"My daughter and my grandchildren shall have everything I could ever wish for them and more. For that, I will be eternally grateful, my lord. But my choice is to remain here, as your steward."

"Are you sure, Aikan?"

"I have given the matter long thought, my lord, ever since I rejected Ewart's offer, and I realized that my home is here." Aikan shifted in his chair. "And now that you know what has been on my mind, what weighs on yours, Lord Cailean?"

Cailean started, almost guiltily, though he wasn't sure why. When Aikan took that tone, he felt like a twelve-year-old boy being questioned about the "mysterious" disappearance of a fresh pie. "It might be nothing."

"My lord, I would rather know about this, whatever it is, and have it be nothing than not know until it becomes something and we are unprepared."

Cailean sighed. "I tried to speak to the royal astrologer, with King Hakon's permission."

Aikan gave him a surprised look. "And?"

"The moment I introduced myself, he knew who I was, and he refused to speak to me more than absolutely necessary. He would not read my future—wouldn't even pretend to try, saying he preferred that his head remained on his shoulders."

Aikan stiffened indignantly. "He thought *refusing* a lord would keep his head *on* his shoulders?"

"Apparently, he thought his chances better if he outright refused me than if he read my fortune. Which leaves me to wonder just what he could tell without even asking my date of birth. Lyan told me once that a stargazer ought to learn at least that much about the person whose fortune he tells."

"Then either he already knew that, or he is a charlatan," Aikan said.

"Or something in a larger prediction included me, and he didn't need my signs to know it," Cailean said. "He did tell me one thing: 'You will receive a visitor soon, bearing an invitation you will not refuse. You'd probably be better off if you did.'"

"A visitor who you will not refuse, but should?" Aikan thought on it, then shook his head. "Vague gibberish that could mean anything, my lord."

"Maybe," Cailean agreed slowly. "But I'm not sure. I'm just not sure." He rested a hand on Solstice and wondered why Lyan, through Equinox, hadn't answered him yet. And he worried.

3

KITHR

*Each village of Eilidh Wood acts like a separate state, sometimes with laws quite different from those of their neighboring villages. Their governance appears simplistic. The village is ruled by a single Elder, and the word of the Elder is law among the people. He is lord, judge, and high priest in one, and the elves claim that the Elder speaks the will of their gods to the people.*
*~Ercole Baeil'Kyn, Royal Archivist of Tather, "Treatise on Eilidh Wood"*

Kithr woke with a throbbing head, and groaned as he rolled from his low bed. The fall was short, but it roused him enough to crawl to his feet and stagger to the washbasin.

*Jahrin, Lord of Sleep, couldn't you have let my evening of celebration end in pleasant dreams rather than nightmares?*

He washed his face, then dressed. Contrary to popular belief, he *did* own clothes in a few colors other than brown, and ordinarily would have worn one of the green shirts, or at least a few ornaments, when meeting with the Elder. But knowing that Lyan was turning notice away from him, Kithr thought he shouldn't intentionally sabotage his friend's efforts, and adopted his typical style.

That thought was on his mind when someone knocked on his door. Kithr opened his mouth, about to invite them inside, but caught himself, remembering his promise. He raked fingers through his hair and opened the door.

Lyan stood on his doorstep. Looking at him, Kithr wondered if Lyan had slept at all. His face was lined, and dark shadows ringed his eyes, while the smile that usually rested on Lyan's mouth was absent. Kithr longed to ask, and his question showed on his face.

"I'm all right, Kithr—I just didn't sleep well. You don't look like you did either." Lyan rubbed his eyes. "I'll let you finish getting ready."

Kithr tied back his hair quickly. It was getting too long, promising to catch on brush and branches. As soon as he had a chance, he would bathe, then chop the ratty ponytail short. By habit, he hooked his quiver to his belt and reached for his bow. Kithr paused and cast a questioning look at Lyan.

"You can bring it," Lyan answered. He wasn't even wearing a belt knife. Equinox remained noticeably absent, and that bothered Kithr. Lyan continued. "Ready?"

Kithr nodded. He wanted to barrage Lyan with questions, much as he wanted to know when to expect whatever disaster could be averted by his silence. Instead, he wordlessly followed Lyan outside.

Dew hung heavy on the ground, and a faint morning mist swirled around their ankles. Early risers had begun clearing away the benches from the previous night's celebration, and they bid the two good morning. Lyan smiled in return and raised his hand in greeting, but didn't stop. Kithr drew a deep breath rich with the scents of trees, tension easing. This was Eilidh Wood—home, and the forest was pleased to have them safely under its branches again.

Eilidh Wood protected its children, and both he and Lyan worried over nothing.

The shadow of Elder Brenhan's walnut tree spread over them as they approached the hedge surrounding the Elder's grove. The hedge offered privacy, seeming to swallow sounds. Kithr followed Lyan through the graceful archway of woven vines onto the stone-lined paths of Elder Brenhan's grove. More hedges separated plants into groups—herbs, flowers, edibles. Kithr paused, brow furrowing. He'd never realized how unnatural the division was, as if it were a human's garden rather than allowing plants to grow where they would. But this was the Elder's grove. If there was anyone who would not go against the ways of Eilidh Wood, it was Elder Brenhan. Kithr had played in the grove as a child, like so many other village youths. Here in the Elder's grove, Lyan's cousin Nylas had discovered his plant magic.

Kithr turned his thoughts away from Nylas. Lyan's cousin now lurked in a forest in Tather, continuing to fight a war that the rest of the elves had ended long ago. Nylas was Lost to Eilidh Wood, turned away from the ways of the elves to follow his own path of blood, vengeance, and death. Lost elves were anathema to Eilidh Wood, rejecting the traditions and rites decreed by the gods and by Eilidh Wood itself. At least Nylas and his men hadn't gone so far as planting crops and raising animals. The idea of behavior so foreign to an elf of Eilidh Wood sent a shiver through Kithr.

*Will Lyan tell the Elder about the Lost in Tather? I almost hope he skims over that portion of our journey.*

They reached the gazebo at the center of the grove. Elder Brenhan waited for them, a mug of tea steaming in his gnarled hands. He wore a light robe, but Kithr saw the cuffs of sturdy breeches under the hem, and expected that the Elder planned to tend his grove once their meeting concluded.

"Come in Lyan, Kithr. Sit and tell me of your travels with the Tathrens."

"Thank you, Elder." Lyan settled on a bench across from Elder Brenhan. Kithr chose a seat to one side, where he could see both Lyan and the Elder, and also keep an eye on the entryway, in the unlikely event that a threat presented itself.

"Now tell me, what drove our village astrologer to leave his duties to follow the descendants of men against whom we warred?" Elder Brenhan asked.

Kithr stiffened. The Elder's tone was pleasant and mild, but the question rose like an accusation, assuming that whatever Lyan said, he had been in the wrong.

"The sky was clouded every night, Elder," Lyan answered. "Without being able to see the stars, I could not perform my duties to Heartshrine Village. It was, therefore, my responsibility to do whatever lay within my power to discover and remove the cause of the unnatural obstruction. From Cailean Dev'gilla, I learned the clouds were the work of a Tathren mage in the service of the Mad God."

Elder Brenhan raised an eyebrow. "The Mad God wished you to be unable to read the stars for your village?"

*He chides Lyan for leaving, then dismisses Lyan's explanation in the next breath?*

"No, Elder," Lyan said. "The mage sought an answer from the stars and didn't want anyone to find that answer before he did. So his master gave him the means to hide the sky. This mage was the enemy of Cailean and his men, so by accompanying them, I served Heartshrine Village by working to reveal the heavens again."

"Yet the Tathrens traveled away from their land, not toward it," Elder Brenhan said. "Did this mage not dwell among his people? Cailean Dev'gilla told us that his home had been overrun and captured. How did accompanying him help to reveal the stars?"

"His home and lands had been captured, yes," Lyan said. "And the mage was among those responsible. With the forces available to him, Cailean knew he couldn't defeat a minion of the Mad God. He and the handful of men we met set in search of power great enough to fight against this force."

"What power?" Elder Brenhan's eyes narrowed. "Did he tell you?"

"He told me, Elder. Cailean sought Equinox, Spear of the Stars." Lyan met the Elder's gaze unflinchingly.

"And you left Heartshrine Village *knowing* this?" Elder Brenhan asked, voice icy.

"Yes, Elder." Lyan's voice held no hesitation or regret.

*Tell him the rest, Lyan. Tell him that you knew the path to the Shrine of Equinox, because you read it in the stars long before the clouds ever covered them. Tell him that you took the trials, not Cailean. Gods, tell him that you accompanied Cailean because he bore Solstice and you knew you had to ensure he would not attempt to claim both Spears.* Kithr looked intently at Lyan, willing his friend to continue.

"Why?" Elder Brenhan demanded.

"The Tathrens were determined to find the Spear, Elder, and the knowledge possessed by Cailean brought them to Eilidh Wood and beyond. By accompanying them, I could make certain they would not defile a sacred place when they found it."

"You guided them to the Spear?" Elder Brenhan asked coolly.

"Cailean led the group, Elder," Lyan answered.

Kithr blinked. *Cailean led the group, that's true. But only Lyan knew where the Shrine could be found. Why are you dancing around this, Lyan?*

"You allowed Tathrens to enter the Shrine of Equinox." Elder Brenhan's voice made it an accusation, skipping over the whole of their journey to reach the Shrine. Kithr thought of the pooka pursuing Lyan, and Kithr saving him. Of battles and ambushes, and Kithr finally allowing the Tathrens to know that he had followed them. Of Vynzent Col'renn capturing and torturing Lyan in an effort to learn the Shrine's location, and how that had been counted as the first of the three trials Lyan overcame to claim the Spear. All that, left unsaid.

"The Guardians of the Spear, who protect the Shrine and Equinox, allowed us all to enter, Elder. The choice of who passed the gates was not mine," Lyan answered.

Before he could continue, Elder Brenhan set aside his now-cool mug of tea and stood. "And would they have been allowed to enter had you *not* been there, Lyan? The Guardians allowed an elf to enter, and with you, our enemies."

Lyan's eyes narrowed. "The Guardians of the Shrine have followed their duty since before any of us were born, Elder. They know their responsibilities. Had they wished any one of us not to enter the Shrine, they possessed more than enough power to deny them entry. Yet they allowed *all* of us to enter the Shrine. The decision of who to allow within belonged to them and to the Spear. And more importantly, the decision as to who was worthy to challenge the Trials of Equinox was theirs."

*Tell him, Lyan! Tell him who Equinox chose!*

"The Spear of the Stars belonging to *our* people was taken by a *Tathren?*" demanded Elder Brenhan, inferring a conclusion that Lyan had never said. The venom in his voice shocked Kithr—for all that Elder Brenhan often reminded Kithr that the war was over, he sounded ready to start a new one.

Kithr's mouth fell open, words on the tip of his tongue. For the first time since they entered the grove, Lyan turned and looked directly at Kithr, holding his gaze. Deliberately, Lyan shook his head, and his eyes carried a message as clearly as if he had spoken. *You promised, Kithr.*

Kithr stared at his friend in disbelief. But finally, he closed his mouth, angry and feeling as if he had somehow been deceived.

Lyan let out a deep breath and spoke. "Elder Brenhan, Equinox chose its bearer, and the Spears are unconcerned with national squabbles. It is we who claim that one Spear belongs to one land, and the other to another land. The Spears are concerned with their wielder's abilities, whether elf or human, male or female. Without Equinox, we stood no hope of overcoming the Mad God's followers. They acted with his blessings, and had at their call magic strengthened by blood and sacrifices. The Mad God sought a foothold in this world, Elder."

Elder Brenhan's eyes narrowed. As if the threat of Murdo was inconsequential, he said, "And without *you*, the Tathrens could never have found a Spear of the Stars that has no right being in the hands of their people. There are many among our people far more worthy to bear Equinox than a *Tathren*."

"If they were worthy, they should have sought Equinox themselves, Elder. Then there would have been nothing for the Tathrens *to* find, and they could have appealed to the Spearbearer for aid," Lyan countered.

*And obviously you don't number Lyan among those "worthy" to bear the Spear, Elder.*

Elder Brenhan continued to glare at Lyan. "Tell me the truth, Lyan. Where is Equinox?"

Though the weight of that gaze wasn't fixed on Kithr, he felt it press on him from all sides, demanding an answer. Kithr gritted his teeth and clenched his fists, stubbornly remaining silent, as he had promised Lyan he would.

Lyan met the Elder's gaze, giving no hint that he felt the same pressure. Then, he lied. "I do not know, Elder Brenhan."

"You would protect Tathrens over your own people?" Elder Brenhan demanded, expression twisting in anger. "The *truth*, Lyan. Where is the Spear?"

Kithr flinched, the Elder's voice striking like a blow, but Lyan remained unmoved. "I do not know."

"You're lying, Lyan. You're hiding something."

"Why should I hide anything from you, Elder?" Lyan asked.

"An excellent question," Elder Brenhan agreed coldly. "I intend to find the answer."

Kithr saw Lyan flinch ever so slightly. "I cannot tell you what I do not know, Elder."

Elder Brenhan stepped toward Lyan, glaring down at him. "Lyan, astrologer of Heartshrine Village, you have abandoned your duties to your people. You have aided and guided Tathrens, enemies of our people, knowing they sought the most sacred treasure of our people: Equinox, Spear of the Stars. If that were not enough, you allowed them to defile the Shrine of the Spear and claim Equinox for their own people. And now, you return to us with lies and deceit."

A surge of anger rushed through Kithr as the Elder's words wrapped around him, invading his thoughts. *How dare you, Lyan? How dare you betray us and allow Tathrens to do such things?*

Then the rage vanished, leaving confusion instead. Kithr blinked, shocked at himself. *What's wrong with me? That's not what happened. Cailean carries Solstice, not Equinox. Lyan hasn't betrayed anyone, least of all our people. Why did I accept Elder Brenhan's words over what I saw with my own eyes?*

Lyan's eyes remained locked with the Elder's, and he didn't speak, didn't acknowledge or deny the accusations.

"What do you say to this, Lyan?" Elder Brenhan demanded.

"I have told you of my journey, as you wished, Elder. I have nothing more to say," Lyan responded.

Fury radiated from Elder Brenhan, and Lyan added to it with every word, but Kithr didn't understand the reason. Lyan claimed he had told the Elder of his journey, yet he hadn't told him anything. And the Elder wasn't asking, wasn't interested in knowing what had happened, but was intent on accusing Lyan of something so… unlike Lyan that no one would believe it.

*Yet, when the Elder said it, I accepted it. I did, even though I was with Lyan, and saw everything that happened. I don't understand what's happening. It doesn't make sense.*

Lyan said something, too softly for Kithr to hear. Elder Brenhan caught the words, though, and raised his hand as if he intended to strike Lyan across the face. Kithr tensed, ready to intervene.

Lyan held the Elder's gaze. "Equinox is in the keeping of one worthy of it. The Spear chose its bearer, as the Spears will do regardless of the whims of gods or mortals."

"Who did the Spear choose?" Elder Brenhan demanded.

Kithr held his breath, waiting for Lyan to answer and finally end this inexplicable duel of words.

"Why?" Lyan rose and stood eye to eye with the Elder. "So you can incite our people to war again? Will you use force to deny the decision of the Spear that you yourself called our people's most sacred treasure? Will you send more elves to bleed and die, to become Lost?" Anger shook Lyan's voice.

"You will answer me!" Elder Brenhan's shout roared through the grove. Kithr felt it like a physical force, seizing and pinning him in place, holding him and demanding an answer. Not a plant stirred, not a bird chirped.

In the silence so stifling Kithr could hear his pulse pounding, Lyan whispered his answer. "No."

The world drew breath, and sounds returned. Elder Brenhan's expression twisted again in outrage. "You dare to defy me, Lyan? You defy me, and you defy our gods, whose will I speak!"

"Do I?" Lyan murmured softly.

"You are unworthy to be astrologer of Heartshrine Village," Elder Brenhan continued coldly, damning words.

"Yet I am the only one we have," Lyan responded as if his very purpose was not being stripped from him. "The only one in our village with skill to read any fortunes, since you banished the Se…"

"Silence!" Elder Brenhan snapped. "You will not speak of

the Seer. And you will not speak of the stars. I will send to the other villages, and instruct that one of them provide a trained apprentice for Heartshrine Village to take the duties you have failed."

Kithr's breath caught. He should be raging, but he was too stunned by the words he heard from Elder Brenhan, the leader of his home, the man he had always looked up to and admired.

The Elder continued. "*You*, Lyan, will remain within your house and not set foot outside. Defy me, and you will be banished from Eilidh Wood."

Kithr's mouth fell open again in disbelief. Lyan? Stripped of the title of village astrologer, and confined to his house for refusing to name the bearer of Equinox? Why? *Why won't you just tell him, Lyan?* A tremor of anger shook him.

For the first time, the Elder's eyes settled on Kithr. "Take Lyan to his house, Kithr. See to it that he remains there."

*Now you expect me to agree with you? To treat Lyan like a criminal, preparing to banish him from Eilidh Wood?* He drew breath to release his building outrage.

Lyan didn't give him a chance. "As you will, Elder." His voice was flat and emotionless. He turned and walked from the heart of the grove.

Kithr ran after him, catching up in only a few steps. He glared at Lyan, but Lyan offered no explanation. They walked in silence, Kithr fuming, Lyan unreadable. If not for the promise Lyan had extracted from him, Kithr would have demanded an explanation from Elder Brenhan. *Why is he doing this to Lyan?*

If anyone had heard the raised voices from within the grove, they showed no sign when they cheerfully greeted Lyan and Kithr. Lyan hurried to his house, avoiding anyone he could. When he reached it, Lyan jerked open the door and rushed inside. Kithr followed, slamming the door closed behind him.

Lyan stumbled over baskets and gifts, the abundance of welcome given to him the previous day. He reached a chair and dropped into it, suddenly shivering and sucking in deep gulps of air. Part of Kithr worried, battling with the part of him that wanted to shake Lyan and demand answers. He stood by the door, unable to decide what he should do.

From outside, Kithr heard the Elder's voice, too muffled to understand. He reached for the door.

Lyan's eyes snapped open. "Kithr, wait!" Fear filled his voice.

Kithr spun around, facing Lyan. *Why?*

"Please, wait. Stay here until the Elder finishes talking, please. Talk to me, yell at me, whatever you must, just don't leave yet."

Kithr stepped away from the door, toward Lyan. "*Now* I can talk? *You* refused to tell Elder Brenhan *anything* about who *really* bears Equinox, while implying something we both know is a lie. You didn't tell him *anything* about our travels. And he didn't care! Elder Brenhan arbitrarily rejected you as our astrologer and threatens to exile you if you so much as leave your home, and *now* I can speak? *Now?* Mad God's Pits, Lyan, what supposed disaster was *averted* by this?!"

Lyan turned away, looking at the wall rather than Kithr. "A greater one than did happen."

"And why should I stay here? Tell me *that*, Lyan," Kithr demanded. "Tell me before I see for myself."

"Elder Brenhan is calling the village together. He'll tell them that I've been accused and sentenced."

"He expects anyone to *believe* that?" Kithr spat on the floor. "Who is going to accept that *you*, of anyone, betrayed our village?"

Lyan closed his eyes. "You did, when he said it."

Kithr stiffened. "I do not believe him! The accusation is ridiculous."

"But you *did*, when he made it," Lyan said.

"Only for a moment, before my sense caught up," Kithr said sharply.

Lyan opened his eyes and locked gazes with Kithr. "And what if it hadn't? You were with me, Kithr. You saw everything that happened, yet none of that mattered when the Elder spoke."

A chill crept up Kithr's spine and he stepped closer. "What are you saying, Lyan?"

"His words hold power, Kithr. I had to allow you to feel it so you would understand." Lyan shuddered and pulled up his legs, breaking eye contact. "Then I interfered again, and shielded you from that power. The Elder didn't know. He barely knew you were there most of the time."

"You're claiming that Elder Brenhan was *enspelling* me? That he's going to do the same to the entire *village?*"

Lyan shuddered again. "If you go outside, Kithr, I will continue to shield you against it, because if I don't, you'll be defenseless. But if you hear what he says, you'll lose your temper, and someone will get hurt."

"Elder Brenhan is *enspelling* our people?" Kithr repeated in disbelief. "That's nonsense! The Elder speaks the will of our gods!"

"The Elder speaks the will of his god," Lyan agreed in a whisper. "You don't have to believe me, Kithr. Only wait. Leave after the Elder has spoken, and see for yourself whether they believe him." He slumped back in his chair.

Kithr picked up a flameless elven lantern and held it over Lyan. Lyan winced. His skin was pale, and a sheen of sweat glittered on his face. He looked as if he might pass out at any moment. Kithr returned the lantern to its hook and worked his way to the shelf with dishes. He found a bottle of wine and filled a mug, then brought it to Lyan.

"Drink."

Lyan accepted the mug and gulped the wine down. Finally

he looked up at Kithr with haunted eyes. "I'm sorry, Kithr. I'm sorry. I can't tell you. Can't explain. I'm sorry."

Despite Lyan's words to the Elder, his attitude had been a front. The Elder's condemnation wounded him deeply. But more than that, Lyan was afraid. Horribly, unspeakably afraid.

Kithr's jaw tightened, and he didn't respond aloud. *Elder Brenhan speaks the will of the gods to our people. If this is the will of our gods, then I will defy even them.*

4

CAILEAN

*Any child knows the gods of his people, and every country has its gods. But there are gods also who hold to no one nation. Cantorelle, the god of roads, is often invoked by travelers. Jahrin, the Dreamer, may be called on to bless sleep, or to inflict nightmares on enemies. Even the monsters have their own god, Nachyne—a name rarely invoked by men.*

"Now, Lady Airla is the daughter of Lord Horlane. By reputation, an attractive girl with a pleasant disposition, and her father has offered three villages, the woods around them, and the crossroads town as her dowry. Are you listening to me, Lord Cailean?"

"I'm listening, Aikan." Cailean sighed, rubbing his eyes. "Lady Airla. Pretty girl, a couple of fields. Father who wants to get rid of her but isn't willing to put up enough dowry to make most nobles look twice. Makes one wonder if she's in poor health."

"Lord Cailean! This is important. You need to secure your family line with a successor!"

Cailean shoved away from his desk and paced around his study, stopping at the window to look out at the clear afternoon sky. "If I have to go through the rest of that stack in front of you, Aikan, I swear, I'm going to go down to the village, invite up the five prettiest girls I find, bring them here for a few months, and formally acknowledge whatever bastard children come from it!"

He turned his gaze down on the outer courtyard, where several men struggled with a yoke of oxen hitched to a wagon. The oxen balked at the gate, blocking traffic. Cailean found himself sympathizing with the animals as he turned back to Aikan.

Aikan watched him, expressionless. "My lord, at this point, I am willing to allow that as an acceptable alternative."

Cailean stared at him. It took a moment, but finally the first twitch of a smile escaped onto Aikan's face. Cailean couldn't help the laugh that broke free, and with that, Aikan joined him, both men laughing until tears ran down their faces, releasing tension and strain.

Cailean finally wiped his face clean and sighed. "I know my family's succession is important, Aikan, but I'm looking for a *wife*, not a brood mare." He rubbed his eyes again. "Mad God's Pits, after all the talk of marriage contracts, dowries, alliances, and trying to choose who to side with and who to alienate, I'm tempted to ask Lyan to recommend a bride from Eilidh Wood. Wouldn't that look fine? Marry an elf of Eilidh Wood, take the first open steps to healing the rift between our countries? Can't you just imagine how *that* would stick in my neighbors' craws?" Even as he spoke, Cailean rested his hand on Solstice, feeling worry stir again. Two days now, and Lyan still hadn't answered him.

Aikan stiffened at the first mention of the elven forest, but now he stared at Cailean as if doubting his lord's sanity. "My lord…"

A rush of air filled the room, coalescing at Cailean's desk to settle into the empty chair. "I wouldn't recommend it. Not when you are the Tathren Spearbearer, and your child will be Spearbearer after you. The idea of a half-elf carrying either Spear raises some unpleasant memories and potential issues regarding Solstice and Equinox." Bare, taloned feet propped on Cailean's desk as the speaker lounged back, balancing the chair on its back two legs. Draconic wings brushed against the stone floor. Sunlight drew to him, the rest of the room dimming in comparison to the glow of his bronze skin. A deep blue swath of silken cloth wrapped around his waist in token acknowledgment of "mortal taboos on nudity."

Cailean recognized the speaker the moment he heard that voice, but his mind took several moments to accept the presence that appeared in his study. However, it was impossible to deny he heard the voice that echoed with power, and equally impossible to deny he saw the nearly naked winged form of Nachyne before him. Cailean's tongue stumbled over the greeting that tried to get out, producing an inarticulate mumble.

Nachyne, the god worshiped by monsters and feared by any sane man, continued. "It might not be common knowledge among mortals anymore, but one reason Murdo succeeded in claiming both Spears was because he had both bloodlines—elven and Tathren. With that in mind, you would be better to leave the marrying of elven women to someone else. Not only that, but almost all offspring from matches between humans and elves are sterile. That's why Murdo has to draw in followers rather than just breeding his own."

"Lord... Nachyne," Cailean managed finally. "This is unexpected. What brings you to my home?"

"You do," the god of monsters replied evenly. "Much as I'm sure you hate to be interrupted in the midst of this review of eligible mortal women, I have reason to believe that bringing a Spearbearer with me will be beneficial." He picked up a missive, glanced it over, and made a face. "This one's close enough to being a harpy that she almost falls into my domain."

"Having a Spearbearer with you," Cailean repeated, feeling like a slow-witted idiot. "With you for what, Lord Nachyne?"

"Some business that needs taken care of," the god replied, setting aside the parchment and looking across the room at Cailean. When Cailean continued to stare, Nachyne continued. "I imagine you will want to pack some sort of supplies."

Cailean drew a deep breath. "Lord Nachyne, I have a duty to my home—a responsibility to be here." He didn't voice the rest of the thought. *I need to be here, a noble in his own home, his own lands, not gallivanting about like some common tinkerer or minstrel.*

Nachyne's eyes narrowed. His tone barely changed, but Cailean felt the force of the god's voice, no longer flippant, but deadly serious, chilling the air. "I heard that in the court of your king, when questioned about your dealings with elves, you gave a fine speech about the duties of the Spearbearers, and how you do not answer to men. As I heard it, you told your own people that a Spearbearer's first responsibility is to stop Murdo, wherever he might be working his schemes, and that matters of state came after that. Or was I misinformed?" He rested the chair on the floor, swinging his feet off the desk and leaning forward, elbows crunching down on loose parchment.

Cailean opened his mouth, then caught himself. His own words were being thrown back in his face, but he could not argue them. "You were not misinformed," he said finally.

Nachyne continued to fix Cailean with his icy stare. "The Mad God does not wait until it is *convenient*, Cailean Dev'gilla. I doubt he will make an exception for *you*."

Cailean forced himself to nod. "I beg your pardon, Lord Nachyne. Could you at least allow me time enough to put my house in some degree of order and warn my people of my absence? It may well be the least of my concerns, but it *is* still a concern." He wanted to ask a great many more questions about what Nachyne needed with a Spearbearer, and why he had chosen Cailean instead of Lyan, but his reading of the god's temper suggested that he pressed his luck even by asking for this much.

Aikan, however, was less willing to capitulate. "And where will you be taking Lord Cailean? Is he to be unattended?"

"You have until the dinner hour," Nachyne said, standing. "You'll be accompanied by the men who were with you the last time—your steward here, Saiboti's champion, and those two brothers. When I return, you and your men will be leaving, prepared or not." Nachyne's tone made it painfully clear that he considered the delay more than generous, and far longer than he wished to wait.

"Our destination?" Aikan asked pointedly.

"Eilidh Wood."

A chill ran down Cailean's spine. He swallowed hard. "Of course, Lord Nachyne. Thank you." He didn't wait to see what dramatic departure the god might employ, and he didn't waste the little time he had been granted by asking the questions tumbling through his mind. Solstice in hand, Cailean left his study at a jog.

*"You will receive a visitor soon, bearing an invitation you will not refuse. You'd probably be better off if you did."* The astrologer's words echoed back into Cailean's mind. He couldn't think, though, how he could possibly be better off refusing the orders of a god and bringing the anger of Nachyne on himself and his people.

"Lord Cailean! What's wrong?" One of his men rushed to him.

"Tell Captain Ralston that I need to speak to him immediately. Also, call Yion, Shiolto, and Dalrian. Send them all to the Great Hall."

"Yes sir!"

*Eilidh Wood. Lyan's home. Why does Nachyne need me, when he's going to the very place Lyan is? And why hasn't Lyan answered?*

Cailean reached the Great Hall only shortly before Captain Ralston. Cailean waved for the captain to join him. "Something has come up."

Captain Ralston straightened indignantly, offended at the thought that someone had reported news directly to Cailean without informing him. "I have not heard anything of note, my lord. No messengers, and no incidents within the keep." The man prided himself on knowing what happened in Cailean's keep.

"I'm going to be leaving the keep this evening, and I don't know how long I'll be gone," Cailean told him.

"What?" Captain Ralston jerked back a step. "My lord, why? You can't—"

"I must," Cailean interrupted. He gestured to Solstice, resting against his chair. "As I was pointedly reminded not long ago, the Mad God doesn't wait until it's convenient for us before taking action. This cannot wait."

Captain Ralston drew a sharp breath. "The Mad God, my lord? I'll assemble men."

Cailean raised his hand to stop him. "I'll be accompanied by Aikan, Shiolto, Dalrian, and Yion. Though I would rather that Aikan remain here."

"And why them, sir?" Captain Ralston clearly disliked being given no say in the matter.

Cailean sighed. "Because the god who appeared in my study to tell me that I'm needed said so, Ralston."

"A... a god, sir?"

For many years, Solstice had been considered a family

treasure—an heirloom and artifact to be protected, but few members of Cailean's line had been called on to use the Spear, and Cailean couldn't think of any in the last hundred years who had directly battled the Mad God's forces. So much knowledge about Solstice had been lost, it was hard to know truth from legend. The idea that he should be called to do so was foreign to his people, and almost as much so to Cailean himself. Cailean nodded. "At the moment, I consider myself fortunate he granted me until dinner to put my house in order."

Captain Ralston saluted with alacrity. He might argue with his lord, but no wise man denied the will of a god. "Yes, my lord. I'll see to it that your horses are brought in and readied for travel, and an escort assembled."

Cailean doubted any escort beyond those Nachyne had named would actually ride with him, but arguing would waste time he didn't have. "See to it, Captain."

When the captain left, Dalrian, Shiolto, and Yion were admitted. Shiolto looked nervous, as if unsure whether he'd done something wrong. Dalrian hung back a little, making Cailean wonder what mischief the brothers had done. Yion approached first, without hesitation or concern, but he stopped when he looked in Cailean's eyes.

"Lord Cailean, you are troubled by matters outside your own walls. What has occurred?"

With these men, Cailean spoke plainly. "Nachyne appeared in my study and told Aikan and I that the five of us are leaving tonight for Eilidh Wood."

"We're going to see Lyan?" Shiolto asked uncertainly.

"I don't know," Cailean admitted. "The god of monsters implied that his reason for going there, and for coming here first, relates to some scheme of the Mad God, and for several reasons I didn't feel I should demand explanations." He looked to Yion.

"I do not know, Lord Cailean. My lord has told me

nothing of it." It was rare to see Yion worry, but his expression hinted at concern. "I shall ask him again."

"Thank you," Cailean said. "What I know at the moment is that we're leaving tonight whether we're ready or not. I don't know what we're going to face, or how long we'll be gone, but prepare as best you can. Assume we won't be back here for some time—better to be more prepared than necessary than to not have what we need. Nachyne returns at dinner."

"Yes, Lord Cailean!" All three men bowed and left.

When Cailean entered his rooms, he found servants already rushing about, packing his bags for travel. They paused when he entered, and bowed to him.

"Lord Cailean. Aikan told me that you have been called away unexpectedly and are to leave tonight." Terrin had been chief of Cailean's servants for years.

"It came as a surprise to everyone," Cailean said.

"We will have everything in order shortly, milord," Terrin assured him, and Cailean believed him. If the black-haired servant couldn't have all Cailean needed assembled and packed before Nachyne returned, no one could.

"Good," Cailean said. "Captain Ralston is seeing to the horses. Make sure baggage goes down to be loaded on packhorses."

Knowing he would only be in the way, Cailean left his rooms, and eventually found himself back in his study. Notices and letters he'd been putting off suddenly became urgent business, requiring resolution before he left. Normally he declined the use of his scribe, preferring to pen his own correspondences, but in the interest of time, Cailean summoned the man from the keep archives and set him to work. Polite apologies were written for those bridal proposals Cailean had already decided against. A notice of taxes to be collected was sent to one of the villages that continually gave Cailean trouble, with permission to the local magistrate to resort to more forceful methods if necessary. He sorted through stacks of parchments, providing replies to those he could, cursing himself for ignoring Aikan's advice to deal with matters as they came to him.

Aikan himself finally relieved Cailean. The steward entered the study, followed by a servant with a tray of stew, bread, and wine. Aikan dismissed the scribe and servant, bringing the tray to Cailean personally.

"Eat something, Lord Cailean."

Cailean rubbed bleary eyes and capped his inkwell, then set aside his quill. "What time is it?"

"You have time enough to dine before the god of monsters is likely to return," Aikan said. "Your bags are packed and loaded on the packhorses, and I've made the necessary arrangements for the administration of your holdings to continue in both our absences. Also, my daughter will leave tomorrow for Ewart's—my new holdings."

"I would have asked that you stay here," Cailean began. Aikan was no young man, and he deserved to stay in a warm house, administering the keep, and not being dragged about the world in the wake of a Spear of the Stars.

Aikan shook his head. "Given the choice, I will follow you, my lord. I am not so old that I must be confined to a chair and eat only mush and custard." He looked pointedly at the tray. "And *you*, my lord, are old enough that I should not have to remind you again to eat your supper."

Cailean chuckled. "Yes, Aikan." He obediently picked up the spoon. "Have you had anything?"

"Of course, my lord. I also recall that some gods have little patience for such mortal weaknesses, and insisted the others eat as well." Aikan looked over the remaining papers on Cailean's desk. "The rest of these should keep, or will be dealt with by Marim as acting steward in your absence. I trust him, and he's an able administrator."

Cailean gulped down stew, following it with bites torn

from the chunk of brown bread. He swallowed the last of the wine, feeling the food settle like a stone in his stomach. Worry fluttered around his mind like a restless moth, unwilling to settle on any one thing. "Let's head out."

Horses crowded the courtyard, packed and saddled, and the escort Captain Ralston had assembled milled around. Shiolto moved between the animals, soothing them amid all the activity. Cailean was pleased to see that the grooms had brought him Sai, the stallion given him by Ohrlan, leader of the Na'Khahra clan, nomads of the Appret Plains. Though they were not trained as warhorses, the plains horses were prized for their speed, stamina, and intelligence.

Yion silently slipped up beside Cailean, and he spoke in a low voice. "My lord has answered me, Lord Cailean, but I fear what he told me still leaves much unknown."

"What did he tell you?" Cailean asked.

"He gave his blessings on our venture, and told me that he and the other gods of Tather have agreed to allow Nachyne to act as an intermediary between them and the gods of Eilidh Wood. He bid me to continue in the task he has given me, and to safeguard the Spearbearers."

"But he didn't tell you why Nachyne wants us?"

"No, Lord Cailean, he did not." Yion dipped a short bow.

*If the gods know what's going on, is it too much to ask them to simply tell us?* But, like lords to peasants, gods revealed only what they wished and no more.

Soldiers shifted restlessly around the courtyard, and Cailean sensed the tension in the air. All these men knew that during the retaking of the keep and the defeat of Ewart and Porephyn, Ahebban had appeared within the keep to fight alongside Cailean and his men, but few had actually seen the god. The idea of personally encountering a god in their midst terrified most of them, and had they known which god they awaited, that fear would only have been stronger, for Nachyne was not a god of Tather.

"How kind of you to assemble an audience for me, Cailean Dev'gilla." Nachyne spoke from the air.

Men jumped and cast frightened looks around, searching for the source of the voice. Horses snorted and whinnied in alarm, leaving handlers trying to calm them. A rush of wind swept over the courtyard. Nachyne appeared in the air above them, massive wings beating lazily to keep him aloft. The sweeping wind tossed at Nachyne's loincloth, rendering it useless for modesty. The god had timed his appearance so that the sun outlined him in a shimmering halo of light.

Cailean bowed, swallowing his anxiety. "Lord Nachyne."

"And you are ready for travel, I see. Good. I am glad you did not waste your time."

"I trust you don't object to my bringing mounts and pack animals," Cailean said.

"Not at all," Nachyne agreed magnanimously. "And *I* trust that your people understand that only those I invited will accompany you."

"I told them so, Lord Nachyne," Cailean replied.

The soldiers gaped at the god, and not even Captain Ralston dared object.

Nachyne alighted on the ground. Tathrens and horses both shied away, clearing space for him. The wind died, and Cailean blinked grit from his eyes as he walked to his horse. A trembling stablehand held the reins for him, but Cailean's horse, like the others of the plains, were the calmest animals in the courtyard. Cailean took the reins and swung into the saddle. Aikan followed his lead, then Yion, Dalrian, and finally Shiolto, who reluctantly left the rest of the horses. Cailean suspected the horses were not going to be necessary for their travel to Eilidh Wood, but wherever they might go afterwards, he would be glad to have a mount.

Cailean looked over the men assembled in the courtyard. "I entrust the protection of my home to you in my absence."

"Yes sir, Lord Cailean!" Captain Ralston responded, straightening and saluting Cailean. "Be careful, my lord."

"I will," Cailean promised. He turned to look at his keep. *Barely a month home, and I'm leaving again.*

Nachyne waved a hand, and the world lurched around Cailean, twisting and leaving his stomach behind as he was swept to somewhere else.

5

KITHR

*"We stand as one, united against our enemy. Together we fight, and bleed,
and send our foes to meet their gods. We do not stand alone, and we will
never leave one of our own to fall alone."*
*~Oath sworn by elven warriors at the beginning of the war with Tather*

"I still can't believe Lyan would do such a thing!"

Kithr's hands strained to clench into fists as he forced himself not to whirl on the woman he overheard in the village common. He wanted to explode, rage boiling to the point of bursting. *If you really couldn't believe it, then you wouldn't! How dare you accept the Elder's lies? How dare you believe that Lyan betrayed us?*

She wasn't the only one. Just as Lyan had warned, the entire village accepted the Elder's accusation without question. Worse, they assumed that Kithr joined in their blind submission. Kithr gritted his teeth to stop the words lurking on his tongue as he stalked toward his house, carrying the bag of nuts he'd gathered in the forest.

"Kithr!" The call reached him as he was about to open his door.

Kithr turned, and saw Declan jogging toward him. The former soldier wore hunting leathers, his black hair tied back, though he was empty-handed if he was returning from a hunt, and late if he was only now, near evening, about to head into the forest. Kithr waited, letting nothing show in his expression. "What?"

"I looked for you earlier, but you must have been out." Declan glanced at the bag Kithr carried, and frowned. "Not hunting?"

"I need more than just meat to hold me through winter," Kithr responded. "You were looking for me?"

Declan glanced around and lowered his voice. "I wanted to ask how Lyan's doing."

Kithr stiffened slightly. *You don't trust me, do you, Elder? Despite everything Lyan's done to protect me, you suspect that I'm not under your hold, and now, you're using someone you think I would trust to test me. I hate you.* "Why don't you ask him?" Kithr responded curtly.

Declan hesitated, looking genuinely concerned. "Because Elder Brenhan has forbidden anyone to speak to him. But he's told you to guard Lyan's house, so if anyone knows whether he's all right, it would be you, Kithr."

"How well do you expect him to be doing, Declan?" Kithr snapped. He could have answered Declan's question. He could have told the other soldier that Lyan sat in his house, barely eating, barely speaking. Surrounded by the gifts showered on him only three days before by the village that had inexplicably turned against him, Lyan did nothing. Kithr knew his friend hurt, and had rarely seen Lyan so withdrawn. At the same time, he felt like Lyan waited for something— something he hadn't told Kithr, and Kithr couldn't be sure if what Lyan waited for was a good thing or not. Most worrisome, since their arrival in Heartshrine Village, Kithr had not seen Equinox.

Words couldn't help Lyan. Words were useless against the

Elder's hold, and Kithr wasn't a man for words. Help for Lyan would come by action.

*"Any trips you take in the near future will be ones you plan for first,"* Lyan had said as they returned to the village. *You knew about this even then. Is that why I felt something was wrong? Is that why you wouldn't look at the stars? You didn't want to see this fate burning down at you?*

Declan responded, ignorant of Kithr's roiling turmoil. Quietly he said, "I would expect that Lyan's not doing well."

The concern in his voice sounded genuine. Kithr wanted to trust him and believe that somehow, someone else in the village remained free of Elder Brenhan's enchantment, but he didn't dare.

When Kithr said nothing, Declan continued. "Does he even have food?"

Kithr nodded. "Lyan has the gifts he was given—that's plenty of food for a while. I bring him water."

"Does he need anything? I can try to look for—"

*He needs people to stop treating him like a criminal!* "Lyan doesn't need anything you could find," Kithr said sharply.

"Kithr! Mad God's Pits, I'm trying to offer you help!" Declan burst. "You look like you haven't slept in days, and you don't talk to anyone."

*Damn you, Elder Brenhan. Damn you for forcing me to distrust even my brothers in arms.* "You want to help me? Well I'm a lot more likely to need help getting enough food to last the winter than I am to need help dealing with a stargazer!" Kithr jerked open his door and stormed inside, slamming it shut behind him.

"Kithr!" The door muffled Declan's protest. Kithr closed his eyes, leaning back against the wood and shaking with rage.

*I hope I passed your test, Elder. Because I don't think I can restrain myself through another.*

Even as he thought it, Kithr knew he would. If the Elder tested him again, he would force himself to hold back again.

He had to. Lyan's life depended on it, and until Kithr had prepared, he couldn't risk discovery.

Drawing a steadying breath, Kithr opened his eyes. His outer room was as stark as ever, with little hint of anything out of the ordinary aside from the unusually large assortment of nuts he'd collected and the sun-shriveled berries he had dried. He hadn't been hunting. Meat took too long to smoke, time he couldn't take. Winter in Eilidh Wood, with little time to prepare, would be difficult. Winter outside Eilidh Wood, with only what supplies he could carry, would be brutal.

*We'll both be named as exiles.* That thought hurt more than he expected. *We will be… we will be numbered among the Lost, but that will be a lie. Lyan will never be Lost. I might have been so once—gods know I could become so again. But Lyan represents everything an elf of Eilidh Wood should be. Nothing anyone says will change that—not men, not gods.*

Kithr set down his bag and strode into his bedroom. The covers of his bed lay in rumpled, unmade lumps, testimony to his futile attempts at sleep. Sometimes he could doze, but never for long before his mind spurred him back to his feet. All around, evidence of his plan lay visible. Kithr's travel bags hung on pegs, already packed with gear. His bow hung next to the bags, with three full quivers of arrows below. His winter gear aired, ready to be packed, though the season only hinted at autumn. The room had an air of a temporary stop, a place used to prepare for a continuing journey, not a home.

*I thought I was coming home when I returned here. I was wrong.*

Kithr checked that nothing had been disturbed. No one should be able to enter his house without his leave, but Kithr didn't trust even the forest itself completely. He hated his suspicions, knowing they pulled him toward a dark path he'd walked once before—a path that had led him, during the war, to take the heads of men, women, and children as trophies.

Kithr's bile rose, and he left the room quickly. He spent the late afternoon packing food into hide pouches. He was relying on the gifts given to Lyan to last them for a time, and not to spoil or rot, and he hadn't even discussed his plan with Lyan. That was a risk, but not one Kithr could easily avoid.

As night finally fell and people around the village prepared for sleep, Kithr returned to his room, packed his winter gear, and collected his bags. He wasn't ready to depart, but he would feel more secure if his supplies were stashed somewhere outside his house. He knew several good spots in the forest to create a cache. Escape would be simplified with his gear already waiting outside the village.

Kithr opened his door to check for anyone who might still be about. He paused, surprised to find a leather pack leaning against the door frame. Cautious, Kithr picked it up. By the weight, it was full of something. He brought it in and set it on the table, where the light of the lamp allowed him to see the emblem on the flap.

"Declan," Kithr said aloud, frowning slightly. He unlaced the flap and opened the pack, then stopped, staring.

"Jerky, dried meat, smoked fish…" Each bundle in the pack was marked with an identifying symbol, and at the top lay a folded note. *Does he suspect what I'm planning?*

The note was brief, wasting few words. *Kithr, if this is all the aid you'll allow me to give, then this is what I will give. We haven't forgotten you, and we take care of our own.*

"Will you still think that when I've taken Lyan and left, Declan?" Kithr asked softly. "Or will you curse me, and curse yourself for giving up your own winter stores to me?"

The wrappings around the dried meat kept the scent trapped inside, so predators wouldn't be attracted to it. Kithr laced the bag closed again. *Thank you, Declan. You've helped me more than you know. I wish I could tell you the truth.*

He added Declan's pack to his bags and slung them all over his shoulders. Outside, Heartshrine Village lay quiet and still. In Lyan's house, a light still shone. Lyan had taken to leaving a lantern lit all the time, day or night. Kithr paused, debating checking on him, but after a moment, decided to deal with the gear first.

Lanterns glowed around the village, lighting the way for anyone out late. Pale moths fluttered around the lanterns, drawn to the light.

The struggles of one fat moth caught Kithr's notice, and he saw the faint shimmer of a spider web in the light, then the dark shape of the spider as it stalked toward its prey. When Kithr had been a boy, Elder Brenhan told him that even spiders were entitled to their prey and served a purpose, but Kithr had never been able to tolerate the eight-legged, skittering creepers. Everything about them, from the way they looked to the way they moved sent chills down his spine.

He dropped a bag and jerked his knife from its sheath. A slash of the blade ripped through the web, separating spider from its prey. The spider clung tenaciously to its threads, climbing resolutely back up the torn web as it swayed in the breeze. Kithr slashed again, cutting the strands that held the spider. It tumbled to the ground, and he crushed it underfoot, shuddering.

Picking up the bag again, Kithr scraped the sole of his boot against a tree root and followed the familiar path from the village into Eilidh Wood. That path led him past the shrine. Kithr's steps slowed as he approached. The stones glowed with the light of elven lanterns. The shrine was always lit, and any elf who passed on this path paused to say a prayer to the gods. Kithr almost walked on without stopping, but in the stillness of night, knowing he was alone, he couldn't restrain his anger.

He didn't kneel, and he didn't find any words of praise or thanks. Brown eyes fixed on the carved image of Soldarr, Feyra, and Tesseia, the gods of the elves, and his hands clenched into fists.

"Why?" Kithr demanded finally of the silent stones. "Why are you doing this to Lyan?"

Wind whispered though the trees and rustled the grass at Kithr's feet as insects and night birds fell silent. He sensed a presence behind him, and was reaching for his bow before the other spoke—a dry, familiar, but unexpected voice.

"You think this the work of *your* gods, Kithr?"

Kithr spat out his answer without turning. "Elder Brenhan has stripped Lyan of everything he loves, denying him the stars and astrology, condemning him to remain within his home until he starves or accepts exile by leaving the village. And the Elder speaks the will of our gods."

A sharp bark of laughed answered him. "Your Elder is an arrogant, self-serving liar."

Kithr spun, his eyes narrowing as he faced Nachyne. The god stood with arms folded across his bare chest, wings folded against his back. In no mood for flippancy or riddles, and in no mood to speak respectfully, Kithr snapped back. "*And* he is the Elder. And the *Elder* speaks the will of the gods."

Nachyne's tone held neither the jest nor mockery Kithr had heard during past meetings. "He might be speaking the will of *a* god, but it's not that of your gods."

"How would you know?" Kithr countered.

"Because if it *was* their will, Soldarr, Feyra, and Tesseia would not have asked me to go fetch Lyan *out* of your village."

Kithr scowled. "Why would *our* gods have asked *you* to come here to get Lyan and not do it themselves? You have nothing to do with Eilidh Wood."

"I asked them for an answer to a question, and this is what they wanted in return for telling me," Nachyne said. He looked over Kithr, noting the bags. "Good, you're already prepared to travel. What about Lyan?"

"I was bringing some supplies to a safer location, not planning to leave tonight. And I haven't discussed my plan with Lyan yet. I intend to wait until I'm ready to leave. It gives him less time to object."

"He's locked in his house after some incident with your

Elder, and you expect him to object to leaving?" Nachyne asked dubiously.

"Yes," Kithr said. "I do."

"Then I won't offer him the option," Nachyne said. "Lyan leaves tonight."

Kithr bristled at the god's tone. "I *have* a plan."

Nachyne made a sound of irritation. "Mortals! It's *obvious* that you have a plan, Kithr, and a perfectly good one, I'm sure. In case you forget, *I* have good reason to want the Spearbearer free as well. You've packed and prepared. What's left to wait for?"

Kithr let out his breath slowly. *I should be the one freeing Lyan, not you.*

Nachyne's eyes narrowed as he watched Kithr's face. The god spoke coolly. "Which is more important right now, Kithr: your pride, or Lyan?"

That stung, as Nachyne doubtless intended. "Lyan," he said. He forced his voice to be even. "I doubt he's packed anything. He'll need his winter gear, and I was counting on taking most of the food he was given as our supplies." Kithr paused. "I haven't seen Equinox since we arrived."

"The Spear isn't here," Nachyne said. "Believe me, I *know* when I'm near that damnable thing. Lyan's sent it somewhere else."

"Equinox isn't here?" Kithr repeated. He'd suspected as much, but hearing his thought confirmed sent a chill down his spine. "Then Lyan won't have it to protect himself."

"Even separated from the Spear, he can use some of its powers," Nachyne told him. "But that isn't a reason for concern. You'll be guarding him, and I brought some additional assistance."

"What sort of assistance?" Kithr asked warily. His gaze roved the dark forest in search of glowing red eyes, expecting to see the pooka that Nachyne had bound to Lyan.

Nachyne chuckled. "Don't look for monsters, Kithr. Look for Tathrens."

For one moment, all Kithr's anger flared to life, ready to lash out at an enemy he had hated for years. Then it passed like a summer cloudburst, and for the first time since Elder Brenhan passed his judgment against Lyan, a small smile found Kithr's face. "You brought Cailean."

"I left him and his men a little way off the main road. It seemed safer until I knew the situation," Nachyne said.

Kithr nodded shortly. "I'll bring them. Get Lyan, and I'll meet you here."

He set his packs in the shelter of the bushes. As Kithr jogged up the path toward the main road, he felt weight lift from his spirit, and he laughed darkly.

*The irony—the Tathrens I spent so long hating are now the only allies I know I can trust to not be corrupted by Elder Brenhan. Mad God's Pits. I can't believe how relieved I am to know that Cailean is here.*

## 6

## CAILEAN

*Eilidh Wood is a strange thing. The forest is more than simply the home of the elves. It is a living thing, with what can only be called an awareness—a consciousness primal, protective, and intelligent, for which not even the elves have an explanation. For all that elves are long-lived, much of their history is lost. Within Eilidh Wood itself lie ruins of stone and wood, telling of structures, even fortresses, implying an age when the inhabitants were more than primitive hunters and gatherers. When asked about such places, though, the elves have no answers but to say "they have always been there." Whatever the secrets of their origins, they are known only to Eilidh Wood itself, and perhaps the gods, if even them.*
*~Ercole Baeil'Kyn, Royal Archivist of Tather, "Treatise on Eilidh Wood"*

Eilidh Wood's shadows loomed over Cailean and his men, dark and foreboding with an air of watchful awareness unnatural to ordinary plants and trees. The blue flames of the fire Nachyne had left offered illumination like bright moonlight, but it didn't soften the oppressive air of the elven forest.

Cailean searched the shadows warily. The forest never offered welcome to Tathrens, though it tolerated them so long as they didn't antagonize it. Even the animals were unsettled by the forest—the packhorses more than the mounts, but the mounts were plains-bred horses, and had stood under the forest's shadows before. The horses had all endured Nachyne's method of travel better than Cailean had expected. Better than some of the riders, certainly. He cast a look of concern toward Aikan, sitting near the fire. Aikan still looked wan, though his stomach had finally settled, and he nursed a mug of wine, resolutely attempting to ignore the looming oppression.

"I don't like this forest," Dalrian said, shifting uneasily as he glanced around.

"The feeling is obviously not mutual, as you are still alive and well," Yion observed mildly. The mercenary sat at ease, leaning against the trunk of a tree and radiating calm. Not even the disapproval of elven forests flustered him.

"Thanks, Yion. That makes me feel *so* much better," Dalrian muttered. "This place makes my skin crawl. Feels like I'm being watched."

"Of course you are being watched. You are in Eilidh Wood, and you are *Tathren*." The word wasn't quite spoken as a profanity by the watcher who stepped from the shadows like a phantom emerging from the trunk of a tree.

Even as his hand closed around Solstice, Cailean recognized both the voice, with its strong elven accent, and the speaker. Brown hair, tan skin, brown clothes, grim face, Kithr demonstrated at every abrupt appearance why elven fighters had been so lethal during the war with Tather. He was near Lyan's age, some one hundred and fifty years old, but those years had hardened Kithr in ways they had not marked Lyan. Shadows always clung around him, but even with the pale light, Cailean saw more shadows on Kithr's face than the last time they had met. His hair had been chopped raggedly short, as if it had been pulled back in a tail, then the tail hacked off and the remainder left untended. Dark circles of sleepless nights ringed his eyes, and exhaustion and anger lined his face. His clothing was creased, rumpled, and dirty, as if worn unchanged for several days.

Cailean couldn't call Kithr a friend, but in their previous journey, a grudging mutual respect had grown between them, and Kithr's devotion to Lyan was unquestionable. "Nachyne brought us—," Cailean began.

Kithr stepped into the blue light and faced Cailean. The weariness in his brown eyes struck Cailean. "I know. He said as much and sent me to fetch you. Come on."

Cailean caught his horse's reins, and the stallion raised his head to eye him warily. Cailean scratched the horse's ears, then asked, "What's happened, Kithr?"

"Nachyne didn't bother to tell you?" Kithr said sharply.

"No. The god of monsters insisted on vagaries," Aikan said almost as sharply, pouring out the last of his wine and climbing to his feet.

"He only told us that he had business in Eilidh Wood and wanted to bring a Spearbearer with him," Cailean said. "I'm sorry, I don't know more."

Kithr stopped and drew a deep breath. "I apologize for my short temper. My anger is not directed at you or yours, Cailean. In truth, I'm relieved to see you."

That wasn't an admission Cailean had expected to ever hear from Kithr. "What happened?" Cailean asked again, more quietly.

"More than I know, probably," Kithr said. "But something is very wrong in Heartshrine Village. When we were to tell Elder Brenhan the tale of our journey, Lyan made me swear to say nothing, then hid the knowledge that he bears Equinox." His eyes narrowed as he focused on the Spear in

Cailean's hand. "He created the impression that you carry Equinox, not Solstice, and the Elder accused Lyan of betraying our people by allowing a Tathren to claim our Spear."

"What?" Cailean said in disbelief.

Kithr continued. "Elder Brenhan stripped Lyan of the title of astrologer and ordered him confined within his house. Lyan offers no resistance, and makes no effort to so much as *see* the stars. And he refuses to tell me *why*!" The elf's frustration filled his voice.

"That doesn't sound like Lyan at all," Shiolto said, speaking Cailean's thought.

"No, horse-tender, it doesn't," Kithr said. He let out a deep breath. "Nachyne told me that the gods of my people sent him to fetch Lyan. We meet at the shrine."

"Lead the way," Cailean told him. "Did Nachyne say why the elven gods found it necessary to send him?" The thought reminded Cailean uncomfortably of the wards Porephyn had created by blood sacrifice in Cailean's own keep. Blessed by the Mad God Murdo, those wards had prevented any of the Tathren gods from entering the keep while Porephyn lived.

"He said Elder Brenhan is a fool and not following the will of our gods. Beyond that, he left to my imagination," Kithr said sharply. "I know that Lyan has used Equinox—somehow he has made the Elder seem to forget that I accompanied Lyan, so he assumes I am in agreement with his judgment against my friend."

"How can *anyone* who knows you ever think—," Cailean started to say.

"Lyan guards you against a danger only he knows," Yion cut in, "yet he will not tell you what it is or why your Elder is a threat."

Kithr's gaze fixed on the mercenary. "What do you know?"

Yion shook his head. "My lord has revealed nothing to me, Kithr. I only infer from your words and my knowledge of Lyan. If I knew more, you have my word that I would tell you."

Kithr cursed. "I was hoping *someone* would know what in the gods' names is going on."

"Should I discover anything or my lord reveal answers to me, I will tell you all I am able, Kithr," Yion promised solemnly.

Cailean expected Kithr to sharply dismiss Yion as a mercenary as he had in the past, but the elf surprised him by nodding and not arguing. "Good. Maybe you can get something from Lyan. I can't."

Those words told Cailean how desperate Kithr grew for answers. Both an admission of helplessness and a plea for aid lay hidden within. "We'll help however we can, Kithr. Without you and Lyan, I wouldn't have my home, my title, and probably not even my life. I owe you anything we can offer. For what good a Tathren's help is."

Finally, a ghost of a smile touched Kithr's face. "Yours is worth more than most. Come on."

Leading the horses, they followed Kithr. Behind them, Nachyne's fire flickered and died. Kithr paused to pick up a lantern from the ground. When he opened the shutter, light glowed like a flame, but the lantern held neither fire nor visible fuel. Cailean stared at it, but when Kithr continued walking, Cailean hurried after, urging Sai on. As they followed the narrow trail, the pack animals snorted and shied. Shiolto soothed them, convincing the reluctant horses to trust him and follow. Kithr glanced over his shoulder at them.

"You're better prepared than I am, Cailean."

Cailean didn't hear sarcasm in Kithr's voice, but raised a questioning eyebrow all the same. "I don't know about that. It's a hasty thrown-together assortment of gear. The god of monsters appeared this afternoon to inform me that I was leaving. He didn't give us much time, so I had to guess what we might need without knowing how long we'll be away from home. I would think that less of a worry for you—you're in Eilidh Wood."

Kithr shook his head, a sharp movement. "We're not staying here. I've been gathering what I can since the Elder's judgment fell, but my ability to do so is limited. I don't have winter stores stashed away—the time in which I would have done so, I was otherwise occupied—and I cannot risk raising suspicion that I am not under the Elder's enchantment. If he discovered the truth, I won't be able to get Lyan out of here." He slapped aside a branch hanging in the path, knocking loose a shower of yellowing leaves.

*No farms, no herds for reliable supplies of food… Do the elves really still live by primitive hunting and scavenging in the forest, with a little trade? How do they survive?* "If the situation here can be settled quickly, you might not have to leave," Cailean said.

Kithr just grunted in reply, and Cailean knew the elf held no hope for a simple, swift resolution. He made a different offer instead. "It might not be your first choice, but if you have need, my keep will always be open to you and Lyan."

Aikan shifted uneasily. "Lord Cailean…"

"My home is open to them, Aikan," Cailean said without turning. He knew what Aikan was thinking, the political ramifications of inviting elves into his lands, and how it would look to the other lords of Tather. But this was far more than mere politics.

"I considered it," Kithr said. "Predictable, though. Pursuit would be heaviest in that direction."

"You expect your own people to chase you if you and Lyan leave?" Dalrian asked.

Kithr didn't answer. He stumbled suddenly, tripping over a root, cursing sharply as he caught himself against a tree.

"Kithr, when was the last time you slept?" Cailean asked.

"I'm fine!" Kithr snapped.

Cailean pressed his lips together, saying nothing as Kithr forged on down the narrow path.

"Three days, I think," Kithr said suddenly.

"What?" Cailean asked.

"Last time I got a full night's sleep. Three days ago, I think. I've slept in snatches here and there since."

*Three days with little to no sleep? Considering that, Kithr's temper is remarkably restrained.*

Cailean didn't voice his thought, and they walked in silence until Kithr held up a hand. The line halted, and Kithr shuttered the lantern, plunging them abruptly into darkness. In the moments while Cailean's eyes adjusted, Kithr disappeared. Tension crept up Cailean's spine, and he tried to suppress it before he thought too long about being abandoned in Eilidh Wood in the dark. He heard horses and his men shifting uneasily behind him, but couldn't see their shapes. The thick canopy of branches overhead blocked even moonlight, as if the forest preferred to leave them blind.

Heartbeats stretched on for an eternity, then a glow of light flickered into being as Kithr returned. Cailean blinked rapidly as his eyes readapted to the light, but he saw Kithr's brow pinched in concern.

"No sentries," the elf said quietly. "There should always be sentries around the village."

Cailean stood straighter. "So, we are near the spot where you first aimed an arrow at my head?"

Kithr nodded. "The road should always be watched. All around the village should, but especially the road." He looked angry and worried over the lapse, but motioned Cailean and his men to follow.

"What would you have done if there *had* been sentries?" Dalrian asked.

"Incapacitate them," Kithr answered. "Normally I could

offer to replace them, but since I've been assigned to guard Lyan, I'm exempt from sentry duty."

"Lyan needs a guard?" Shiolto asked.

"He is accused of treason, horse-tender," Kithr snapped. "He is to remain in his house until he starves. If he chooses to leave his house, his guard is supposed to tell the Elder immediately so the rite of banishment can be performed, which would, according to our laws, make him an exile and Lost."

"If he has been found guilty of treason, why wasn't he executed?" Aikan cut in.

Cailean jerked and looked sharply at his steward. The thought hit like a punch in the gut. "Aikan!"

Aikan's gaze remained on Kithr. "In Tather, that would be the punishment."

Kithr tensed, his free hand clenching in a fist. "Lyan is *not* a traitor," he hissed between his teeth.

"I did not claim he is," Aikan said sharply. "But the accusation remains one of treason—a capital crime in Tather. Are elven laws so different?"

A long silence followed from Kithr. "No," he said finally. "That would normally be the punishment for treason. With the village under the Elder's spell, no one asked why he passed the sentence he did, while I didn't think to consider what other fate could await Lyan."

"Your Elder believes you under his spell as well?" Cailean asked. He wanted to ask a great deal more about this spell, but those questions would wait.

Kithr nodded curtly. "Lyan protected me from it."

"And the Elder assigned you to guard Lyan?" Cailean continued.

Another sharp nod. "Your point, Tathren?"

"It sounds intentionally cruel," Cailean said plainly. "Confine Lyan to his house and deny him the sight of the sky, turn his people against him, then use his best friend as his guard. If your Elder thinks you agree with him against Lyan, then he would know that making you into Lyan's enemy would hurt him more than anything else."

Kithr stiffened, then hissed something angrily in Elven. He didn't speak the rest of the way.

Cailean remembered the shrine to the elven gods. It held an air of age, an inexplicable sense that he looked upon something ancient and sacred. The massive blocks of carved marble depicted three figures—one god and two goddesses. He knew little about Soldarr, Feyra, and Tesseia except that Feyra and Tesseia were sisters, and Soldarr was lover to both. Some fanatical Tathren priests claimed that Soldarr was also brother to the goddesses, but Cailean dismissed the charge as an effort to further sully Tathren opinion of the elves.

The ground before the shrine was worn and flat, and small offerings lay arrayed before it. The last time Cailean had been here, the elves in his company had taken care to kneel and offer prayers at the shrine. This time, Kithr appeared determined not even to look at it. His gaze raked the dark forest as he hung the lantern on a hook beside the shrine.

"Nachyne. Are you back yet?"

Cailean flinched at Kithr's sharp tone and its lack of respect for the god. He shifted uneasily in the following silence. The elven village lay only a little way down the path, and at this late hour, Cailean couldn't think of any plausible excuse he could offer for his presence, aside from the truth, should any other elves come upon them.

Yion stepped in front of the shrine and gave it a deep, formal bow. The action surprised Cailean, but Yion offered no explanation and addressed no words to the shrine. Whatever message his actions conveyed, it was not intended for mortals.

Footsteps crunched in dry leaves from the direction of the village. Cailean tensed, motioning for his men to move away from the light of the lanterns around the shrine. The approaching steps were in no hurry, almost plodding in their advance, and Cailean guessed there was only one person. He tugged his horse with him back toward the shadows, praying the animals wouldn't give away their presence. Kithr held his bow, warily watching the path.

Cailean had been wrong—two figures walked into the pools of light around the shrine, though only one made noise. Nachyne's bare, clawed feet didn't rustle the leaves as he walked beside Lyan, a bundle of packs slung over one shoulder. The god of monsters spied Kithr and, without preamble, demanded, "Is he *always* this stubborn?"

Lyan stood with head bowed, gazing at the ground as if it held something of utmost importance. He wore leather breeches and a shirt too thin for the night's chill. His red hair was tied back loosely, but strands hung free, dangling around his face and eyes. Lyan didn't look around, and his slumped stance was that of a man facing a trial, not one being rescued and released from imprisonment.

"Lyan?" Shiolto asked uncertainly.

Lyan raised his head slightly and looked toward Shiolto. He gave a slight nod that might have been agreement or greeting, but he didn't answer.

Kithr didn't answer Nachyne's question. "Did anyone see you?"

Nachyne rolled his eyes. "Yes, Kithr, I decided to take Lyan from your village by announcing myself with trumpets and lightbursts, so everyone would know. No, we weren't seen." He dropped the bags at Kithr's feet with a thump. "Clothes, the books he wanted, and whatever else I could prod Lyan into telling me he expected to need."

"Food?" Kithr asked pointedly.

"The gray bag, Kithr." Lyan's gaze shifted toward Kithr. Cailean heard the words in perfect, unaccented Tathren, but he knew that Lyan was speaking Elven, and the words were translated by the enchanted earcuff Lyan wore. Lyan sounded... not tired, but resigned. The dull, weary voice was so unlike the vitality Cailean remembered. A new jolt of distressed concern washed through him, coming from Solstice. Equinox was not within Solstice's senses.

*I'm sure the Spear is safe. Lyan probably sent Equinox away to keep it from being discovered. He can call it back at any time.*

Aikan stepped up beside Cailean. He frowned at Lyan, then looked at Nachyne. "And this is why you insisted on dragging my lord away from his home and duties?"

Again, Cailean winced at the disrespectful tone. Nachyne wasn't a god of their people, but all the same, he *was* a god.

"Hardly," Nachyne scoffed in response. "I wasn't aware there was a problematic situation here until I arrived."

Cailean started. "Then..."

"Get to the point!" Kithr snapped at the god.

Nachyne fixed a glare on the elf fit to send reapers fleeing for cover. Cailean spoke quickly, trying to avert divine retribution. "Lord Nachyne, I'm sorry. We're all short of temper and confused over the current situation. If you could please enlighten us as to why we are gathered here, I'm sure we would appreciate it."

"You are here because both Spearbearers are needed, and I foolishly thought it would be faster to start by getting you. You are away from Tather because you and Lyan as Spearbearers must deal with the havoc being caused by Murdo's new champion. *I* am here because I was promised an answer to a question, and I'm still waiting for it as if I have nothing better to do than listen to the complaints and squabbles of *mortals!*" Nachyne replied, his eyes glittering with anger.

*A champion... of Murdo?*

"And we will answer your question, Nachyne." The new voice was rich and female, a lovely alto that begged to be singing rather than speaking. The shrine glowed, and Kithr sidled away from it as three figures shimmered into view on the bare ground before the shrine, drawing moonlight until they became solid. Cailean's eyes opened wide and he found himself kneeling, just as the elves and the rest of his men did. One of the two women spoke, the same voice as before. "We will tell you, and we will explain to the mortals why we asked you to bring both Lyan and the Tathren Spearbearer here."

7

———————

KITHR

*"Should the Mad God or his minions find their way into the Shrine of
Equinox, they must not be allowed to take hold. For that reason, our
guardianship becomes all the more important, not less, when the Spear has
a bearer, for then the Spear's power is not here to aid in the protection of
its place of power."*

Soldarr, Feyra, and Tesseia glowed with the light radiating
from the ancient shrine. Kithr's anger and weariness gave
way to awe as he stared. He had met gods before, but never *his*
gods.

Nachyne's stance implied boredom. "I'm sure you can
handle matters from here. Just what you asked for—two
Spearbearers. Now, the answer to my question?" The god of
monsters sounded irritated and impatient.

Feyra's golden hair glittered as she turned to Nachyne.
Over one shoulder, she carried a hunting bow, over the other,
a quiver of arrows, and at her waist, a slender blade, identical
to the weapons carried by her sister. Both goddesses wore
decidedly unfeminine studded leather jerkins, and Soldarr

wore gleaming armor, battle axe slung across his back, as if they prepared for war.

Feyra answered Nachyne. "You asked us how you could be freed from the hold of Equinox. The answer, Nachyne, is that the bearer of Equinox alone has the power to release you."

Nachyne's gaze moved to Lyan. The god growled in anger. "Bah! You are *sure* that is the only way?"

"We are," Soldarr answered. "You know the powers of the Spears are unique. You were bound by the Spear—you must be freed by the same."

Nachyne spat in the dirt. "Why didn't you just *tell* me, rather than demand a favor in return?" The god of monsters was rapidly growing more irate.

"We need both Spearbearers, and you have had direct dealings with them," Soldarr responded. "Also, your presence is more tolerated in Tather than mine. And I *do* trust you noticed the wards surrounding Heartshrine Village?"

Kithr stiffened, looking up sharply at the gods. *Wards? What kind of wards?*

"I noticed," Nachyne said, eyes narrowing. "I also noticed you neglected to mention them, or that there might be other difficulties to your request. Quite a lot of trouble for me to get an answer you *knew* I wouldn't like."

"You're right, Nachyne," Tesseia agreed quietly. Her hair was pure black, the night to Feyra's golden sun. "Had we told you more, we doubted that you would have agreed."

"You would have been right," Nachyne snapped.

Kithr's anger rose again, pushing away the awe. *You complain about mere mortals wasting your time, and now you waste ours by bickering while in the village, the Elder continues to manipulate and deceive everyone?* "What is all this about?" he snapped in the pause, climbing to his feet. "You wanted us here. So here we are!"

At his outburst, the gods finally deigned to notice the

mortals around the shrine. Kithr didn't flinch from their gazes, defiantly staring back.

Feyra answered. "We called the Spearbearers and their companions because Murdo has raised up and empowered a champion, and this new champion must be stopped before he grows stronger."

Kithr tensed. "The Elder?"

She shook her head. "No. Not Brenhan. We do not know his name, and he is not in Eilidh Wood."

"And what about Elder Brenhan?" Kithr demanded. "He condemned Lyan of treason! He lied to us! Was *that* your will?"

"No, Kithr of Heartshrine Village, it was not our will."

"Then why didn't you *do* anything about it?" Kithr burst. Part of his mind quailed, shocked that he dared speak with such disrespect to his gods. But anger held him and refused to be pushed down.

"We did," Tesseia cut in. "We asked Nachyne to bring him safely out of the village."

"Leaving the Elder to continue to do as he pleases? Letting him lie and enspell our village? Why haven't you gone yourselves?" Kithr asked sharply.

Lyan rested a hand on Kithr's shoulder and spoke quietly. "Because they can't."

Kithr jumped, then looked at his friend. "Why not? Why *can't* the gods act among their own people? This is *Heartshrine Village,* by the First Seed! This is one of the most sacred places in Eilidh Wood!"

"Wards," Lyan answered softly.

"Wards? What, like those that damnable mage crafted at Cailean's keep, blocking entry to the Tathren gods?" Kithr fervently hoped he misunderstood Lyan.

But Lyan simply nodded, silent.

"The leader of your village is using some kind of power to

keep your gods out?" Shiolto asked uncertainly. "That's not a good sign."

"There are no good signs," Lyan said. He glanced to the sky, but only for a moment, then shivered. "No good signs at all."

Uneasy silence fell. Nachyne broke the stillness after a long moment. "Very encouraging, Lyan." He tried to sound dismissive, but Kithr heard unease in the god's voice. That unsettled Kithr as much as Lyan's words.

"Truth is not required to be encouraging," Lyan said.

"Signs or not, you have a duty to stop Murdo's champion," Soldarr cut in. His gaze moved between Lyan and Cailean.

*Lyan was imprisoned on false charges, and the only reason you intervened was to send him away to fight somewhere else?* Kithr's eyes narrowed. "And our home? Heartshrine Village? Elder Brenhan? You want us to simply *leave* like this?"

Tesseia gazed at Kithr. "You were already planning to take Lyan and leave, were you not?"

Kithr faltered. "Not permanently," he said. *You're here now! We shouldn't have to!*

"You already chose to leave Heartshrine Village," the goddess said. Her voice was soothing. "We have not changed that. We have given you a destination."

"And the Elder?" Kithr insisted. "We're supposed to let him have his way? Let him continue to deceive our people?"

"This shrine's magic is great enough to overcome the wards here, allowing us to appear before you now, Kithr," Feyra said. "But unless those wards are broken, our powers are limited."

"Kithr."

Kithr turned when Lyan spoke his name.

Lyan held his gaze. "We have no proof and no support. We can't fight him yet. We aren't ready. No one will believe us.

Without something that will break the wards, we won't beat him."

Kithr's jaw tightened, but finally he nodded, acknowledging Lyan's words. "This 'champion.' He has something we can use to defeat the Elder or break the wards?"

Lyan hesitated, then nodded.

"Fine. I'll trust you, Lyan." Kithr looked back to the gods. "So where *are* we going?"

"East, to the land of Joski," Soldarr said. His expression and tone betrayed impatience at the delay in proclaiming the reason for their decision to grace the mortal world with their divine presence.

Cailean frowned. "Pardon me, Lord Soldarr, but isn't that near the Shrine of Equinox?"

Soldarr studied the Tathren lord with only slightly less distaste than Ahebban had looked on Lyan and Kithr in Cailean's keep. "You are correct. Murdo undoubtedly knows that the Spear has a bearer, but we believe his champion seeks the Shrine."

"We heard rumors of unrest and battle in that area when we traveled through it," Cailean said. "Even before Equinox chose Lyan. Armies on the roads, villages attacked and looted."

"Murdo thrives on chaos," Feyra said simply. "It provides him with cover to hide his schemes."

Kithr remembered ragged bands of refugees in the forest. He hadn't cared much about their plight at the time, focused instead on finding Lyan and freeing him from the clutches of Vynzent, but he remembered them all the same. "So that's where we're going."

*That's several months of travel. Winter will be on us by the time we reach that land, unless some god or Spearbearer can magic us there.*

"It is," Soldarr responded. His tone indicated that he considered the matter to be settled.

Kithr, however, was less ready to leave the matter as it

stood. "And this champion will delay his plans long enough for us to *walk* there?"

Cailean cleared his throat pointedly. "We don't need to walk, Kithr. Solstice can take us."

Kithr felt an irrational stab of anger at Cailean for offering a solution that didn't inconvenience the gods, the same anger he'd felt earlier when the Tathren had placated some of Nachyne's anger with apologies and excuses of exhaustion and confusion, no matter how true those excuses had been.

"Good." Soldarr's tone was brusque. "Wait until you are outside Eilidh Wood before using the Spear to speed your travel. The forest can be unpredictable in its reactions to such magic under its boughs. I trust there is nothing else."

"Lord Soldarr, my lord wishes me to extend his greetings to you and to Ladies Feyra and Tesseia," Yion said. "He has bid me assist the Spearbearers as I am able."

Soldarr paused, assessing Yion. The god frowned. "He does, does he? I find it strange that Saiboti, who claims to be the god of honorable warriors of Tather, should choose a Quereshi assassin as his champion."

Yion expressed no offense or indignation at the statement, only bowed. "You are not the first to say so, Lord Soldarr, and I doubt you shall be the last, either."

"Watch over them well," Feyra said to Yion.

The mercenary bowed again. "I shall, Lady."

Lyan frowned at the gods, as if puzzled by their words. When he noticed Kithr watching him, Lyan shook his head, dismissing whatever troubled him.

The gods offered no additional farewells. The trees rustled in an unfelt breeze, then drew back to let the full light of the moon shine on the shrine. Kithr sensed Eilidh Wood, the spirit of the forest responding to the presence of the elven gods. He was always aware of the forest while under its boughs, but less often did Kithr feel that the forest was, in turn, aware of him.

But Eilidh Wood was undeniably aware of the elven gods. He wasn't certain the forest welcomed their presence, but his own feelings may have colored that impression.

The three elven gods stood in the moonlight, and their forms evaporated into glittering motes, shimmering in the night. Nachyne snorted softly, then spread his wings and launched into the air. As Kithr watched, the silhouette against the moon shifted in the air, changing from a winged man into a massive reptilian form, obliterating moonlight until it flew past. The tree branches settled back into their normal places, and only mortals remained, earthbound in the shadows of night.

At first, no one spoke. Yion and Cailean had both risen when they spoke to the gods, but Dalrian, Shiolto, and, somewhat surprisingly, Aikan, remained kneeling. Aikan groaned stiffly as Cailean helped him to his feet. The older man glowered—some things never changed.

Shiolto and Dalrian approached. "Lyan, are you all right?" Shiolto asked.

Lyan shook his head, then spoke quietly. "We shouldn't linger."

Kithr gathered the bags he had stashed and added to them those brought by Nachyne. Dalrian eyed the pile, then asked, "Where are your horses?"

"Mine went with Shadowstar," Kithr answered. "So, I expect they are on the plains."

"You mean you had a horse and you just let it go?" Shiolto asked in disbelief.

"I don't have use for a horse within Eilidh Wood," Kithr said. "And I wasn't expecting to be leaving again so soon."

Shiolto looked at Lyan. "But you can call Shadowstar and Kithr's horse back, can't you Lyan?"

Lyan's gaze drifted away. "I'm not calling him."

Kithr started. "You aren't going to call Shadowstar, Lyan? Why not?"

"He's needed where he is. The Appret Plains need their guardian spirit," Lyan said. "I will not call him."

Shiolto cast a look to Cailean, as if expecting his lord to somehow change Lyan's mind. Dalrian, however, chose not to take up the battle. "The packhorses still have some spots. You want your gear loaded on, Kithr?"

*Did I actually think I could carry everything myself? Even splitting the load with Lyan, we would be encumbered.* Kithr nodded. "Yes. Thanks." He slung bags across his shoulders and followed Dalrian to the pack animals.

Lyan snatched up one of the packs Nachyne had brought, sliding his arms though the straps and settling it on his back with a protective air. Kithr didn't know what Lyan carried within, but he didn't argue. He had his own share of gear that he intended to keep close at hand.

As Dalrian strapped bags onto the packhorses, Kithr turned to Cailean. "You can really use Solstice to get us there faster?"

"Yes, I can, and that wasn't just something I said to avert divine anger," Cailean said. "However, Kithr, I don't think picking a fight with your gods is a wise idea."

"Saying what I see is picking a fight?" Kithr countered.

"If a peasant in my lands spoke to me the way you were just speaking to the gods, he would consider himself lucky to only receive a flogging as punishment," Cailean said grimly. "You were insulting *gods*, Kithr. Not mortals. *Gods.*" He shook his head. "Arguments between gods and mortals rarely end in favor of the mortals. And if *that* doesn't convince you, then ask who will be there to help Lyan if you are struck down by divine wrath?"

"I give my respect to those who deserve it," Kithr growled. He let out a deep breath. "It doesn't matter. It's done now. We need to go."

He took a lantern from the shrine. The act of theft against the village was hardly worth mentioning in the face of the other crimes he was committing tonight. Abandoning his assigned duty. Freeing a convicted traitor, and helping that convict escape from Heartshrine Village and from Eilidh Wood. Consorting with the Tathren Spearbearer—perhaps not officially a crime, but it could easily be called an act of treason as well. Against such charges, stealing one lantern from the shrine was insignificant.

Kithr glared at the path leading into Heartshrine Village. *I will not forgive you, Elder, and I will not forget what you have done here. I swear, I will find a way to break whatever hold you have on my home, and I will see true justice done.*

The Tathrens swung into their saddles, and Kithr grabbed the last of his bags, slinging them over his shoulders and leading the way toward the main road, Lyan behind him.

*We will return, I swear it.*

8

## CAILEAN

*Behind him the shadows lay, thick and dark, lurking on feet shod in
silence. No light graced their eyes nor touched their faces, condemned ever
to walk in night, their flesh painted with blood.*
*~Fragment of "The Shadowed Ones," translated from Quereshi.*
*Accuracy of the translation is suspect.*

Kithr walked at a quick pace, confident in his navigation
of Eilidh Wood. Cailean followed, wishing the lantern
light extended further. The forest stood still and quiet around
them, making the crunch of hooves through dry leaves sound
unnaturally loud. A cricket began to chirp, but the sound
faded away uncertainly when it went unanswered.

Cailean's eyes found Lyan. The astrologer walked behind
Kithr, giving more attention to the ground and his footing
than Cailean had ever seen him do during their previous
travels together. Even when the sky had been utterly obscured
by clouds or trees, Lyan's gaze had always roamed upward,
searching. Now, his eyes avoided the sky, as if the answers he
had been seeking now brought him no joy.

Aikan's horse stepped up beside Cailean's, crowding the narrow path and pleasing neither animal. Cailean looked to his steward.

"Lord Cailean, are you sure of this?" Aikan asked in a low voice.

"Sure of what, Aikan? Going to battle against a champion of the Mad God? I find the idea more than a little unsettling, but I'm sure I need to fight this battle."

"About using Solstice to bring us closer to this battle," Aikan said. He looked uneasy. "Are you certain you can do so?"

"I've done it before," Cailean said in surprise.

Aikan blinked. "When, my lord?"

"When we rescued the elves from Ewart's keep," Cailean said, wondering why Aikan didn't remember.

His steward frowned. "Lord Cailean, Lyan claimed Equinox was responsible for our transportation from the dungeon."

"Gods. I forgot that I didn't tell anyone what we really did," Cailean said, understanding. "Lyan and I agreed that those elves could not learn that I carried Solstice. Lyan knew about the curse and how it drained my strength when I used the Spear, but Equinox doesn't have the power to transport people. I used Solstice to free us from the dungeon, and Lyan, using Equinox, gave me his strength to counter the effects of the curse. To everyone else, it looked like Lyan used Equinox, then collapsed."

"Then *you* were responsible for freeing those savages without bloodshed, my lord?" Aikan asked, aghast.

"Aikan, if it had come to bloodshed, far more Tathren blood would have spilled than elven. I don't regret the choice I made."

Aikan fell silent. When he spoke again, he avoided the subject of the elves of Malgor Forest. "Then you don't know how far the Spear can carry us, or how taxing it will be on you."

"True," Cailean allowed. "But it will hasten our travel. Especially with Lyan and Kithr on foot." At least Lyan's ankle didn't appear to be troubling him anymore.

"Um, Kithr," Shiolto called softly from behind Cailean.

"What?" Kithr's reply was clipped and curt.

"How far are you planning to go tonight? It's late, and the horses need rest."

Kithr didn't slow, but he answered after a few moments. "We can stop for a while after we reach the road. The further we are from the village before pursuit begins, the better."

"When is pursuit likely to start?" Dalrian asked uneasily. Cailean heard him shifting in the saddle.

"That depends on which is discovered first: the absence of Lyan and myself, or the horse tracks all around the shrine."

*What will we do if elves attack us? I don't want to harm Lyan's people. They are victims, even if they don't know it.*

"We should have time for a little rest," Lyan said, breaking Cailean from his thoughts. "If anyone comes to the shrine tonight, they'll notice the missing lantern before the tracks, and will leave to replace it."

Kithr made a sound of agreement. "It ought to be a while before anyone actually notices they haven't seen me." Though Kithr said it as an advantage, Cailean heard bitterness in the elf's voice.

Trees rustled and branches creaked. At the edge of the light, Cailean glimpsed movement. "Are you sure it's going to take so long?" he asked, voice low.

The horses snorted and sidled away from something. Something that skirted the edges of the light and moved between trees without a sound. Then, abruptly, it stood in the middle of the path. Kithr jerked to a stop, raising the lantern.

Pale light washed over the figure of a female elf. Cailean's horse danced back with a whinny and a snort, eyes rolling back. He soothed the animal even as he tried to identify why the woman unsettled him as well. Her limbs seemed too thin and too long. Her eyes caught the lantern light and glowed amber, like a cat's. Her skin was brown and rough as bark. In the light, her hair looked green, like trailing vines, and it moved without a breeze.

"Ash and rot." Kithr stepped back.

"What is that?" Shiolto asked.

Her glowing eyes found him. "We are a Splinter of Eilidh Wood." She raised a hand in what might have been a greeting. Overlong fingers tapered to tips like the branches of a tree.

"A what?" Shiolto gulped.

"A Splinter of Eilidh Wood," Lyan repeated quietly. "A mouthpiece of the forest. An elf with plant magic who has surrendered all 'self' to Eilidh Wood and become part of it."

"Yes," she agreed.

Cailean eyed the woman with caution. He'd heard tales of strange creatures that lived in Eilidh Wood, but not even those stories had described a being that was as much plant as elf. "Eilidh Wood has means of speaking?"

Kithr cast a scowl over his shoulder. "You've witnessed the forest's will before. You didn't think that just a pretty turn of phrase, did you?"

Cailean didn't answer. The forest always radiated the impression that it was watching him, and it certainly reacted to the actions of others. However, he'd never considered that it might have both the capability and the desire to speak directly.

*Until a few months ago, I didn't think the Spears could do either. Should I be surprised that Eilidh Wood can?*

"Our children are uprooted, and you are removing them," the Splinter said.

"You intend to stop us from leaving?" Kithr's voice was tight, but he didn't reach for his weapons.

"No, we do not intend to stop you." Her gaze moved to

Cailean. "Last time you walked under our boughs, you took two of our children. One of them returned a Spearbearer."

"Yes," Cailean agreed cautiously. "Though I did not think you were pleased with our presence at the time."

"Not pleased?" she repeated. "You did as we wished. We put our stargazing child where he would need to be found, and turned your path to find him so we could send him with you."

"You dropped Lyan down a ravine and sprained his ankle on *purpose*?!" Kithr burst.

The Splinter ignored him. "A corrupt seed grows in our soil and we cannot uproot it yet. So we send more of our children with you, Spearbearer."

"Not even Eilidh Wood can stop Elder Brenhan?" Kithr stared at her as if he could will answers from the Splinter by look alone.

"If we possessed force enough to consume the Mad God's power, we would need no Spearbearers," she replied, turning to him.

Kithr flinched, looking away from her as he had not done when arguing with the gods.

She continued. "Search out fire sufficient to burn the rot from beneath our branches. Return with whatever tools you must to carve away the blight before it spreads further."

Kithr dipped his head in a stiff nod. "As you will, Eilidh Wood."

"This Splinter will accompany you."

Cailean stiffened. His mouth opened, then closed. He glanced to Lyan and Kithr, but the idea discomfited the elves as much as it did him. "Are you certain you want to send your representative with us? It may be dangerous."

"We are capable of defending ourselves. This Splinter will accompany you."

"It's not a request, Cailean," Lyan said softly.

"I think the forest has made that clear," Cailean said as

quietly. "Do you need any gear? Special food?" What *did* a plant-elf eat? Did one eat at all?

"This Splinter will be supplied." She gazed again at Cailean. "This Splinter will join you when you come to our border." She stepped back out of the light and was gone.

No one spoke for several long moments. Finally Kithr started walking again. Cailean kicked his horse into motion, following the elf. "Does Eilidh Wood send emissaries to speak to people often?"

"I've never seen a Splinter before," Lyan said. "Their appearances are very rare."

"And usually herald a coming disaster," Kithr added, not turning.

"Or the fact that not even Eilidh Wood agrees with the things your Elder is doing, and wishes to make that objection abundantly clear?" Cailean suggested.

"Maybe," Kithr said. "Doesn't make a difference now. The forest has made up its mind, and it won't change it. It's sending that Splinter with us whether we like it or not." From his tone, Kithr's opinion tended toward the second.

Behind Cailean, Dalrian and Shiolto exchanged low, anxious whispers. The few words he caught told him that the Splinter was the subject. Cailean straightened in the saddle, remembering his responsibility to project calm and confidence to the men who depended on him. He might not be any more comfortable with the forest's representative than the brothers, but he could at least present the proper front. He glanced to Aikan, but his steward, for the moment, kept his thoughts to himself.

The path met with the main road, and Cailean relaxed with more space between himself and the looming trees. Kithr, however, remained tense and wary.

*We're more exposed. I know that, but, gods, I'd rather be more exposed than smothered by the trees.*

Kithr didn't stop immediately, but continued down the road until he found an acceptably sheltered site.

"We can rest here for a little while. I want to be moving again before dawn."

Cailean climbed stiffly to the ground. He was sure he would want more sleep than Kithr would grant them, but he didn't complain. No one did, though Aikan visibly winced as he climbed from the saddle. Shiolto tended to the horses, and Dalrian lay out bedrolls.

Yion walked around the camp's perimeter. Cailean remembered that the mercenary had done the same during their travels, though he hadn't known or asked why. Yion noticed Cailean watching him.

"My lord grants me the power to place protections around our place of rest, Lord Cailean. With no offense meant to Eilidh Wood, I find that sleep comes more easily knowing that my lord watches over us as well." Yion finished his circuit and sat down.

Cailean hesitated, then spoke in a low voice. "Yion, I would like to speak to you about something."

Yion met his eyes. "In regards to Lord Soldarr's words to me?"

How the mercenary knew Cailean's thoughts so easily, he didn't know. But Cailean nodded.

"Then let it wait until morning, Lord Cailean, and not disturb the sleep of others."

Cailean opened his mouth, then closed it, realizing to his astonishment that he, a lord, had just been dismissed by a mercenary, the conversation ending before it began. Try as he might, he couldn't find a way to reassert authority without sounding childish, and so, reluctantly, Cailean let the matter lie.

Lyan shivered as he settled on the ground. Kithr asked something in Elven, and Lyan shook his head. Kithr muttered under his breath, walking to the horses and retrieving blankets. Lyan accepted them, and lay down without a word to the Tathrens.

*It's as if someone took everything that makes him "Lyan" and locked that away, leaving a shell behind. Is this going to last? Maybe things will improve once we are out of Eilidh Wood.*

"You should rest as well, Kithr," Cailean said.

Kithr scowled stubbornly. "And who will keep watch, and know the signs of an ambush creeping up on us?"

*As obviously exhausted as you are, Kithr, I think any one of us have a better chance of it than you do.* Cailean barely restrained himself from speaking the thought aloud.

"What, after such a show of support from this damnable forest, you don't trust it to watch over our camp?" Aikan snapped, voice thick with weary irritation.

"Do you?" Kithr countered as sharply.

"I shall keep the watch," Yion said.

Kithr eyed the mercenary. Yion met his gaze and waited patiently. Finally, Kithr capitulated. "Wake me before dawn."

"Of course," Yion agreed.

Kithr sat beside Lyan, pulled his bow forward to rest by his feet, then leaned back against a tree, closing his eyes. Cailean nodded to Shiolto, Dalrian, and Aikan. The men hesitated.

"Do you want the rest of us to take watches as well, Lord Cailean?" Dalrian asked.

Yion shook his head. "No need. I shall keep the watch. You should sleep rather than waste the time."

"Get what rest you can," Cailean ordered. "We'll leave early."

Forcing himself to follow his own instructions, Cailean found the bedroll Dalrian had laid out for him and lay down. Despite the unsettling air of Eilidh Wood, when he closed his eyes, sleep came.

Cailean started awake when someone shook his shoulder. Muzzy and confused, he wondered if he'd somehow rolled out of his bed and a servant was trying to rouse him. He lay on a hard, lumpy surface, not his comfortable mattress.

"Lord Cailean," Yion said softly. "If Solstice has the means of diverting eyes from our camp, you should employ it."

*Camp? Oh… Eilidh Wood. The elves.* Cailean wormed one hand out from the blankets to massage his forehead. The fog of interrupted sleep hung over him. *"Solstice?"*

The Spear responded, and Cailean sat up slowly, pulling a blanket around his shoulders against the chill. "That's more within Equinox's talents, but Solstice can shelter the camp. As long as we stay within its confines, we shouldn't be noticed." His voice was thick with sleep.

"Thank you, Lord Cailean. I apologize—I should have requested such before you lay down to sleep," Yion said. The mercenary was a dark shape, barely visible. Cailean wasn't entirely sure whether he actually saw Yion, or only tricks played by his eyes in the near-darkness.

"Are elves close?" Cailean asked.

"I cannot be certain, Lord Cailean, but I believe there might be searchers in the forest," Yion answered. "The land is quiet, and we are near dawn."

That was a long time for Yion to have waited before "remembering" to ask Cailean and Solstice to add protection to the camp. It was also not enough time to go back to sleep. Cailean rubbed his eyes and let his chin rest on his knees. "Did you really wake me just for this?"

He heard a rustle of movement, then Yion sat across from him, a shadowy figure holding a mug to Cailean. "This is better when warmed, but in the absence of a fire, I fear I can only offer it cold. It will help you wake, Lord Cailean. You wished to ask questions of me."

Cailean took the mug and sniffed the contents. He couldn't identify the mixture of herbs, and took a cautious sip. Cailean grimaced, swallowing before he could spit it back out. "Gods, that's bitter. What in the Mad God's Pits is in it?"

"Nothing harmful," Yion answered. "I prefer it as tea, but it maintains its effects hot or cold."

"I've known few men who know herbs and potions as well as you do, Yion," Cailean observed. He kept his voice low, trying to avoid waking anyone. "I've never asked *how* you know them, or what else you know." Not only herbs and potions, but he had seen Yion employ drugs without hesitation. Cailean eyed the mug warily.

"I trained in such arts in my youth, Lord Cailean. That training was later refined and focused into certain areas."

"What areas?" Cailean asked.

"Poisons and drugs, Lord Cailean." Yion's voice lost none of its sangfroid. "I further used that teaching to learn of medicines. Many poisons, properly diluted, can find uses less unhealthy."

Cailean cautiously took another drink from the mug. The bitter drink was hard to stomach.

Yion spoke again. "What you wish to know, you would be best to ask directly, Lord Cailean. You know of my skills, and I doubt that Kithr was alone in questioning my former life."

"Kithr?" Cailean repeated, feeling like an idiot.

"He questioned Lyan regarding me, distrusting me, during our previous journey. Lyan asked the questions of me, but Kithr raised them first."

Cailean set aside the mug. "Yion, are you an assassin?"

"Not any longer," Yion answered without hesitation. "That was my former life, before my lord called me to serve him."

For a moment, Cailean couldn't breathe. *An assassin. And I never questioned him. He could as easily have come to kill me as to help.*

Yion waited. Cailean couldn't see his face, yet he couldn't imagine Yion's expression being anything but serene, even as he declared himself to be a deadly killer.

*But if I'm honest, I knew or suspected this already. I never asked, but I knew a man doesn't gain Yion's skills as an untrained mercenary.*

Cailean drew in a deep breath. "Soldarr called you by a certain title. Was that the name of your homeland?"

"It was," Yion agreed.

"I've heard the name before. Quereshi? That was what he called you, wasn't it?"

"Indeed," Yion said, but he didn't expound.

Cailean tried to remember. "I think—the warrior-mages of Queresh?"

Yion snorted in amusement. "I know the tale you speak of, Lord Cailean. The translation into your tongue is abysmal, and far too glorified."

He tried not to feel too offended by Yion's assessment of the particular story—it had been one Cailean had enjoyed as a boy. "That isn't what you are, is it?" he asked.

He caught the shift of movement as Yion shook his head. "The warrior-mages come only from the noble caste, Lord Cailean. Those of the assassin caste do not attain to such arts. There is another work, found only in fragments in this land, called 'The Shadowed Ones' that relates to the assassins. The translation, however, is even worse than the other, and I would not recommend attempting to read it."

Cailean blinked, taken aback. "You were born into assassinhood?"

"My parents were matched for their honed skills, in the belief that they would produce offspring of exceptional talent. Such is a tradition among the assassins, and it has proven successful. Is it so different from lords marrying women of good breeding to produce strong heirs?"

Cailean hesitated, then avoided the question altogether. "But you left there."

"I did, and that land is far from here. I chose to leave my former life when I chose to spare and defend a life I had been instructed to end. Lord Saiboti found me, and guarded me against those of my caste who pursued. He then offered me a place at his side, and became my lord."

"And now, you're here," Cailean finished.

"Indeed, Lord Cailean."

"Who else knows this, Yion?"

"I have told Lyan, and Kithr knows. I have spoken of that life to no others," Yion told him. "I prefer that others know me as a mercenary, not as a taker of lives, and mercenary sounds less presumptuous than claiming the title of champion of Lord Saiboti, no matter the accuracy of the claim."

Enough light had seeped into the sky that Cailean could finally see Yion. As Cailean had expected, the mercenary appeared unperturbed by the conversation, sitting at ease and drinking from his own mug. Cailean tried to imagine Yion as a hardened, cold killer, but he couldn't. Yion had the skills of an assassin, yet the person he appeared to be was not that assassin. Cailean picked up his mug and attempted another gulp of the bitter drink.

Yion smiled slightly. "I fear it is an acquired taste, Lord Cailean."

"I don't know that I could stand drinking it enough to acquire the taste for it, Yion. Couldn't you mix some honey into it?"

Yion considered. "Perhaps. That should not alter its effects. It is better when hot."

"It couldn't be much worse." Cailean rubbed his eyes, then looked to the sleeping figures around the camp. He hated to disturb them from their rest, but reluctantly rose. "Is it time?"

Yion stood. "It is, Lord Cailean."

"Yion?" Cailean hesitated even as he spoke.

Yion gave him a questioning look. "Yes, Lord Cailean?"

"Do you ever miss your old life?"

"No." Yion's answer was immediate and firm. "I miss nothing of that life." He walked to Kithr and lightly shook the elf's shoulder.

Kithr jerked, his eyes snapping open. He relaxed slightly when he identified Yion.

"It is near the time you wished to depart, Kithr," Yion said.

Kithr climbed slowly to his feet. Shadows of weariness still hung over his features, but at least he appeared to have slept. Cailean offered him the half-full mug.

"Yion mixed up some concoction he claims will help a person wake up. The taste is wretched, but it seems to work, if you want to try some."

Kithr raised an eyebrow, then accepted the mug and took a large gulp. His expression twisted as he swallowed, then he began to cough. "'Wretched' doesn't begin to describe that, Tathren," he gasped. "That is foul."

Cailean nodded. "I know. I drank it too."

"And had to share your misery?" Kithr retorted. He handed the mug back to Cailean. "Get your men ready. We need to leave." He moved to Lyan's side and roused the astrologer.

Yion had already woken the others. Cailean rolled his bedroll for Dalrian to pack onto the horses. Aikan moved slowly around the camp, walking out stiffness. Cailean doubted he was alone in dreading a long day in the saddle.

*Lord Saiboti, please let us reach the edge of the forest before the elves find us,* Cailean prayed. "Eat in the saddle," he ordered. "Pack up."

Lyan said something in Elven. Cailean looked over to him, but whatever he had said appeared to be meant for Kithr only. The astrologer looked little different from the previous day— no more alert, no more rested.

"How're you doing, Lyan?" Cailean asked.

Lyan turned to him. "I'm here," he said in response. "Take the food from the gray bag first, Shiolto. It won't keep as long as the rest."

"All right," Shiolto agreed, disquieted by Lyan's lifeless

tone. Digging into the indicated bag, he exclaimed in surprise, then pulled out bread and sweet rolls. "Gods, Lyan, these look wonderful!"

"Gifts," Lyan said. "To celebrate my return."

Awkward silence fell. After a moment, Shiolto passed out the food, unsure what else to do. As the sky lightened with dawn, the Tathrens climbed into their saddles. They'd cleaned up as many traces of their presence as they could, though Cailean didn't hold great hope for their efforts fooling any skilled trackers. Kithr led the way, and Lyan walked behind him. The horses tossed their heads, ears flicking in irritation and unease as they left the camp and the protections that had sheltered them during the night.

Mist hung over the ground, shrouding Eilidh Wood and giving the trees a ghostly sheen. Cailean pulled his cloak tight around his shoulders. He all but expected to see restless spirits wandering along the side of the road. As the sun finally crept high enough to piece the forest canopy, the mist burned away. Sounds of animal life gradually began, softening the heavy air. Cailean couldn't guess how far they were from the forest's edge—Eilidh Wood didn't thin, as a normal forest would. He remembered the last time he had been here, how the forest had simply stopped, as if someone had drawn a line on the ground and declared that the forest would go no further.

Lyan abruptly froze, head jerking up and eyes raking the trees. "What's wrong?" Cailean asked.

Lyan answered in Tathren. "Someone's following us. Someone is here, and I don't know who."

Kithr spun sharply, setting an arrow to his bowstring. His eyes narrowed, threatening bloodshed. "Come out and face me."

9

———

KITHR

*"May the gods guide your path, with shade and water ever near at hand."*
*~traditional elven farewell*

Kithr couldn't remember when he'd become aware of Lyan's talents. His friend's interest in the stars had bordered on obsession since his introduction to astrology. His parents, the village astrologer, and Elder Brenhan had encouraged him to pursue it. Somehow, in the push to train Lyan as an astrologer, his other abilities had been overlooked even as they began to manifest. Animals always responded well to him, even when he did something as foolhardy as stealing an egg from the nest of one of the viciously protective silverwing eagles. Gravity, unfortunately, had been less forgiving to Lyan in that incident.

Kithr had always envied another talent possessed by the astrologer, and had often thought it wasted on Lyan. By some unexplainable sense, Lyan always knew when he was being followed. Once, Kithr had doubted the ability, but it had proven right too many times to be ignored. When Lyan spoke his warning, Kithr's gaze raked the forest, an arrow ready at the string. The Tathrens drew weapons, and Cailean held Solstice defensively.

Leaves crunched under feet. Kithr spun toward the right. "Who's there?"

"If I'd been trying to sneak, you wouldn't have heard me, Kithr." Declan stepped away from a tree, just enough movement for Kithr to locate him. The former soldier wore forest browns, a cap covering his black hair. He held up empty hands in a gesture of peace.

"I wouldn't wager on that," Kithr said, voice cold. *Damn you, Elder. Damn you to the Mad God's Pits if you force me to fight my comrades.* "I know you didn't come alone. Who else?"

"Seine, Pyrn, Ihm, and Fitch," Declan answered, meeting Kithr's gaze without flinching. Kithr read tension in his shoulders despite Declan's projected calm. No one wanted to stare down a friend's arrow.

Kithr's arm held steady, arrow to the string and ready to draw. "Do you intend to stop us?" Behind him, horses snorted and stomped as the Tathrens closed protectively around Kithr and Lyan's flanks.

"Gods, no, Kithr!" Ihm's voice rose from slightly ahead. "We intend to come with you! When did you turn this suspicious of your friends?"

"Probably when the entire village turned against Lyan without good reason," Declan said, eyes not leaving Kithr.

Kithr glanced to Lyan, suspicious but hoping that, against all likelihood, Declan and the others had escaped Elder Brenhan's manipulation. They said the right words, but he couldn't bring himself to trust them on only his own judgment. Lyan stood tense, gaze fixed on Declan. From the intensity of the stare, Kithr was sure that somehow, Lyan would know if they dared trust the warriors.

"Declan's not lying," Lyan said. In a lower voice, he added, "I'm less sure about the others."

Kithr slowly lowered his bow. "All of you, out in the open."

Declan let out a breath of relief and motioned for his companions to leave cover.

Ihm brushed leaves from his hair as he stepped onto the road. Pyrn emerged from the opposite side of the road with Fitch. Seine was the last to leave concealment, and the only one to give Lyan a long, suspicious look.

Kithr fixed a hard stare on Declan. "For intending to come with us, your positions look remarkably similar to an ambush."

Declan shifted uncomfortably. "We wanted to be sure you and Lyan weren't under duress, and we couldn't be sure you would be the first or only group we saw on the road."

"You've been planning this." Kithr's gaze moved from Declan to the other elves, noting their gear and packs.

"I suspected you were planning to take Lyan and leave," Declan said.

"I *hoped* you were planning to do so," Pyrn cut in. "Gods know it was hard to tell whose side you were on, Kithr."

"Good," Kithr retorted curtly. "That *was* the intent."

"Yes, and you did it well enough that I worried we'd have to kidnap you and get Lyan out ourselves," Pyrn said.

"Kidnap me?" Kithr repeated, raising an eyebrow.

"Just until you came back to your senses and could recognize that the Elder's judgment was unjust," Fitch put in.

"I didn't think it would come to that," Declan said. "However, I did think we would have more warning. We weren't expecting you to leave so abruptly."

"Plans changed," Kithr said. He turned to Lyan and lowered his voice. "What do you think?"

"They should come," Lyan told him.

"We can trust them?"

Lyan hesitated. "I'm not sure. Safer to keep them close."

Kithr nodded slowly, accepting that. He gazed at the five

elves. "If you're joining us, you need to know some things. First, these Tathrens are allies."

Elven gazes studied Cailean and his men with little hostility. Unlike Kithr, they had not engaged in the worst atrocities committed by the elven forces in Tather, and in the years that had followed, they had put the war behind them more effectively than Kithr had.

Declan indicated Cailean. "And the second is that this Tathren carries a Spear of the Stars, right?"

Kithr raised an eyebrow.

Seine snorted in derision. "There must be some truth in Elder Brenhan's accusations. So, that is Equinox."

"No," Cailean said. "I bear Solstice."

Startled consternation ran through the elves. They stood unsure how to react to suddenly learning that they faced the wielder of the weapon over which their countries had warred.

"Then what about Equinox?" Ihm asked. He looked from Cailean to Kithr to Lyan.

"I refused to tell Elder Brenhan who Equinox chose as its bearer," Lyan said. "He drew a conclusion I never claimed."

"If not this Tathren, who *did* claim Equinox?" Seine demanded. Declan rested a hand on his wife's shoulder to calm her.

Kithr longed to prove the Elder a liar, but bit his tongue. Only Lyan had the right to answer.

Yellowing leaves lazily drifted to the ground around them. Lyan stood in silence for a long moment, then softly spoke. "I did."

Seine stared at the astrologer, her mouth opening and closing as she searched for words. Kithr braced for a burst of doubt and derision, a defense of Lyan on the tip of his tongue.

"What? Why didn't you tell the Elder, Lyan?" Pyrn burst. "Why... why did this happen instead?"

Lyan didn't answer. As the silence grew awkward, Cailean

cleared his throat and spoke. "Could we continue this discussion while moving? You might not intend to stop us, but I don't know that others will be so well-intentioned."

Kithr nodded sharply, gaze challenging the other elves to argue. Not even Seine did, still dazed from Lyan's revelation.

Lyan walked beside Kithr on the left. Declan fell into step on Kithr's right. "Did you take a lamp from the shrine, Kithr?"

Kithr automatically matched stride with the other former soldier. "We needed one, and I didn't want to risk returning to the village."

"It offered me the first clue that something had happened. When I looked closer, I found horse tracks around the shrine." He frowned. "To be honest, that alarmed me. Horses meant outsiders—outsiders at a sacred site and so close to Heartshrine Village. I went back to the village to wake Seine and the others, and saw that Lyan's house was dark. Checked yours as well and found you gone."

Kithr frowned. "Who had sentry duty near the shrine last night?"

"I did," Declan said.

"And you were gone from your post long enough that you didn't see us arrive *or* leave. I checked before I brought the Tathrens to the shrine and when we left." Kithr's eyes narrowed.

"I was dealing with something else," Declan said.

"Something worth leaving the path unwatched?" Kithr gave him a long, hard look.

"Strange creatures have been lurking around the village. Some sort of shadow-like thing that turns to ash when killed," Fitch said. "Others either don't care about them, or somehow aren't seeing them at all. We hunt them when we're on sentry, especially at night."

"Shadow creatures that no one but you sees?" Lyan interrupted sharply.

"Yes," Declan said. "Whenever I tried to tell anyone else about them, they just brushed the matter aside like it wasn't important." He glanced to the side and lowered his voice. "Even Seine."

Lyan's eyes narrowed. "Why didn't you believe the Elder's accusations?"

Declan blinked at the apparent change of topic. "Because they didn't make sense. Accusing *you*, of all people, of treason? He also charged you with aiding Tathrens, but the war is over. That shouldn't be a crime. Certainly not treason, even if most of us wouldn't choose to help them. Something about the Elder's accusations just felt… wrong."

"Everyone else accepted them," Lyan said.

"Kithr obviously didn't," Declan countered.

"I know why Kithr didn't. I don't yet know why you did not." Lyan studied Declan.

Declan shrugged, but he shifted uncomfortably. "The village is accustomed to accepting Elder Brenhan without question. We're just a little more willing to question things since the war."

Yion's smooth voice whispered up to them, though the mercenary didn't approach. "You are protected."

Declan hesitated, glancing to the Tathrens, then back to Kithr and Lyan. He was on the verge of saying something, but the words didn't come out.

Kithr's eyes narrowed. "Lyan told me that Elder Brenhan has enspelled our entire village. Lyan used the Spear to shield me. What protects *you*?"

At his blunt, harsh words, the other elves paled, but only Seine's face reflected the shock and denial that Kithr had felt at the revelation. She shook her head quickly. "That's absurd!"

Declan slowly let out a breath. "Gods. We were right. He *has* been controlling people."

*You knew this already? How? Have I been utterly blind all this time?*

Pyrn stepped ahead of them, turning and walking

backwards, confident of his steps in Eilidh Wood without watching his path, even ducking from a low-hanging branch that nearly snagged his dark brown hair. He pushed up the long sleeves of his tan shirt, revealing etched metal bands around his muscled upper arms. "In the war, our company faced a small group of Tathren mages who held a strategic fortification. Those mages used magic to enspell some of our men and use them against us."

"Ridiculous," Aikan cut in sharply. "We never allowed the practice of such dark magic. Not even against *elves*."

Pyrn's blue-gray eyes turned to the older man. "They weren't liked even by their own people. I wouldn't be surprised if they scoured memories of their existence from the mind of those who knew of them. But they did indeed fight against us, and used our own to inflict devastating harm to our company. They might have succeeded in killing or enslaving us all if we hadn't had a Crafter among us."

Aikan scowled, displeased, but Pyrn's explanation denied him a chance to pursue the argument. Shiolto listened with interest, and asked, "What's a Crafter?"

"One of our people with an inborn skill to make and..." He paused, searching for the Tathren word.

"Imbue," Lyan said.

Pyrn nodded his thanks. "Yes, to imbue the things he makes with an ability. Our Crafter's skill was with metal, and he gave these bands the ability to guard the wearer against magic that clouds the mind. He also crafted tools to free those already under the thrall of the mages. These protected us from the mages, and we wore them always, day or night, waking or sleeping."

Shiolto urged his horse forward and peered at the metal bands. Often Kithr thought the horse-tender showed little in the way of sensible, natural caution toward the people who had attacked and slaughtered members of his grandparents' generation. "So why did you decide to wear them after the war?" Shiolto asked.

Pyrn chuckled softly and tugged at one of the bands. It barely shifted. "I was accustomed to wearing them. But more importantly, we had all worn them long enough that attempting to remove them again proved difficult. So, we continued to wear them."

"When we first came home, I wasn't surprised that life in the village felt strange," Declan said. "I thought I just needed time to adjust. But…" He trailed off.

"How long have you known what the Elder was doing?" Kithr demanded.

"*Known?* I *didn't* know, Kithr. All I had were suspicions without proof and the gut feeling that something wasn't right." He hesitated, turning to his wife. "But Seine didn't think anything was different, and, well, I doubted my instincts."

Around Declan, the others nodded in agreement.

"You were protected. Seine was not," Lyan said quietly. "Tell me one more thing. When clouds hid the night sky, did you notice?"

"Clouds hid the sky?" Seine cut in. "When?"

Declan nodded slowly. "Yes, I noticed, and I also saw that no one aside from you acted bothered by them. That troubled me."

Lyan glanced away, toward the forest. "Even his influence couldn't prevent me from noticing when the stars were taken from me."

"Why wouldn't the Elder want us to notice a thing like that?" asked Fitch, shortest of the elves. His blond hair was pulled back in a braid. He looked at Lyan with puzzlement.

"Because the stars were hidden by the will of his god," Kithr snapped sharply.

"His g… What god would want to do *that?*" Fitch said.

"The mad one," Lyan whispered.

Silence fell again as those words struck.

"Elder Brenhan? Following the Mad God?" Fitch repeated. "Lyan, that's blasphemy! How dare you say such a thing?"

"*Your* gods said it first," Aikan cut in coldly.

"And what *Tathren* claims to know the words of our gods?" Fitch growled.

"The gods of your people appeared when we were gathered at the shrine," Cailean answered, playing the peacemaker once again and shooting a warning look at Aikan. "How far are we from the forest edge?"

"We'll be there by midday," Kithr said. "Unless we meet other delays."

"Kithr!" Declan demanded. "Is this true? Our gods denounced Elder Brenhan? They appeared at the shrine?" He stopped, stance stiff as he stared at them.

"It's true," Kithr snapped. Leaving Eilidh Wood, allowing Elder Brenhan this victory infuriated him, and his voice was clipped and curt. "So did Eilidh Wood, for that matter."

"And you're *leaving*, knowing that?!"

"Despite his efforts, Elder Brenhan had yet to succeed in turning Eilidh Wood over to the Mad God," Lyan said. "We are going east to face a champion of Murdo, newly raised to power. Stay with us and fight him, or stay in Eilidh Wood and discover that you can do nothing to break the Elder's hold on Heartshrine Village."

"What? The Mad God has champions?" Ihm asked.

"He does," Cailean answered. "And the Spearbearers have a duty to stop those champions before they can carry out the Mad God's schemes."

Declan's expression hardened. "We're coming with you."

"Declan, you *believe* these accusations?" Seine argued. "It's absurd! Elder Brenhan, enspelling people? Following the Mad God?" She shook her head. "There has to be another explanation."

"An explanation other than the one our gods gave?" Kithr snapped.

She glared at him. "You have no proof of this supposed appearance of the gods except for the testimony of *Tathrens*, Kithr, and your word is certainly suspect enough, under the circumstances. Give me one good reason I shouldn't return to Heartshrine Village and ask the Elder myself."

Kithr tensed. *We can't let her return to the village.*

"You will not go back, because I say you should not," Lyan said.

"Elder Brenhan condemned you, Lyan. Why should *your* word mean *anything* to me?" Seine demanded.

Lyan held out his hand. Equinox appeared in his grasp. He pointed the Spear at her. "As Spearbearer of Equinox, I say you *will* come with us."

Seine sucked in a sharp breath, eyes growing wide. "By the First Seed..." She looked to Cailean and Solstice, then back to Lyan and Equinox, comparing the Spears. She hesitated, and Kithr could only wonder what thoughts fed the mix of emotions that flashed across her face. Finally, she bowed her head. "You. The Spear. You really are..." She swallowed hard. "As you will, Spearbearer."

Equinox vanished, returning to wherever Lyan had called it from. He glanced to the other elves. "Does anyone else object?"

They gaped at him, then quickly shook their heads. "No, Lyan, no objections."

Kithr's shoulders relaxed. Seine seemed the only one who'd been unconvinced, and he was relieved that her agreement had come without requiring force. *I don't know what a champion of the Mad God can do, but I expect we will need all the help we can gather.*

"Planning to ask horses of the nomads?" Ihm asked as they resumed walking at Kithr's quick pace.

Kithr shook his head. "We have another means of travel once we leave Eilidh Wood."

"He does have a point, though," Dalrian said from behind him. "Won't you want mounts?"

Kithr had never been overly fond of riding, but it did have advantages. He wished that Shadowstar and his horse had not left.

"The nomads need their horses. They shouldn't spare any for us." Lyan stared ahead, as if he could see past the trees to the Appret Plains and the horse-herding tribes who roamed them.

Kithr gave him a puzzled look. "*All* of their horses, Lyan? Ohrlan alone has at least twice as many horses as his tribe has members. You said earlier that Shadowstar was needed on the plains, but you didn't say anything about this." He tried to keep his voice from betraying the sting he felt that Lyan was keeping things to himself, only revealing fragments of what he knew.

"He'll need them," Lyan said grimly. "And they need Shadowstar to guide them."

"Why?" Kithr pressed. "And how do you know?"

Lyan closed his eyes and shook his head. "I read it in the stars, Kithr. Even Shadowstar might not be enough to save them."

"Save them from *what*?" Fitch demanded. "Stop talking in riddles and half-empty explanations and just tell us what in the gods' names is happening on the plains!"

"Nothing has happened yet." Lyan finally looked at them. "But it's coming. They are in the way of the Mad God's plans." He shivered. "May the Horselord and the Thunderer guard them all."

"The plans that we're on our way to stop," Kithr said.

Lyan nodded.

"Then as long as we succeed—" Kithr began.

Lyan shook his head sharply. "Some pieces are already in

place, Kithr. Some things we have no way to stop. Even if we tried, we would delay ourselves, and the Mad God's champion *will* use any advantage we give him."

"You're certain of this, Lyan?" Fitch asked. "The nomads are in danger and we can't do *anything?*" Kithr had often noticed him courting, whether in jest or in earnest, young nomad women when the tribes took shelter from the punishing summer sun and sought shade at the fringes of Eilidh Wood.

"*Yes!*" Lyan snapped sharply. "Yes, I am sure, Fitch! Read the stars for yourself if you don't believe me!" His hands clenched into fists. "You think I would invent this for my own amusement? Do you think I *want* to know that people I call friends might die? Is that what you think?"

Fitch blinked, taken aback at the fury of Lyan's response. "I just…"

"Lyan, calm yourself," Yion murmured.

Lyan stepped toward Fitch, clenched fists trembling, as if he hadn't heard Yion. Kithr grabbed Lyan's shoulder and pulled him back. "Lyan, stop."

Lyan spun around to face Kithr, and for an instant, Kithr thought his friend would swing at him. In Lyan's green eyes, he saw frustration, anger, and fear.

Kithr spoke in a low voice. "We're asking questions because you won't tell us what we need to know, Lyan. You dole out information like the final drops from the last waterskin on a scorching summer day, and I don't understand *why*! Don't you *trust* us?" He paused a moment, then asked, "Don't you trust *me?*"

Lyan flinched, looking away. The anger retreated from his face, leaving only fear in its wake. "Don't do this," he whispered.

"Don't do what?" Kithr pressed.

"I can't tell you what you want to know, Kithr!" Lyan burst. "I can't!"

The others stared at them, but said nothing at Lyan's outburst. Kithr barely stopped himself from shouting back. Forcing his voice to be as steady as he could, he spoke. "Then will you at least tell me the things I *need* to know?"

Lyan jerked his head in a nod, but he didn't meet Kithr's eyes.

*I don't believe you, Lyan. I trusted you when you asked me to say nothing before the Elder. Why don't you trust me now?*

They walked in uneasy silence. Kithr couldn't guess what thoughts and questions tumbled through his companions' minds, but his own churned in endless repetitions until he wanted to scream them to the sky. He welcomed the distraction when he saw the sharp, straight line where the trees ended and the plains began.

Brush rustled and parted. The Splinter of Eilidh Wood stepped onto the road, facing them. Beside Kithr, Declan jerked to a stop, eyes opening wide. Kithr tried to act like he wasn't surprised by her appearance, pretending that he had not hoped the forest would change its mind about sending her with them.

Leaves and vines covered her body with the semblance of clothing, green and yellow over her brown bark. On her back she carried a leather pack. Her amber eyes studied them all. "More of our children join the Spearbearer. Good."

"A Splinter?" Ihm's voice rose to an undignified squeak.

"A Splinter," Kithr agreed. "I said that Eilidh Wood denounced the Elder."

Ihm gulped audibly. "A Splinter."

If the words bothered the Splinter, she gave no indication. "This Splinter is prepared."

"For what?" Seine's voice trembled slightly.

"This Splinter will accompany our children beyond the forest," the Splinter said.

"You can do that?" Ihm asked.

"We can, and we do." Her amber eyes were unreadable.

"We have tasked our Spearbearer with finding the means to purge the corruption at our heart. We task you with the same, by whatever tools are necessary."

Declan, Seine, Pyrn, Ihm, and Fitch looked at one another, then bowed their heads. "As you will, Eilidh Wood."

Without hesitation, the Splinter turned and walked down the road. She crossed the border of the forest and waited for them on the dry, yellow grass of the Appret Plains. Cailean rode to the front of the group as they followed her. He held Solstice, the Spear gleaming in the midday sun, beautiful and deadly.

Kithr scanned the horizon, but found only the empty grassland, the stalks stiff and dry. Sensible people were gathering in their stores for the winter, heeding the predictions for a harsh, cold season marked by heavy snow. Only the fools or the desperate planned a long journey during the winter months.

He looked away from the plains, back to the group around him. *So which does that make us? The desperate, or the fools? Perhaps both.*

"Gather close," Cailean ordered. "It's time we moved a little faster."

Kithr stepped to Lyan's side, next to the Tathren lord. Cailean projected confidence, but Kithr glimpsed sweat beading his brow and saw how tightly he gripped Solstice. Not as confident as he pretended to be, but Kithr pretended not to notice. He would grant Cailean that dignity.

Once more he looked to Eilidh Wood. *We will return, Elder. We will return, and we will end this deception once and for all.*

# 10

## CAILEAN

*"Both Spears of the Stars are weapons of great magical power. They are aware—sentient and opinionated. They are also impulsive. It falls to the bearers of the Spears to temper impulse with reason, and to remind the Spears that mere mortals must know their limitations and abide by them."*

Cailean fought a surge of irritation. He should be grateful for the addition of the five elves and the Splinter, but he found himself angry at them instead. More people to transport. More people eating their supplies. More elves, disrupting the balance of their group and outnumbering the humans.

*Why should that bother me? They say they want to help us. Lyan and Kithr trust them. Isn't that reason enough to be glad of their presence?*

Cailean's irritation only grew at that thought. *Gods, what's wrong with me? I should be glad for the help, not ready to start snapping.*

Regardless of what he told himself, the irritation remained, pricking at him as the elves gathered with Cailean's men. It occurred to Cailean that he could simply leave them behind, and he was tempted for a moment. But it was both petty and foolhardy, and he forced aside the impulse. Declan and the other elves watched him expectantly. Cailean closed his eyes and focused on Solstice.

Doubt, insidious and clever, crept up on him. He had used Solstice to move people across distances only once before. That time, Lyan had used Equinox to channel strength to Cailean, countering the effects of Cailean's curse, but wreaking harsh punishment on Lyan. They had moved only a day's journey, and Lyan had needed at least a full day's rest to recover.

*"That was the curse."* The response, sensed more than heard, came from Solstice, answering his doubts with calm confidence.

Cailean had to trust Solstice. The Spear knew more about its abilities than Cailean ever could, and right now it was telling him that he could cross far greater distances than just a day's travel with minimal drain on his strength.

He opened his eyes and turned them to the broad stretches of dry, yellow grass. The air was dry, and the sun warm on his skin, welcome after the looming shadows of Eilidh Wood. The air smelled of dust and haze hung in the sky. Across the grassland lay a range of mountains, dividing the Appret Plains from the Forests of Cossette. Cailean thought of the road winding through those mountains, a week's ride on horseback. Around him, the elves shifted restlessly, and Shiolto fidgeted with his reins, waiting for something to happen.

*Take us to the mountains,* Cailean told Solstice.

The Spear grew warm in his hand, radiating a glow nearly unseen under the midday sun. Pressure built in the air, like a thunderstorm hanging overhead, ready to break free. His head began to throb and his ears felt stuffed up.

The pressure grew like a bubble around them. It burst with darkness and nauseating vertigo as ground and sky fell away. Cailean clenched his teeth, trying not to vomit. Light returned in a painful burst, bringing back up and down, returning sense to the world. A crisp rush of wind brought the smell of rock and dust, with hints of snow.

*It's not late enough for snow yet, is it?* Cailean's muddled thoughts tried to sort themselves out.

His mount's back muscles tensed, and he automatically tightened the reins, checking the animal's instinct to bolt. The horse settled again. Cailean blinked rapidly, trying to orient himself.

To the side, someone was retching. He felt a perverse hope that it was one of the elves, but remembered that Aikan had taken poorly to Nachyne's magic. He looked around for his steward.

The older man sat stiffly in his saddle. His face was pale, but set. He met Cailean's eyes and waved one hand in a sharp, dismissive gesture to indicate that he was fine.

Solstice radiated smug satisfaction. *"I took his sickness and gave it to one of the elves."*

Cailean stiffened. He hadn't known his Spear could do that. His eyes focused on the shortest of the elves, the blond Fitch. The elf finished retching and slowly pushed to his feet. "Ugh. Well *that* was fun."

A petty feeling of delight ran through Cailean. Guilt followed on its heels. He dismounted. "It can hit some people harder than others," he said in vague half-apology. "The sickness should pass soon."

Fitch nodded, finding his water skin and rinsing his mouth. At least the elf's braid had kept his hair out of his face.

Lyan glanced around. Cailean had the unsettling suspicion that the astrologer knew what Solstice had done. Lyan shivered as wind buffeted them.

"Where are we?" Declan asked. He pulled off his cap before it could blow away. His black hair was cut short, and didn't whip around in the wind like Yion's horsetail.

The grassland lay behind them, visible, but far below.

They stood in the middle of a road, next to a sign marker carved into the stone. One arrow pointed back toward the grassland. The script beneath it was written in the Trade tongue, and read "Appret Plains." The other pointed up the road, and it bore the name "Kamael." Plant life along the road was sparse, but shrubs and stunted trees clung tenaciously to the rocks in defiance to the wind. The Splinter drifted to a clump of weeds among the stones, reaching down to run long fingers over the leaves.

"We're on the road through the Vashom Mountains," Cailean answered. "The Appret Plains are behind us."

Fitch turned and gazed at the plains. His face fell, and his voice held a plea. "Lyan, are you *sure* there's nothing we can do to help the nomads?" The anxious expression on his face made him look like a youth barely old enough to carry a weapon.

Lyan crouched, picking up a handful of dirt and stones, letting them run between his fingers. "This was where we debated whether or not dragons could have carved the road from the stone," he murmured.

Cailean frowned, but nodded. "Yes, it is, but why bring that up now, Lyan?"

"*Lyan!*" Fitch burst. "Stop acting like an accursed Seer and answer me! Is there anything we can do for them?" Cailean heard an unexpected note of anguish in the elf's voice, and regretted again his secret satisfaction at seeing him get sick.

Lyan flinched and stood. "I brought it up because it was a pleasant memory, Cailean." He didn't turn to Fitch. "Do as you believe you should, Fitch. I won't tell you not to."

"Then tell me what danger is coming to them! Tell me what you've seen in the stars, Lyan."

Lyan closed his eyes and sighed. "Come with me." He walked up the road a little way, but when Kithr started to follow, Lyan shook his head. "Just Fitch. This is for him alone."

Kithr stopped, taken aback, expression hurt. Fitch stopped as well, uncertain. "If this is a problem…," he started.

"Do you want your answer or not?" Lyan's tone was sharp.

Fitch hesitated, then followed Lyan. Cailean looked at the other elves and saw confused concern. Among his men, Dalrian and Shiolto exchanged worried looks. Aikan frowned after Lyan. Yion simply watched the astrologer intently.

*This isn't like Lyan. He's keeping secrets and he's even pushing Kithr away. Why? His behavior clearly baffles those who know him well just as much as it does me.*

Cailean couldn't see Fitch's face as Lyan spoke to him, but he saw the shorter elf tense. Fitch's back stiffened, and he shook his head sharply. Lyan nodded. Fitch spun around and marched back to the group, his face grim.

"I'm going to the plains."

"Are you sure?" Declan asked him.

Fitch nodded. "I am."

Cailean expected argument or discussion, but none followed, no attempts to dissuade Fitch. The elf picked up his bag, dropped when nausea had hit him, and slung it over his shoulder.

"Be careful," Cailean bid him.

Fitch turned to him, surprise crossing his expression, then he nodded. "Soldarr's blessings to you, Tathren."

Without further farewell, he walked down the road back toward Appret Plains.

Dalrian watched the elf leave with puzzlement. "I know in Eilidh Wood you do things differently than we do, but you really don't care that he's just leaving?"

"Of course we do," Pyrn answered. "But Lyan gave him permission to choose."

Aikan snorted and looked to Lyan, who rejoined them. "Stargazers have the authority to countermand other duties?"

"Our *Spearbearer* has that authority. Just as he had the

authority to order Seine to accompany us." Pyrn's voice grew cool. "His orders outrank any other elven authority. Even that of an Elder."

"So, by being a Spearbearer, Lyan is like a lord?" Shiolto asked.

Kithr laughed sharply. "Not a lord, horse-tender. Though some Elders might argue about whether or not his word supersedes theirs, by being Spearbearer, Lyan's authority would be better equated to that of your king."

Shiolto blanched, his eyes widening.

"I am no Elder, and I am neither lord nor king!" Lyan burst sharply. "I am bearer of Equinox, and Cailean is bearer of Solstice. That's enough!"

*By equivalent rank, if what Kithr says is true, Lyan wouldn't be my equal. He would be my superior.*

The thought startled Cailean, but not as much as the surge of outrage that followed it did. He didn't expect elves to treat him with the deference that men of Tather would, but to think that one of his companions, even if it *was* Lyan, outranked him rankled.

As if Lyan heard his thoughts, the astrologer repeated, "I'm not a lord. If you want someone to give you orders, look to Kithr, or Cailean. Not me. We should keep going."

Shiolto hesitated. As a servant in Cailean's house, he had known his entire life that nobles were not to be treated the same as common men, no matter how they had attained nobility.

Lyan closed his eyes and spoke quietly. "Shiolto, please, I'm not a lord. I'm just a fool stargazer."

Shiolto snorted. "You're no fool, Lyan, and anyone with a bit of sense knows *that*." Lyan's words had the intended effect, though. Shiolto relaxed.

Cailean also relaxed. Order and rank had been established again, and Lyan clearly wanted no place at the head of it.

Aikan cleared his throat. "My lord, are you planning to visit the temple of Toirni?"

The temple stood high in the mountains off a trail from this road. The priestess who attended it had helped Cailean and his band the last time they had come through the mountains.

Cailean shook his head. "I didn't plan to, and don't know of a reason we should. Do you, Lyan?"

"They can't tell you anything more than you know already," Lyan replied.

"Then we continue. There are places on this road where I don't care to linger." Cailean glanced up at the cliff walls, watching for movement.

Men had tried to kill Cailean on this road. That attack had forced them to seek shelter in Toirni's temple. Cailean didn't wish to test fate by lingering.

"None of the rest of you intend to leave, I trust?" Aikan asked the elves.

"Fitch has a woman in one of the nomad tribes," Declan said. "He's never said, and we haven't asked, but we suspect he has a child there as well. He has reason to go."

"The rest of us are staying, though," Pyrn added firmly.

*"This time, don't make any of them sick, Solstice."* Cailean felt another surge of guilt over inflicting such humiliation on Fitch when the elf had worries enough. He hardly seemed old enough to be a father.

Cailean didn't sense any guilt from Solstice, but neither was there disappointment about not embarrassing another elf, just agreement to his request. Cailean swung back into the saddle as he sought for their next destination. *Somewhere near the edge of the Forests of Cossette where we won't attract attention.*

A laugh from Solstice rang in his mind. *"Which end of the forest?"*

*"We can reach the far side?"* Cailean asked in astonishment. That lay at least three weeks ride from the mountains.

*"Of course."*

*"Then take us there."*

Pressure built again in the air. Cailean winced, and his stallion snorted uneasily, disliking the idea of another fall through darkness. Lyan stepped over by Cailean's horse, and the animal calmed a little. The rest of the group clustered closer, and then black, empty nothingness swallowed the world.

Pain stabbed through Cailean's head. His senses fought to find any grounding point. He could feel Solstice clutched in his hand, but nothing else, not even the saddle beneath him. No sounds, no light, no smells. The first jump through darkness had been quick, over before he had time to be aware of the sheer emptiness of it. Now, panic dug claws into his mind.

*"Let me out! Gods, please, let me out of here!"*

The darkness tore open and Cailean fell through the gap back into the world of light. His horse whinnied in fear and jerked sharply to one side. Balance failed Cailean, and he tumbled from the saddle to the ground, gasping for breath. Sounds rushed in his ears, nonsensical noise. He panted, pain shooting through his body and stabbing into his skull. Rocks jabbed into his back and side. Finally Cailean rolled onto his side and tried to sit.

The pounding pain in his head almost overwhelmed him, but Cailean somehow managed to keep his eyes open. The horses had scattered, with only Yion's and Shiolto's remaining close. Yion kept his mount walking in a tight circle until he managed to calm it, speaking soothingly in a low voice. Aikan doubled over, sick again, as were two of the elves.

"Catch those horses!" Kithr ordered

Cailean shook his head, then regretted the movement. He found Kithr standing beside Lyan. Lyan sat, eyes closed, sucking in deep breaths. Kithr looked pale, but he was keeping his stomach, and ordering elves after the horses as the animals vanished between the trees.

Trees. Cailean finally took in his surroundings. They had arrived somewhere in a forest. Massive trees towering over them, untouched by axes. Insects gradually began to chirp and buzz, and a few birds warbled out songs.

*The Forests of Cossette. That must be where we are, somewhere in the middle of the forest, not at the edge as I wished to be. But that's my own fault, isn't it? I forced Solstice to pull us out before we reached our destination.*

"Lord Cailean?" Dalrian asked. "Are you all right?" He staggered over to Cailean. "You don't look so good."

"I'm all right," Cailean mumbled. The headache refused to relent, but he tried to get up.

"Stay there, Cailean," Kithr said. "We'll gather your horses—you aren't going anywhere until we have them again."

Cailean sank back down, relenting. "We can move on after that."

"On foot, if we do," Kithr said firmly. "I've had quite enough of magic travel for one day. And I think your steward would agree."

Cailean grimaced. He wanted to argue, but simply for the sake of argument and to assert his authority. Kithr was right, and they both knew it. The thought of venturing into that emptiness again made Cailean's skin crawl. Lying back on the ground, he drew deep breaths, taking in the rich, earthy smells of the forest.

*"I'm sorry, Solstice. You might have the power to take us that far, but I'm afraid this mortal isn't yet strong enough to endure it."*

1 1

———

KITHR

*"Some places in this world are ancient. Men have forgotten their legends, but they can feel it in their bones, and know that they tread upon mysteries. The Forests of Cossette, the Ruins of Cha'que, the Spines of the Sleeping Dragon, to name only a few. Wonders still roam this world, but few see them, and fewer still live to tell the tale."*

To Kithr's relief, Cailean didn't protest. The Tathren lord closed his eyes and lay back on the ground. Kithr wished he could do the same. His skull pounded, and sudden movement brought waves of vertigo that threatened to empty his stomach. Kithr gritted his teeth and took several deep breaths until the nausea passed.

He wasn't alone in feeling sick and disoriented. Declan and Pyrn followed the horses, but neither moved quickly, while Ihm and Seine still recovered from the gut-wrenching fling through darkness. Kithr hoped the horses weren't in much better condition and wouldn't go far. The Splinter didn't appear to be sick, but she also wasn't trying to catch the horses. If anything, she looked disoriented, her long toes digging into the ground like roots and her expression blank. The Tathrens looked dazed at best, and even Yion was unsteady on his feet when he dismounted. The mercenary tied his horse to a branch and lifted down his saddlebags.

"With your leave, I shall make a fire, Kithr, and brew tea. It will aid our recovery."

Kithr nodded curtly. "A small fire."

"Of course." Yion busied himself arranging twigs on a patch of bare ground.

Kithr left the mercenary to his task, and turned to Lyan. "Are you all right?"

Lyan's face was sallow and his voice was thin and strained. "As much as anyone else is, I think."

"Do you know where we are?" Kithr asked. He looked around at the trees, and shifted uneasily. This wasn't an elven forest, and it lacked the alertness and welcome he took for granted in Eilidh Wood. The indifference this one projected dismissed him without notice.

"The Forests of Cossette, probably," Lyan answered. "But I'm not sure where in the forest we are."

"Are we near where we should be?" Kithr asked.

Lyan closed his eyes. "We could be in worse places." His voice grew softer. "We could have made it to where Cailean intended us to be."

Kithr stiffened. "We could what? What do you mean, Lyan? Where?"

"The chances are high that someone would have been waiting for us there. Don't blame Cailean—he doesn't know."

"But you do!" Kithr protested. "You knew before Cailean began. So why didn't you say anything, Lyan?"

Lyan flinched and looked back to him. "There were worse possibilities than *that* too, Kithr, and most of them stemmed directly from me telling Cailean before he made the second jump."

"The stars told you that the *best* possibility was for us to be dropped blind somewhere in the Forests of Cossette, with no idea how deep in the forest we are or even which way is the quickest way out? And how could you be sure that this *would* be the most likely result if you didn't say anything?"

Lyan shivered. "The further we travel, the longer we have to be in that dark place. I know that I couldn't have stood being in there for long enough to bring us to the other side of the forest. I hoped Cailean wouldn't be able to either. Also, using the Spear in that manner is exhausting. He didn't give himself much time to rest between uses."

Kithr glanced over his shoulder to the Tathrens, hoping none were listening. Gods only knew what offense Aikan would take if he overheard. The older man, however, sat against a tree, eyes closed. Shiolto and Dalrian stood anxiously near Cailean, fussing with such gear as hadn't been carried off when the horses bolted. Yion built a fire and hung a small pot from a metal tripod frame. He emptied water skins into the pot, then added powder from a cloth bag.

A new thought occurred to Kithr—one he should have considered sooner. He kept his voice low, speaking in Elven. "You said that there would most likely have been someone waiting for us if we'd gotten where Cailean intended to arrive, and they wouldn't have been waiting with good intentions. But how could they know where to wait for us? No one told them. None of *us* knew where Cailean planned to arrive."

Judging from his expression, Lyan had hoped Kithr wouldn't think to ask that. "I'm not the only one who can predict the future, Kithr," he said softly.

Kithr drew a sharp breath. "The Mad God's champion can?"

Lyan nodded.

"What sane astrologer would become a champion of the Mad God?" Kithr demanded.

"I never said he was an astrologer, Kithr," Lyan said quietly. "There are other means of divination."

"Then what? Some mad Seer?" Kithr asked.

"Don't ask what blessings the Mad God can bestow on those whom he favors. You do not want to know, Kithr, and you do not want to know the cost at which his gifts come." Lyan shuddered.

"He can predict what we will do? But can't you also predict him, Lyan?" Kithr asked. "Can't we use that to our advantage?"

"There's far more to it than just that, Kithr. I don't just know what *he* will do, but also what you do, Cailean does, *everyone* does and what will happen, and…" Lyan trailed off for a moment, then drew a deep breath. "Believe me or don't, Kithr, but I am trying, with everything I do, say, or *don't* say, to shift the odds in our favor."

*And you aren't sure if you will be able to do so. Is the situation you see so desperate, Lyan?*

Lyan suddenly grabbed his arm. "Kithr, please don't tell the others what I just told you."

Kithr blinked. "About the champion? Or about you trying to stack the odds?"

"Both, preferably," Lyan admitted. "But especially about what I'm doing."

"Is this part of manipulating the odds?" Kithr asked.

Lyan shook his head. "No. It's purely selfish on my part. When… *if* something happens, and I could have stopped it but didn't, I don't want to be asked why I made one choice and not another."

A chill ran down Kithr's spine. "I think everyone should know that the champion can predict us, Lyan. It will help explain when you tell us to do strange things. But I'll keep the other part to myself."

Lyan considered, then bowed his head in acceptance.

"Damned animal. Come *here*!"

Kithr turned to see a cursing Declan clutching a pair of reins and trying to pull one of the horses into their makeshift camp. The horse snorted and tossed its head, stamping its hooves in protest.

Shiolto bolted over. "Not like that!" he objected, catching hold of the horse's bridle and snatching the reins out of Declan's hands. He stroked the horse's nose. "It's all right, Chestnut. Did the elf scare you? You're all right now." He scowled at Declan. "Don't you know *anything* about horses?"

"They're animals, humans ride them, and I've heard they make a good stew," Declan responded.

"*Stew?*" Shiolto exclaimed, aghast.

Declan gave him a grin, releasing the horse into Shiolto's care. "So how *am* I supposed to get these animals to come with me?"

"Well, first, you don't tell them you plan to eat them," Shiolto said indignantly.

"I assure you, I've never knowingly eaten one. I only repeated what I've been told," Declan said cheerfully.

"Careful what you say to the horse-tender," Kithr said, seizing on an opportunity for a lighter conversation. "He's also our doctor."

Shiolto fidgeted uncomfortably as Declan gave him an appraising look. "Not a doctor, Kithr. I just know how to take care of horses, and I can bandage people when they need it."

"Lord Cailean offered him the opportunity to study medicine once matters at the keep were settled. Shiolto declined." Aikan stood, steadying himself against a tree.

Shiolto shifted from one foot to the other. "I'm just a common man. Wouldn't have been right for me to be book-learning like a noble." He quickly tethered the horse. "I'll help find the rest of the horses."

As Shiolto hurried into the forest, Yion rose from the fire and brought a mug to Aikan. Aikan considered the steaming liquid with mild suspicion. "What is this?"

"It is a tea meant to settle the stomach and clear the

mind," Yion answered. "Also a touch of honey to ease the bitterness—Lord Cailean objected to my last brew."

Kithr remembered the foul drink Cailean had shared with him in the morning, and didn't blame Cailean in the least for complaining.

Aikan cautiously accepted the mug and took a gulp, as if he intended to take it like any wretched medicine: quickly. Yion waited. Aikan's expression was surprised, and he swallowed the rest of the tea with less haste. "It's not bad," he admitted.

Yion inclined his head in thanks. "I am pleased to hear it. I found it too sweet for my liking, but I must remember that Tathren tastes are less refined."

"Refined." Aikan sniffed, but showed no further signs of taking offense. Kithr decided the older man must be feeling worse than he admitted to pass up such an opportunity.

Yion moved to Cailean next, rousing the Spearbearer from his doze. Cailean was muzzy, but drank the offered tea, then lay down again. Dalrian declined when Yion offered, but both Ihm and Seine accepted the drink. The elves treated Yion with less suspicion than Kithr had when he first met the mercenary, but, he realized, they trusted his judgment. Kithr hadn't had that same luxury.

Only after he had served everyone else did Yion bring his brew to Kithr and Lyan. "Kithr, have you need?" Yion asked.

He remembered again the other drink, and hesitated. Kithr's stomach still churned, though, and with a hint of reluctance, he nodded. The tea was pleasantly hot, and when he took a drink, Kithr tasted a pleasant blend of spices, winter's breath, mint, and other herbs, sweetened with honey. He didn't notice any immediate change in how he felt, but at least the brew didn't add a new misery.

Yion refilled the mug once more. "Lyan? Do you wish some? I promise you, it holds no drugs."

Lyan stared into the forest, and didn't respond immediately. Kithr nudged him. "Lyan?"

Lyan started and looked at him. "What?"

"Do you want some tea?" Kithr asked.

"Oh. Yes, that would be fine."

Kithr took the mug from Yion and handed it to Lyan. The astrologer's gaze was distant and distracted, and he frowned about whatever was on his mind. He drank the tea and returned the mug to Kithr.

"Thanks."

Kithr wondered why Lyan addressed the thanks to him rather than Yion, but the mercenary didn't take offense. Or if he did, he didn't show it. Yion was difficult to read. The mercenary simply bowed his head to both of them. "It appears that Lyan Stargazer has much on his mind. I shall not intrude on his thoughts."

Shiolto proved more adept at recovering the horses than the elves were. Kithr wasn't surprised. Aside from Lyan, few elves of Eilidh Wood cared much for horses. They didn't need them to traverse the forest. By the time Shiolto, Declan, and Pyrn returned, the elves were comfortable enough with the Tathren to jest.

To Kithr's inexpert eye, the horses looked weary, their heads hanging and steps plodding. The packs appeared intact, if scuffed. Kithr glanced around the forest. This spot didn't make an ideal camp; it offered little shelter and no quick access to water.

Dalrian looked to Cailean, whose breathing indicated that he dozed, then Aikan. "Should I wake Lord Cailean? Are we going to stop here for the day?"

Aikan's expression was uncertain. Dalrian would have done better to ask someone experienced in living off the land, but Tathrens constantly seemed to think nobility, rather than experience, granted the answers to all questions. "Lord

Cailean needs to rest, but…" With obvious reluctance, Aikan turned to Kithr, silently asking his opinion.

"Kithr, I saw animal tracks while we were following the horses," Pyrn said, speaking in Tathren. "Fresh and large." He made a small swiping gesture at the air, indicating that the tracks had been clawed.

Lyan looked up. "Bear tracks?"

Pyrn shook his head. "They looked more like an oversized wolf's prints."

"Bear?" Kithr asked in an undertone. The animals were sacred to the chief Tathren god, Ahebban, well-known for his dislike of elves.

"The first time I saw Venycia in her bear form was in this forest," Lyan answered. "Just a hopeful thought."

Kithr nodded, understanding. He wouldn't complain if Venycia turned up nearby. She might be the daughter of Ahebban, but she was also a Guardian of the Shrine of Equinox, and a strong ally. Not only that, but Lyan liked her, and she seemed to return the sentiment. *Maybe she would have better luck drawing Lyan from this malaise.*

"Large animals?" Shiolto glanced around nervously. "We're in the Forests of Cossette, aren't we? That's where we saw the temple to the god of monsters." He gulped. "Meaning no offense to him, of course!" he added hastily. "But I don't think all his worshipers like us very much."

Nachyne had a temple in this forest? Kithr hadn't known that, but the thought of countless monsters wandering the length and breadth of the forest made his decision. "Wake your lord. We'll find a more secure camp."

He glanced up to the sky, barely glimpsed through the trees. Could it really be only afternoon? Had they still stood at the edge of Eilidh Wood this morning? Now the Appret Plains and a range of mountains stood between them and the forest.

*Even if the Elder sends hunters to track us, they'll never be able to find us now.*

Aikan shook Cailean's shoulder. "My lord? We need to leave."

Cailean groaned, eyes fluttering open. "What? Aikan?"

"Come, Lord Cailean. Dangerous animals lurk nearby, and this is not a safe place to rest."

Aikan helped Cailean to his feet. The Tathren lord leaned heavily on Solstice, and remaining upright took most of his strength. "The horses?"

"We found them, Lord Cailean," Shiolto answered.

"I'm not planning to go far," Kithr told Cailean. "We just need to find a good campsite."

"No need to coddle me, Kithr," Cailean snapped. "I'm fine."

Kithr barely restrained himself from responding in kind. He would have expected the response from Aikan, but not Cailean, surprising in its venom. Kithr swallowed the first words that came to mind, and forced his voice to be even. "Your horses aren't, Cailean. They need rest."

Cailean scowled, but nodded.

"He's got a burr up his ass," Seine muttered in Elven.

Kithr spun to face her. "No more than you would if you'd just dragged a dozen people with horses across a month's travel in less than a day."

She flushed. "Sorry."

*You should be grateful, Cailean. I just defended your behavior to one of my own people, despite agreeing with her, and you didn't even know you'd been insulted.*

Shiolto brought Cailean his horse, and Cailean took the reins, preparing to swing into the saddle. He stopped suddenly and turned to Kithr and the other elves. "Sorry. I shouldn't be snapping. Head's hurting."

Pyrn shrugged. "Well, I'd be ungrateful if I didn't thank you, even if the trip wasn't overly pleasant. We could still be just starting across the plains instead of here."

Cailean appeared mollified, and climbed into his saddle. "I'll leave this part to the experts. Take the lead, Kithr."

"Of course." That was the closest Kithr allowed himself to speaking his thoughts. *I don't need your permission to do what I'm good at, Tathren.*

Finding a camp took longer than Kithr hoped. Eventually they found a stream, and Ihm scouted downstream. He returned with some of the most welcome news Kithr had heard all day.

"The stream runs into a large pool just a little way from here. I didn't see any predator tracks, just elk and deer."

*Thank Soldarr.* "Let's go," Kithr said, following Ihm.

He kept an eye on Lyan, and saw his friend relax when they reached the pool. Lyan caught Kithr's eye and gave a small nod. The stream fed into a pool twice as long as an elf was tall, then lazily trickled out from the far end to continue its course. Red and gold leaves floated on the pool's surface, and tiny fish puckered the water as they sought food. A flock of grouse startled from the tall grass in a rush of feathers at their intrusion, prompting birds in the trees to start scolding.

He didn't have to issue any order to make camp. Elven soldiers knew a good place to rest when they saw one, and they settled in with efficiency. The Tathrens wasted no time either. For now, elves and Tathrens were united in their simple desire for rest and what comforts they could have.

Kithr glanced at Cailean. *Something is eating at you, though. How long before it breaks free, and what will happen when it does?*

## 12

### CAILEAN

*"I cannot afford to turn away anyone who can aid me, whether Tathren or elf, mortal, monster, or god. Knowing the enemy I face, I dare not refuse any ally."*

Cailean massaged his throbbing forehead. At least moving his head no longer sent lances of light stabbing into his eyes.

"Lie down for a little while, my lord," Aikan said. "I've set out your bedroll."

Cailean looked at his steward. "Lay out your own and do the same," he said.

"I will as soon as you do, my lord," Aikan said stubbornly. His face was pale and he moved slowly, clearly aching, but he would not rest until Cailean did, regardless of who needed it more.

Cailean's gaze moved from Aikan to their surroundings. Dalrian, Shiolto, and Yion helped the elves set camp. Kithr had picked a good spot. The babble of the water running into the pool created a soothing sound, and the air was fresh and clean. The forest felt less oppressive than it had during their previous passage through its depths. Despite the apparent peace, though, worry nagged at Cailean, and he gripped Solstice. If he went to sleep here, and something crept up on them…

*I've trusted Kithr to keep watch before. I have no reason not to do so now. He won't let harm come to Lyan.*

Finally, Cailean moved to the bedroll. With a weary, sore groan, he lay down. Had he been home, servants would draw a hot bath while he rested with a cup of mulled wine. And Aikan would be reading yet more names from his ledger of eligible marriage prospects for his lord.

*I suppose there is at least one benefit to not being home.*

Cailean closed his eyes and listened until he finally heard Aikan lie down. Cailean opened his eyes slightly, making sure his steward really was going to rest. Aikan wasn't a young man anymore, and he shouldn't be sleeping on the hard ground in the middle of a forest far from home.

Eventually, Aikan dozed. Once he was confident his rising wouldn't wake Aikan, Cailean got up again.

The elves and Cailean's men sat near the pool, far enough from Cailean and Aikan that conversations wouldn't disturb them. Dalrian appeared to be teaching two of the elves to play a dicing game. Shiolto spoke with another of the elves—Declan, Cailean thought—near the horses. Kithr checked the fletching on his arrows, while Lyan gazed into the pool as if he found some wisdom in it. The Splinter drifted around the edge of the pool, examining each plant intently. Yion and the remaining two elves were nowhere to be seen.

Kithr looked up when Cailean approached and nodded to him. "Feeling better?"

His head still ached, and weariness still dragged at Cailean, but he nodded and lied. "Yes. What's the situation?"

Kithr gestured toward the trees. "I sent Yion and a couple

of our men out to hunt and scout. We'll stay here tonight. Tomorrow, move on. That's my plan, at least."

Cailean nodded curtly. He couldn't argue with anything Kithr said. "How's Lyan?"

The shadow of worry crossed Kithr's face. "He's concerned. Once everyone has returned and woken, we need to discuss some things about the Mad God's champion."

"Things Lyan told you?" Cailean asked.

Kithr nodded.

"So, he'll reveal everything to you, then let you dole out scraps to the rest of us?" Cailean muttered testily.

Kithr stiffened, setting aside his quiver and standing. Anger flashed in his eyes, but his voice was remarkably calm, if tight. "Cailean, could I have a word with you in private?"

Cailean scowled, but nodded, his own voice falling into the overly courteous tones he used with nobles he didn't like. "Of course."

He followed Kithr away from the others, out of direct sight of the pool and among the trees. When Kithr stopped, Cailean folded his arms across his chest. Kithr stood slightly taller than him, and Cailean felt a stab of irritation that he had to look up to meet the elf's eyes. "Well?"

"What is the problem, Cailean?" Kithr asked sharply. "You've been acting like something crawled into your bedroll and died, and you suspect that one of us is responsible. So *what* is the *problem*?"

Cailean's jaw tightened. "No problems, Kithr. Everything is just *fine*."

"Horse turds," Kithr snapped.

"And what difference does it make?" Cailean countered. "You seem to have taken charge here, haven't you?"

Kithr stared at him. "What in the Mad God's Pits does *that* mean? You think that doing what I know how to do is 'taking charge' as if I'm trying to what, usurp you?" He spat in the dirt. "I didn't hear you offering a better idea."

"I did not come here to be insulted by elves with no sense of protocol and no respect for nobility!"

Kithr's eyes narrowed. "No, you didn't. In fact, I was under the impression that you came here to face a champion of the Mad God—you and Lyan. The rest of us are here to help get you there."

Cailean gripped Solstice. "Then where is Equinox? Why does only *one* Spearbearers have his *Spear*? And why isn't Lyan talking? Why does *he* act like we're marching to our doom?"

"I don't know where Equinox is, or why Lyan doesn't have the Spear with him," Kithr said plainly. "He won't tell me. He won't tell me a lot of things, in fact, and *that* worries me more than you can imagine, Tathren."

"Does it?" Cailean snapped. "You hide it well." He was being unfair and unkind, and he knew it. Kithr's worry about Lyan was constantly evident, as was his frustration at being unable to help his friend. Cailean couldn't take the words back, though, and more followed them. "But regardless, that makes this 'Tathren' the one person here who is most likely to have a chance against the Mad God's champion."

"I've called you 'Tathren' since our first meeting. So why are you taking exception to it now, Cailean?" Kithr said, his use of the name made with precision.

"I don't expect a bunch of *elves* to care," Cailean said. Even in his own ears, the words sounded petulant.

Kithr gave a short, sharp laugh. "Is *that* it? Too many elves for refined Tathren tastes? Maybe we'll corrupt your good Tathren peasants into thinking for themselves and not relying on nobles to tell them when to breathe? Or you just can't stand the idea that you're outnumbered by people who don't fall over themselves to tell you how wonderful you are?"

Cailean's lips curled back in a snarl, and his clenched fists shook with anger. Before he could gather a coherent response, a quiet voice interrupted.

"Kithr, that's enough."

They both turned, startled, to see Lyan. The astrologer gazed at Kithr and Cailean with haunted eyes. He leaned against a tree, looking ready to topple over at any moment.

Kithr looked to the side. "My apologies, Cailean." The words were strained and forced.

Cailean gave a short nod, acknowledging the apology, however insincerely it was given, then nodded to the astrologer. "Lyan."

Lyan started to push away from the tree, then wavered and caught himself against it again. His green eyes met Cailean's. "We need your help, Cailean. We don't have any chance against the Mad God's champion without it."

"Lyan, where is Equinox?" Cailean demanded.

Lyan paused, considering his answer. Finally, he closed his eyes and spoke. "The champion seeks the Shrine of Equinox, Cailean, and he is being guided by his god. Without the Spear, the Shrine's defenses won't be sufficient. Equinox is where it needs to be."

"It should be with *you*," Cailean said sharply. "The Spear should be with the Spearbearer."

Lyan shook his head. "That's not what the stars tell me, Cailean. If the Shrine falls into the hands of the Mad God, we've already lost."

"So you think we should go to the Shrine," Cailean said.

Again, Lyan shook his head. "With Equinox, the Guardians can shield it from him. We have to find the champion before he grows too strong."

"Too strong for Spearbearers to defeat him?" Cailean asked dubiously.

"The Mad God doesn't care if his minions are eventually consumed by the power he feeds them," Lyan said. "But even without that, he isn't sitting idle. If our confrontation would be just you and I against him, that would be one thing. But it won't. When we find him, we won't face just him. We'll face him and the army he is collecting. If it's at all possible, we want to fight him on our terms, not his."

Kithr started. "You never mentioned *that*, Lyan."

"I know." Lyan continued to gaze at Cailean. "I know we don't follow Tathren conventions, Cailean. They baffle us."

"I don't expect you to——," Cailean began.

Lyan cut him off. "You don't expect *me* to, but what about the others? Declan, Pyrn, and the rest? We aren't Tathrens, and we can't act like we are. But we are allies, aren't we?"

"Of course we are," Cailean said.

"I didn't ask them to make me their leader, but they did so whether I like it or not. And if that makes you and I equals according to Tathren conventions, it doesn't make me anyone other than Lyan. The same fool stargazer I was before." Lyan sounded exhausted. "Or maybe even more of a fool."

"Maybe so," Cailean said. "Are you going to tell us what's going on?"

Lyan hesitated again. "I'll tell you what I can, Cailean."

"That isn't a promising answer, Lyan," Cailean told him, annoyed.

Lyan drew a deep breath. "I cannot tell you everything, Cailean."

"Why *not*?"

"Because I need enough time to think!" Lyan snapped, hands balling into fists. "Barely seven *days* ago, I was forced to confront the fact that the Elder of Heartshrine Village, a man who I have trusted and respected my entire life, betrayed us and serves the Mad God. He stripped my title from me. He imprisoned me. He turned my entire home against me. And while you may be angry about leaving your lands and lordly duties, at least *you* can be assured that when you return, your people will *welcome* you back! Do you know how many elves believe my innocence?" Lyan didn't wait for an answer. "Six. *Six* elves of our entire village, and all of them are now here, except Fitch." He gripped a low tree branch, and it snapped off in his hand. "I had to leave Heartshrine Village when I *knew* it was under the Mad God's spell. My home, Cailean. *Murdo* has his claws sunk into the very core of my home, and I can't do anything to stop him. I can't even keep Equinox with me, much as I want to, because the Spear is the strongest protection the Shrine can have. So damn us all, I *need* some time to *think* before I say or do something that gets us all *killed!*"

*Lyan has just lost almost everything he's ever known, and I'm getting upset that our group contains more elves than it does humans. Gods, does that ever make me feel like a self-centered ass.*

Cailean walked to Lyan and rested a hand on his shoulder. "I'm sorry, Lyan. I've been a fool, and I wasn't thinking."

"You don't have sole claim on that, Cailean," Kithr said. He joined them and held out a hand to Cailean. "Long overdue and probably unofficial according to any council of law, but a truce between Tather and Eilidh Wood?"

Cailean took Kithr's hand. "We've had one on record for quite a few years now, Kithr."

"Then call it a truce between your house and us," Kithr said. "As long as we agree that we're on the same side."

"We are," Cailean said. *And I will remember why we're really here, and that my friends need my help now, just as they helped me before. This isn't about Tather and Eilidh Wood. It's about stopping the Mad God.* "Can I do anything to help, Lyan?"

"You can listen to Solstice."

Cailean frowned. "About the Mad God's champion?"

Lyan shook his head. "No, just learn to listen to Solstice."

Cailean bristled. "Lyan, you haven't even born Equinox for a quarter of a year. I have been Spearbearer of Solstice for nearly five years."

"And you didn't know the Spears were sentient until we came to the Shrine of Equinox," Lyan said. He rubbed his eyes wearily. "I'm not trying to imply you haven't fulfilled your duties as Spearbearer. You have, using what you did know. But when did a member of your family last directly fight the Mad God's forces? When did someone last have to *use* Solstice?"

He started to argue, stopped, and considered the question. His father hadn't, nor his grandfather. How many generations back did he have to look to find a Dev'gilla who wielded the Spear against more than mortal foes?

"You're no novice with the Spear as a weapon," Lyan added. "I'll never have your skill there. But you need to know *Solstice* too, so you don't make mistakes as I have with Equinox."

Kithr looked sharply at Lyan. "Mistakes?"

Lyan shook his head. "Not now."

"I do listen to Solstice, Lyan," Cailean said.

"You do when you hear the Spear, but Solstice has to shout for your attention." Lyan shook his head again. "I'm sorry, I don't know how to explain. Just... try to listen when Solstice is being quiet too. Like... like Solstice is a friend you want to talk to, not a subordinate bringing a report."

Cailean looked to the Spear in his hand. Lyan's reproach stung. "What do you expect me to hear that I don't already?"

"Equinox speaks to me, Cailean. Sometimes Equinox uses images and impressions, but sometimes, the Spear uses words, and we have actual conversations. Do you? Have you?"

Cailean hesitated, then finally admitted, "Rarely."

"You asked what you could do to help, Cailean. This is what I can tell you. If you strengthen the bond between yourself and Solstice, that... that is help none but you can offer."

"I'll try," Cailean said finally.

"Thank you."

When the three of them returned to camp, eyes turned toward them. Even if the words hadn't been clear, the sound of raised voices would have carried. Ihm reminded Cailean once again that elves didn't hold to the same rigid class structure as Tathrens when he spoke.

"No bruises, Kithr? I didn't think you could have an argument without coming to blows."

Kithr shot the other elf a scowl, though it lacked venom. "We were not arguing. We were discussing plans."

Ihm raised a thin eyebrow. "Whatever you say, Kithr."

A smile flickered across Lyan's face. The astrologer took his seat again near the edge of the pool, and seemed slightly more relaxed, though it was difficult to say for sure.

Not long after, the hunters returned with a young buck. The two elves, Seine and Pyrn, eyed Yion with wary respect, and Pyrn hurried to Kithr and asked something in a low voice. Kithr nodded, then responded, nodding his head in Yion's direction. Cailean guessed that the mercenary was the subject of the conversation.

*I wonder what it is about Yion that makes the elves able to recognize his past so much more quickly than I ever did?*

These elves were soldiers, though. Their appearance often made Cailean forget how much older than him they all were —at least one hundred years his senior. They had fought in a war, and some might even have faced assassins during that time.

*They are experienced soldiers, and their loyalty is evident in their decision to follow Lyan and Kithr. Gods only know, they blessed us when they sent this handful of elves to us. And I am going to remember that, and not resent them for it.*

While Kithr spoke with Pyrn, Shiolto and Dalrian fanned to life the fire they had started earlier. Yion and the elves had dressed the meat before bringing it into camp. The brothers set to work transforming that meat into a meal.

Declan walked up beside Cailean. "Horse-tender, doctor, *and* cook?" He indicated Shiolto. "Gods know you're lucky to have him with you."

"I am," Cailean agreed. "I was more lucky than I imagined when Shiolto and Dalrian were among the few who volunteered to accompany me on the journey that first brought me through Eilidh Wood."

"The same men as those you brought this time?" Declan asked. "I remember one more."

"There was another," Cailean told him. "One of my guards. Torqual." He couldn't say the name without venom. "He betrayed us."

Declan's expression was grim. "The Mad God has mobilized his forces." He forced a thin smile. "Well, that's why the gods gave us Spearbearers, right?"

"I guess it is," Cailean agreed softly.

Deliberately returning to a lighter subject, the elf asked, "So, does Shiolto hold more hidden talents yet to be revealed? Is he also secretly a bard?"

Cailean winced. "No. I can attest with great certainty that he is *not* a bard. I've heard him sing. Dogs and small children flee the room."

Declan laughed. "That's a pity. Well, no one's perfect, I suppose."

"Lyan can sing," Cailean remarked. "I heard him once."

Declan nodded, growing serious again. "He could have become a bard, if he'd wanted. Or a loremaster. Or—gods only know, Lyan could have become just about anything he might have wanted."

"Did he choose to become an astrologer?" Cailean asked.

"I guess... sort of," Declan said. "He always liked it, but he liked lots of things. The Elder pushed him to become the astrologer's apprentice. Lyan didn't seem to object to the idea, though."

"So he made Lyan into an astrologer in the first place, and now he's taken that title away from him," Cailean said quietly.

Neither of them spoke for a time. Cailean eventually drifted to the bedrolls, where Aikan still slept. The smells of cooked meat hinted at a meal nearing completion. Cailean shook Aikan's shoulder.

"Dinner's almost ready."

Aikan stirred, blinking away sleep. "My lord? Did you rest?"

"Of course I did, Aikan," Cailean told him.

Aikan slowly sat up, then frowned at Cailean. "Did you rest for longer than it took me to fall asleep?"

"Yes, Aikan," Cailean answered with an amused smile. It wasn't *quite* a lie.

The elves had already gathered around the fire in the fading daylight. The Splinter avoided the fire, but she too drew toward the gathering. Cailean and Aikan joined the rest of the group. Shiolto carved off the first prime cut of meat for his lord, the second for Lyan, and the third for Aikan. After that, he didn't worry about rank and protocol, serving whoever was closest until everyone had fresh, hot venison. It might not have been a meal fit for a lord's table at home, but the meat tasted better than anything Cailean had eaten in a long time. He helped himself to a second serving.

Lyan noticed. "You should have eaten earlier, Cailean. You ought to eat immediately after you use Solstice to carry us across distances."

Cailean quickly chewed and swallowed, then answered. "Didn't think about that at the time. And I'm not sure there will be another time of doing that."

Lyan shifted uneasily, picking at his meal for a moment before sawing off a slice of meat. "I think we should."

Silence fell over the camp, broken only by the crackle of the fire and the babble of running water. "You *want* to make another jump like that, Lyan?" Cailean finally asked.

Lyan shivered. "No. I don't want to. Neither do you. Neither does anyone else here. That is *why* I think we *should*."

"If there's some logic to that, Lyan, I'm not seeing it," Pyrn said.

Kithr sat up straighter. "I do. Gods, this is why I told you everyone else needs to know what you told me earlier today,

Lyan." He looked across the fire at the rest of them. "The Mad God's champion uses some form of divination. He can predict what we are likely to do, the same as Lyan can predict what he's likely to do."

Aikan frowned at Kithr and Lyan both, but slowly nodded. "You are implying, then, that if Lord Cailean moves us again using Solstice, we will be taking the less likely choice —the one we least wish to do."

"That's right," Lyan answered quietly. "He will probably still have soldiers stationed where we would be most likely to arrive, but not as many as he will have waiting should we decide to travel on foot."

"So it will be a fight either way," Ihm said. "But they won't expect us, and there won't be as many of them. For that, I can accept another passage through the darkness, if the Spearbearer is willing."

Lyan gazed at Cailean. "The choice is yours."

Cailean forced himself to smile. "What kind of a choice is that, Lyan? Accept a little discomfort, or throw my men into a pitched battle?" He drew a deep breath. "Tomorrow morning, at first light, we'll make another jump."

Only after he said it did Cailean realize that when he had spoken of "my men", he had meant all of them—humans and elves both.

## 13

## KITHR

*"Using the same tactics repeatedly only works until your opponent learns those tactics. Then, he knows exactly where to strike."*

Kithr woke before dawn, surprised to discover that he finally felt rested. Perhaps it was only his imagination, but the air felt clearer and less tense in the camp. Even Lyan's uncharacteristic quiet seemed less strained.

*Or maybe I finally understand what he's been trying to tell me with and without words. Gods know I should have realized Lyan's had no time to regain his balance after what's happened.*

Peaceful quiet lay over the forest, and cold dew glittered across the ground in the light cast by the campfire. Mist rose off the pool, curling across the water's surface. Knowing Nachyne had a temple somewhere in this place, Kithr wondered if the god had ordered his monsters to watch over their camp.

He looked around the clearing again. Nothing about it made him think of the god of monsters or his followers, though Kithr did have the sense that they were safe here, perhaps even protected by something unseen.

*Maybe Nachyne's not the only god who has a presence in the Forests of Cossette.*

Kithr shook his head. Speculation gained him little. He walked to the pool and washed his face. There, while crouched by the water's edge, he murmured, "I don't know who might be watching over us, but I thank you for allowing us to rest here in peace." He felt a little foolish expressing gratitude to something that might be no more than a figment of his imagination. However, in the mist rolling across the surface of the pool, he thought he saw a shape like a stag looking back at him. Kithr blinked and it was gone, leaving him to wonder whether he had seen it at all.

"Gods, mortals, and Spearbearers," Kithr said under his breath, shaking his head. He stood, dipped his head in a small bow toward the pool, and moved toward the fire.

He almost walked into the Splinter, who paced restlessly. She stopped sharply, her long toes digging into the ground for balance. Her glowing amber eyes fixed on Kithr as if she hadn't noticed him. Neither of them moved, eyes locked. Kithr stepped back.

"Sorry."

She blinked and didn't respond.

Kithr waited a moment, then prompted, "Is something wrong?"

"We are alone."

Kithr frowned, glancing around the camp. The rest of the group sat near the fire, a low murmur of conversation rising. "Alone? What are you talking about? The others are right there."

Her brow furrowed as if his response confused her as much as her words confused him. She touched her chest. "We are alone. This place belongs to another and does not speak to us. When our roots delve into the earth, we do not feel our home."

Kithr finally realized that she just meant herself when she said "we." "We're a long way from Eilidh Wood."

Her amber eyes fixed on him sharply. "We are well aware of that."

"So why are you surprised that you can't feel the forest?"

"We are not surprised. We knew we should expect such," she snapped. "We knew all this when we were sent with you."

"If you already knew it and expected it, then why is it a problem?" Kithr asked, exasperated.

"Because we are alone now," she said, more quietly than he expected. "Then, we were not. We are... splintered from our whole, and we might never return."

*The Splinter is as much an exile as the rest of us.* Kithr wasn't sure what to think of that. A small piece of Eilidh Wood, broken off from the forest and sent with them. "We'll return to Eilidh Wood," he told her. "You'll go home again. Come on. Breakfast is ready."

"We do not need to eat as you do," she said. But she followed him, and settled into the dew-coated grass at the edge of the group.

Shiolto handed Kithr a bowl of stew. With a nod of thanks, he ate quickly. He was the last to sit down to breakfast.

Cailean set aside his bowl. "I thought about what we discussed last night, and I think we should adjust the plan."

Eyes turned to the Tathren lord, questioning. For a moment, Kithr wondered which discussion Cailean meant.

Cailean continued. "If the champion of the Mad God can divine the actions we're likely to take, we should try to use that against him. Our options at the moment are to travel on foot or to use Solstice, and he expects us to shy away from using Solstice at the moment."

Kithr nodded slowly. "Do you know of a third option?"

Cailean shook his head. "Gods know, I wish I did. But last

night I said that we should leave at first light. Now that I've given the matter more thought, I don't think we should be in such a hurry."

Around the fire, puzzled looks met Cailean. Abruptly, Ihm brightened, sitting straighter. "Because that's what anyone would expect us to do! We want to get it over with first thing. That's why an ambush is waiting in case we do let the Spear move us, but the longer we don't appear, the less they'll expect us."

Cailean nodded. "Exactly." He turned to Lyan. "What do you think?"

Lyan considered. "It's a good plan."

"Will he expect it?" Cailean asked.

"He's new to his gift," Lyan answered. "He hasn't learned how to predict the finer shifts as they are affected by sudden decisions or actions."

Kithr blinked. *How does Lyan know that? I could believe that the stars might reveal the Champion is a diviner, but how can Lyan know how long he's been able to do so, or how skilled he is? What else does Lyan know about the Champion that he isn't telling me?*

"How long do you wish to wait, my lord?" Aikan asked.

Aikan's voice made Kithr bite back his questions. He and Cailean might have reached a truce, but Aikan seized any opportunity to heap blame on elves. Lyan needed no more of that, and if Kithr asked his questions in front of everyone, he would fill Aikan's quiver with far too many arrows.

Unaware of Kithr's turmoil, Cailean answered his steward. "A turn of the hourglass—or my closest guess to one. Not too long, or I might lose my nerve after all."

Nervous laughter rippled through the group. Kithr wiped his bowl clean with his fingers and set it aside. Cailean's strategy made sense. Kithr didn't *like* the idea of waiting, but that only emphasized the cleverness of the plan.

*If the Mad God's champion can divine anything about me, he'll be well aware that patience is not my strength.*

Declan signaled his men. They rose as a group and walked toward the middle of the clearing. Pyrn paused and looked over his shoulder. "Kithr. You coming?"

Kithr started from his thoughts and frowned in puzzlement. "Where?"

"Preparing for battle," Pyrn said, tone implying that the answer was obvious.

During the war, the series of stretches and exercises had been as much a part of Kithr's daily preparations as dressing had. Once he'd returned to Eilidh Wood, Kithr had fallen out of the habit. He hadn't taken it up again even after following Lyan out of Eilidh Wood, relying on his skills as a hunter more than those as a soldier.

He followed Pyrn and began the series of basic stretches. Kithr felt awkward and stiff. He tried not to dwell on the memories such simple actions raised, yet he felt as if he stood only a stone's throw away from cold mornings when he had dressed, stretched, taken up his bow, and prepared to kill Tathrens. Days to which he had no desire to return.

Declan, Pyrn, and Ihm moved smoothly through the routine, as if they still practiced it regularly, over sixty years since the war. Seine moved with them, not as smoothly as her husband, but clearly practiced. Kithr forced himself to keep pace, though his body complained at the unfamiliar activity. He knew if he pushed himself too hard, he would do more harm than good, but his pride demanded that he not fall behind.

A reprieve came unexpectedly. The Tathrens just watched the elves in mild puzzlement or curiosity, but Yion began preparations of his own. While the mercenary stretched, the elves gave him little notice. However, as Yion began a complex series of turns and thrusts, gazes drifted more and more toward him. To Kithr's relief, the pace of the elven exercises slowed as the others became distracted watching Yion.

The mercenary moved with smooth grace, no movements

wasted, and each deadly in its precision. He could have been dancing on a stage, but Kithr had only to picture blades in Yion's hands to recognize how lethal the mercenary was. Lethal and possessing skill that came only with years of training.

*Anyone who knows fighting could watch this and know that Yion is no brute mercenary. I've never seen him practice before. I doubt anyone here has, and knowing that he takes pains to conceal his past, I understand why.*

Kithr finished his exercises without embarrassing himself thanks to the mercenary's timely decision to display his skills. Whether it was coincidence or deliberate, Kithr silently thanked Yion for it. Sweat streamed down his face and soaked his clothes as he sank down by the pool. Kithr stripped off his shirt, dunked it in the water, and used it to wash. The cold water and morning air felt good against his bare skin. Kithr lay back in the browning grass, taking deep breaths.

Lyan sat beside him. "You're going to hurt yourself if you keep that up, Kithr," he cautioned.

Kithr rolled his head to the side to look at his friend. "Prediction?"

"Common sense. Declan and the others practice every other day. I used to see them sometimes when I stayed up all night. You last practiced when?"

"Don't remember," Kithr admitted. "I stopped when I decided to stop being a soldier and go back to being a hunter."

Lyan considered saying something, and Kithr wondered what it was. Finally, Lyan murmured, "Soldiers are predictable even without divination, Kithr. Especially elven soldiers. Hunters are the ones who must adapt to new prey with each hunt."

Kithr frowned, then his expression twisted with distaste. "That sounds like something that traitor *Torqual* said."

"Does that make it any less true?" Lyan stood before Kithr answered.

"The truth is I should have carved out the bastard's guts when I had the chance," Kithr muttered.

He climbed to his feet and found his pack. After changing into dry clothes, he tested the draw on his bow. His shoulders ached, but not unbearably, and his hands were steady. Ready for battle.

"Break camp!" Aikan ordered.

*It's time.*

The group assembled. The elves positioned themselves in a loose circle around the horses. Kithr stepped back, casting a critical eye over his companions. He didn't need to remind anyone that they expected battle, nor did he need to remind them of the sickness that accompanied Solstice's gut-wrenching transportation. "Lyan, stay near the packhorses, calm them after we arrive. Tathrens, remember that your horses don't like this travel any better than you do, and don't have the advantage of understanding the need for it. If you see shelter, head for it. Lacking that, high ground. We'll spread out and take cover as we find it to make sure you have a clear path." He looked up at Cailean, who settled into the saddle. Kithr smiled faintly. "Try not to drop us in the middle of a lake."

Cailean returned a tight smile. "I'll do my best."

The Tathren lord's grip tightened around Solstice. Kithr took up a guard position to one side. He felt the unpleasant pressure growing in the air, and tensed, knowing what would come next. The ground plummeted away, taking his stomach with it, and Kithr fell into empty darkness.

Heartbeats passed with agonizing slowness. Kithr counted them to focus his mind on something other than his wish to scream and create *some* sound in the void.

*Seven… Eight… Nine…*

His feet hit solid ground. Kithr staggered. The contents of

his stomach lurked somewhere near the back of his throat, but didn't demand to go any further, and the nausea seemed less severe than the last time. He opened his eyes, hearing horses snorting and stamping. The Tathrens struggled to keep their mounts in check, but they had expected the reaction and no one spilled from the saddle. The packhorses snorted and clustered around Lyan, as Kithr had hoped they would. The astrologer's natural affinity for animals gave them the comfort and reassurance they sought.

Kithr's gaze raked their surroundings. Wherever they now were, the trees grew in thin clusters like the last unruly tufts of hair clinging to a balding man's head. One clump stood to their left, and a glance at the spindly trunks told Kithr that they would not support his weight. They offered little cover, but as consolation, enemies couldn't use those trees for shelter or as posts for archers.

Ahead of them, a rise promised a good view of their surroundings. Between Kithr and that rise, a band of armed men staggered into a line. Knowing his own disorientation, Kithr was surprised the men hadn't seized advantage of the moment. Even if surprised by the group's appearance, they should have attacked immediately.

Several of the stumbling men doubled over as if in pain. Next to Kithr, Cailean murmured, "Thank you Solstice." The Tathren had his horse under control and sat straight in the saddle.

"Cailean?" Kithr asked, not taking his eyes from the men.

"Thanks to the Spear, they feel as ill as we do," the Tathren answered. "It won't last long for us or them."

*Couldn't Solstice have revealed that convenient little trick earlier?*

A broad-shouldered man wearing a steel skullcap raised his blade. "In Murdo's name, attack!"

Ragged, lackluster shouts answered the order, but men broke into a run toward Kithr, Cailean, and their group. Kithr counted at least twenty men with no visible archers.

*Time to even the odds.* He grabbed arrows from his quiver and began to loose them into the attacking line, hearing the hum of other bowstrings as Declan and his men did the same.

A scattering of arrows answered, rising from the enemy camp like a flock of startled sparrows. Kithr cursed, springing to one side. Cailean's horse shied, dancing the other direction.

"Spread out!" Kithr called. *Where are the archers?* He ducked as an arrow zipped overhead. *There!* Kithr sent a shaft flying toward what he had first mistaken as a pile of bags at the ambushers' camp. He heard a scream of pain, and sneered. *You think you're clever, human?*

A moment later, Kithr realized that the archers didn't have to be clever. They only had to be clever enough to delay the elves. They were a distraction and bait. While the elven archers tried to pick them off, the foot soldiers had closed the distance. A black-bearded man with a ragged scar across his face and three missing teeth grinned as he charged at Kithr, mace swinging.

Kithr swore in Elven, rolling back and jumping to his feet. He hated fighting this close, and his nascent plan had never counted on the ambushers forcing him into melee range. Kithr kicked the man in the unarmored shin and sprang back. Black-beard growled and spat, straightening just in time to catch Kithr's hastily loosed arrow in his neck. Snatching another shaft, Kithr found a new target and sent another man sprawling to the ground.

Cailean held his ground, skillfully wielding Solstice as he turned his horse toward their attackers. The animal might not understand magic, but battle was familiar. One man caught a vicious bite from Cailean's mount.

The Splinter carried no visible weapons, but around her, clumps of plants burst from the ground and lashed at the attacking humans. Men shouted in alarm and surprise, their cluster splitting apart to avoid the grabbing, stabbing plants.

*Where's Lyan?*

Kithr scanned swiftly for the packhorses, and saw Shiolto, Dalrian, and Seine clustered protectively near them. Lyan clutched a knife, but stayed back as best he could. As if sensing Kithr's gaze, Lyan turned toward him.

"Hunter or soldier?" Lyan mouthed the words. Perhaps he said them aloud, but the crash of battle drowned his voice.

Kithr didn't have to hear Lyan to understand. *Elven soldiers are predictable.*

His gaze swept over the battle again as he loosed an arrow toward one of the men. He saw Pyrn near him, moving back to gain enough range and a better position for his bow. Elven soldiers often preferred the bow to melee.

*If I knew that, I would set traps.*

"Pyrn!" Kithr called in Elven. "Swords!"

Pyrn skidded to a stop, startled by the order. "I have a good spot," he called back in the same. The chestnut-haired soldier took a step back, drawing his bow to prove his point. His back foot came down, and sticks broke under the weight. Pyrn stumbled, dropping his bow and trying to catch his balance as the thin camouflage fell, revealing a pit.

Kithr lunged for him. As Pyrn started to fall, Kithr caught his wrist. Pyrn grunted, and Kithr winced at the sharp jerk of weight. Pyrn grabbed hold of his arm. Muscles already strained and sore from the workout of the morning howled in protest, and Kithr felt his grip slipping.

"It's not deep," Pyrn panted. "Let go."

Kithr grimaced, but his weakening grip decided the matter before he could attempt to argue. Pyrn released his hold, and Kithr couldn't hold on. He winced at the following thump, but no cry of pain rose from the pit. Kithr looked over the edge and saw Pyrn gingerly picking himself up.

Kithr shoved back onto his feet, and shouted in Elven. "Traps at our backs. To blades!" Drawing his sword, Kithr lunged into the fray.

## 14

## CAILEAN



*"Following Murdo's imprisonment, his followers scattered to the winds. Hunted and unwelcome, many sought refuge in the harshest of lands, struggling to survive. Those who endured held to the belief that one day, their god would call on those who held true and stood firm, and raise them again in glory."*

Cailean heard Kithr yell in Elven, but was surprised to see the elves drop their bows and draw swords. Cailean rarely saw Kithr voluntarily enter close combat. Not that Kithr lacked skill in the sword; it simply was not his weapon of choice.

The change startled the ambushers as well. Men hesitated as the elves rushed them. They recovered, but the elves of Eilidh Wood seized the opportunity while they had it, pushing the offensive. Cailean kicked Sai forward with them. He blocked a sword swing and kicked the man, his boot catching the other under the chin. The impact probably rattled teeth loose, not that the wild-eyed man had many to spare.

Tremors of weariness shook Cailean's arms. He longed to

call on Solstice to sweep these men from their path, but admitted the limits of his strength. Using more of the Spear's powers now would be foolhardy. Even without calling on its magic, the Spear was a deadly weapon, slicing through leather armor and flesh alike.

Aikan fought near Cailean. His face was wan, but his blade was steady. He handled his horse and his weapon with skill. Most of what Cailean knew about mounted combat, he'd learned from his steward.

Shiolto, Dalrian, and one of the elves protected Lyan and the packhorses. If Lyan would call Equinox, the battle would be over already. Cailean had to trust the astrologer had a good reason for not summoning his Spear. Lyan held a long knife, though with the horses clustering around him, he had little opportunity to fight even if he wanted to.

On foot, Yion swept through the men around him as smoothly as if he were still practicing by the pool. His movements appeared effortless, almost enough to make one forget that he carved a path of blood and death.

Assured that his men held their own, Cailean urged his horse forward, gaze fixed on the broad-shouldered man with a steel skullcap who shouted orders. Beads ornamented Skullcap's brown beard, and he wielded a curved sword of a style unfamiliar to Cailean. He met Cailean's eyes and grinned, showing blackened teeth.

Cailean's horse shoved through the few men between them, and Cailean poised Solstice like a lance on the saddle. Behind him, weapons clashed as Aikan engaged the men he left in his wake. Skullcap sneered, ducking low and dodging aside as the horse thundered toward him. Cailean wheeled Sai around. Skullcap closed the distance, giving Cailean no opportunity for a second charge.

Cailean blocked Skullcap's first powerful swing, but numbing vibrations ran up the Spear's shaft and through his hands. Cailean twisted in the saddle, shifting his grip on

Solstice. On Skullcap's second attack, Cailean swung Solstice in response, catching the curved blade in the flanged base of the spearhead. With an ordinary spear, such a block would have been foolish, more likely to result in a severed spearhead than an effective parry. Solstice, however, was no ordinary spear.

Cailean saw surprise in Skullcap's eyes at the unexpected block. Cailean twisted the Spear, nearly tearing the sword out of Skullcap's hand. The man jerked his sword free, chipping the blade.

"I'll use your skull for a whetstone," Skullcap snarled, slashing not at Cailean, but his horse.

Sai danced aside, but the blade bit, opening a gash. Sai stumbled. Cailean hissed a curse. From Sai's movements, he knew the horse was hurt. He kicked at Skullcap and dropped to the ground.

Cailean landed hard, weariness robbing him of grace. Skullcap lunged at him. Cailean braced Solstice, and the Spear stabbed into Skullcap's left shoulder.

Skullcap bared his blackened teeth, enraged. Rather than pull back, he shoved forward, driving the Spear deeper into his shoulder. Paying no heed to the blood flowing from the wound, he raised his blade.

Cailean tried to tear Solstice free, and the rough jerk threw off Skullcap's balance, but the Spear remained firmly impaled. Skullcap spat out a glob of something black and sneered. "Die, in Murdo's name."

"Not today," Cailean growled. He released Solstice and jumped back. "Solstice!" He held out his hand, and the Spear appeared in his grasp once more. Blood rushed from the wound in Skullcap's shoulder.

Skullcap swung viciously, moving faster than an injured man ought to. Cailean deflected the blow, but the blade tore through his sleeve and opening a stinging gash. *Dammit, how can he keep going? And how long can I keep this up?*

An arrow slammed into Skullcap's neck. Skullcap staggered, blinking in surprise. He opened his mouth, but only a gurgling sound came out. Even so, he raised his blade. Cailean drove Solstice into Skullcap's chest. The man finally fell to the ground.

Cailean jerked the Spear free. Panting for breath, he spun around, praying that he was ready if anyone else attacked him.

A man rushed at him with a howl of anger, but before he reached Cailean, he toppled, one of Yion's throwing blades buried in his back. The rest of the men were engaged or bled out on the ground. Belatedly, Cailean glanced around to see who had loosed the arrow. It couldn't have been Kithr; Kithr was still locked sword to sword with another ambusher. He saw Declan slinging a bow over his shoulder. The elf gave Cailean a brief nod and drew his sword once more, moving to dispatch another man.

Aikan was at his side in a moment. "Are you hurt, Lord Cailean?"

Cailean shook his head. "Just a nick. You?"

"A few cuts, little worthy of notice," Aikan answered. "That was reckless, my lord. Did you honestly expect such a man to hold to an honorable fight?"

Cailean paused. "I suppose I did. I don't know how he kept fighting after I stabbed the Spear into his shoulder. He acted like it was nothing!" He planted Solstice in the ground and leaned against the Spear, feeling worry to match his own from the weapon.

A man shrieked and Cailean saw the last ambusher fall to the ground in a spray of blood. Kithr wiped his blade clean before sheathing it. Cailean took a quick assessment of the situation.

Twenty-three men lay dead around him, along with the handful of archers who had been hidden in the camp of the ambushers. Cailean counted them more fortunate than they deserved that none of the dead came from their own band. Shiolto sat on the blood-stained ground, dazed and bleeding from a gash on his head. Dalrian retrieved bandages, and Shiolto gestured as if to claim he would be all right. The elves bore injuries and moved with less spryness. As Cailean made a quick count, he came up one elf short. In the moment of alarm, he couldn't identify who was missing. Lyan was safe, Kithr, Declan...

Kithr snatched a coil of rope from a packhorse, rushed. Cailean followed him. Kithr glanced over his shoulder, noticed Cailean, and warned, "Watch your step. The bastards dug pits."

*Pits? Why would they....?* "Who fell?" Cailean asked, concerned. *Gods, I pray they didn't line the bottoms of their pits with stakes.*

"Pyrn. He was moving for a better vantage." Kithr's voice was clipped.

Kithr slowed cautiously as he approached a hole. Leaves and dry grass clung to the edges of the pit.

Sounds of movement rose from the hole. Cailean started to lean forward to see if Pyrn was injured, but Kithr grabbed his shirt and jerked him back. "Bad idea, Tathren. Never give a trapped elf a target without identifying yourself first."

"I heard you talking," Pyrn called from the hole. "I wasn't going to attack him."

*But he could have, and I would have been unprepared.* Cailean flushed. "I'll remember that."

"Assumptions are dangerous," Kithr said simply. He uncoiled the rope and let it drop into the pit.

Cailean helped him brace the rope and lift Pyrn out. The elf was scraped and cut, coated with dirt. When he stood, he favored one leg. Pyrn gave Cailean a nod of thanks, then met Kithr's eyes. "I should have listened to you."

"You should have," Kithr agreed tersely.

Cailean expected further chastisement from Kithr, but for the elves, the brief exchange proved sufficient.

Lyan led the packhorses toward the rise, and the rest of the group drifted after him. Cailean caught Sai's reins and checked the bloody gash from Skullcap's attack. The horse snorted and stomped a hoof. Cailean grimaced and stroked Sai's neck. "Easy, boy. Let's get you over to Shiolto and get that looked at."

Yion paused beside Skullcap's corpse, searching the man's body. Cailean stopped next to the mercenary. Yion opened a pouch from Skullcap's belt and plucked out a pinch of dried, black root, sniffed it, then brushed his fingers clean.

Yion glanced to Cailean. "Dried kalumyun root, Lord Cailean. A man who chews this will feel no pain. Even with the gravest of wounds, he will battle until death. Continued use stains the teeth black." He nodded to Skullcap. "His teeth tell me that he kept the habit many years. This man traveled far to come here. Kalumyun is used as a drug by warriors in the lands south of the land of my birth, and the plant grows few other places."

Cailean just nodded. His legs trembled as he followed the others to the rise. Declan scrambled to the top to take a look around, but the others were less inclined to exert that much effort. Cailean sank down in the dry, brown grass, grateful for the moments to rest. Shiolto made noises of concern at Sai's injury and took the horse from Cailean without so much as a by-your-leave. For a time, everyone focused on tending their wounds. Finally, Cailean's gaze turned to Lyan.

"You said that taking this route, we would meet a small ambush. Twenty-three footmen as well as archers is your idea of small?"

"I said it would be smaller than the band we would face had we gone on foot through the forest," Lyan corrected quietly as he bandaged Seine's shoulder. "If we had walked through the forest, we would have faced more than twice this number."

"Fifty men simply to stop us?" Aikan asked dubiously.

"Fifty men to weaken and slow us," Lyan replied. "The Mad God's champion doesn't expect to *stop* us. But for the chance to weaken the Spearbearers, slow our progress, and possibly cause serious harm and kill our friends? He'll gladly sacrifice fifty men for that. He also knew that if we traveled on foot, his ambush would need enough strength to try to overwhelm us with Cailean at full strength and using the powers of Solstice."

Pyrn waved off a handful of bandages from Shiolto. "These men set a good trap. Decent fighters despite their scraggly looks, and those pits were clever. Wicked, but clever."

"Our preference for bows is well-known," Kithr said sharply. Cailean thought him more irate that he hadn't anticipated the trap than that one of the elves had fallen into it. "As I have been reminded, repeating comfortable tactics only works until the enemy learns to counter them."

"Lyan, what size of an army are we going to face?" Declan climbed back down to join them.

"If we were to face him right now? Not quite enough to besiege a Tathren stronghold," Lyan answered grimly. "And he's gathering more. He intends to lay siege to the Shrine of Equinox."

"He's what?" sputtered Dalrian. "How?"

"He is the champion of the Mad God," Lyan answered. "His master has blessed him with power and with the guidance of at least two of his priests. When he finds the Shrine, at least half his army will become sacrifices to summon demons from the Mad God's prison to battle the Guardians: reapers and worse."

"Won't the gods stop him?" Shiolto protested.

"The Mad God has had centuries to perfect methods of hiding his followers from the gods' eyes. He uses them all now.

Nachyne and the rest of the gods sent *us* because the champion and his army are shielded from their sight. They must rely on us: on mortals and the Spears." Lyan closed his eyes a moment. Cailean saw lines of anguish and fear on his friend's face.

"The Mad God has raised a champion. The fact that he dares do something so brazen, so *open* as a declaration of strength means he's confident in his plans." Lyan opened his eyes and looked at each of them. "Murdo has blessed a man with the powers of a champion and begun calling his mortal followers together because he is *certain* the gods cannot stop him from breaking free of his prison. If *that* thought doesn't terrify you, then you're a fool."

*Did Lyan always know so much about the Mad God? I don't think he did. When did he learn all this? How?* Cailean's worry sat in the pit of his stomach like a rock.

Declan looked back at the battlefield, considering. "I can't say I know anything about fighting a champion of a god, or about magical weapons, but if you and Cailean are the two people who can stop this man, I do know a few things. He is going to continue targeting you and determining how much force he needs to crush you. He is going to continue gathering men. Judging from the ones who attacked us, he's taking a lot who aren't the sorts to line up neatly on a battlefield and face you head-on. He's gathering some prime scum, and with no offense to you Tathrens, you don't know how to think like scum."

Cailean smiled faintly. "None taken. What do you recommend?"

"We need more men," Declan answered plainly. "Preferably some who *can* think like scum."

"Such a fine characteristic to seek in a soldier." Aikan glowered.

"Soldiers aren't what we need. Thieves, brigands, pickpockets, mercenaries, any of those could have the skills."

Declan shrugged and looked at Cailean. "I understand that Tathren nobles sometimes keep that sort of men in their dungeons. Do you know of any who might let you borrow their prisoners for a suicide mission?"

Blunt and to the point. Cailean could appreciate that about elves, sometimes. "My own dungeons are empty, and I don't know about others. My neighbors and I have had differences of opinions in recent times, and I'm not certain I would be welcome even asking. We could try recruiting from local towns, assuming we find one soon. The issue I foresee, though, is funds. If we hire men, I have to pay them, and most mercenaries, excluding Yion, expect prompt payment."

"If we could convince anyone in Eilidh Wood, other soldiers would join us," Ihm said. "Maybe the Splinter would be enough to convince—"

Lyan shook his head sharply. "We cannot look to Eilidh Wood for help. The Elder's web is too wide-spread."

"But—" Ihm protested.

"No." Lyan's answer was forceful and final. "No elf of Eilidh Wood will help us."

Cailean caught Lyan's emphasis on Eilidh Wood, and frowned. "Are there elves who are *not* of Eilidh Wood?"

He thought it an innocent enough question, but abruptly all the elves except Lyan stiffened, looking sharply at him. Cailean looked back, unsure why the sudden reaction.

Finally, Declan spoke, voice tight. "Yes. There are the Lost. They are elves who have been banished or who have fallen so far from the ways that an elf of Eilidh Wood should follow that they are cut off from any connection to the forest."

"Lost?" Shiolto repeated. "Isn't that what you called those elves in Malgor Forest, Lyan?"

Lyan nodded. "Yes."

Pyrn drew a sharp breath, sitting up straight. "You've encountered Lost elves? You know where they are? Kithr, you never said anything about this!"

Aikan sprang indignantly to his feet. "You don't expect us to recruit those savages, do you?"

Cailean watched Lyan's face, and he spoke quietly. "You do. You expect us to recruit them." *If we're looking for, as Declan calls them, scum, they are ideal. They've survived in a land that hates them for decades after the end of the war, killing Tathrens while horribly outnumbered. However.* "I see a couple of problems with that idea, Lyan."

Kithr responded to Pyrn. "They're in Tather. Soldiers who never left the war, led by Nylas."

"Nylas is still alive?" Ihm burst in astonishment.

"He's Lost, and he's cold as ice," Kithr said. "Given your parting words to him, Lyan, I hardly expect he'll welcome an invitation to fight alongside us or the Tathrens."

"He doesn't have to welcome it." Lyan spoke with cool confidence. "Nylas doesn't have to welcome it, but he *does* have to accept. He and his men owe a life-debt."

Aikan made a sound of scorn. "The savage refused to even acknowledge our help. What makes you think he will acknowledge any debt?"

Kithr frowned at Aikan. "He didn't acknowledge *your* help in rescuing him and his men from the dungeon. Did he acknowledge Lyan's?"

"He did," Lyan answered.

"Then Lyan's right. Like it or not, Nylas and his men will come. They must repay that debt."

Declan eyed Lyan with a mix of unease and respect. "Lost elves owe you a life-debt?"

"*These* Lost do," Lyan told him. "We freed them from a Tathren dungeon without any of them dying."

"Lyan!" Aikan said sharply. "You are serious about this?"

"Declan says we need fighters who can think like scum. Who do not follow the 'rules' of battle. Can you think of any better, Aikan?" Lyan stood. "Nylas has just enough honor left that he will answer a debt he acknowledged. He doesn't *have* to like it. *We* don't have to *like* it. But we don't have to pay him and we don't have to question his reliability. He *will* answer this debt. He *must*. And Cailean must go tell him so."

Cailean started. "Me? Why not you, Lyan? You're the one who he owes the debt to."

"And the one who forced them all to see that they were Lost. Cailean, one of us should go, and it would be better that it be you." Lyan held Cailean's gaze.

*He's not going to expound, is he?* Cailean could tell from Lyan's gaze that he had gotten as much of an explanation as he was going to. "All right, but I would like at least one elf with me as well. And how are we going to get there quickly? Last time we traveled to Malgor Forest, it was either the Shrine of Equinox or one of the Guardians who sent us there."

Lyan paused. "I can't command the original Guardians of the Spear, but I can ask their help."

"We're really going to be calling on the *Lost* for help, Lyan?" Pyrn asked, clearly liking the idea no more than Aikan did. "The Lost! It's practically defilement to *speak* to one!"

Kithr's eyes flashed. "And what do you think *we* are right now, in the eyes of Heartshrine Village? What do you think the Elder says about *us*? We *need* their help, and you *will* accept it!"

The Splinter spoke for the first time since before the battle. "We will use whatever tools are necessary to attain our goal. Even those Lost to us."

Pyrn opened his mouth to argue, then closed it again, scowling. "Fine," he said through clenched teeth. "The Lost. Next you're going to claim we need to track down the accursed Seer."

Lyan winced, but didn't respond.

"I'll accompany Cailean," Declan said.

"Thank you." Cailean wasn't sure whether having an elf at his side would be any help in Malgor Forest, but it made him a little less worried. He recalled the looming shadows and the air of malevolent anger in that forest, and shivered. Forcing down the chill of fear, he asked Lyan, "Can the Guardians help us?"

"Lyan Spearbearer has asked my assistance for a little while, and I admit, I'm glad to have an opportunity."

Everyone jumped at the new voice—a calm, mild male voice that felt vaguely familiar to Cailean. He turned to see an older elf dressed in unremarkable leather pants with a russet tunic. His feet were bare. A woven headband held back his reddish-brown hair. Light blue eyes twinkled as he greeted the group with a bow.

*I've seen him before. The gatekeeper at the Shrine of Equinox.*

"To those of you who I have met before, a pleasure to see you once again. To those I have not yet met, it is a pleasure as well. I am Sirex, Guardian of the Shrine of Equinox and son of Cantorelle, god of roads."

15

## KITHR

*The chill upon the spine, the whispers in the darkness; it is said these are signs of the followers of the Mad God. But far worse are the other kind. The secret kind. The ones who act not with rituals, sacrifices, and fear, but who wield words, soft and sweet. For there lies the true danger—the knife that strikes you in the back, held in the hand of one you trust.*

The rush of battle faded, leaving Kithr exhausted and aware of every aching muscle. At the appearance of the gatekeeper from the Shrine of Equinox, he reflexively reached for his bow. The movement sent sharp pain through his shoulder, cutting the motion short even before he recognized the man.

*I'll be useless if we have to fight again today. Gods preserve us.*

Declan and the other elves had snatched up weapons, but stood startled by Sirex's calm assertion that he was a demigod. They looked uncertainly at Kithr, then Lyan, waiting for an order to either fight or stand down.

"I asked for his help; Sirex is not an enemy," Lyan said firmly. He spoke to the demigod. "Thank you."

For the son of a god, Sirex looked unremarkable. He was certainly of elven decent, but where Venycia was breathtaking in her beauty, Sirex could have blended into a crowd without effort. Wearing tunic and trousers instead of the robes of a Guardian of Equinox, he might have been any traveler on the road. Although most travelers were not barefoot, as the demigod was.

Sirex nodded in reply to Lyan. "The Shrine held against the Mad God's first assault. I can be spared for now."

Despite his aches, Kithr sat straighter. "The Shrine is under attack already? I thought the Champion was still looking for it."

Sirex nodded, grim. "The Mad God sent minions as advance scouts. We killed many, but one slipped past the protections and found a path to the Shrine. It led others in an attack. Their goal is less to take the Shrine, and more to prevent us from closing the path they have opened. They are a constant distraction as we prepare for a larger assault. Venycia and Waldros lead the defense and agreed that I should aid you as I can."

"Cailean needs to travel to Malgor Forest, gather the elves there, and return with them," Lyan told him. "Declan is going with him, and—" He looked to Cailean. "Who else?"

Shiolto and Dalrian both shifted uneasily, but Aikan scowled fiercely at Lyan. "I will not see my lord sent to treat with those savages alone. I am going as well."

*The Tathren Spearbearer and his elf-hating steward. This will put Nylas's honor to the test.* Kithr shoved aside the twinge of guilt over his relief that Aikan intended to accompany Cailean rather than continue to inflict his dislike on everyone else.

"Easily done," Sirex said. "I need only a few moments to build the pathway."

"Does that mean you're leaving right now, Lord Cailean?" Dalrian asked, surprised.

Cailean hesitated. He looked worn, and if Nylas saw him

in such a state, he would strike without questions. The Tathren lord rubbed his forehead and brushed back sweat-damp hair. "I need food first. I trust our departure can wait *that* long."

For a moment, no one responded. Aikan frowned, then cleared his throat pointedly. The sound spurred Dalrian into movement. Shiolto started to stand up, but sat back down heavily. From his dazed expression, Kithr guessed that the horse-tender's head wound left him more off-balance than he wanted to admit. Dalrian pulled a loaf of bread, somewhat worse for wear, from a grey bag. Cailean accepted it without complaint.

Kithr groaned as he stood. He found the pack Declan had given him back in Heartshrine Village and retrieved a bundle of dried meat. Tossing the bundle to the Tathren lord, he said, "Take what you need, Cailean."

Cailean fumbled, barely catching it. "Thank you."

Kithr nodded, gingerly sitting again. Cailean tore into the bread and devoured the meat with an unrepentant lack of dignity. Aikan checked the horses, frowning at Cailean's injured stallion.

"Lord Cailean, you will need to ride my Ember," the steward said. "Sai is in no condition for such a venture as this."

"Mmph." Whatever Cailean meant to say was muffled by a mouthful of bread.

Yion spoke. "Lord Cailean may borrow my mare, Miska. I am comfortable afoot, and should you need to cross swords with someone, you are at an advantage when mounted, Lord Aikan."

Cailean nodded vigorously in agreement as he stuffed the last of the food into his mouth. He wiped his sleeve across his mouth. "You should ride, Aikan. I'll take Yion's horse."

"What about the ones Dalrian and I ride, sir?" Shiolto

asked. "Since there will be four of you." He clearly second-guessed the idea of allowing Declan on a horse.

"Your beast would sooner bite me than let me ride," Declan chuckled. "I'll walk."

Sirex smiled warmly. "A generous offer, my friend, but I too prefer my feet upon the earth."

Cailean levered to his feet, brushing crumbs from his clothes. A full loaf of bread and the bundle of dried meat had reenergized him in a way that made Kithr fiercely jealous. Lyan had told Kithr that food was the fastest means for a Spearbearer to restore his strength after using the Spear's powers, but that knowledge was little comfort when Kithr still ached as if a horse had dragged him through a forest.

The Tathren looked over the group. Injuries had been bound, and the air was uncertain, waiting. Yion had removed his packs from the saddle and buckled Cailean's in their place. Declan kept a healthy space between himself and the horses, pack and bow slung over his shoulders. Seine murmured something in his ear, making Declan smile. He kissed her and whispered something in return. Seine shook her head with a soft laugh and stepped back. Sirex didn't pace, but he radiated a sense that he was eager to be moving, now that he was temporarily released from the Shrine.

"I don't know any reason to delay further." Cailean sounded resigned, as though hoping someone would provide an excuse to postpone departure.

Kithr didn't fault his lack of eagerness. When Lyan had led the conversation to the Lost elves, chill dread had settled over Kithr. The last time he'd seen Nylas, they had exchanged harsh insults and nearly come to blows. Nylas made no secret of his hate of Tathrens or his contempt for Lyan as foolish, ignorant, and useless. He had also made no secret of the fact that he despised Kithr for not continuing the war and for allowing Lyan to number Tathrens among his friends.

*If I had to call Nylas's debt due, could I do so without bloodshed?*

*Maybe Cailean really is the best man for this task. At the least, it means less to him that Nylas and his men are Lost.*

"Be careful," Kithr said.

Cailean nodded. "We will."

Sirex perked up. "You're ready?"

"We're ready," Cailean said.

"We will continue on from here, once we're ready," Lyan said. "You can find us, Sirex?"

The demigod smiled. "Unless you take to the air or find some tract of land without road, path, trail, or tracks, I can find you. Cantorelle will guide us." He crouched briefly, and as he stood again, a doorway shimmered into being next to him. "Malgor Forest awaits, Spearbearer Dev'gilla."

Cailean swung into the saddle and kicked Yion's horse to the doorway. The animal entered without hesitation and vanished. Aikan made a sound of annoyance and urged his horse to a fast walk, following his lord. Declan saluted Lyan and Kithr as he entered the portal. Sirex stepped through last, and the portal vanished on his heels.

The shimmer had barely faded from the air when Pyrn whirled to glare at Lyan and Kithr. "You've been dealing with the Lost. I'm astonished Elder Brenhan didn't even mention *that* in his accusations. At least they would have had *some* truth then! How *dare* you defy the laws of Eilidh Wood?"

Lyan didn't flinch. "They are not all Lost, and they are not all beyond redemption. To find their path back to the ways of an elf of Eilidh Wood, they had to first recognize that they *were* Lost, and they wouldn't have done so on their own. Yes, we dealt with the Lost to force them to see the truth of what they have become."

"And what are they?" Pyrn demanded.

"A bloodlord ruling over his winterborn blooddrinkers," Lyan said harshly. Worse insults could barely be found among elves. "That's what Nylas and his warriors have become. I don't call on this life-debt for *their* sakes. Nylas can rot in his accursed forest for all I care. I'm calling on this debt for the sake of a handful among them who are not Lost, in the hope that they, at least, can be saved."

"The Elder doesn't know, does he?" Seine asked suddenly. "You didn't tell him."

Kithr laughed bitterly. "Elder Brenhan didn't care about our journey. He heard only enough to make inferences and hurl accusations at Lyan."

"Elder Brenhan always listens," Ihm protested.

Kithr's jaw tightened. Remembering that morning still infuriated him. "Lyan told the Elder that he left with the Tathrens and found the Shrine of Equinox. Nothing else, and the Elder didn't care to know anything more. We were attacked time and again, but the Elder didn't hear. Lyan was captured and tortured by a Tathren who wanted the Spear for himself. We found Lost lurking in a forest of Tather. Lyan was pursued and tormented by a pooka, and finally bound the creature. We met *gods*, and Elder Brenhan knows *nothing* of it, because he *would not listen*!"

Pyrn, Ihm, and Seine stared at Kithr. Ihm ventured, "You met gods? You mean like him?" He waved toward the spot where Sirex had been.

"Sirex is a demigod," Lyan corrected. "One of his parents was mortal. Twelve demigods chose to become the first Guardians of Equinox. He is one of them."

"Then he is not what you meant about gods," Ihm said.

"No. I think by gods, Kithr meant Lord Ahebban and Lord Nachyne," Shiolto said. The Tathren shifted nervously when gazes shifted to him.

"The Lost *and* Tathren gods?" Pyrn said sharply.

"We *were* in Tather helping the *Tathren* Spearbearer," Kithr responded. "And the god of monsters isn't bound to any land. If it makes you feel better, Soldarr, Feyra, and Tesseia appeared at the shrine to give *this* journey their blessings." He couldn't keep the bitterness from his voice.

His tone made the others uncomfortable, but only Ihm was brash enough to address it. "You sound angry about that, Kithr."

"They told me that Elder Brenhan will continue to have free reign to manipulate and control our home, and however much of the rest of Eilidh Wood is under his sway," Kithr snapped. "At least until this champion of the Mad God is dead." He glanced to the Splinter. "*Eilidh Wood* offered us more help than the *gods* did."

The Splinter turned to face him. "We have waited long enough for them to purge the rot. We wait no longer."

"Oh." Ihm paled and fell silent.

Kithr clenched his fists and let out a deep breath. "We should leave before the scavengers gather." He looked at the corpses strewn across the ground at the ambush site. He didn't even want to loot the bodies or the ambushers' camp.

"I gathered such as was salvageable of their belongings, Kithr," Yion said, as if reading his mind. "They carried little of value, I fear, and their coins are foreign, unlikely to be accepted in these lands."

Kithr nodded and dragged himself to his feet. Walking might help work out the stiffness. "Let's go."

Conversations were minimal. Lyan took the lead, and Kithr walked at his side. Once the trees that marked the battle site had shrunk behind them, Kithr finally broke the silence. Remembering the morning when he and Lyan had entered Elder Brenhan's garden to tell the tale of their journey had brought back questions that had plagued him.

"Lyan, why did you make me promise to say nothing that morning?"

Lyan drew a sharp breath. He answered in a low voice. "You asked me to read your fortune the night before, Kithr. I saw…" He stopped and shook his head, starting over. "I saw that Elder Brenhan followed the Mad God and that he had the entire village under his sway. I made you promise to stay silent because as long as you didn't speak, I could turn his attention away from you. If you had spoken, he would have known you weren't under his spell, and that something protected you. He would have struck you before you could act, and before I could stop him."

A chill ran down Kithr's spine. "Elder Brenhan? Elder Brenhan would have killed me?" Despite his knowledge of the Elder's manipulations, he could not reconcile the idea of cold-blooded murder with the man who had schooled him, been a mentor and a leader, always ready to offer advice, or to just listen.

Lyan shuddered, wrapping his arms around himself. "No. He wouldn't have *killed* you."

Kithr's stomach dropped as if the earth had fallen away. *Elder Brenhan? Torturing someone? That's impossible. He couldn't. He wouldn't.*

"He's had all of us under his spell, Kithr. His magic and the years we spent under his sway makes us reject the idea even now, and that makes him stronger. We hesitate in the face of the truth, certain that it's somehow a mistake. We give him the chance to strike because we cling to the lie that he wove. You would have hesitated to attack him, even in your rage, and he would have used that to imprison you. I would have hesitated, and he would have used that to do worse. We would both have fallen into his hands."

"How long, Lyan?" Kithr whispered. "How long has he done this? When did the Mad God sink his claws into the Elder?"

"Before you or I were even born, Kithr," Lyan said as softly. "Our entire lives."

Kithr stopped in his tracks. "What? You're saying that even…" He trailed off. Thoughts tumbled together with memories. Elder Brenhan speaking of the need to go to war against Tather. Elder Brenhan calmly and quietly refuting arguments against the invasion. Elder Brenhan gravely charging the elven soldiers with their mission, blessed, he claimed, by the gods, to claim Solstice. Elder Brenhan, sending them to die. "The entire *war* with *Tather* for possession of Solstice, we were doing the will of *Murdo*?" His voice rose. "The war was a farce? A lie? We were puppets dancing for *Murdo*?"

All eyes fixed on Kithr. He shook with anger.

"Yes," Lyan whispered.

"And what about the gods?" Kithr demanded. "Did they not *notice*? Our *Elder* followed the Mad God, and what did they do? Ignore it? *Allow* it? *Nothing*?"

A female voice spoke, though no one appeared. "Murdo is a master of manipulation and deception, Kithr."

Kithr jumped. He hadn't expected his rage to receive a response. He thought the voice was Tesseia's. Collecting himself, he scowled fiercely. "And?"

"We knew he was working in Eilidh Wood, and maneuvering his schemes. When he set his plot into motion and rioted your people against Tather, he also mobilized followers on another front. We could not ignore the other threat, because if it had taken root, we would never have been able to weed it out completely. It took all three of us years of hunting to thwart that plot. Yes, years that you and your fellow warriors spent at war with Tather."

"And the rest of the gods?" Kithr demanded. "You talk like you were the only one who cared about whatever this other threat was. No one else could deal with it? Help with it?"

The goddess sighed. "Despite what you might think, we gods are rarely united to one purpose. We deal with those outside our own circles only when we must, and we are no more immune to petty squabbles than mortals are. You have only to look at Soldarr and Ahebban to see that. The last time we united for a common goal was when we joined together against Murdo, and in truth, we were almost too late when we *did* do so."

Kithr spat. "So I should be *glad* it *only* took more than an elven *lifetime* for you to admit that you needed help?"

"Kithr?" Seine said uneasily. "This is one of our *gods* that you're shouting at."

"Our gods. Yes, our gods. We went to *war* because we thought it was *your* will!" Kithr snapped. "We fought and bled, killed and died, and we thought it was *your* will, and you did *nothing*! Not a word! We were outside the village, outside Eilidh Wood. You *had* opportunity. All it would have taken was a word! One appearance and an announcement that you didn't condone the invasion. You had a damned *army* you could have *used*, and you let us march into Tather and *die* for a cause that was *Murdo's*!"

The Splinter gazed at a point in the air. "These are the seeds you have sown. This is the harvest you reap."

"You speak as if you were outside Elder Brenhan's influence once you left Eilidh Wood, Kithr," Tesseia said. "You were not. Though he was not with you personally, his acolytes were among you. They stirred your people to battle, rioted flagging spirits, and incited fresh fury against Tather. Was there not a whisper in your own ear, seeding a harvest of revenge when your father fell, Kithr?"

He froze, chest growing tight until he finally remembered to breathe. "You knew. You *knew* what we did. What *I* did! Every head taken, every atrocity, and you *still* didn't intervene? *Why*, damn you?"

The goddess didn't respond.

"Answer me, dammit!" Kithr demanded.

Only silence met him—silence from the goddess, and silence from his companions.

16

---

# CAILEAN

*The Lost. Among the elves of Eilidh Wood, this term was first applied to those elves who willingly followed Murdo, the Mad God, when he challenged the true gods. Since that time, it has been used to describe elves who no longer follow the teachings of the elven gods or the traditions of Eilidh Wood, as well as exiles from the forest. They are viewed as outside the laws of the forest, no longer under the protection of the gods, laws, or traditions of Eilidh Wood.*
*~Ercole Baeil'Kyn, Royal Archivist of Tather, "Treatise on Eilidh Wood"*

Thorns and brambles rose in a menacing wall, threatening any who approached the forest. Autumn's colors had begun to tint the leaves of the towering trees, but they didn't soften the forest's foreboding air. Cailean shivered as he gazed at the looming, threatening tangle called Malgor Forest. The horses snorted and shifted uneasily, pawing at the dry yellow grass. They had arrived just outside the forest's border.

"So Nylas lurks here?" Declan asked. The elf studied the forest warily.

"He commands the elves within," Cailean answered.

"It's worse than I expected," Declan admitted, which didn't bolster Cailean's confidence. "You actually entered this forest?"

"The first time, not exactly. We left the Shrine of Equinox and found ourselves in the middle of it." Cailean cast a look at Sirex as he spoke.

"The Spearbearers were needed there," Sirex said. "And it was close to your intended destination, without being close enough to draw the notice of the Mad God's followers." He frowned at the trees. "It *is* a remarkably unwelcoming place, though, isn't it?"

"You have a talent for understatement." Aikan reined his horse sharply to stop her sidestepping prance. "How do you wish to proceed, Lord Cailean?"

"If you don't object, I'll try something," Declan offered.

"Go ahead," Cailean agreed. "Gods know an elf might have a better idea how to pierce this forest's defenses."

Declan approached the forest edge. Brambles rustled as if some large beast lurked within, ready to pounce. The elf spoke firmly in a steady voice, his words in Elven.

"Interesting." Sirex watched Declan.

Cailean turned to the demigod. "You understand him?"

"He gave his name, rank, and what I presume to be the name of his company. Now he requests permission to enter with three companions. I am curious to see if his request will be granted."

*Could it be as simple as that?* Cailean watched and waited.

Declan fell silent and stood at parade rest. The branches stopped their restless rustling, but the elf didn't approach. Finally, the wicked thorns drew back, opening a passage into Malgor Forest. Declan stepped up to the entry, then motioned for Cailean, Aikan, and Sirex to join him.

*Solstice, guard us against arrows.* Cailean eyed the brambles. *And against thorns.*

The horses balked. Cailean kicked his mare firmly, and she reluctantly obeyed. He was tempted to leave her outside the forest and proceed on foot, but Cailean doubted he would find her again if he did so.

Under the looming shadows of the broad-leafed trees, branches shifted and thorny vines slithered across the narrow path. Thick undergrowth peeled back grudgingly as Declan advanced. When Cailean cast a look over his shoulder, he saw it closing on Sirex's heels. No one spoke. Cailean gripped Solstice tightly, and Aikan's hand hovered near his sword.

The choking undergrowth thinned as they entered the depths of the forest and the trees shrouded more sunlight. Malevolent rage continued to seethe from the trees, but the feeling of claustrophobia eased a little.

"Do you know which way to go, Declan?" Cailean asked in a low voice.

"Not precisely," Declan said. "However, the sense of the magic is stronger to the north-east."

How the elf told direction under the dense canopy, Cailean could only guess. He followed Declan's lead, eyeing the shadows. His chances of seeing any elves were slim, but he wanted to at least give an impression of being alert and aware.

Feet and hooves crunched through dry leaves in the eerily silent forest. During their previous intrusion into Malgor Forest, Cailean had heard the elves signal one another through birdcalls, but he didn't hear even those now. Plants shifted sometimes. One oak tree abruptly released a flurry of acorns as they passed under its branches, stinging, but causing no real harm.

Leaves crackled as something hissed rapidly across the ground, then lashed up to strike at Declan. The elf jerked back with a sharp profanity as a vine prickling with savage thorns slammed against Cailean's barrier. Both horses snorted, nostrils flaring as they danced away from the vine as it slid back to the ground.

"Nylas!" Cailean shouted, shattering the tense stillness. "I have a message for you!"

An arrow stuck the barrier with enough force to crack the shaft.

"I am here to *speak* to you. We don't *have* to make this difficult," Cailean said coolly.

The arrows came from several directions on the next flight. Cailean didn't flinch when they hit the barrier, nor when a coiling mass of vines were repulsed in their attempt to burrow under the barrier. Anger surged through Cailean. He couldn't tell if it came from him or Solstice, and he didn't care.

*Do you think I came here because I want to? Lyan needs help, damn you, and I will get him that help whether you like it or not!*

A vine probed around the barrier, then drew back, taunting in its movements, daring Cailean to pursue. Cailean jumped to the ground. Solstice appeared in his hand. "Stay here."

"Lord Cailean, what are you doing?" Aikan demanded.

"Accepting a challenge. Stay here." Cailean stepped through the barrier.

Aikan tried to follow, but the magical shield that protected them against arrows became solid, keeping Aikan inside. Cailean's steward beat his fist against it. "Lord Cailean!"

Cailean spoke to the forest. "My men cannot come to my aid. Will yours hold their attacks as well, or are you too great a coward to face me alone, Nylas?"

"You are a fool, Tathren." The words hissed from somewhere among the trees.

"I'm sure you find that normal enough. The question is, are *you* a coward?" Cailean taunted.

"You think you can best me in my own element, Tathren? Let's see you try."

No more arrows flew. Instead, the forest itself exploded into motion. Roots burst up around Cailean, grabbing for his limbs and neck. Cailean sprang aside, grateful that he wore only a leather jerkin and nothing heavier. Mobility promised to be far more valuable than armor when an entire forest was trying to kill him. A vine whipped around Cailean's legs, jerking him off his feet. He landed hard, knocking his breath away. Solstice's barrier protected Aikan, Declan, and Sirex, but outside of it, Cailean was exposed.

He slashed at the vine, slicing through it and rolling aside as a tangle of green lunged after him. Cailean panted as he got his feet under him again. *I have to find Nylas first.* He didn't see the elf, but he was sure he was near.

Reckless, Cailean plunged from the trail and through masses of ferns. They slapped at him, but the leafy fronds offered only minor distraction. The hawthorn bramble just beyond them, however, sliced gashes across his face and nearly hit his eyes. Cailean jerked and ducked, and the thorns bloodied his forehead instead. As blood trickled down his face, he stabbed reflexively at the bramble. Solstice stuck into the wood, and Cailean felt a jolt of the Spear's power strike the plant.

He sensed more than heard the sharp sound of pain, not from the plant itself, but from the one controlling it. The bramble withered and crumbled to ash. Cailean stepped over it, feet grinding the powder into the ground. *We could destroy this whole perverted forest. Let these elves try to hide then!*

He caught himself, pushing the thought back. "No. Solstice, *we need them. This isn't the time. Lyan is depending on us.*"

The Spear relented, though Cailean received the strong impression of a sulk. As he advanced, plants near Solstice wilted. Vines lashed out, only to blacken and shrivel to dry husks. Sweat trickled down Cailean's face, stinging in the cuts from the thorns, but his lips curled in a savage smile when he sensed another muffled sound of pain.

*So, it hurts when your plants die, does it?*

The burning *need* to punish Nylas for attacking him left Cailean breathless. *"Stop, Solstice. We need Nylas, and we need him alive. Lyan needs him. Equinox needs him!"*

The Spear's anger continued to batter at his mind. Cailean gritted his teeth. *"I can't fight you and Nylas at the same time. So unless you want him to win, stop!"*

*"Any who try to harm my bearer deserves to suffer."* The Spear's response quivered with fury.

Glimpsing movement at his feet, Cailean stabbed down. The Spear pinning a retreating vine. It squirmed and thrashed like a serpent.

*"If you want to make Nylas suffer, guide me to the one controlling this vine."*

Cailean jerked the Spear free, allowing the vine to slither away into the undergrowth. Following the Spear's lead, he advanced.

A stone hit him in the back. Cailean whipped around, Solstice raised defensively. A branch creaked, and another stone launched at him. He evaded, spitting a startled curse. All around, plants shifted and moved, none drawing too near him. Vines became slings, tree branches could nearly be catapults.

*I don't have time for this!* Rather than unleash an attack on the plants as Solstice urged, Cailean turned and ran through the forest toward the source. He jumped over fallen branches, trusting the Spear to wither plants in his path before he tripped and broke an ankle. Behind him, a flurry of stones and debris flew. Most missed, but Cailean winced as something struck his shoulder with bruising force. He stumbled, thrown off balance. Using the Spear to lever back to his feet, Cailean staggered on.

He slowed as Solstice directed him straight toward a tangle of vines and thorns between a cluster of gnarled trees.

Cailean kept his eyes on the plants as he edged closer, expecting a renewed assault.

Dirt crumbled under his feet, and Cailean fumbled for balance. As his feet slipped, he drove Solstice into a thick root, clinging to the Spear. A deep trench ringed the tangle, hidden under a thin net of vines covered by leaves. Stakes lined the bottom of the trench. Cailean swallowed hard, panting for breath. His arms ached, and at any moment he expected the root to fling him into the waiting spikes. Bracing his feet against the side of the trench, he released Solstice and let himself slide slowly down to the bottom. His limbs trembled and his breath came in short gasps.

*If I had been moving any faster…*

With a thought, he called Solstice back into his hand. Cailean gave himself several moments to let his pounding heart slow. He wiped blood and sweat from his forehead, smearing it across his sleeve. Finally, he climbed out of the trench on the side closest to the tangle of brambles. He expected the ground to come alive with plants and assault him or push him back onto the stakes, but nothing happened. Branches shifted and rustled behind him, as if hunting for him. Cailean dragged himself to level ground and touched Solstice to the brambles. The plants recoiled from the Spear, revealing their heart.

A tall stump had been shaped like a chair, and in it, an elf slumped. His head rested back against the wood, eyes closed and breathing rapid. Under the lids, his eyes moved as if he searched for something, but he didn't react to Cailean's presence before him. His skin gleamed with sweat, and his reddish-brown bangs lay plastered to his forehead. Blood ran from a puncture on his left arm. Vines wove around him, and Cailean bit back a sound of revulsion. Tendrils pierced the elf's arm, burrowing under his skin like parasites. The skin around the vines had an unhealthy yellow hue.

Cailean raised Solstice with an arm that trembled wearily

and rested the tip of the Spear against the elf's throat. The elf looked at least as exhausted and strained as Cailean, so if it came to a fight here, they might be nearly evenly matched. "If I wilt these vines digging into your body, would it actually kill you, or just hurt enough to make you wish it would?"

The elf's eyes snapped open, icy blue orbs fixing on Cailean with pure hate. He started to move, then felt the press of the Spear against his skin. His hands twitched, an aborted reflex to grab weapons. Cailean met his gaze coldly, and Solstice didn't waver.

"What did you do, Tathren?" the elf hissed.

"I accepted your challenge," Cailean answered. "Do you acknowledge defeat, Nylas?" He hadn't been certain of the elf's identity until he opened his eyes, but Cailean remembered those cold orbs well enough.

"Defeat? To a *Tathren?*" Nylas sneered.

Cailean shifted Solstice slightly, touching the Spear's tip to one of the vines that pierced the elf's skin, and sent a pulse of power into it. Spots of brown decayed the vine, spreading toward Nylas's arm.

Nylas grabbed the vine and ripped it from his skin, doubling over and clenching his teeth against a cry of pain. The rest of the vines rapidly withdrew of their own accord. Cailean lowered Solstice as Nylas cradled his arm. He bled where he'd jerked the vine free, though the rest had extracted themselves without leaving wounds. Ice-cold eyes glared up at Cailean.

"Do you acknowledge defeat?" Cailean repeated.

Nylas panted for breath, then spat, "On what terms, human?"

"On the terms that you will actually *listen* to the message I'm here to deliver," Cailean told him.

Nylas's eyes narrowed. "Is that *all?*"

"You and your followers will agree not to attack or try to harm or kill me or my people," Cailean said. If they were going to be conscripting these elves, he decided to negotiate a little additional protection, especially given the rage he saw in Nylas's eyes. Assuming, of course, that he could trust this elf to keep his word.

"And who are 'your people'?" Nylas snarled. "All filthy Tathrens?"

"My people are any who swear fealty to me, Lord Cailean Dev'gilla, Earl of Ihvako, or to lords under me."

Nylas's narrow eyes were suspicious. "I hear your message, and we do not seek to harm you or your followers. Those are your terms?" He clearly suspected a trap.

"Yes, those are my terms."

The elf gazed grimly at the Spear once again pointing toward his throat, considering whether he would actually prefer death to defeat at the hands of a Tathren. Finally, voice quivering with restrained fury, he spoke. "I accept your terms, and acknowledge defeat. Now say your blighted message and be done with it."

"There is one more thing you should know first," Cailean said. Nylas would either honor his word or not, and Cailean intended to find out which now, while the sting of defeat and the pain of the process remained fresh. "Your army invaded Tather with the goal of stealing Solstice, Spear of the Stars. That Spear is the one currently pointing at your throat."

Nylas jerked, coming to his feet and snatching a knife from his belt. He shook with fury, teeth bared. "Treacherous, filthy Tathren *bastard!*" He panted for breath, gripping the knife tightly enough to make the leather bindings creak. His body tensed, on the verge of lunging at Cailean, when he spun around and slammed the knife into the tree trunk, the blade sinking up to the cross guard. His back to Cailean, he spoke in a tight, strained voice. "Speak your message and begone, Tathren."

Kithr regularly complained that Tathrens gave speeches when brevity would do. For once, Cailean took the idea to heart. "You and your men owe a life-debt to Lyan. He's calling that debt due."

Nylas's back stiffened and he drew a sharp breath. Cailean didn't wait for the elf to find words. He turned and walked around the tangle, searching for a path away from it that did not require climbing back through the trench. Before Cailean, plants shifted and wove together, forming a bridge. He eyed it warily, not trusting Nylas.

"It will not drop you."

Cailean started at the female voice. Across the trench from him stood a girl of fourteen or fifteen years. Her worn, brown clothes nearly blended with the forest, and he had not heard her approach. Her golden brown hair was cut boyishly short, exposing ears too pointed to be human, but not so sharp as those of the elves he knew. A blotchy purple birthmark ran down the right side of her face, from just above her eye down to her chin, making her left eye look larger than the right.

"Patch." The name came unbidden from his mouth.

She simply smiled. "I heard the Captain's promise to you. We are not to bring you to harm. I won't drop you to the stakes."

Half elf, half Tathren, and able to manipulate plants as Nylas did. Cailean remembered the girl and how she had spoken, if not exactly in their favor, not actively against him and his men. He cautiously stepped onto the bridge. It creaked, but held him.

Behind him in the tangle, Cailean heard the thud of a knife being driven repeatedly into wood. Less certain that Nylas would actually keep his word, Cailean quickly crossed the trench.

"Thank you," he said to Patch.

She nodded. "You left your friends over here." She started walking, and Cailean followed. She paused suddenly, turning back to him. "The Captain will keep his oath, both to you and to Lyan. I'll take you all to camp."

Cailean shivered. "Are you sure that's a good idea? We won't be a welcome sight there."

"If Lyan has called on the debt the Captain owes him, then the others shall have to get used to seeing you," Patch responded. "We might as well begin now, don't you think?"

"Um…" Cailean couldn't find a response to that logic.

"I've already told them what the Captain promised. We will not attack you." Patch smiled, as if that made everything right. Cailean doubted that Nylas would see the matter as so settled.

Aikan paced within the confines of the barrier. Declan and Sirex watched Aikan pace. Cailean released the barrier as Aikan saw him. The steward rushed to him. "Lord Cailean! That was foolhardy and reckless!" He drew a deep breath. "And, I am forced to acknowledge, probably the best way of settling the matter quickly. How seriously are you hurt?"

"Bruised, battered, and scratched up, but I'll be all right," Cailean promised. His cuts and scratches had already stopped bleeding, thanks to Solstice. Though they could not mend anyone else, both Solstice and Equinox could heal their individual bearers. "Were any of you threatened?"

"Glared at, cursed at, and insulted," Declan answered. "I'm glad your man doesn't understand Elven."

"Some of their epithets were very creative," Sirex added. He sounded amused rather than insulted over whatever had been said.

"What's the situation, Lord Cailean?" Aikan asked.

"Nylas accepted defeat, with the agreement that he and his men will not attempt to do any harm to me or any of my people," Cailean said. "And I delivered Lyan's message."

Declan drew a sharp breath, then looked at Cailean cautiously. "Did you tell him about…" He indicated Solstice with a nod.

Cailean nodded.

The elf whistled softly. "Then extracting that promise from him was an act of brilliance. Pure brilliance, Cailean."

Cailean blinked. "Pardon?"

Declan smirked. "How well can they continue to claim that they remain in Tather to steal Solstice now? Nylas has sworn that he and his men will not attack you: the Spearbearer of Solstice. He *cannot* claim he will continue the war for the Spear now."

"You mock us?" The rustle of leaves announced Nylas's arrival—more noise than the elf usually made. Seeing the heaviness of Nylas's steps, Cailean didn't think the noise was intentional. "We have fought, bled, and died in this war, and you *mock* us?" Blood stained his ratted shirt, and his exhausted eyes burned with anger.

Declan cast him a look of open contempt. "Should I care about the fate of the Lost? Your blood is worthless, shed in vain."

From the twist of Nylas's expression, few things Declan could have said would have enraged him more. He could barely speak for his fury. "And you... you follow this *Tathren*?!"

"No," Declan answered, his voice flat. "I follow the elven Spearbearer, Lyan. As you *should*, but undoubtedly do not."

"You would do the bidding of that stargazing *mooncalf*?"

"I follow the elven Spearbearer," Declan repeated coldly. "If there is any act over which he could be accused of being a mooncalf, it would have to be saving your life, as you are evidently without enough honor left to repay your debt to him."

*It will be a miracle if Nylas doesn't try to murder Declan.*

Nylas's eyes narrowed to thin slits. "Call no man an oathbreaker until he's actually broken his word, Declan of Heartshrine Village. And I have not broken any oath I have taken." He said the last through clenched teeth. "Follow me." He stormed away.

Cailean dragged himself wearily into the saddle. Declan,

Aikan, and Sirex waited for him. Nylas stopped, spinning around to glare at all four of them. "I said follow me!"

"I don't take orders from Lost," Declan said.

Nylas's face twisted with anger. "And who *do* you take them from? *Him?*" He jabbed a finger at Cailean.

"I take orders from Lyan. Lyan designated Kithr as his second-in-command. And in Kithr's absence, he designated Cailean. So yes, I do."

"From a *Tathren*, but not from a superior officer."

Declan's eyes narrowed. "You're a Lost elf, Nylas. I'll take orders from this horse before I'll take them from you."

Outrage. Then, as Cailean watched, something shifted in Nylas's expression. The elf's clenched fists slowly uncurled. "Very well. If you would, *please*, follow me." Anger and sarcasm dripped from the words.

Cailean urged his horse to follow Nylas. He looked to Patch, wondering what she thought of the exchange. She simply smiled at him, as if to say that she'd told him Nylas would comply, then caught up with the elven captain.

Declan followed Cailean's gaze, and frowned. "Who is that?"

"Her name is Patch. We met her the last time we were here. She's half—"

"Half Tathren," Declan said. "I can see that. They have women in the camp?"

Cailean shook his head. "Not that I saw. But there were five half-Tathren children, including Patch."

Declan frowned, but didn't ask more.

Cailean looked at Patch again and thought of the other children. They couldn't stay here alone, but he couldn't in good conscience bring them into battle. Taking them to Eilidh Wood was out of the question, given the apparent situation in the forest. But they had to go somewhere. Somewhere safe.

Hostile eyes followed them, making the hair on the back of Cailean's neck stand on end. Nothing attacked them, though the air was tense with threat. Nylas led them to a living wall of thorns. The aged wood creaked and protested as it opened a passage into the home of the elves of Malgor Forest.

The thorn wall encompassed the camp. A few huts held stores, but Cailean knew most of the camp lay in underground tunnels. Elven warriors entered silently after them, spreading around the camp. Weapons hung openly on racks, close at hand and ready to spill blood. Targets lined the walls, and wooden practice dummies dressed in tattered Tathren uniforms marked a training ground. The children, three boys and one girl, were collecting arrows from the targets, though they turned to watch Cailean and his small group enter. A dairy goat browsed around the edge of the wall, to Cailean's surprise. He had not seen any animals in the elven camp last time.

Elven warriors gazed coldly at Cailean, then assessed Nylas, wondering how Cailean could have forced their leader to surrender. Nylas glared around the camp, but said nothing to break the tense silence.

An infant's wail ended the stillness, startling Cailean. A moment later, a second cry joined in chorus. The children set down their bundles of arrows and ran to the goat, catching hold of her halter and leading her toward one of the huts. Several elven warriors ducked into the hut.

Declan frowned at Nylas. "What in the gods' names?"

Nylas's eyes narrowed, as if he expected derision from the other elf. "You think the children grow from trees? Their mothers abandon them in the forest. If they're alive when we find them, we bring them here and do what we can." He nodded toward the goat. "Like steal livestock to feed them. These two, a boy and a girl, we found less than a month ago. They're sickly, and probably won't live."

The words sounded cold, but Cailean realized that they weren't meant to be so. Nylas simply stated facts. These warriors did their best, but this camp was ill-equipped to care for newborns left to die of exposure.

*They are not just savages. Savages would leave sickly infants to die, not do everything possible to save them.*

That decided Cailean. He swung down to the ground and approached Nylas. Patch had already disappeared into one of the tunnels, leaving Nylas alone in the center of the camp.

"Nylas," Cailean said in a low voice. "Lyan is calling you and your men to battle. The children should stay somewhere safe."

Nylas gazed at him narrowly. "You have yet to tell me where Lyan is, Tathren, or why he feels the need to call this debt due."

"The gods have called the Spearbearers to stop the champion of the Mad God," Cailean said plainly. "The gods of *your* people spoke to both Lyan and me. The Mad God's champion is gathering an army to assault the Shrine of Equinox."

"The elven gods spoke to *you*." Nylas seemed to find that more questionable than the idea of fighting a champion of Murdo.

"Yes."

"And *Lyan* is fighting the Mad God."

"That is what the Spearbearers do. We fight Murdo and his minions."

Nylas looked Cailean in the eyes without a word for a long moment. Finally, he said, "And where, precisely, do you think the children will be *safe*?"

"They will be safe in my keep," Cailean answered.

Nylas's eyes narrowed and his expression grew dark. "You put that little faith in my word, Tathren?" he growled.

Cailean blinked, taken aback. "They won't be hostages. They'll be guests, not prisoners." *Unlike the demand your men made of us when we came here.* He looked toward the cluster of elves who were feeding goat's milk to the pair of squirming, fussing infants, then he met Nylas's eyes again. His voice was quiet. "They might live."

Nylas hesitated. "You swear this, Tathren?"

"I swear by Solstice that in my keep, these children will be safe. They will be cared for, and they will be treated as well as any Tathren child in my home would be."

Nylas looked back to the infants, not replying immediately. One of the little ones began to wail, and Cailean read helpless frustration in the stance of the elf who rocked the child.

Aikan elbowed his way through the gathering and stormed to the elf, snatching the child from him. The elf was too startled to protest. Aikan lifted the infant to his shoulder and patted the tiny bundle on the back. A moment later, the infant spat up on Aikan's shoulder, but finally stopped crying. Aikan said something sharply to the elves, then returned the infant to them. The warrior holding the other child frowned, then imitated Aikan. The steward gave a curt nod of approval. After a pause, one of the elves offered Aikan a rag to clean his shoulder.

Nylas watched the entire exchange before he spoke. "If you break your word, Tathren, and any of them come to harm, you will wish the forest had torn you apart."

"I believe you," Cailean said.

"Then we've wasted enough time, and should be moving. I have a debt to pay." Nylas turned from Cailean and began snapping sharp orders in Elven.

## 17

## KITHR

*The gifts of the gods must not be taken lightly. They are given for a
purpose, and that purpose will be fulfilled, regardless of the will of men.
Beware, lest the gift you receive prove a punishment in disguise.*
*~proverb of the Na'Khahra tribe of the Appret Plains*

Kithr knew he should be worried. He should fear the
wrath of the gods for his tirade, but he felt only rage.
Rage that the gods whose guidance he'd always trusted had
left their own people under a minion of the Mad God. Rage
that when Elder Brenhan claimed that the invasion of Tather
had been the will of the elven gods, he had deceived them all.
Rage that he could have been so blind.

*The gods betrayed us. We believe that they were guiding us into war,
and they did nothing while we fought for Murdo!*

He slammed his knife into a thick chunk of firewood. The
loud thump in the silent camp made several people jump.
Kithr's gaze raked over the clump of elves and Tathrens
sitting uneasily around the small fire.

"What?" Kithr snapped. "Am I *wrong*? We bled, died, and

became Lost thinking it was *their* will, and what did they do to stop us? Nothing!" In the back of his mind, Kithr realized the sudden outburst might sound like rambling nonsense without the context of his thoughts.

Shiolto and Dalrian looked at him with bewilderment. Kithr stopped to think whether he'd spoken in Elven or Tathren. *No, I said that in Tathren. They could understand the words, at least.*

The elves shifted uncomfortably. Pyrn glanced around nervously, then spoke. "Kithr, it's not… well, it's not whether what you said was true or not, but… You were insulting our *gods*!"

"Is it an insult when it's true?" Kithr growled.

"When you scream it at the top of your lungs? *Yes*!" Pyrn burst. "What are you *thinking*?"

"I'm thinking the gods should pay less attention to petty grudges over a family squabble, and more to what's actually going on!" Kithr shoved to his feet to storm from the camp. "But if you're afraid they're going to strike me down, I'll make sure I'm far enough away that you don't get hit." Anger and sarcasm dripped from his tone.

"Should it offer any manner of consolation, Kithr, my lord agrees with you." Yion finally spoke. The mercenary sat cross-legged on the ground, calm and collected even in the face of Kithr's outburst.

Kithr stopped, looking at Yion. "Does he?"

"He says it is difficult for a god to admit being in the wrong, especially to mortals. But he offers to you an apology for such part as he has had in the strife between your people and his."

Ihm gave Yion a puzzled look. "Your lord? I thought your lord was Cailean."

Yion shook his head. "Lord Cailean has my service, but my lord is Saiboti."

"The Tathren god of warriors?" Ihm asked uncertainly.

"He has called me to serve as his champion," Yion said. "I name no other as my lord."

"What? You're not even Tathren!" Ihm exclaimed.

The thick air of tension in the camp eased as attention turned from Kithr to Yion. His role as the champion of the Tathren warrior god was not one Yion spoke of often, and Kithr knew he ought to be grateful to the mercenary for choosing to do so now. Perhaps he would feel that way later. Free from the watch of the others, Kithr strode out of camp.

One set of footsteps followed him. When Kithr turned, he saw Lyan. He slowed, allowing his friend to catch up. Neither spoke immediately, and Kithr had the feeling that Lyan waited for him to break the silence.

Kithr tried a weak attempt at dark humor. "Not afraid that Soldarr might rain lightning on my head?"

Lyan shook his head with a thin, forced smile that faded after a moment. "Our gods won't strike you down, Kithr. Even if they want to, they need *me* too much to attack my friend."

Kithr almost tripped over his own feet. "What?"

"They need the Spearbearers, Kithr. The gods are afraid, and they don't dare risk letting Murdo break free. They need Solstice and Equinox against the Mad God's followers, because without the Spears, he *will* succeed. He might do so even with the Spears against him. I sent Equinox back to the Shrine because that thread of prediction offers the best chance. But if the gods try to strike you, I *will* call Equinox, and I *will* use every power that the Spear possesses to fight them."

Kithr drew a sharp breath. "You would fight the gods?"

Lyan's expression was grim. "Kithr, I will do whatever I can and whatever I must to save my friends. Even defy the gods."

The words carried the weight of a vow, and Kithr had

nothing to say for a long moment. They walked in silence, Kithr's violent rage fading, replaced by concern for Lyan.

"Don't fight the gods for my sake," Kithr said finally. "I'll try to keep my thoughts about them to myself."

"The Mad God is a poison, Kithr. Not everything he does is obvious. Most of it isn't. Instead, it's the subtle slip of a seed that seems harmless. By the time the poisonous flower comes to bloom and becomes evident, the roots have burrowed deep, and the corruption can't be purged without killing the healthy, innocent plants around it as well."

"Heartshrine Village," Kithr said.

"He planted his poisonous seed in the heart of Eilidh Wood, in one of our most sacred sites," Lyan said quietly. "He struck a place he knew would hurt us."

"Then we need to hunt down this 'champion' of the Mad God, kill him, and go home to deal with the Elder," Kithr said firmly. His anger was finally settling on a target he *could* attack. Rage seethed and boiled, but he knew it would settle into a steady burn, fueling and driving him. Such rage had been the fuel that drove him on against the Tathrens in the war, and now, it would drive him against the champion of Murdo.

Lyan nodded, and they returned to camp. The air of tension had eased in Kithr's absence, and only rose slightly with his presence. Shiolto boiled something over the fire, and the smell of food drifted around the camp.

"Come morning, we'll move out," Kithr said. "The further we go on foot, the less distance we have to travel by the Spear." He made no mention of his outburst, and no one else brought it up.

"You know where we're going, Kithr?" Seine asked.

"Our enemy expects us to continue eastward. He must have a good reason for thinking so," Kithr responded.

The others accepted that answer without argument. No one seemed inclined to argue with him at the moment. They all ate Shiolto's stew, which seemed made of "whatever was convenient to toss in the pot." Conversation was sparse.

Kithr was not given to long fits of introspection, and as he ate, he turned his thoughts to the problem of the Mad God's champion. Assuming Nylas *did* have enough honor to fulfill his promise, they would still number less than one hundred warriors. Against them stood an army, and they had to defeat that army. Nylas and his men had been waging their war on Tather in the face of such odds, but they'd had the advantage of an entrenched, defensible position.

*We don't have that unless we plan to fight this battle at the Shrine of Equinox. Lyan already spoke against going directly to the Shrine, and I agree with him. Even with the magic and defenders there, the Shrine is the champion's goal. If we must fight there, it will be as a last resort.*

As night closed around them, Kithr put aside the thorny matter of finding a plan that would not get them all killed and focused on the more mundane matters of preparing for the night. They had seen no one since the ambush, but Kithr didn't intend to take chances. He gave Dalrian first watch, Ihm second, and Yion fourth, taking the third himself. He didn't *want* to take a watch, but everyone was as tired and worn as he was, and it seemed the only right thing to do.

Kithr cursed his own sense of responsibility when Ihm woke him. Blearily, he pulled his cloak around his shoulders and paced around the camp until the cold air pushed back sleep.

"Anything?" he asked Ihm.

Ihm shook his head, but he looked uneasy. "I didn't see or hear anything, but there's this lingering feeling that *something* lurks out there, where I can't see it. It could be nothing, but… I'm not sure."

"I'll keep a watch for it," Kithr told him. "Get some sleep."

"Yes sir." Ihm sketched a weary salute and slunk to his bedroll.

The banked fire offered little light or heat. The stars glittered overhead. Kithr looked up to them, reminded once again that Lyan was not practicing his astrology even on the clear nights like this one, which should have delighted him and occupied him for most of the night. Kithr looked over to the curled lump that was his friend.

*What's going on, Lyan?*

A sharp chill ran up Kithr's spine. He spun around, sensing as much as hearing movement. His sharp gaze picked out the form of a man standing in the camp, inside the warding circle of protection that Yion always laid around their camps. Kithr reached for his bow, and the other flinched.

"I remember the bite of your arrows well enough. No need to remind me."

Kithr froze. He recognized the silky, smooth voice, tinged as always with an undertone of arrogance and scorn. "What do you want here, monster?" he growled, shifting his bow into his hands.

"What I *want* is unfortunately immaterial in this situation." The pooka's smooth tones took a steely edge. "My god Nachyne informed me in no uncertain manner that regardless of the liberty my master granted to me, I must be present to protect and safeguard him." He took a step closer to Kithr, and the starlight glittered off metal around the pooka's neck.

Kithr didn't relax his wary stance. "Your master. You mean Lyan?"

The pooka's handsome features twisted with anger, and he shook back the ruffled sleeves of his shirt—probably silk, knowing the creature's vanity—to reveal a matching pair of simple black metal bands fitted tightly around his lower arm, just above the wrist. "Who *else* would I mean, elf?" he hissed. "My god ripped my freedom away and made a *gift* of me to him. You think I *could* serve any other even if I wished to?"

"I don't know," Kithr answered flatly. "You're a pooka. Your kind are renowned for their ability to deceive."

"I cannot lie to you, Kithr of Eilidh Wood. My master has forbidden it. Nor can I act to harm you or any other who he calls a friend." The pooka's red eyes glowed with sullen light.

"Does Lyan know you're here?" Kithr glanced again at Lyan's sleeping lump.

"I don't know. He should, if he cared to look, but he has not acknowledged my presence." Anticipating Kithr's next question, he continued. "I have been following you since the middle of this day."

"I haven't seen you since the defeat of Ewart and Porephyn. Where have you been?" Kithr demanded.

"Don't you remember? You were there when my master gave me the order. He told me that, to the best of my abilities within the confines placed upon me, I was to act as a free creature. I have been obeying him. I have been doing so as far away from him as possible." His scowl twisted into a wince. "Lord Nachyne was not pleased by that, and demanded that I attend my master at all haste."

"*Just* what we needed," Kithr muttered. "*You.* Well, obviously you know who I am. Do you have a name, or do I continue to call you 'that damned pooka'?"

"My master gave me a name, mortal," the pooka said, eyes narrowing. "I am called Praett."

"Good. Then we can, in theory, converse like civilized people. And you will call me Kithr. Not 'elf,' not 'mortal,' not whatever creative epithets you are thinking up right now. Kithr."

"Oh, but they are such *creative* epithets," Praett purred. "It would be a shame to let them go to waste."

"Save them up for the Mad God's champion, for all I care," Kithr snapped. "Why are you here, talking to me instead of Lyan?"

Praett grew serious. "Because I believe that if he knew I was here, my master would attempt to send me away, and I cannot do that. I have no wish to be caught between my master's orders and the duty required of me as his slave. So I will do my duty without informing him of my presence. You, however, are the one most likely to run yourself into the earth by trying to watch over his every move."

"You'll be watching over Lyan," Kithr said.

"Whether you wish it or not, whether I wish it or not, I must protect my master. Yes, I will be watching over him."

Kithr let out a deep breath, wondering whether to feel angry, jealous, or relieved. He finally nodded sharply. "Good. We'll need the help." *Especially if Nylas and his men are on their way. If there's anyone Lyan needs to watch his back against, it's Nylas.*

Praett strode out of the camp. "I will be near. I will be watching you." With those soft words, the pooka vanished into the darkness.

"Ancients preserve us from the gifts of the gods," Kithr whispered, gazing into the night.

# 18

## CAILEAN

*In Eilidh Wood, it is said that each elf has a tree—a sapling that sprouts on the day of the elf's birth. When an elf dies, so does the tree. Some claim, though, that an elf is not limited to one tree alone in his lifetime, and that those of power can bind more trees, even whole forests, to themselves.*

The half-elf children perched uncertainly in the saddles of Cailean's and Aikan's horses. Patch chose to walk alongside and spoke softly to the younger half-elves. A pair of elven warriors carried the infants in slings and led the animals.

Nylas and his men stripped their camp efficiently, as if it were a practiced maneuver. Perhaps it was. They exhibited no sentimentality over leaving the place that had been their home for many years. Cailean expected them to bring nothing but the necessities, and was surprised at how many elven warriors carried trinkets, tokens, or other items unrelated to battle. He was especially surprised to see Nylas pack a fiddle into a case and stow it with his gear. If there was anyone he did not expect to play an instrument, it was the grim, cold leader of the elves of Malgor Forest.

"A fine instrument," Cailean said.

The elf fixed him with a glare, suspecting mockery. Finding none in Cailean's face, he snapped, "Its previous owner doesn't need it anymore."

"May I see it sometime?" Cailean asked.

Another glare and a curt nod answered him.

Under the cover of night, they left the camp. While they moved along the paths of Malgor Forest, Cailean didn't see or hear many elves around them, but once they reached the grassland, shadows flowed from the tree line, silently joining their ranks. Cailean couldn't see faces, only dark hoods covering heads and hiding pointed ears. He pulled up his own hood. Although Malgor Forest lay within his land's borders, it specifically lay within the holdings that had belonged to Ewart. Without knowing how many of the locals retained loyalty to the traitor, Cailean didn't wish to announce his presence, whether or not he was in the company of elves.

"The forest is clear. We're ready to march," Nylas said.

In the darkness, Cailean couldn't tell how many elves surrounded him, but the air was heavy with hostility. "I hope you can muster as much hate for the Mad God's champion as you do for Tathrens," he said under his breath.

Nylas probably heard him, but the elf didn't reply. Cailean took the lead. Aikan walked at his side, with Declan and Sirex behind him, then Nylas and his men. The elves moved quietly, but with so many, they couldn't march without some noise. Grass rustled and crunched. Clothing added whispers of sound, with the occasional creak of leather or clink of metal. The horses snorted in weary protest to the night march. The dairy goat added her bleats of complaint. Several elves cursed. Cailean glanced over his shoulder, but he couldn't see enough to tell if there was a problem. The goat quieted shortly.

The night passed without incident, to Cailean's relief. He

set their route to skirt as many villages as he could. Internally, he chafed at the time it would take to reach the relative safety of holdings whose loyalties he could trust.

Dawn found them on a road. Cailean searched uneasily for a campsite where a band of armed men could rest undetected. Anyone who saw such a large group would have reservations, even without knowing that most of the hooded figures were elves. He didn't immediately recognize the area, with no noteworthy landmarks and no convenient shelter. The children drooped wearily in the saddles of equally weary horses, and the infants fussed. Cailean rubbed tired eyes.

One of the elves spoke a sharp word. The warriors stood straighter, reaching toward weapons. The children all sat up, looking around with a wariness to match the adults.

"What is it?" Cailean asked, scanning the horizon.

"Riders," Nylas answered coldly in Tathren. He pointed, and Cailean squinted against the rising sun.

Aikan shaded his eyes and followed Cailean's gaze. "At least a dozen men." He frowned. "I can't see their banner, but they aren't wearing the keep's colors."

"No one's been wearing Col'renn colors recently," Nylas said.

"They had better not be," Cailean said curtly. "Ewart's dead and his holdings have a new lord, who shouldn't be going out of their way to engage Malgor Forest. Can you tell who the riders are, Nylas?"

"Looks like Olbrieh's cronies," the elf answered.

Cailean straightened with a startled oath. Of all the names he didn't want to hear, he would place that of his antagonistic neighboring lord near the top of the list. "Olbrieh's men, *here?*" As he squinted at the riders, he recognized the distinctive long, jagged three tails blowing in the morning breeze. The riders advanced toward them. Cailean gripped Solstice tightly, eyes narrow.

Sirex stepped up beside them. "Do these men serve the lord of this land?"

"No," Cailean said tightly. "They serve the neighboring lord, and should not be here. Their lord is no friend of mine, and certainly no friend of elves. I think he blames *me* for the actions of the elves of Malgor Forest." He shot a glare at Nylas.

"And why would he—" Nylas's eyes narrowed. "These are *your* lands, Tathren?"

"I didn't even know your people lived in Malgor Forest, Nylas. That's how little Ewart revealed about the state of his holdings even *before* he rebelled and besieged my keep," Cailean growled. "We can discuss the matter later." His mind raced as he searched for a way out that didn't require them to engage the riders.

Sirex pushed back his hood, under which he wore a tight-fitted cap, effectively hiding the shape of his ears. "Allow me to handle the matter, Lord Cailean. All I request is that no one else speak, even if words are addressed to you, and that you bring the horses and children to the head of the line."

Startled from their respective thoughts, Cailean and Nylas both frowned at him. The elves had shifted protectively around the horses. Nylas eyed Sirex, then Cailean, and finally he made a sharp gesture. "Do as he says."

Even weary as they were, the children shifted nervously atop the horses, fidgeting with their hoods and trying not to appear frightened. Patch, walking beside the horses, smiled up at the other children and spoke quiet words of reassurance. Cailean wasn't sure how she could be so confident—he was tense with worry and the lingering fear that the only way he would reach home would be over the dead bodies of Olbrieh's men.

The riders came within shouting distance, and a heavily armored man rode ahead of the rest. "Halt and identify yourselves!"

Sirex answered in a clear, confident voice. "I am Freewarden Sirex, escorting these children."

Cailean blinked. *Freewarden?*

The mounted man pulled his horse to a sharp stop. "A Freewarden?" His suspicious tone echoed Cailean's thought. "I was unaware that Freewardens normally traveled with armies."

Sirex raised an eyebrow and cast a look back over the band. "An army? I see no army, friend, only weary refugees. These men have been charged with guardianship of the children until they reach their destination, and I have no complaints with their company. They have been vital to our journey, especially when some of my wards are so young." He indicated the bundled infants in their slings. "While men respect the rights of a Freewarden, I fear that the wild animals are less accommodating."

Lord Olbrieh's captain frowned. "Where do you hail from, Freewarden?"

"A Freewarden calls no land home, friend. My home is on Cantorelle's roads, wherever they lead me."

"Your destination?"

"Beyond this land," Sirex said.

"Where?" the captain insisted.

"Our destination is not here, and does not fall under the authority of your lord," Sirex answered firmly. "As such, you have no need to know it."

The rest of the riders joined the captain. All looked over the band with open suspicion. The captain's scowl did not relent. "That is true, if you *are*, as you claim, a Freewarden." He uttered a sharp string of foreign words.

Sirex smiled and said something in return, the words flowing easily from his lips.

Surprise crossed the captain's face, and he sat back in the saddle. "Your pardon, Freewarden." His tone was genuinely apologetic. "There are too many who would make a false claim, thinking to gain undeserved protection."

"Cantorelle casts no blame on those who test that a Freewarden is what he claims to be. Only on those who refuse to honor a Freewarden's rights," Sirex answered.

"Of course." The captain looked over the band again, and his gaze remained untrusting. Cailean kept his head down, and saw that most of the others did the same. It gave them the appearance of worn, weary men, but under cloaks, hands lingered near weapons.

One of the infants woke and raised his voice in a thin wail. The sound made people in both groups jump. Sirex smiled in apology. "Pardon us, friends, but the little ones need rest. Do you know of a sheltered place where we could stop for a time?"

The captain shook himself. The child's wails seemed to decide him. Cailean could all but see the man mentally shifting the group from being a potential attack force to being what Sirex implied they were—refugees from some other land, brought on this road by unknown, but surely dire, circumstances. Why else would they travel with infants?

The captain's expression warmed to one of detached sympathy. "Of course. On the other side of this hill you can find the site where our men made camp last night. They have moved on by now, and you are welcome to rest there as long as you need."

"You are patrolling your borders?" Sirex asked. Cailean frowned at the question. They were well beyond Lord Olbrieh's borders, though one might presume that a traveler wouldn't recognize the border marks.

"My lord is concerned by reports of restless behavior from his neighbor," the captain answered. "Soldiers have made incursions into our lands—border disputes and skirmishes. So far, diplomacy has proven ineffective."

Next to Cailean, Aikan stiffened in outrage. Cailean put a

hand on his arm to warn him not to speak, though his own anger flared at the lies flowing from the man's mouth.

"Your offer is kind; thank you, friend." Sirex dipped his head in acknowledgment. "May Cantorelle guide you."

"And you as well, Freewarden." The captain signaled his men, and they turned their horses, ready to ride. He paused, gaze settling on Nylas. "Out of curiosity, what land do you come from?"

"Our journey has been long, and we have far yet to go," Sirex cut in, polite but firm. "Thank you for your hospitality, friend." The words had an edge of finality to them, clearly ending the conversation.

The captain's jaw tightened slightly, but he nodded. "Safe journeys, Freewarden."

The riders thundered up the road, leaving the band to walk at their own pace. Sirex took the lead, setting a quick pace in the direction that the captain had indicated. The pace didn't encourage conversation, weary as everyone was. The infants continued to fuss and cry despite attempts to sooth them. Cailean breathed a sigh of relief when he saw the camp area—flat, trampled ground nestled in the shelter of the hill, near a trickling stream.

"We will rest here," Sirex said.

The children slid down to the ground stiffly, rubbing aching legs and bottoms. Patch fetched the dairy goat and helped to feed the infants. Nylas cast a critical eye over the land, then over Cailean and Sirex. "I don't recognize this area, and I am well acquainted with the land within three day's walk of Malgor Forest. Where are we, and what is this matter of a Freewarden?"

"All roads belong to Cantorelle," Sirex said. "With his blessing, I sped our travel. As for my being a Freewarden, what else is there to say? I am the first Freewarden. I trust you are familiar with our order?"

Nylas answered with a sharp nod. "I have encountered a

few in the past. A very few. Even Freewardens hesitate to enter the forest, though we allow them to pass when they do."

The children lingered nearby, listening. The girl asked, "What's a Freewarden?"

Sirex smiled warmly at her. "Freewardens are the protectors of Cantorelle's roads. They don't serve any land or people, and go wherever Cantorelle leads them. As protectors of the roads, they also protect and guide travelers in need, especially women and children. Where refugees are found, fleeing from whatever drove them from their homes, a Freewarden is often found among them."

One of the boys spoke, frowning. "Don't people try to stop them? That Tathren dog we met—he didn't want to let us go. Why did he?"

"I proved that I was a Freewarden when he tested me. Because I claimed protection over you, he had no authority regarding you," Sirex said. "The Freewardens answer to their god alone."

Nylas spat in the dirt. "No one with any sense attacks a Freewarden. The god of roads takes it personally when one of his priests is assaulted."

*And knowing that, I don't want to imagine how he would respond if someone attacked his son.* "I appreciate your help, Sirex," Cailean said. "If that man had recognized me, things would not have gone well." He sat down, looking around the camp, and a realization pushed through his weariness. *The men who camped here intend to attack my people and lands.*

"A pity we're leaving," Nylas said. "With his forces focused here, Olbrieh's lands are prime for raiding."

Cailean's gaze darkened. "He's lying about the attacks," he said sharply. "It's nothing more than a thin excuse to do what he wants."

Nylas snorted, not caring about Tathren politics, but Declan asked, "Are you sure about that?"

"I *am* the neighbor in question," Cailean snapped. "Yes, I am *quite* sure I have not invaded Lord Olbrieh's lands."

"Lord Olbrieh is a treacherous liar," Aikan fumed. "But I didn't think he would stoop to *this*."

"Well, either he's lying, or someone else attacked his borders and made it look like your men, Cailean," Declan said.

Cailean started and looked at the elf.

Declan continued. "You're facing the Mad God. You know he doesn't fight honorably."

Cailean inhaled sharply. "He's attacked Lyan through Eilidh Wood. Of course he would attack me by stirring up jealousy here."

The elves near enough to hear Cailean stiffened. Cailean abruptly found Nylas in his face. "What do you mean that the Mad God has attacked Lyan 'through Eilidh Wood'?"

Cailean took a step back. Nylas might deride Lyan at any opportunity, yet at a hint that the astrologer was under direct attack, all the elves were ready to launch into battle. "Declan, would you explain? I think you understand the situation better than I do."

Declan answered with a curt nod. "Yes sir." He fell into Elven, and eyes turned to him.

Cailean sat and closed his eyes. "We won't get much rest at this rate."

"We will get enough, my lord." Aikan sat down beside him. "And if we move as quickly tonight, we can reach your keep by dawn."

"Warn my men that Lord Olbrieh is pressing at the borders, send some out to defend… Send someone out to engage in the diplomacy he claims has been 'ineffectual'." Cailean groaned. "I'd hoped to bring some of my men with us as well, but that would deplete the keep's defenses. Damn him for starting this *now*!"

Aikan was quiet for a moment, then said, "Lord Cailean,

much as I agree that we are badly outmanned against an army, I do not think that adding more Tathren soldiers into our ranks would be wise."

Cailean opened his eyes and looked at Aikan, surprised.

His steward watched the elves. "With the addition of the savages, the situation will be tense enough. Though I have no great love for being outnumbered by elves, more of your men could add sparks to tinder-dry grass. The Mad God's champion would not *need* to stop us—our 'alliance' would destroy itself."

"I did not expect to hear that from you, Aikan," Cailean said.

His steward scowled. "It's obvious enough, Lord Cailean. Which is why you need me, and will not be leaving me behind when we return to your keep, nor sending me to help my daughter. I trust her judgment."

Cailean smiled wryly as Aikan rejected the idea before he even had a chance to say it. "Stubborn."

"Rest, Lord Cailean," Aikan ordered firmly.

Cailean woke to late afternoon sun hitting his face. Stifling a groan, he rolled over, then peeled open stinging, gritty eyes. Most of the elves slept, wrapped in cloaks. Some kept watch, and eyes opened when Cailean climbed to his feet. He stumbled to the stream and washed his face in the frigid water. His stomach growled, reminding him of how long had passed since his last meal.

When he turned back toward the camp, he wasn't alone. Cailean started, calling Solstice to his hand before he identified the other as Sirex and relaxed. "Sorry. I didn't hear you."

"No need to apologize, Spearbearer Cailean," Sirex assured him. "I hoped to have a few minutes to speak with you. With you both."

"Both?" Cailean frowned, confused until he felt a pulse of

agreement from Solstice, and realized Sirex referred to the Spear. "Of course."

"Thank you." The demigod walked a little way down the bank of the stream. Cailean followed. "How long have you carried Solstice?"

"Five years," Cailean answered. "But I was trained to wield a spear since my youth."

Sirex nodded, thoughtful. "I've been watching how you and Solstice interact. I imagine you had little training on that matter."

Cailean shifted uncomfortably. "No, I haven't."

Sirex continued. "Solstice has been sleeping, so I'm unsurprised that bearers before you could not offer you instruction."

"Sleeping?" Cailean repeated. "What do you mean?"

"Human lives are short, compared to those of elves or demigods, and the Spears are far older than that. Solstice has had many bearers, but not all have been called to fight the Mad God directly or have needed to call on the Spear's full powers. As such, there have been periods when Solstice slept, never forming a true bond with its bearer." The demigod's keen eyes fixed on Cailean. "Now, however, Solstice is awake."

Cailean held the Spear possessively. "You speak like that's a problem."

"The Spear's waking is not the problem. The problem lies in the bond between you and Solstice."

"I'm not a new, green Spearbearer," Cailean snapped, irritated. *Lyan is far more a novice than I am. Why don't you lecture him instead?*

"No, you are not. That is, in fact, the greatest difficulty. You've developed habits, ways of thinking and using the Spear that have served you in the past. They do not, however, offer room for Solstice to speak. You wield the Spear as a weapon, not as a partner." Sirex sighed. "I would far rather have a conversation like this with a novice. A novice, at least, *knows* they don't know everything yet."

That stung.

Sirex was silent for a long moment. When Cailean didn't speak, he continued. "I know that Solstice's temperament is not the same as Equinox's, but I would suggest you converse with the Spear in times of calm and quiet as well as in battle. I know Solstice rejected the idea of trials for its bearers, but they do have a certain advantage of opening the new bearer to communication with the Spear."

Cailean scowled, but said, "A pity there aren't Guardians of Solstice."

A wave of something—anger or irritation—radiated from Solstice. Sirex's expression grew carefully neutral. "That is a matter you would have to discuss with Solstice. It's not my place to comment."

Cailean looked from the demigod to the Spear. *"What?"*

Another pulse of emotion with a strong sense that the subject was not open for discussion.

Cailean snorted. "Yes, clearly I should spend more time trying to talk to Solstice, so the Spear has more opportunities to tell me to piss off."

"That particular topic is a sensitive one," Sirex said. "I hope that Solstice will, in time, be willing to explain. I know it's hard to change the habits of a lifetime, whether yours or Solstice's. I hope you will both consider the matter, though, and be willing to learn new ways."

Cailean just shook his head and returned to the camp. Elves stirred as he passed, and those on guard eyed him or the Spear. Cailean was not surprised when Nylas joined him, though he hadn't noticed the leader of the elves among those keeping watch. The elf's face didn't show weariness and his movements were crisp and alert, as if their battle the previous day had never happened.

"You did not tell us the situation in Eilidh Wood," Nylas said without preamble.

"I don't *know* the situation in Eilidh Wood," Cailean retorted.

"And Lyan's state?" Nylas said.

Cailean let out a long breath. "Not well. He barely talks—most often to Kithr. Since we rejoined him, I have yet to see Lyan look at the stars."

Nylas raised an eyebrow. "He can look somewhere else?"

Cailean wasn't sure if the elf meant it as a joke, but neither of them laughed. Cailean shook his head. "I think he's seen something in the stars that he doesn't want to tell us, but I don't know for certain." He eyed Nylas. "You're worried about him."

"The mooncalf is kin, like it or not," Nylas snapped, "and I have promises to him to keep." He raised his voice. "Up!"

It was the tone of a commander issuing an order. At that single word, the camp roused. They moved with the quiet efficiency of practice, packing such gear as they had used and passing out dry rations. Cailean accepted the leathery strip of jerky and lump of hardtack offered him. The meat took enough chewing to make him wonder if it was worth the effort, while the hardtack had as much flavor as dirt.

He was still gnawing on the jerky when they continued the march. Sirex took his place at the head of the line without any mention of his conversation with Cailean. Cailean tried to look for signs of Lord Olbrieh's incursion, but found the landscape difficult to watch. During the night, he hadn't noticed the effect, but with daylight, Cailean felt a headache starting to throb in his temples when he tried to focus. Whatever Sirex did to speed their travel made the land around them seem to warp and ripple, like looking through a wall of water. Dusk and nightfall were a relief to Cailean's aching head.

At dawn, he found himself gazing at the gates of his own

keep. Home. The gates stood closed; the morning's flow of commerce between keep and the village below had not yet begun. Cailean threw back his hood and took the lead up to the gates.

"Halt! Identify yourselves!" The shout came from the wall above the gate, an uneasy guard faced with an unexpected band of cloaked, hooded men.

"Lord Cailean Dev'gilla," Cailean called back. "The men with me are here in peace, Sherod." He recognized the guard's voice and the nervous movements of the silhouette above him.

"Lord Cailean? You're back? But…" Scrambling on the wall, and a moment later, the smaller guard door opened beside the gate. Sherod stared at him, then Aikan. Then his gaze moved to the men behind Cailean, and he stiffened, gripping his sword.

"They're here in peace, Sherod," Cailean repeated.

Sherod jerked his head in a nervous nod, stepping back inside. The gates swung open with a groan, and shouts ran through the courtyard, rousing everyone from their morning rituals. Cailean and Aikan entered first, followed by the elves. Soldiers scrambled to attention, most of them in rumpled, unbuttoned uniforms, some of them only half-shaven, wiping lather from their faces. Captain Ralston, at least, was fully collected, and he watched warily, studying the situation for any indication that his lord was under duress. Cailean cast a look over his shoulder. The children gaped at everything from horseback, though they were obviously nervous and anxious. The elves were all tense, disliking being confined within stone walls and surrounded by heavily armed and equally tense Tathren soldiers.

Aikan scowled at everyone. "Lord Cailean has arrived with guests!" he snapped. "Stop gawking and bring refreshments!"

That finally sent servants scurrying into motion. Captain

Ralston exchanged glares with Nylas as he strode up to Cailean. "Welcome home, my lord. Are you back for a time now, sir?"

Cailean shook his head. "Not long. Once we've rested, we need to be on our way again. I returned to Tather to find Nylas and his company, so they can assist Lyan."

Captain Ralston stood straighter. He didn't particularly like Lyan or Kithr, but he knew his lord's opinion. "Sir, if your friend is in danger, then we should…"

"No," Cailean interrupted, even as Nylas and the other elves tensed. "As much as I would like to have my own men joining us, I cannot. I'll explain later."

Captain Ralston frowned. "Then what has brought you back home, sir, if not that?"

"We're going to be facing battle," Cailean said. "I offered the children shelter here." He nodded to the horses.

A kitchen maid approached cautiously. The servants had met Lyan and Kithr, but even Kithr projected more warmth than these hardened warriors. Still, the plump woman smiled and raised a platter toward the youths on the horses. "Cook made honey rolls. They're still warm from the oven. Would you like some?"

One of the boys licked his lips, but none of them reached to take a sticky roll. Instead, the eyes of the children flickered to Nylas.

Cailean gave the brave woman a smile and plucked two rolls from the platter. He tossed one to Nylas, who caught it by reflex. Cailean took a large bite and made a sound of genuine pleasure. "I have missed Cook's meals."

"He'll be pleased to hear that, Lord Cailean."

Nylas eyed the roll suspiciously, sniffed it, and took a bite. The children waited as he took a second bite, then gave a nod of permission. Between blinks, the rest of the honey rolls vanished from the platter. Though some were devoured on the spot, Cailean was sure any number vanished into sleeves and pockets as well. He didn't envy the laundress who would have to deal with the clothes later.

Cailean's men chuckled, relaxing some of the tension, and the serving woman laughed. "That's the sort of healthy appetite that Cook loves to see. Don't worry, young'uns, you won't go hungry here."

"Dismount," Nylas ordered. The children slid down to the ground and stood alert, looking at him. "As we agreed with the Tathren lord, you will stay here. Act in obedience to those assigned to your care. Do nothing to tarnish our honor."

"Yes sir," four voices answered.

"I am going with the rest of the company," Patch said.

Nylas looked at her sharply.

She met his gaze. "I have promises I must keep as well. Breaking it would tarnish my honor and that of our company."

"Then you come with us," Nylas said, voice giving no hint that the words were any manner of capitulation. He looked over the other children with eyes that dared anyone else to argue. When no other challenge came, he spoke in Elven. The children nodded solemnly.

"They'll rob you blind," Aikan whispered in disapproval.

"I doubt it," Cailean whispered back. "They aren't just here for their safety. They are also a guarantee—a binding promise that Nylas and his men won't attack us. Even if the offer wasn't meant that way when I made it, I know Nylas will see it as one. Knowing that, I don't think the children will be stealing beyond stashing food."

"My lord, if you and your guests are ready to break your fast, food is ready." The servant didn't come too close to the elves, but his voice carried clearly.

"Thank you." Cailean saw that Nylas had finished giving his instructions. "Please come inside and join me in a meal." To the servant he instructed, "Prepare quarters for our guests, and for the children. And the infants need a nursemaid."

"Lord Cailean, your servants will see to the matter," Aikan said firmly, and Cailean realized he was starting to ramble in exhaustion.

For having no warning, Cook and his staff outdid themselves preparing breakfast. Porridge, fresh bread, smoked meat, and mulled wine awaited them. Cailean made a point of taking some of everything, knowing that years of war and distrust wouldn't be easily set aside by elves dining at the table of a Tathren lord.

He didn't have to worry much about whether the elves would eat. Before Cailean had taken more than two bites of his food, Nylas's men were filling plates and devouring food with little evidence of table manners. Aikan watched them for a moment, a disgusted scowl on his face, then he ate his own meal with exaggerated decorum.

Once the table had been cleared, servants offered to show the elven guests to their quarters. Most accepted, but Nylas remained, as did Declan, who kept a cautious eye on Nylas. Cailean wanted little more than the chance to sleep in his own bed once again, but it was clear Nylas had something to say. Cailean met the icy blue gaze. "Yes?"

"You wanted to see it." Nylas set the fiddle case on the table and opened it.

Cailean had almost forgotten the elf's reluctant agreement to show him the instrument. He stepped closer, looking in the case, and his breath caught. Polished maple caught the light of the torches. Silver knobs held the strings, and the body was inlaid with gold leaf.

"What bard did you murder for this?" Aikan asked in a voice more astonished than accusatory.

Nylas snorted. "The thief I killed for it saw no value beyond the gold and silver. Who *he* killed for it, I don't know, but it's mine now." He ran his fingers across the strings, teasing music from them.

Cailean longed to do the same, but restrained himself,

recognizing Nylas's possessive air. "I've rarely seen finer craftsmanship. I'm glad it's in the keeping of someone who can appreciate it."

Nylas's icy eyes narrowed. "Are you mocking me, Tathren?"

Cailean shook his head. "No. You and your warriors took only what you need and what you value. If you didn't treasure it, you would have left it behind. No mockery, Nylas."

The elf silently closed the case. "Why do I sense elven magic within these walls?"

*Elven magic? Oh.* Cailean rose. "Follow me; I'll show you."

He led the way down halls, eventually reaching a small, isolated courtyard. A gate had once hung at its entrance, but now the stone doorway was empty, and the edges smooth and polished in a manner few mortal craftsmen could achieve. Cailean had left it that way rather than have a new gate set into the stone. Few frequented this courtyard anymore.

Stone rubble littered the ground, overgrown by tall grass and creeping vines. The shattered remains of walls formed a crumbling enclosure around a tall oak tree. The leaves were turning red and gold in a herald of autumn and harvest. Nylas strode toward the tree, but stopped abruptly to snatch something from the ground. He brandished it toward Cailean —the twisted remains of a lantern with no wick and no fuel. It still glowed faintly, shedding ghostly light.

"Where did you get this, Tathren?" Nylas demanded. "Where did the likes of *you* acquire an elven lantern? We do not give them to outsiders."

Kithr had taken such a lantern from the shrine in Eilidh Wood. Elven lanterns—magical, flameless, and found, to Cailean's knowledge, only in Eilidh Wood. *And here. Why did I never question that? I should have asked and wondered, how did Ewart and Porephyn have elven lanterns?*

Cailean answered, his voice grim. "Someone gave them to outsiders, but not to me. This was where my enemies built their shrine to the Mad God." He held Nylas's gaze. "Those lanterns lit that shrine."

Nylas dropped the lantern as if it had burned him. "And the tree?"

"Lyan and Equinox. The tree ripped through the shrine, and it killed the Mad God's high priest."

Nylas marched up to the oak. The tree rustled rudely in response, projecting a sense that it did not welcome the elf. Nylas scowled at the oak, and a branch slapped the top of his head. Nylas snorted.

"I think Lyan will be *delighted* to see me, if this overgrown lump of firewood is any indication."

Cailean's mouth twitched in a smile in spite of himself. The tree had never been anything but pleasant to him during his visits. "Perhaps it just likes Tathrens better."

"No." Nylas moved away from the tree, eyeing it. "It's tied to Lyan, and its responses mirror his feelings. Little wonder he didn't come himself." The elf spun on his heels. "Well, he has called due our debt. He will have to deal with what he gets."

19

KITHR

*"When the skies clear, I shall find you once again, and you will keep your*<br>*promise, cousin."*

Kithr massaged his temples as he studied the map Yion had provided. The leaps across distance that Solstice had employed badly skewed his perception of their location, and he still struggled to orient himself.

His finger hovered over a forested patch toward the left side of the map. "This would be where we encountered Vynzent?" he asked quietly. He glanced toward Lyan as he said it, knowing that his friend still flinched to hear that name. Lyan sat across the camp, nursing a mug of tea, and didn't appear to have heard Kithr's question over the low crackle of the fire.

Yion nodded. "It is, and the Shrine lies further in that direction, I believe."

"But if we turn north, we'll go toward—what city is this?" Kithr couldn't read the script on the map.

"Ceolvost," Yion answered. "A trade city built upon the

river. When the city was built, they constructed many canals and diverted the river to flow through the midst. By such means, they control all travel upon the river, and gain prosperity by the taxes they level on the traffic."

"You've been there?" Kithr asked.

Yion nodded again. "My path carried me through the city once. Mercenaries there can find employ from the merchants with little difficulty."

Kithr gazed at the map again. "What are the chances that the Mad God's champion already has men there, recruiting those mercenaries?"

"Very high," Yion told him. "I would do the same, in his place."

Kithr stiffened. "You think *we* should hire sell-swords? Men loyal to money alone?" He caught himself, remembering whom he spoke to.

Yion didn't take offense. But Yion didn't take visible offense to anything. "Some abide by a code of honor. Others do not. I could find among them those who would remain true —*if* we have the gold to pay them."

"I don't like the idea," Kithr said, scowling.

Yion smiled. "Precisely."

Kithr frowned at him.

"You dislike the idea of purchasing loyalty with coin, and distrust those who sell themselves so. I think that the rest of your people, or at least your warriors, feel much the same. For that reason, our enemy will not expect you to augment our forces with mercenaries." Yion's tone was patient without being patronizing.

"Cailean would think of it," Kithr argued.

"Indeed, Lord Cailean would. But the decision lies with you, Kithr. It is you who lead here," Yion said.

Kithr wanted to argue, but he didn't. He hadn't intended to take charge of the group when it grew beyond him and Lyan, but someone had to, and he could hardly leave Lyan's safety entirely to Tathrens. With the addition of Declan and the others, Cailean had, reluctantly, accepted that elven warriors would not readily accept the Tathren Spearbearer at their head.

*And gods know there is no way I'll let Nylas take charge.*

He looked at the map again and grimaced. "Mercenaries, is it? I don't know if we have a way to pay them even if we try to hire them, nor do I know if they would accept my coin."

"The stamp on the coin matters less than the weight of it to most," Yion said. "But the question of whether we have the means to pay them is not one I can answer."

Kithr let out a deep breath. "Where are we?"

"Near here, I believe," Yion answered, letting a long finger hang south of the city. "But I am not certain."

"Lyan!" Kithr called.

Lyan started from his thoughts and crossed the camp. Yion stepped aside to allow Lyan full view of the map. Lyan didn't say anything to the mercenary as he glanced at the map, then gave Kithr a questioning look. "Yes?"

"Where would you say we are right now?" Kithr asked.

Lyan indicated an area north of the one Yion had pointed to. "By the stars, we're near here, two day's steady walk south of the main road. While it's a good landmark, we don't want to travel on the road."

Kithr grimaced. "Agreed. We'd stand out too much on a road. Though we might need to use one eventually. What would you think if we made for Ceolvost? We can hunt for information there and get supplies." He was reluctant to admit that he was considering Yion's suggestion about mercenaries.

Lyan looked at him in surprise. "You want to go to Ceolvost?"

"Is that a problem?" Kithr asked. "If it is, we can—"

"No." Lyan said quickly. "We should go. I just... didn't think you'd like the idea. I expected to argue with you to convince you to go there. I… wasn't looking forward to that."

"Then you are fortunate that I held the argument in your stead," Yion said with a small smile. "Does it bother you, Lyan?"

Lyan gazed at the map and didn't respond.

Kithr frowned. "Lyan?"

Lyan gave him a puzzled look at the expectant tone. "Yes?"

"Does that bother you?"

"Does it bother me that I don't have to argue with you? Of course not! It's a relief, Kithr," Lyan answered.

"Does it bother you that Yion convinced me of the idea?" Kithr asked plainly.

Lyan blinked, brow furrowing in puzzlement. "Yion?" he repeated, glancing around the camp. "He's here?"

Kithr opened his mouth, but words wouldn't come. The mercenary sat beside Lyan, yet Lyan seemed unaware of him.

"I am beside you, Lyan Stargazer," Yion said.

Lyan completed his scan of the camp and looked back to Kithr, his gaze still bewildered.

"Lyan, you really don't—" Kithr began.

Yion stood. "Let it be, Kithr. I believe that Lyan is indeed ignorant of my presence. He has no reason to lie about such a thing. There is more to this matter than we see upon the surface, and I must think on the possibilities."

Kithr watched Yion walk across the camp. Lyan tried to follow Kithr's gaze, but his eyes never focused on Yion.

*Lyan hasn't been ignoring Yion. He really doesn't see or hear him. But why not?*

The rest of the group tried not to be obvious in their staring as they looked between Lyan and Yion. Shiolto opened his mouth, on the verge of saying something. Kithr caught the Tathren's eye and shook his head. Dalrian cleared his throat and valiantly broke the uneasy silence.

"If you've decided which way we're going, shouldn't we get started?"

"Yes," Kithr said decisively, grateful for the question. He rolled the map and slid it into the scroll case.

He set a steady pace, sending Pyrn to scout ahead and Ihm to watch their backs. Shiolto and Dalrian rode, leading the packhorses. Yion walked, followed by the horse with the broken saddle girths. The elves accepted Shiolto's invitation to load some of their gear on the packhorses, though they could have easily kept Kithr's pace even without doing so.

Lyan walked by himself for a time, but eventually moved up with Kithr.

"Doing all right?" Kithr asked.

Lyan nodded, but his expression was hard to read. "Kithr, please don't look at me like I've gone mad when I ask this, but, is Yion actually here?" His voice was quiet.

"Yes, he's here. He came with Cailean and the rest of the Tathrens. Been with us the whole time. Even spoke to our gods at the shrine outside the village." Kithr gazed at his friend. "You didn't know that?"

"No, but now Soldarr's remarks at the shrine make a lot more sense." Lyan stared into the distance. "None of the predictions I've seen even hint at Yion's presence. He's really with us?"

"Yes, and he's as much the annoyingly calm, know-it-all mercenary as ever." *How must it feel to be told everyone else can see someone you can't?*

Lyan's shoulders relaxed in relief. "Thank the gods."

"Lyan?" Kithr frowned.

"Don't you see? None of the predictions say anything about Yion! It's like he's invisible to them."

"And to you," Kithr said.

"That's not the *point!*" Lyan said. "Kithr, it means that the Mad God's champion can't predict him! He doesn't know what Yion will do or how that might change events."

"Doesn't it bother you that you can't even tell where Yion *is*?" Kithr pressed.

"It is unsettling," Lyan admitted. "But if that is the price for this, I accept it."

"Why?"

Lyan gave him a questioning look.

"Why can't you see or hear him? And why do you seem to think this is a *good* thing, Lyan?"

"Can't you just believe me that it is?" Lyan asked plaintively. Kithr gave him a hard look. Lyan's shoulders slumped. "No, I suppose you can't."

"Would you, in my place?" Kithr countered. "I need to know, Lyan."

Lyan hesitated. "Before I answer, Kithr, I need you to promise to accept that what I tell you is all I can tell you. I know you'll want to know more, but I can't answer the questions you will have."

"As long as you tell me *something*," Kithr said, waving a hand in frustration. "Would it kill you to explain?"

"It's not my death I'm worried about," Lyan whispered. He let out a heavy breath. "Do you remember how, during our travels with Cailean, I told you about the curse on him?"

Kithr nodded slowly. "The Mad God's priest cursed him to limit his ability to call on Solstice's power, and prevented him from discussing the curse itself."

"Yes." Lyan waited.

Kithr stiffened. "You mean that you—" He lowered his voice. "Lyan, are you under some sort of curse? Is that why Equinox isn't with you? But I know you've used the Spear's powers."

"It doesn't interfere with my connection to Equinox," Lyan said. "This has different effects. Solstice was one of Cailean's greatest strengths—that curse targeted it to weaken him."

"The curse targets your strengths." Kithr frowned. "This

curse—your curse has something to do with astrology and divination, doesn't it?"

A nod answered him.

"When did this happen, Lyan? How? Who? Elder Brenhan?" *How could I let this happen to Lyan? I promised I would protect him! How could this happen under my nose? Who do I kill to fix it?*

"Not the Elder. No one here. I can't tell you more than that."

"Cailean's curse broke when you killed the Mad God's priest. Will killing the champion break yours? You said he's using some form of divination. Is it connected?"

"They are connected. And killing him will help." Lyan hesitated, about to say more, but closed his mouth, leaving the words unspoken.

*If this curse works anything like Cailean's, maybe he can't say more.* "But you can still read the stars?"

Lyan shivered, gaze shifting from Kithr to a point on the horizon. "It doesn't stop me from reading the stars. I almost wish it did. It shows me more than the stars do, and all of it tainted by the Mad God's touch." His voice grew quiet. "Every time I'm looking to the stars. Sometimes, even when I'm not."

Kithr stiffened. "Like a..."

"Don't say it!" Lyan cut him off. "Please. Just... don't say it."

Kithr closed his mouth. *Like a Seer. I know we call Seers cursed, but this… Lyan's not a Seer. He can't be. There's only one Seer of Eilidh Wood, and it's not Lyan.*

Lyan looked to him again and spoke softly. "Kithr, please understand. Even telling you this much opens a possibility for things to get much, much worse. I'm trying to turn us away from that path, but now it's open, and I don't know if I'm strong enough to keep us off it."

Kithr's stomach sank. "I'm sorry." *If I hadn't demanded an answer, he wouldn't have had to do this. I'm putting us in more danger.*

Lyan shook his head. "I chose to tell you, Kithr. I want you to know. I want to tell you more, but I can't. I'm sorry. Everything I tell you, or anyone else, I must weigh the consequences of telling or not telling. And sometimes, the consequences of not telling—of you, Cailean, or the others being angry and frustrated at me—are better than those that would come from my telling you more. I can endure being the target of everyone's anger if it means no one dies."

A chill ran down Kithr's spine. "Maybe you can't tell me this either, but I still don't understand how this form of divination relates to Yion."

"I'm not certain, but I have a guess," Lyan said. "Would you ask him to come here?"

"Sure." Kithr caught Yion's eye and motioned him to join them.

Yion approached, leading the horse with him. "I trust that the horse remains visible to Lyan. While we travel, at least, he may use it as reference to my location."

"Thanks. Lyan, Yion's here. He's leading the horse, so if you need to find him, that's where he will be."

Lyan turned toward the horse. "Thank you. I need to ask, does Saiboti shield you from divination?"

Yion raised one eyebrow. "Oh? Yes, my lord does. It was necessary to prevent my homeland from locating me."

Kithr repeated Yion's answer. Lyan nodded. "Thank you. I hope that Kithr will tell me if you say something to me." He paused. "You could try writing messages, too."

"I shall test that, though not at the moment," Yion said. "And I am most grateful to Kithr for being willing to serve as my translator."

Again, Kithr repeated the words, though Yion's way of speaking felt odd to his mouth. He added, "So what does that have to do with what you told me, Lyan?"

Lyan fixed a pointed look on the horse Yion led. Yion inclined his head and returned to his previous position in line. Lyan turned to Kithr again. "This. What I told you about, it's not like a Seer's visions, but sometimes I see and hear things just when I look at someone. Because Yion is shielded from divination, the, um…"

"Curse," Kithr supplied quietly.

Lyan nodded. "It can't 'see' Yion. And because it's affecting my senses, I can't perceive him either."

"Ash and rot," Kithr said quietly. He was sure he didn't want to ponder the implications of Lyan seeing things and divinations beyond astrology. Because that sounded far too much like a Seer's cursed visions.

"The Mad God's champion won't be able to see him either, and he won't be able to plan for whatever actions Yion may take," Lyan said. He gazed intently at Kithr. "Please listen to his advice. And if there's a chance for him to take down the Mad God's champion, give it to him. I know you'll want to kill the champion yourself, but he truly cannot see Yion coming."

Kithr grimaced, but forced the expression into a tight smile. "I understand. I'll listen to him, and I'll let him take the first stab at the champion, don't worry."

"I'll worry less than I did," Lyan responded soberly.

A little after midday, Kithr saw a shimmer in the air, like waves of heat rising from the grassland in summer. This day, though, had none of summer's heat, carrying strong hints of autumn and a chill breeze. Kithr raised his hand, calling a halt. Stringing his bow and nocking an arrow, he watched the shimmer warily.

For a moment, he saw ghostly, insubstantial forms, then they became solid. Kithr raised his bow but did not release the arrow, waiting until he could identify the hooded men. Around him, the rest of the group drew together, hands seeking weapons and bows creaking as arrows were nocked.

"Another warm welcome, I see." Nylas threw back his hood and scowled at Kithr.

"It's all right, Kithr." Cailean pushed back his own hood.

Kithr slowly lowered his bow. "I didn't loose any arrows—consider that welcome enough," he said. "It's as much of one as I extend to anyone appearing from gods-know-where right now."

Nylas sniffed scornfully, and his icy blue eyes shifted to Lyan. Folding his arms across his chest, he said, "Well? We're here. Surprised?"

"No," Lyan answered. "You always keep your word, Nylas."

Nylas paused, frowning. The air remained tense. Nylas's men watched the group like feral animals studying prey, their faces cold and hard. Cailean and Aikan left the company of the elves to rejoin Kithr's group, followed by Declan and Sirex. Kithr felt the barrier between the two groups, unseen yet seemingly impenetrable. Only one person seemed pleased with the situation, and Kithr was taken aback to see her among the elven warriors: the half-Tathren girl Patch.

Patch made straight for Lyan, brushing golden brown hair from her face. She'd gotten taller in the months since Kithr last saw her, now nearly as tall as Lyan, though willowy thin. "I kept my promise, cousin: I found you. So you have one to keep to me as well."

For the first time in far too long, a genuine smile formed on Lyan's face. "It is good to see you well, cousin. As I promised, I will read your fortune tonight."

"Cousin?" Nylas demanded, striding after Patch as if he meant to pull her away from Lyan.

Lyan's eye met Nylas's. "Patch told me that none claim her as kin except the other half-breed children. I offered, as is the way of Eilidh Wood, and she accepted."

Behind Nylas, elves shifted uncomfortably. Lyan was right—in Eilidh Wood, an orphaned child would be offered kinship by other families, regardless of whether a blood relationship existed. Patch and the other children had grown up among the warriors in Malgor Forest, but none of those elves had done what Lyan had. And Patch had accepted, though Lyan had been in her life only a few meager days.

Kithr's gaze shifted from Patch to Nylas, who wavered between disbelief and outrage. Speculation among Nylas's men, the Lost elves, ran that Patch might be Nylas's child, which would make her Lyan's cousin in truth. But Nylas never openly claimed her, and there was no proof.

For the first time since leaving Eilidh Wood, Lyan looked to the sky without hesitation. A few clouds drifted lazily across the blue expanse, and a bird wheeled on the wind. The astrologer watched it for a moment, then spoke. "I don't know the signs of your birth, but I will use what I do know to read your fortune, as I promised."

"On her naming day, she was under the Huntsman, with the Torch rising and the Willow waning," Nylas said.

Lyan turned to Nylas and raised an eyebrow.

Nylas scowled, crossing his arms. "Regardless of whether or not we placed much value in them, we still maintained *some* traditions."

Lyan gave a brief nod, then he looked up again. "Huntsman, Torch, Willow, Blade, and Blood."

A shiver ran down Kithr's spine as Lyan said the last two signs. Nylas stiffened, as if he wanted to argue. Patch looked at Lyan curiously. "Blade and Blood?"

"For your parents," Lyan answered. "An unusual combination, but it feels right for you, Patch Warborn."

Patch smiled. "Thank you, cousin."

"Where are the rest of your siblings?" Lyan asked her.

"The younger siblings are in the home of the Tathren Spearbearer. He offered them shelter," she answered.

"Thank you, Cailean," Lyan said, turning toward the Tathren.

"We would have returned sooner, but I thought the side trip would be wise. Sirex sped our travels," Cailean replied.

Nylas scowled at the gatekeeper of the Shrine of Equinox. "If you could simply have moved us all in one instant, why didn't you do so before, Freewarden?"

"I could have," Sirex agreed. "However, using such power is much like lighting a beacon fire on a starless night. Casual use attracts the attention of people whose interest we don't want. It's useful for crossing long distances, but was unnecessary within Tather."

"People whose interest we don't want." Nylas snorted. "Such as?"

"Such as those priests of the Mad God who aren't currently involved in the assault on the Shrine of Equinox," Sirex told him. "I assure you, we need no more of them converging on the Shrine or on the Spearbearers."

The chill wind whipped through the grass, drawing a shiver from Kithr. He slung his bow and straightened. "Nylas. How many warriors do you bring?"

Nylas responded to the tone of authority that Kithr took. "Eighty-four warriors, including myself. I don't count Patch, though she's handy with a bow. Each man carries a week's rations."

That week's worth of rations apiece was probably the entirety of their food stores. Kithr nodded curtly. "You're fit to march?" Now that Nylas was closer, Kithr could see lines of weariness on his face.

"Of course," Nylas answered coolly. "*You* are taking charge?"

"Lyan is Spearbearer of Equinox. He is in charge, but he appointed me as second-in-command. Do you intend to challenge that?" The question was a calculated risk. Nylas's men well outnumbered them if a challenge descended into a battle, but challenging Kithr's leadership also implied a challenge against Lyan—a far more thorny prospect, when

Nylas was duty-bound to fulfill his debt to Lyan. As long as Nylas accepted Kithr's claim, his men had little choice but to do the same.

Nylas glared, and for a moment Kithr thought him about to issue the challenge regardless. They locked eyes. Kithr didn't blink.

Nylas finally turned aside. "No. No challenge. But we will not accept orders from a *Tathren*."

"You will if Cailean gives them," Kithr said icily. "Let me make this *very* clear, Nylas. The chain of command here runs Lyan, me, and Cailean. You and your men are under all three."

Nylas stiffened, on the verge of lashing out, when Patch turned to him. "The Tathren Spearbearer has allowed himself to be placed under the authority of Lyan and Kithr, Captain. Will we do less?"

Nylas caught himself, forcing clenched fists to relax. He jerked his head in a nod. "Very well." His gaze raked over Pyrn, Ihm, and Seine, then Shiolto, Dalrian, and Yion. When his eyes fell on the Splinter, he turned away sharply. "This is the extent of your forces?"

"It is," Kithr said, unflinching. "Declan's told you the situation in Eilidh Wood?"

"He has, as he knows it. Anything to add?"

"The Elder has been deceiving and manipulating Heartshrine Village since before we were born, and we can't kill him until the champion of the Mad God has been dealt with." Kithr was pleased that his voice only shook a little from his anger. "We have the support of Eilidh Wood, though not of its people." He nodded toward the Splinter.

A ripple of uneasy murmurs ran through Nylas's men. They eyed the Splinter warily, edging back from her. Kithr had acclimated to her presence and appearance, and their reactions reminded him just how unsettling she was.

The Splinter gazed at Nylas without blinking. He turned

to face her. A grimace of pain touched his face and he gripped his left arm. She looked him up and down. Her hair twisted and coiled across her body, and a tendril curled down her arm and reached toward Nylas.

He jerked away with a hiss. "Keep that to yourself."

"You refuse our invitation?" she asked.

"If I wanted to plant myself, I could do so without your help," Nylas snapped. "I have work to do."

"You reject Eilidh Wood." The Splinter's voice grew chill.

Nylas laughed sharply. "Haven't you listened to Kithr and the mooncalf? We're not yours. We're Lost."

The tendril withdrew. The Splinter's tone was cold and her eyes hard. "So you are."

Turning from her, Nylas eyed Dalrian and Shiolto, who shifted uncomfortably under hostile stares. "The Tathren Spearbearer already extracted my agreement not to fight him or his underlings."

"Good," Kithr said. "We'll add more warriors to our ranks as we can."

The slight cock of Nylas's head and his frown asked a silent "How?"

Kithr ignored the unspoken question. "Cailean. A moment?"

Cailean nodded, and they walked a little ways from the rest, leaving the groups to glower at each other. Kithr spoke in a low voice. "We're heading for Ceolvost. Lyan and Yion both think it's a good idea. Yion convinced me that we should consider hiring sell-swords."

Cailean's expression was surprised. "Hire mercenaries? What does Lyan think of that?"

"I don't know. Didn't discuss that specifically with him. We also learned something odd regarding Yion and Lyan, which I'll explain as best I can later. However, I don't know what a sell-sword costs or if we *can* afford to hire any."

A wry smile touched Cailean's mouth. "So, I'm the purse of this venture, am I?"

"Eilidh Wood trades with the Appret Plains, and little beyond that. Mostly barter, and we use coin only infrequently. You've mentioned several times that Yion doesn't expect prompt payment, but I assume other sell-swords would. I have some trinkets I can part with, but I don't know their worth." The issue of money had lurked in the back of Kithr's mind since Yion brought it up.

"That may not be necessary, Kithr. I also considered mercenaries, and collected money from my treasury during our brief visit to my keep, in case I could convince you. We won't be able to hire many—five, maybe six."

"Five or six men," Kithr repeated. "That's all?"

"If we want skilled men, yes," Cailean said.

"Hardly sounds worth the effort," Kithr said, frowning.

"Would you say that if we found five men of Yion's skill?" Cailean countered. "We don't need archers, certainly, but swordsmen are a different matter."

"You expect to *find* men with Yion's skills?" Kithr asked.

"Well, not with his background," Cailean admitted. "I doubt there are many other former assassins turned champion of Saiboti for hire. But men who find themselves far from their homelands often become mercenaries for lack of any other legitimate source of employment, and they bring their own styles of fighting to a battle."

Reluctantly, Kithr nodded. "Then we will have to hope those five or six will be enough." He spun and marched back. Raising his voice, he shouted, "Let's move!"

## 20

### NYLAS

*"What fate awaits the Lost? Only madness and, if they are fortunate, death."*

Dawn saw Nylas already awake, checking the perimeter of the camp. The sentries for the final watch were mainly his men, but Kithr had ensured at least one of his own people joined each watch. Despite the company he kept, Kithr was no fool.

Nylas's path drew him toward what he first mistook for a scraggly tree. Then it opened amber eyes, looked at him, and spoke. "Rejecting us will not stop what has begun."

One hand clenched. His left arm ached. "I didn't ask your opinion."

"You would prefer to grow wild? Plant your roots far from our boughs? You wish to be reduced to a mindless weed, consuming any living flesh to feed your branches until you are cut down and burned?" She gave him a cold look of disdain.

"That will not happen!" He caught himself gripping his left arm, and forced himself to release it. The closer he stood to her, the more he felt the ache in his arm, the magic eating into his limb and transforming it from flesh to something akin to wood, his blood to sap.

"It will," she said with cool confidence.

"It will not," Nylas repeated. "I don't need *you* to contain me when I turn."

"You are not so blind as to think you will be able to retain your self." The Splinter eyed him, then her gaze moved to the camp. "You expect the girl to control you? Have you trained her? Has she ever seen the fate of a Lost shaper?"

He bristled, but her tone was not one of accusation, but curiosity. "Patch knows the fate of the Lost. I'd trust myself to her long before I would give charge of that fate to *you*. I'm not interested in your assessment of my state."

"We do not care what interests you. We care what tools our children need to succeed in their task. You have already declared yourself not one of our children. Thus, you are a tool." She pointed a long, twig-like finger at him.

Sharp pain lanced through his left arm as if thorns bristled from his bones. His breath hissed between his teeth. He gripped his forearm and felt moisture seep through the shirt sleeve.

"We will use the tools available to us, whether they wish to be used or not," the Splinter said.

"Go rot! I'm no one's tool!" Holding his arm close to his body, Nylas retreated, eyes never leaving the Splinter.

She watched him go and did not follow. Her voice, however, whispered in his ear. "If you were not a tool, our Spearbearing child would not have summoned you."

He bared his teeth in a snarl at her and withdrew to the campfire. He'd noticed her giving the fire wide berth the previous evening. Nylas stirred the coals to life and fed tinder until a small blaze crackled. He settled on the ground beside it, rubbing his arm as if that would banish the pulsing pain. Yellow liquid oozed from a puncture at the crook of his elbow.

Kithr sat across the firepit from him and set a kettle of water to heat. Though he didn't say anything, Nylas was certain he'd witnessed the conversation with the Splinter.

Pain gave Nylas's voice a sharp edge. "Why did you let that *thing* come with you?"

"The Splinter?" Kithr gave him a long, dubious look. "After the great success you just had arguing with Eilidh Wood, what makes you think I was given any choice in the matter? The forest does as it pleases." His eyes narrowed. "How correct was she about your state?"

"What difference does it make to you?" Nylas growled. "My men and I are tools for you."

Kithr didn't blink. "It makes as much difference to me as it would to you if one of your warriors stood at risk of losing himself to his magic."

"It's under control."

"She didn't think so."

"She doesn't know me. You do. Do you really think I would allow mere plant magic to prevent me from fulfilling my oath?" *If you say yes, I swear I will gut you where you sit.*

"No, I just want to know whether or not you'll still be aware that you're doing so," Kithr said.

"If I'm not, Patch knows what to do." Nylas stood.

"Well, that's reassuring." Kithr checked the kettle, then nudged it closer to the coals. "If you lose yourself to the plants, everything's in the hands of a fifteen year old girl. No reason for concern at all."

Nylas glared at him. "Oh, should I instead leave everything in the hands of the mooncalf? I'm sure that would be *much* wiser."

Kithr raised eyes as cold as Nylas's. "You don't have the slightest idea what's going on with Lyan."

"I know he wouldn't call my debt due if he had another choice." Nylas folded his arms. "But he did, and we're here, wherever 'here' is. Are you going to tell me where we are and what plan, if any, you or Lyan have? Or should I assume that what I've seen so far *is* as much of a plan as you have?"

Kithr remained predictably easy to nettle. "We're about five days south of the city of Ceolvost. We're taking a detour there to pick up supplies and see about hiring on mercenaries."

"First Tathrens, now sell-swords." Nylas spat. "You truly are desperate."

"Yes, desperate enough to call even Lost elves to our aid," Kithr retorted. "At least a mercenary's loyalty stays bought as long as he's paid."

"Until he gets a better offer, at least," Nylas said, sneering.

"If a mercenary wants the Mad God's gold, we don't want him here," Kithr said. "Let them chase coins, if that's all they want. They're more likely to end up on the wrong end of a priest's blade than they are to enjoy a long life or wealth."

"And just how do you propose to root out who will stay bought and who will follow the Mad God's coin?" Nylas asked. He cursed the moment of hesitation before he spoke of their enemy. *Lyan and Kithr intend to do battle against a champion of the incarnation of madness. What sell-sword will be lunatic enough to accept that job?*

Kithr nodded toward a short, black-haired human who brewed something in a kettle over his own small fire. "I'll let Yion sort them out first. He's a mercenary himself, after a fashion."

Nylas remembered the man from his first encounter with Cailean, in a Tathren dungeon. Even outnumbered and surrounded by hostile elves, Yion had projected the air of a man confident in his skills and not intimidated by anyone. His confidence should have been foolish, yet somehow his calm had proved intimidating. Nylas looked back to Kithr, eyes narrow. "That is no mercenary."

"Yes, he is. He's also a former assassin."

Nylas stiffened. "You allow an assassin near Lyan?"

"Former assassin," Kithr repeated without flinching. "Now he's a mercenary. And a Champion of Saiboti."

"A Cham... You say that like it's *nothing*, Kithr? What *else* are you not telling me? Cailean carries Solstice, the mercenary is champion of a Tathren god, Lyan bears Equinox, and the Freewarden Sirex is a demigod. What aren't you telling me? Is the old man Ahebban in disguise?" *What in the First Seed has Lyan been doing?*

"No, thank the gods, Aikan is Cailean's steward without a drop of divine blood in him," Kithr said. "But I suppose you ought to know that Lyan has a pet pooka."

"He has *what?*"

"A gift, personally given to him by the god of monsters, who was apparently feeling particularly petty and vindictive at the time," Kithr said.

"You're serious."

Kithr nodded.

"A pooka."

"Yes, by the name of Praett. You may or may not see him. Look for either a black horse with glowing red eyes or a human dressed impractically well for the terrain. Don't loose arrows at him; he gets testy."

"Anything *else* I should know?" Nylas demanded.

"The Mad God's champion possesses some form of divination and intends to besiege the Shrine of Equinox. We need to kill him before that happens. Ideally, well before he gets close to the Shrine. Any more questions?" Kithr moved the steaming kettle to rest on the ring of stones around the fire.

"Just one." Nylas gazed across the fire at Kithr. "Do you trust Lyan as Spearbearer of Equinox?"

"Of course I trust Lyan," Kithr said, voice sharp.

"No. Not just 'Lyan, astrologer of Heartshrine Village.' I am asking whether or not you trust him to bear Equinox."

Kithr rose. "I know of no one whose hands I would trust

Equinox in more. Yes, I trust Lyan as Spearbearer. I trust him to lead us where we need to go and do everything he can to protect all of us—even the Lost—from whatever sadistic schemes the Mad God's champion plots."

"Good. Then I don't have to challenge you for leadership."

Kithr frowned, suspicious.

"Believe it or not, Kithr, we both want my mooncalf cousin to succeed. If he is going to succeed, he needs a second in command who trusts him. If you were not up for the task, I would ensure the post was held by someone who was."

"You want him to succeed? Considering the accusations you leveled during our conversation in Malgor Forest, I have my doubts." Kithr sat again and poured steaming water into a battered mug.

Nylas didn't deign to respond. Words wouldn't settle Kithr's doubts, so he didn't waste them on the effort. He strode from the fire, making a fresh circuit of the camp. After several minutes, Patch joined him. Tension eased from his shoulders, and when she touched his left arm, the pain dulled.

"So, did Lyan read your fate last night?" Nylas asked her. Once night fell, Lyan had called Patch over to a spot on the edge of the camp and banished the sentries near enough to hear them.

"No, Captain. Lyan read my fortune. My fate follows yours," Patch said.

"My fate is not yours," Nylas said sharply. "You're half human, and I have yet to hear of one of *their* magic-users transforming into something other than the form they were born with." He had to believe Patch wouldn't be consumed by the magic she possessed, that she and the other half-Tathren children would be protected from the fate of the Lost by their mixed blood.

"But mine still follows yours if I am to be your guide once

you change, Captain. That's why it isn't my fate that Lyan read, but my fortune." Patch lowered her hand from his arm.

The pain remained a dull ache, soothed by her touch. "What fortune did he predict, then?"

Patch shook her head. "I'm sorry, Captain, but he asked that I keep it to myself. He did tell me that if you wish it, he will read yours tonight. After he read my fortune, others of our warriors sought Lyan out as well. I think they kept him up quite late."

That surprised Nylas less than it might have before Lyan's visit to Malgor Forest. "They should know better. Gods know Lyan would stay up all night looking at the stars if we let him. I'll make sure they don't keep him up after midnight tonight."

"And will you ask him to read your stars, Captain?" Patch asked.

"No." His answer was curt. "I don't care what hold either fortune or fate thinks they have over me. They don't change what I need to do, and they won't stop me from doing it."

# 21

## CAILEAN

*"Lord Murdo, grant me strength. Save me now from the hands of my enemies, that I may rise again and strike them down in your name."*

Despite Nylas's apparent contempt of astrology, at least half his men had asked Lyan to read their stars by the second night, to Cailean's count. To judge by the troubled expressions on some faces in the morning, not all the fortunes Lyan provided favored the recipients.

He found Lyan by the fire, shoulders hunched, staring into a steaming mug. Cailean sat beside him, and Lyan flinched back.

"Sorry," Cailean said quickly. "Didn't mean to startle you."

"No, it's… sorry," Lyan said. Dark shadows ringed his eyes.

"How late were you up?" Cailean asked in concern. "You look exhausted, Lyan."

"Not too late, last night. Nylas ordered everyone away at midnight. And he didn't want his stars read, fortunately."

246

"Fortunately because he didn't keep you up later, or because you worry what the stars would tell him?" Cailean asked.

"Yes."

Cailean considered his next question carefully. "If he had asked, would you have done so?"

"It's my duty as an astrologer of Eilidh Wood." Lyan shivered, shoulders hunching more. "Even if Elder Brenhan claims I am not one."

"He doesn't have the authority to make that claim," Cailean said.

"He is elder of Heartshrine Village, Cailean. His word is seen as the word of our gods."

"You are Spearbearer of Equinox, and he's a follower of the Mad God. Nothing he says follows the will of your gods. If you doubt me, ask the Splinter."

"I don't doubt you, Cailean. Just…" Lyan shook his head. "I didn't sleep well, and I'm afraid. I need to have my wits, because…" He bit his lip. "Today I'll need them."

A chill ran down Cailean's spine. "Why?"

Lyan looked into his mug. "We will probably meet trouble today."

*Was that so hard to say, Lyan?* Cailean thought, exasperated. "I suppose the Mad God's champion plans to throw more men at us to test our new additions." That didn't explain why Lyan looked so miserable, though.

Lyan gulped down the contents of his mug and rose to refill it. Cailean watched him, the chill growing into a knot of worry in his gut. *He's almost acting like he feels guilty about something. Why would Lyan hide things from me?*

He wanted to demand an explanation, but pressing further would draw the attention of Nylas and his warriors. The last thing they needed was any sign of division between himself and Lyan, especially now that the Tathrens and the elves of Eilidh Wood were united in their distrust of the Lost elves.

Cailean rose to find Shiolto and learn the state of breakfast. Lyan stiffened. Cailean followed his gaze. He'd thought Lyan uneasy speaking to him, but when Nylas strode purposefully toward them, the astrologer visibly tensed.

Nylas ignored Cailean and scowled at Lyan. "So, what is the prediction for today, stargazer?"

Lyan held his mug like a protective talisman. "Rain."

Nylas glanced to the sky, clear with only wisps of clouds. "Rain. Is that all you have to say? My men are not on edge and worried because you predicted *rain* to them last night, Lyan."

Ihm and Pyrn joined them and stood to either side and slightly behind Lyan, watching Nylas warily.

"Cold, driving rain," Lyan said. "It will turn the ground to mud that grabs your feet and slows you. The darkness will make shadows look like solid things. The wind will make your arrows all but useless."

"And will we *need* our arrows?" Nylas demanded, stepping closer. Pyrn rested a hand on his weapon. Nylas ignored the unspoken warning.

"You'll wish you had them," Lyan said.

"Yet your prediction is *rain*?" Nylas loomed over him. "Not 'battle,' 'an ambush,' or just 'trouble'?"

Lyan raised his head to meet Nylas's icy blue eyes. "You expect battle, ambush, and trouble. It's the rain you aren't prepared for. And I don't want your fiddle ruined."

Nylas stopped. He searched for a retort, but finally whirled and left. Lyan's shoulders relaxed slightly.

"We're going to be attacked?" Ihm stared at Lyan. "Were you going to *tell* us?"

"I just did," Lyan said. He gulped down his tea, ignoring the worried looks cast toward him.

Kithr joined them. From his expression, he'd heard. To Cailean's surprise, he didn't voice any frustration over Lyan's announcement. "When should we expect the attack?"

"Sometime after the rain starts. I can't be more specific," Lyan replied. "I saw it last night." He paused, glanced around to see who was close enough to hear, then spoke in a low voice. "The Mad God's champion isn't sending more of his men to harry us. Today, he'll be there himself."

"Then we have a chance to stop him, here and now," Cailean said.

"He wouldn't come himself if he wasn't confident of victory, Cailean," Lyan said. "And he is very confident. If I thought we could avoid this encounter, I would try."

"We'll be prepared," Cailean said firmly. He fixed a pointed look on Lyan. "More prepared now that we know what we actually face."

Lyan's hands clenched, then relaxed. "Sometimes, being more prepared is worse in the end, Cailean. Sometimes, it's better to act before you think. It makes you less predictable."

"And this is one of those times?" Cailean asked, dubious. "It would be better to run blind into battle against the Mad God's champion?"

"Yes." Lyan glanced at the others, then met Cailean's gaze. "The champion can predict you, Cailean. He can predict all of us with a form of divination far more clear than astrology. He doesn't have to spend years learning how to interpret what he sees; he can take the answers he receives and act on them immediately. He knows that you will go to great lengths to protect your men. He knows Kithr's temper. He knows that I want to protect my friends, and he knows that if he can goad me into calling Equinox from the Shrine, the Mad God's minions can exploit the weaknesses in the defenses."

"But how does being less prepared thwart his plans?" Pyrn asked, frowning.

Lyan shivered, then answered. "We react differently when we're expecting an action than we do when we're not. And the stars tell me that most of the time, the actions you would take when you've had time to plan give the champion better opportunities to achieve his goals. Your reactions in the moment are less predictable, and right now, the less predictable we are, the better."

"So divination doesn't show everything," Cailean said.

Lyan shook his head. "It never has. It shows the most likely outcomes, based on the most likely actions taken and choices made."

"So can you give us any ideas?" Ihm asked. "If we can't prepare for whatever the champion is planning, is there something we *can* do?"

"Something you can do, Ihm? Not really, except remember that elven warriors tend to follow familiar tactics, which makes them—"

"Predictable, right." Ihm nodded.

Lyan continued. "Much of how the coming battle goes depends on Cailean and Solstice, and how well they trust each other."

Ihm looked confused. "Why wouldn't Cailean trust his weapon?"

*This again?* "I do trust Solstice, Lyan," Cailean said sharply.

Lyan didn't blink. "Does Solstice trust you?"

"Does that make sense to anyone else?" Ihm asked.

Kithr reached over and smacked the other elf in the back of the head. "If Lyan needed you to understand, he'd have told you."

"So it *does* make sense to someone, just not me," Ihm persisted.

Cailean shot the elf an irritated look. "Yes, Ihm, it does."

"Good, because Lyan was starting to sound almost as vague as the See—"

"Ihm, shut up," Pyrn interrupted. "Try being unpredictable by not spewing out every thought in your head."

Ihm's mouth snapped shut. He bowed his head. "Sorry."

"You can tell your men that we're facing the champion, Cailean. Kithr, Pyrn, Ihm, you can tell Declan and Seine."

"And Nylas?" Kithr asked.

"He knows we'll be fighting today. He doesn't need to know *who* we're going to face."

Even knowing that Lyan had a reason, vague though it was, Cailean stirred uneasily at the idea of intentionally withholding information from the majority of their warriors and from their leader. Kithr looked uncomfortable as well, but he didn't argue.

The small conference separated to break their fast. After eating, Kithr found Cailean again. "We should reach the main road sometime today. Might have to wait there to avoid attention."

Cailean nodded. The road would serve as a landmark, but traveling it would make them far too easy to find, as well as potentially endangering people who had no part in their fight. If the road was particularly busy, they could be forced to wait for nightfall before leaving cover. And not knowing when Lyan's predicted rain might arrive, he couldn't guess how far they would travel before coming under attack.

"We should leave soon," Cailean said.

"Agreed." Kithr raised his voice. "Pack up and move out!"

Cailean caught himself looking at the sky again, searching for rain clouds through the light canopy of yellow leaves.

Near midmorning, they entered a lightly wooded land that offered more shelter than the open grassland. The elves spread out accordingly, scouting for farms and other habitations.

One of Nylas's men spoke to Kithr, who nodded then waved for the elf to return to his post. The division between their groups grew less distinct as they all watched for enemies.

*Maybe a fight against a common enemy will do us good, and forge a sense of unity we lack.* Cailean rubbed the mare's neck.

Shiolto led the packhorses, Sai among them. The stallion carried a very light load, still healing from his injury. Dalrian and Yion both scouted, at Kithr's instruction. Aikan, as always, rode by Cailean.

Patch walked with Lyan, sometimes talking, sometimes quiet. Cailean puzzled over her presence. She'd obviously wanted to come with Nylas and the warriors, but he was still surprised that Nylas hadn't objected. The girl had an air of innocence at odds with the hardened elven warriors who had raised her. Innocence and wisdom, as if she understood some mystery hidden from the rest of the world.

*Perhaps she's been taking lessons in composure from Yion,* he thought with a silent laugh.

Dalrian interrupted Cailean's thoughts. "Kithr, there's a small village ahead—five houses. It's abandoned, and someone came through and burned the place to the timbers. No sign of anyone near now, and the buildings are barely smoldering. Pyrn says it's been a few days since the place was torched. Nothing salvageable left."

Kithr frowned and nodded. "Fane found a single cabin, also burned about the same time. Watch for tracks."

"We didn't find bodies. People had probably left already," Dalrian said. "Hard to say which way they went."

Cailean shivered and tugged his cloak over his shoulders. Small communities, isolated and undefended, were the first to suffer when war came. He hoped the peasants found refuge.

*I'm not sure whether to hope their homes were burned by the champion's forces, who are less likely to linger, or by one side or the other in the region's ongoing conflicts. At least the soldiers in the local unrest probably don't worship the Mad God.*

Early in the afternoon, they reached the road. Overhead, dark clouds gathered in the sky. Cailean looked up and down the wide road. It cut like a knife through the wooded land, defying its untamed surroundings. The paving stones were worn with ruts, telling of countless travelers who tread it. A road so obviously well-traveled stood barren at a time when farmers should be bringing goods to markets, travelers making journeys, stragglers hurrying to their homes before the storm struck, even soldiers marching to one battle or another.

*We could be the only people for miles, from the look of this. I know we must not be, but this is eerie.*

"Where is everyone?" Pyrn wondered aloud.

"Kithr. Smoke ahead," Nylas said, tone clipped and curt.

Cailean sniffed the air. Perhaps he only imagined the hint of wood smoke. *Someone else must be here.*

"It could be shelter from the rain," Declan said.

"Or bait," Nylas countered sharply.

"Then we'll take the bait expecting it to be trapped," Kithr ordered.

Nylas accepted the decision, though Cailean expected an argument. If he'd known they would face Murdo's champion, Nylas might not have consented so easily. With a curt nod, the elf took the lead. They crossed the road and returned quickly to the shelter of the trees. Cailean's back itched, and he expected an ambush to strike at any instant as they were exposed.

*I don't like this. It doesn't feel right.* Cailean gripped Solstice, and felt the Spear's worry to match his own.

Thunder rumbled overhead, then fat drops of rain began to fall. Tathrens and elves both cursed, pulling up hoods and hunching low as the air lost the last hints of warmth. They followed a trail barely wide enough for a wagon between the trees toward the smoke's source.

The trail opened into a man-made clearing. Under Cailean, Miska snorted, tossing her head, catching something in the air that she didn't like. The other horses caught her unease. Trees had been chopped down and lay in piles, awaiting use in the half-built huts around the clearing, attempts to add permanent shelters among a mass of wagons and rude tents. As Cailean entered, he only saw the shelters that formed the refugee camp. Then he realized what he really saw and stopped cold.

The rain washed much of the smoke from the air, but even in the growing downpour, Cailean smelled it. The unfinished huts smoldered and hissed as rain and fire fought, though the flames that licked at the timbers were dying. Dark shapes lay around their bases, and several dangled from a beam. Cailean swallowed the bile rising in his throat. Throughout the clearing, bodies lay scattered like broken dolls on the ground, their blood turning the puddles deep crimson. Some had probably died quickly, but the woman nearest to Cailean bore cuts and gashes all over her body, and her face twisted in a scream of agony, dead eyes open and staring into the sky.

Shiolto made a sound of horror, one hand rising to cover his mouth. "Who? Why?"

Kithr's gaze swept coldly over the sprawled corpses, then settled on the one unmarred building, a meeting hall. The door stood ajar, and shadows from inside flickered on the ground. "No shelter here," the elf said.

Outrage swept through Cailean. His hand ached from his grip on Solstice. The Spear's fury pulsed through his thoughts. Were these the same men who had razed the other village? Did the bodies of those helpless peasants lie here, among the other men, women, and children?

A scream of pain and fear rose from the meeting hall. Cailean jabbed his heels into his mount's side, urging her through the elves in front of him. Kithr seized the bridle. "Stop, Tathren," he ordered.

"I'm going in there!" Cailean snarled, jumping down to the ground in a splash of muddy water."

"Don't charge blindly into the trap," Kithr said coolly.

"You'll leave someone else to die like the rest of these people?" Cailean hissed.

"Captain, we shouldn't be here." Behind Cailean, Patch spoke in an urgent, frightened voice. "We should leave. We can still go. There's time, if we hurry." Then she drew a sudden, sharp breath and whispered, "No. It's too late."

The door crashed open, spilling light across the muddy, bloody clearing. A figure stood in the doorway, torchlight gleaming across his black cuirass. A shield hung on his left arm, and he carried a sword in his right. His head was uncovered, but with the light at his back, Cailean couldn't see his face. Undaunted by the warriors facing him, he strode into the center of the clearing.

"Is this your doing?" Cailean demanded, stepping forward. "Who are you?"

The armored figure stopped, then threw back his head and laughed. "You didn't tell them, Lyan? How kind of you not to spoil my entrance."

Cailean glanced over his shoulder at Lyan. The astrologer stood stock still, tension in every line of his body. "I know what you would have done as an 'entrance' if they expected you," Lyan said.

"A pity—I was looking forward to seeing them all thrashing in the bale vines."

The mocking voice was familiar, sending chills down Cailean's spine, but it was Dalrian who said the name, barely a whisper. "Torqual."

Another laugh. Smoldering fires flared to unnatural life, illuminating the clearing with flickering yellow light. Finally, Cailean saw the features of the armored man. Torqual's face was thinner than Cailean remembered, the shadows dark in his hollow cheeks. His eyes gleamed with arrogant confidence. His mouth curled in a sneer that Cailean remembered all too well. His blond hair was cut short, and he'd shaved his beard.

"Cailean, I'm glad you finally arrived. I suppose I should apologize for the accommodations—my men grew bored while we waited for you, and I had to allow them some entertainment. If you'd gotten here sooner, some of these refugees might still be here to greet you. We could have saved a few for your elven friends."

"You bastard," Cailean hissed.

"You knew quite well when to expect to see us, Torqual," Lyan interrupted. "If anything, we're earlier than you anticipated. So don't place blame on us for what you've done."

"Bold words from someone who didn't tell his 'friends' to expect a reunion," Torqual scoffed. "Such a secret to keep from them. Don't you *trust* them? And why do I only see one Spear, Lyan? Did you forget something?"

*This is what he was hiding. He knew Torqual was the champion, and he didn't tell us. Why did he keep this from us?*

A bowstring hummed, and an arrow flew at Torqual's face. Unflinching, he raised his blade and batted it aside, grinning. "Elves never change." He raised the sword. "My Lord, by the blood I have shed here in your name, grant me the power to show these pretenders your majesty!"

Cailean had never known that darkness could glow. A pulsing antithesis of light enveloped the sword, then radiated across Torqual's armor. The ground trembled, and the horses shrieked in terror. The air pulsed with force, and Cailean felt it trying to drive him to his knees. He staggered, bracing with his Spear.

*"Solstice, help us!"*

Solstice lashed out, reaching to the clouds and hurling a bolt of lightning at Torqual. The blinding flash slammed into a barrier. Torqual staggered back a step, but straightened again, unharmed.

"Do you really think it will be *that* easy to stop Murdo's champion, Cailean? The chosen warrior of the *true* Spearbearer?" He laughed scornfully.

"You should be dead already!" Cailean shouted. "You should have bled out in whatever dark hole you crawled into!"

"My god preserved me. He healed me, made me stronger, gave me his blessings. He granted me the blade Soulreaper to consume his enemies. He gave me a gift—the same gift he gave to Lyan. Tell me, Lyan, do you enjoy it as much as I do?" Torqual's teeth gleamed in a wicked grin.

"*You* still talk too much," Kithr said icily.

Despite the rain and the wind, the elven arrows soared for Torqual like a flock of crows. Torqual swept his sword through the air before him, and a burst of darkness rose to meet them. Arrows shattered and splintered. Then Torqual sprang forward, moving far faster across the swampy ground than a man in full armor should. Cailean shoved forward, raising Solstice to meet the attack, but Torqual veered to the left, lunging into the midst of the elven warriors instead.

Elves fell back, drawing blades as Torqual stabbed and slashed. The black sword tore across the chest of a scarred elf whose name Cailean didn't know. The elf fell with a scream, jerking and twisting on the ground. Dark tendrils flowed like smoke from the wound to the blade.

"Is this the best you can do?" Torqual mocked. His blade swept in a slash through the air. Black spines burst from the muddy ground to stab at the elves.

Warriors shouted in alarm and sprang away. The undergrowth around the edge of the clearing knit together in a wall, blocking the spines as the elves scrambled aside. Even the trees leaned down, offering their branches. Warriors leapt from the ground, accepting the shelter.

Torqual sneered. "Go ahead, hide. Abandon your companions. Elves are good at that, aren't they?"

Cailean rushed at Torqual. Torqual spun, meeting the attack and deflecting Solstice with his shield. The last time Cailean had seen Torqual, the traitor had been bleeding from a spear wound to the gut and a bone-deep gash in his sword arm. Now he moved as if he'd never been injured, as if he had been trained by the greatest swordsmen in the world. Cailean parried a numbing slash. Solstice poured fury into him, replacing weariness with rage.

He sensed a presence on his right. A quick glance showed Aikan beside him, glaring at Torqual. Cailean smiled faintly, glad to have his steward at his side.

Torqual laughed. "Ever your master's loyal dog, Aikan." He raised his voice. "Leave the Spearbearer to me. Take care of the rabble however you like."

"The 'rabble' is more than a match for whatever ditch waste you've collected," Aikan retorted.

"So *you* are the Mad God's champion, Torqual? He couldn't do better than a second-rate traitorous gate guard?" Cailean demanded.

"My lord saw potential in me that you could never imagine!" Torqual roared. His next swing missed Cailean, but carved a gouge in the ground between them. He swung the shield at Aikan, forcing the older man back a step. "And he has given me gifts the likes of which you could never *dream*! He has given me the Soulreaper." He raised the black blade, letting light shine off the blade. "He bid me use it on the Spearbearers. But don't worry—I won't *kill* you, Cailean." The sickening smirk. "Not immediately, at least."

"You think *you* can defeat *me*, Torqual?" Cailean jabbed at Torqual's stomach, and was rewarded with a momentary flash of alarm in Torqual's eyes as he blocked.

Torqual recovered as if the lapse had never happened. "You don't think I can? Why don't you ask Lyan, then? Ask what *he* has seen coming from this battle. Perhaps he knows something else he doesn't want to tell you."

Despite himself, Cailean glanced back. He caught a glimpse of Lyan's expression, a mixture of fear and guilt, and then Torqual's foot hooked Cailean's, and he was falling to the blood-soaked, muddy ground.

## 22

### KITHR

*"Blood and rain. I know, that sounds like the end of some tragic ballad.
But you asked what I remember about that day, and that is the only
answer I can give. Blood… and rain."*

**I**should have killed that son of a dog when I had the chance! As
Cailean tripped and fell, Kithr drew his bow and let an
arrow fly at Torqual's smug face.

Torqual half-turned, raising his shield to block, and
laughed. "Is that all you can do, Kithr? You didn't expect *that*
to work, did you?"

Kithr didn't respond. He didn't need to—the arrow had
served its purpose. Cailean rolled aside and pushed back to his
feet, guarded by Aikan. *Just because you somehow know it's coming,
Torqual, doesn't mean you don't have to defend yourself. You talk too
much. In fact, anyone who can talk as much as you do in the middle of a
swordfight isn't even trying. You're playing. This is a game to you.*

"Keep that piece of dog meat busy," he ordered in Elven.
"If we can kill him, we can finish this right now."

Ihm cursed as the wind sent his arrow off mark. "We can rush him," he said, reaching for his blade.

"No!" The response, sharp and urgent, came from Lyan. "His blade. Keep away from it, whatever you do."

The curling tendrils of black mist radiating from Torqual's sword gave Kithr reason enough to keep his distance. He wasn't sure what magic resided in the blade, but Torqual had killed one of Nylas's soldiers with a blow that should barely have slowed the warrior. Cailean made full use of the greater reach of Solstice to keep Torqual back, equally wary of the weapon.

*He has us on the defensive. He's only one man, even if he is a dung-eating champion of Murdo. Why aren't we attacking him? Why am I not attacking him?*

Kithr watched Torqual wield his sword effortlessly and recognized the sensation crawling in his gut: fear. He'd felt the same fear months earlier when he and Lyan were attacked by reapers, demonic minions of the Mad God. Now it rooted his feet to the muddy ground and threw off his aim.

"He's not alone," Lyan warned.

Kithr tore his gaze from the traitor. Shadows moved near the buildings, circling toward them. Torqual was arrogant, but unfortunately, not an idiot.

*He probably already has men in the forest working to surround us.*

"Stop anyone from leaving that building!" Kithr ordered sharply over the storm. "Nylas, Patch, find anyone nearby who's not one of us and keep them busy!" Manipulating the plants would occupy both Nylas and the girl to the exclusion of most anything else, but they had the best chance of finding men creeping through the shadows. "Splinter, do something about those spikes and thorns."

A volley of arrows flew, some for Torqual, some for the silhouettes at the door of the hall. The light from the fires offered unnaturally strong illumination in the midst of the sheeting rain, but it also added dancing shadows, and Kithr couldn't be sure how many shafts found their targets. Torqual raised his shield to protect his head, and let the rest of the arrows strike where they would.

Nylas's warriors spread around the clearing. Kithr heard sounds of fighting as they encountered Torqual's men. A few shadows moved toward Kithr and Lyan's position, but someone dispatched them with swift efficiency before they got close.

*I should be in battle with them, not just watching!* But someone had to take command, and he'd already given Nylas orders.

The mud grew deeper. Torqual, Cailean, and Aikan were splattered as they circled and jabbed at openings. Cailean and Aikan fought in comfortable synchronism, despite Torqual's unnatural speed and strength. Cailean slipped, but Aikan lunged, drawing Torqual's attention before the armored man could strike.

"Nylas! If there are roots, try and trip up the bastard in armor!" Kithr shouted, hoping Nylas wasn't already so entangled in the forest that he didn't hear.

His yell received no response, and might not have reached Nylas at all. Kithr cursed and angrily shoved soaked hair from his eyes. With a sharp gesture, he signaled the end of the ineffective volleys of arrows. With the wind and rain, they were as likely to accidentally hit Cailean and Aikan as they were to score a strike on Torqual, and no more shadows advertised themselves in the lit doorway across the clearing.

"Declan! Find out the situation in that hall. Shiolto, Dalrian, go with him. And you as well!" He gestured to the nearest clump of Nylas's men. "Free any prisoners, if possible. If you can find a way, burn it!"

"*Burn* it?" Shiolto burst incredulously, startled from his gaping at the battle between Cailean and Torqual. "In *this*?"

"The other buildings are on fire, aren't they? Figure out how," Kithr snapped, though he knew the answer almost certainly involved magic.

He drew three arrows and loosed them in rapid succession at Torqual. One bounced off Torqual's black cuirass, another missed completely, but the third caught in a joint at the top of his left greave. The arrow snapped when Torqual shifted his footing, and Kithr hoped that the barbed iron head managed to work its way to skin. An annoyance could become a distraction, and a distraction to Torqual was an advantage to them.

Torqual turned toward Kithr with a sneer and crooked one finger like a lord summoning a peasant.

Kithr's lips curled back in a snarl. "Are you challenging me, Tathren?" He slung his bow and jerked his sword from its scabbard.

"Kithr, don't!" Lyan said urgently.

Torqual swung his shield at Cailean's face, making the Tathren lord stagger back. Rather than pursue the advantage, Torqual spun and slammed the blade down into the mud. "My lord, show these fools the power you have given me!"

Writhing black tendrils burst through the mud, swarming toward Kithr. He raised his sword in a token acknowledgment to defense and lunged forward.

Someone seized his arm in an iron grip and threw him out of the path of the tendrils. Kithr landed hard with a splash, the wind knocked from him. He gasped for breath and swallowed a mouthful of water that tasted of mud and the coppery tang of blood. The mass of tendrils whipped out as they reached the spot where Kithr had stood, snatching at anything near them. Screams of pain rose over the roar of the storm, then the Splinter's shout of outrage. The ground trembled as a tangle of tree roots tore apart the writhing mass. For a moment, Kithr sensed Eilidh Wood. The sensation vanished as the roots dragged the tendrils into the earth.

Kithr struggled to get his feet under him. Cold water soaked through to his skin. A firm, strong hand pressed against his chest as a figure loomed over him. Light caught the gleam of red eyes. Praett spoke in his ear as the pooka leaned over him. "Torqual wishes my master alive, Kithr—alive and suffering. He feels no such inclination toward preserving *your* life. In fact, he would love to see you dead at his feet, because he knows what it would do to my master."

Kithr coughed and gasped, finally hissing breathless words. "So why don't *you* stop him?"

The pooka effortlessly hauled him to his feet. "If I could, I would already have done so," he said grimly. "The Mad God protects his champion, and the magic shielding him inflicts debilitating pain on those who are directly bound to our gods the closer we are to Torqual. I *could* attack him, but I would fail, and my death would accomplish nothing but to leave my master with one less protector." Praett spoke quickly. "For that same reason, Saiboti's champion cannot confront the traitor directly."

"Where is Yion?" Kithr demanded. "And *you* can see him, even if Lyan can't?"

"I can. He attempted to move into position to attack, and was disabled by the magic I spoke of. I was able to move him away so he could recover." Praett gestured toward the nearby trees, pulling Kithr with him.

"Let go of me," Kithr ordered, trying to pull from the pooka's iron grip.

Metal crashed against metal as Torqual blocked Cailean's attack, returning Torqual's attention to the Spearbearer before he launched another attack at Kithr. Praett's grip didn't loosen. "So you can charge into battle and die?"

"I have to do *something*, dammit!"

"Then do what he does not expect," the pooka said. As suddenly as he had appeared, he vanished, leaving Kithr standing alone.

*Do what he doesn't expect.* Lyan had said something similar not so many days ago, and Kithr had accused him of talking like Torqual. *Were you warning me, Lyan? Did you tell me who we would face, and I ignored it? What won't Torqual expect of me, of elves?*

"Yion! Are you near?" Kithr said.

"I am." The mercenary's voice was thin and strained. He staggered away from a tree, catching himself against another.

"How serious?" Kithr asked quickly. Yion moved like a man bleeding to death.

"It is pain only, no wound. I will recover," Yion answered, though the tremble of his voice undermined his attempt to dismiss the matter.

"Good." He didn't curse aloud, didn't voice the frustration as he recognized that, for once, Yion was in no condition to fight. "Get back to the others. We have to…" The word tasted bitter in his mouth. "Withdraw."

Yion didn't argue. Kithr half-ran across the mud-slick ground to Lyan. The bodies of three elves sprawled in the mud, their faces contorted in pain though their bodies showed no wounds. *You will pay for their deaths, Torqual. I swear it. Not today, but you will pay.*

Lyan grabbed his arm. "Keep away from him, Kithr. Don't listen to Torqual."

"Sorry. It was stupid of me."

Lyan shook his head. "Worse. It's what he wanted you to do."

"Then let's try something he doesn't expect." Kithr turned toward a figure crouched on the ground, hands pressed to the earth and apparently oblivious to the cold and rain. "Nylas or Patch, tell Declan to pull back here! If they can't burn the hall, leave it."

The figure lifted her head slightly and answered, her voice distracted. "They are coming. We are leaving? We should. We should leave now. I will tell the Captain."

Kithr looked at her sharply. "Isn't he with you?"

"He is near," she promised.

"Have his men pull back into the trees." He didn't need to tell them how to deal with pursuers.

"They will do so," Patch said. She stood, put her fingers to her lips, and blew a sharp whistle. Kithr heard the whistle repeated back from other ends of the clearing.

Cailean jabbed at Torqual. Torqual deflected the blow, but Solstice tore a gouge across the black armor. The combatants backed apart.

"Cailean! Back to the trees!" Kithr yelled.

He didn't hear any response, but Cailean and Aikan backed further from Torqual.

Torqual sneered. "Giving up, milord? Going to hide with the elves and hope none slit your throat for a chance to claim Solstice?" His voice carried through the clearing.

Cailean's steps faltered. Aikan said something, and Cailean's head jerked in a nod. They continued their cautious retreat. For reasons Kithr couldn't guess, Torqual didn't pursue.

Beside Kithr, Lyan's gaze fixed on Cailean. "Trust him. Please trust him," he whispered.

"Trust who? Aikan?" Kithr whispered back.

"Cailean. Solstice, please trust Cailean."

*Cailean never answered when Lyan asked him before.*

"You and I both know Nylas would rather impale your head on a pike, Cailean!" Torqual took two long steps toward Cailean. "Kithr's no better."

"If I take any heads, yours will be the first, not his."

Kithr hadn't seen Nylas lying in wait among the bodies of the slaughtered refugees. Clearly, neither had Torqual. He jerked away in surprise when Nylas sprang to a crouch, but not before Nylas stabbed a slim blade into the back of his leg, where the sabaton didn't cover. The champion roared in fury and pain. Nylas rolled away from Torqual's wild, reflexive swing.

The ground trembled. Nylas splashed to his feet and shot a glare at Cailean and Aikan. "*Move*, Tathrens!"

Torqual's men abandoned their pursuit of the elves, retreating toward the hall. Spikes and black tendrils erupted from the ground around Torqual. Nylas, Cailean, and Aikan dodged away from them. Some of Torqual's men weren't quick enough. A tendril seized one man's ankle and flung him onto an impaling spike. Kithr couldn't tell whether any elves had been caught. He tensed, ready to rush from cover should he see any of their people get tangled. Cailean and Aikan reached the trees, but he didn't see where Nylas had gone.

Arrows flew from Kithr's left. At least one found flesh, sinking into Torqual's leg. Torqual's eyes burned with fury. He pointed his sword at the trees from which the shafts had flown. Branches erupted in flames. Elves screamed.

"I'll burn you out like rats!"

"If he can do that, why didn't he before?" Kithr hissed, scrambling toward the burning trees.

"Because he didn't want to make her mad," Lyan answered.

"Who—" Kithr started to ask.

The sense of Eilidh Wood's presence drove him to his knees. The Splinter stepped from between two burning trees. Sparks smoldered in her hair, and she swept them away with a sharp motion, then raised her hands toward the sky. The ground buckled. Hundreds of roots burst through the mud. The plants surrounding the burning trees swarmed together into a smothering wall to envelop the flames.

In the clearing, someone climbed to their feet. Kithr saw Nylas raising his hands in mirror to the Splinter's. Around the elf, plants lashed at Torqual's black tendrils, ripping them from the ground.

"What is he doing?" Kithr hissed.

Behind him, Patch spoke urgently. "I cannot break him from her hold!"

"The Splinter is controlling Nylas?"

"She will use any tools available to her," Lyan said softly. "Even him."

*The Lost are tools to her.* "Keep trying!" Kithr yelled to Patch.

Torqual's gaze moved between the Splinter and Nylas, and he backed warily away from their plants. Black spikes formed a wall between him and the Splinter. Her expression twisted in fury, and her plants attacked the barrier. Nylas's gaze followed Torqual, and creeping vines swarmed across the ground to seize Torqual's ankles.

*This could be our chance to strike.* Kithr looked to Lyan. "Lyan. Do we attack while he's distracted or withdraw?"

Lyan watched Torqual slash through the vines. "Withdraw," he said.

Nylas stumbled. His hands clenched in fists and he shot a baleful glare toward the Splinter.

"Patch, do you have Nylas?" Kithr demanded.

"He is in control of himself," she answered, relief evident in her voice.

Kithr saw Nylas withdrawing to the far end of the clearing. Other than the Splinter and their fallen, all of their people had found shelter in the trees. He should have felt relief, but tension held Kithr.

Torqual smirked. "Well, Lyan, it looks like you managed to pull the right strings to get your friends out of reach. Does my lord's gift tell you what happens next?"

Lyan's hands clenched. Kithr rested a hand on his shoulder. "What do we need to do, Lyan?" Kithr asked in a low voice.

"We need to leave, now," Lyan whispered.

"Solstice!" Torqual shouted, his gaze raking the dark trees. "You really think these *elves* can keep Equinox out of my lord's reach? Go on, run away. I'll gladly deliver your brother to Murdo."

Lyan stiffened and bolted in the direction Kithr had last

seen Cailean and Aikan. Kithr followed, but the appearance of a second figure with Torqual gave him pause. The newcomer wore no armor and bore only a long, serrated knife in his hand. Torqual raised his shield to protect the newcomer from any arrows that might fly.

"Who is—?" Kithr started to ask, but Lyan was already ahead of him. Kithr hissed a curse and pulled an arrow from his quiver.

The new man bent and scooped up a handful of mud. Torqual stepped between him and the trees, blocking Kithr's view. He didn't see whatever the knife-wielder did, though a grimace of pain flashed briefly over Torqual's face. The knife-wielder tossed something to the ground, and shadows swarmed to it, forming a shape that grew to the size of a man, then larger, until it towered over Torqual and his companion.

"What in rot is *that*?" Kithr whispered, stepping back involuntarily.

"Nothing I want to fight." Declan had reached his side. "Couldn't burn the hall, sorry. Found a handful of prisoners and brought them along." He wiped a streak of blood from his forehead. "Took care of a few of the champion's men."

"Good." Kithr blew a sharp whistle, trusting that their people either knew the signal or could figure it out.

He heard Aikan speaking in a low voice as he neared Cailean and Lyan. "My lord, you know full well that I would not say this if the situation were not dire, but I agree with Lyan."

Cailean scowled, but conceded. "Fine. We'll just let Torqual gloat."

"He can gloat from a distance, or he can gloat over our corpses. I prefer the former," Aikan said.

Cailean cast a glare toward Torqual, took in the looming shape, and finally nodded.

"Follow me," Kithr ordered, getting their attention.

"What is that thing?" Aikan demanded as they withdrew.

"A construct made with Torqual's blood and the Mad God's magic," Lyan answered, urging them faster.

"It's large, dangerous, and under our enemy's control. That's all I need to know right now," Kithr said. The shadows and rain made it impossible to tell if everyone had heeded the signal to withdraw, but he heard movement in the forest around them. He also heard heavy steps behind them and felt the ground tremble.

Lyan, Cailean, and Aikan followed him through the trees. Kithr wasn't sure exactly where the road was, but neither was he sure he wanted to leave the shelter of the forest for the exposed road.

*I don't care if staying in the trees is what Torqual would expect of me. I won't expose us to unnecessary danger just because it's the less sensible decision to make.*

Seine joined them. "Kithr! That construct is immune to arrows. Not even hits to the head or the eyes slow it. It crushed one of Nylas's men, nearly grabbed a couple more."

*Can we even elude it? Constructs don't tire.* Kithr glanced to Lyan, hoping for ideas.

"Still running, milord Cailean?"

Kithr spun. Torqual's voice sounded like it spoke from just over his shoulder, but he saw no one.

Lyan grabbed Cailean's arm, all but dragging him along, away from the clearing. "He's trying to lure you back. Don't listen to him!"

Torqual continued. "Is *this* your bearer, Solstice? A soft, weak noble who scurries off and cowers away from a real fight?

Cailean stopped in his tracks, face twisting in fury.

"This isn't the time, Cailean," Kithr hissed. Behind them, the crashing in the trees grew closer.

"This is the *only* time!" Cailean snarled. His eyes looked almost black, and Kithr was sure it wasn't a trick of the shadows. "If you won't help kill him, then get out of the way."

"I want that treacherous son of a blight rat dead as much as you do," Kithr snapped. "But I don't want it to happen over the corpses of your men! And if you hadn't noticed, something *large* and *angry* very much wants to start making more corpses!"

"Solstice, please," Lyan said. "I won't let him reach Equinox."

Cailean's gaze flickered to Lyan, then over the warriors around them. Kithr saw more of them now as the elves gathered defensively around them, ready to enter futile battle if necessary. When Cailean spoke, he sounded more like himself. "We won't outrun that thing. We need to move faster."

Solstice glowed faintly in Cailean's hand. Kithr felt pressure build in the air and realized Cailean's intent. "Are we all near enough? Can you actually move everyone, Cailean?"

"Everyone who matters."

He had only heartbeats to realize it hadn't been Cailean, but the other presence who answered. Then he was flung into darkness.

Vertigo and nausea knocked Kithr off his feet as the world returned. He fell to the muddy ground, reeling. "What do you mean, 'everyone who matters'?" he demanded, turning to either side in search of Cailean.

Beside him, Lyan retched. Shiolto, Dalrian, Aikan, and Yion showed varying degrees of misery from the abrupt jump through darkness. The others, including three human women and two human men he didn't recognize, staggered or retched. Only the Splinter appeared unaffected.

"Where's Lord Cailean?" Dalrian asked, alarmed.

Kithr found his feet, shivering with a chill unrelated to the frigid damp. "He didn't. Blight and rot, he didn't." He turned to Lyan. "Tell me he didn't stay behind."

Lyan rose, arms wrapped tight around himself as he shivered. "It wasn't Cailean who decided. It was Solstice." He met Kithr's eyes. "Solstice, who doesn't trust us and who didn't wait to be sure everyone was within his reach."

"What?" demanded Aikan. He looked around sharply. "He wouldn't! Where is Lord Cailean? Someone get my horse!"

"Who's missing?" Kithr raised his voice to be heard by everyone. "And where in blight are we?"

"The Captain was outside the reach of the magic," Patch said. She shot a glower at the Splinter. "Though he would have been near enough if he hadn't been forced to follow another's whim."

"So he's still back in the clearing, or near it?" Kithr asked. "How far?"

She pointed south-east. "Twenty, perhaps twenty-five miles."

He should consider them lucky not to have been sent halfway to the Shrine of Equinox, but Kithr still cursed.

"Sir, in addition to those confirmed fallen during the fight, we're missing Captain Nylas and six warriors." He didn't know the name of the warrior who gave him the report.

Shiolto brought Aikan's horse. The older man climbed into the saddle with more haste than grace.

Kithr started to ask what he thought he was doing, but Lyan gripped his arm and spoke first. "You're riding ahead, Aikan?"

Aikan paused, but only for a moment. "I will not leave my lord to face that traitor alone."

Lyan nodded. "We'll follow as quickly as possible." He pointed southward. "You'll find the road that way. It'll get you back faster."

Aikan gazed at him, then gave a curt nod. "Don't dally."

Kithr glanced to Lyan as the horse splashed through the mud at a quick walk. "Shouldn't someone go with him?"

Lyan shook his head. "Not this time."

Patch watched Aikan, then looked at Lyan with a small frown. "Cousin."

"It's his decision, Patch."

"Form up," Kithr ordered. Much as he wanted to press for the meaning of that ominous yet vague statement, they didn't have time. "Patch, lead the way. We're going back, and unlike Solstice, I'm not leaving anyone behind."

23

CAILEAN

*The warrior must trust the weapon, as the weapon must trust the*
*warrior.*
*~Tathren proverb*

R ain spattered Cailean's head. The crashing drew closer. He waited. Solstice hummed in his hands, radiating fury.

Torqual, the traitor, would die.

Branches splintered as a hulking shape formed of shadow and mud stomped toward him. It paused only a moment upon seeing him, then raised a massive fist to slam down on him.

Cailean braced Solstice. The Spear flared with light that condensed into a single, brilliant beam. The light pierced the construct's head. The hulk gave a groan like falling rocks and dissolved into soggy debris.

"Your pathetic toy broke, Torqual," Cailean called. "Come face me yourself."

Torqual's mocking laughter echoed between the trees.

"Oh, you're not going to scurry off after all? Well then, milord, I'm right here, awaiting you."

The sound of his voice filled Cailean with blind rage. He didn't remember charging back to the clearing, though his burning lungs and aching legs said he must have done so. He didn't see anything beyond Torqual, smug and confident despite the blood that oozed through the joints of his armor and trailed down his leg. Nothing mattered more than Torqual's death.

*Die, traitor!*

He must have spoken the words, because Torqual grinned. "Traitor? You're the one who betrayed your true bearer, Solstice."

A scream of fury rose from Cailean's throat. He lunged.

Torqual blocked with his shield, and Solstice sank deep into the wood. Torqual released the shield, leaving it impaled on the head of the Spear. Ignoring the obstruction, Cailean lunged at him again. Torqual continued to give ground, but never lost the smug smirk.

Sharp pain stabbed into Cailean's right leg and something stopped his advance. Snarling in anger, he glanced down.

His focus on Torqual had been so complete, he'd given no heed to the swarms of spined tendrils. One gripped his leg, digging the thorns into his skin. Torqual stopped, his smirk growing. He raised one hand, and more tendrils rose around Cailean.

He slashed at them, but the wreckage of Torqual's shield crippled the blow's effectiveness. Tendrils seized his arms, their spines drawing blood. Cailean thrashed and struggled.

Torqual raised his glowing black blade and pointed it at Cailean. "How long can you protect your bearer from Soulreaper, Solstice? If I bid the sword to drink his essence, how long can you keep him alive, screaming in agony? Shall we find out?"

Cailean roared in pain and anger. Solstice flared with

light. The grip of the tendrils weakened, then gave way. He jerked free. Another pulse of the Spear's power, and the tendrils crumbled like rotten wood. He raised Solstice and lunged at Torqual again.

The world lurched sideways and spun. Cailean stumbled and fell to his hands and knees, gasping. He couldn't see straight.

"Oh, my apologies, milord. Did I fail to mention that balevines are poisonous? But not to worry. I'm sure Solstice will counter the poison before it stops your lungs completely."

Each breath grew harder, heavier. Cailean clutched Solstice, willing his arm to rise and impale Torqual. The limb would not obey. Solstice screamed in wordless fury within his mind, but Cailean couldn't even draw breath enough to voice it.

His vision grew dark. Cailean's arms buckled and he fell into the mud. His lungs burned. As his last precious gasp of air escaped, Cailean heard Torqual's mocking laughter.

Sweat dripped down Cailean's face and stung his eyes. An attempt to wipe it away sent pain burning through his arms and shoulders. He gasped for breath, and drew in air tainted with smoke and the scent of blood. His head pounded. Though he heard a voice, the words were an indistinguishable garble of noise.

He knelt on a wooden floor. His arms were bound behind his back and pulled upward at an angle that left him bowed forward in futile effort to ease the strain. His legs were bound as well, though the pulsing pain in his right thigh would probably have prevented him from standing even if the ropes had not. Chill air raised goosebumps on his bare arms and back.

Cailean raised his head and looked up into Torqual's smirking face.

Blind fury surged through him. An inarticulate sound of anger rose from his throat. Cailean lunged at him.

Pain flared in his arms and shoulders again, turning his sound of rage into one of pain.

Torqual chuckled. "Tsk, tsk, Solstice. You're going to break him if you keep that up." He still wore the black armor, though he'd cleaned off the mud and blood.

*Solstice.* Cailean's hands twitched, gripping at the air.

Nothing happened.

Torqual chuckled again. "Trying to call the Spear, Cailean? That won't work. You and Solstice are both within restraining wards. You can call all you like; Solstice can't answer."

Cailean snarled. "You're no mage."

Torqual smirked. "I don't have to be, when my lord has provided his priests to take care of such things. So try however much you want. The Spear's powers are beyond your reach. Although it seems its ability to manipulate you remains intact. Do you even know how completely under its hold you are?"

"Lies!"

"Oh? You never even saw the balevines until they seized you. I doubt you ever noticed my men surrounding us."

The fight with Torqual was a blur of confusion driven by rage. Cailean glared at Torqual in silence.

"I hope you aren't expecting someone to sweep in to free you. Solstice already took care of *that.*" Torqual chuckled. "Do you even know where you sent them?"

"Sent who?" Cailean growled. "What are you talking about?"

"I'm talking about Solstice's teleportation trick. You used it to send your men and the elves elsewhere."

A chill ran down his spine. He couldn't remember doing so, but Torqual's words felt true. *What happened? Solstice?*

A cold smile formed on Torqual's lips. "You don't remember, do you? Solstice doesn't trust you at all, it seems." He leaned closer, as if to whisper in Cailean's ear. "Solstice sent them far beyond reach. They couldn't help you now even if they wanted to. And after what you did, I wouldn't be sure they *do* want to."

"You're lying!"

"Am I? Ask the Spear yourself, then."

A mud-spattered man approached. "Champion, what should we do with the bodies of the elves?"

Torqual turned and straightened. "Be certain they're dead. Cut off the heads. Leave the corpses to rot."

"Yes sir." The man tromped away.

"It seems I must attend to other matters for a little while. Make yourself comfortable, Cailean." Torqual reached over and gave a sharp tug on a taut rope tied to a ring on the floor. It jerked Cailean's arms higher for an agonizing moment, drawing a choked cry of pain.

Torqual left him. Cailean panted for breath. Sweat dripped down his face. *"He's lying. He's trying to make me doubt. Isn't he, Solstice?"*

He felt the Spear's presence, but Solstice didn't answer. Cailean closed his eyes and tried to focus. *"Solstice, I know Torqual is lying."*

Guilt. It washed over Cailean as fiercely as the rage he'd felt earlier. He gasped, sagging under the force of it.

*"Solstice, tell me that isn't true!"* He nearly screamed the words aloud. *"Answer me, damn you!"*

*"I sent them away, and let them think you intended to go with them."* The Spear's voice was a whisper in his mind. *"Torqual did not lie."*

*"Didn't lie about that, or didn't lie about any of it?"* Cailean demanded.

Solstice didn't answer.

Cailean gritted his teeth and raised his head again. Lamps

lit the building, throwing amber glow over the blood-stained wooden floor. The air smelled of smoke, unwashed bodies, and death. Whatever furnishings the building might have held had been stripped away, replaced by crates and bags, presumably the supplies needed to feed Torqual's followers. Or maybe what remained of those gathered by the refugees, assuming he was still in the clearing, and this was the hall.

He was restrained near the center of the hall. The rope pulling his arms at their unnatural angle looped over a low, thick ceiling beam. The floor around him was scored with jagged, twisting symbols. The longer he looked at them, the harder his head pounded, as if they rejected his efforts to read them.

Twisting his head to see as much of the building as he could, Cailean couldn't find Solstice, though he knew the Spear lay near. Near, yet out of reach.

*"Was anyone else captured? Did I send everyone else to safety?"* A second, chilling implication of Torqual's taunt hit him. *"Did I send them to safety, Solstice? Where are they?"*

*"I do not know,"* Solstice finally admitted. A pause, then, *"I might not have taken all the elves."*

Cailean stiffened. *"What?"*

*"Some may have been outside my reach. I'm not sure."*

*"You 'may' have left some people behind to be murdered by Torqual and his lackeys?"*

Solstice didn't answer.

A stab of pain without source ran through Cailean's leg. He gasped with a sharp cry, and felt an echo of it from Solstice.

A tall, thin man in red shirt and black pants walked to Cailean and looked him over, lip curling in a sneer. "Your bearer leaves much to be desired, Solstice. If you wish to keep him intact, you'd be wise not to test your bonds again."

"What did you do?" Cailean snarled.

The man chuckled. "I did nothing but craft the wards as

my lord instructed me. Solstice chose to test them. And you—you are but the Spear's minion, the recipient of the punishment my lord inflicts until you bow before him."

"I *will* never bow to Murdo," Cailean growled.

"All will bow to him, in time. Even the false Spearbearers."

A shout rose from outside. Cailean looked toward the sound and saw two men helping a third inside. The third man clutched his stomach, blood flowing between his fingers.

Torqual followed them in, giving the wounded man a look of disdain. "I told you to ensure the elves were dead first." He gestured.

The red-shirted man before Cailean strode to the door. The wounded man shied back, but his comrades practically shoved him to the other. The red-shirted man caught him easily and looked to Torqual.

"There was an elf, Champion?"

"One of them was still alive. He's not any longer. Take care of this one."

"Of course, Champion."

The wounded man's eyes went wide in panic. "No, please, don't let him take me! It's not bad! I'll be all right!"

Torqual just laughed. "Your life is as cheap as a two-copper whore. Your death, however—now *that* will be worth something."

A second figure in red and black joined them. He was taller than Torqual and shaved bald. Jagged, twisting tattoos crawled across his scalp. He took the wounded man's free arm, and with his companion pulled the bleeding man toward a far corner of the hall.

Cailean stared at him. Gold hoops pierced long, pointed, decidedly elven ears. An elf, here, among Torqual's people.

Steps on the floor drew his attention quickly back. Torqual returned to smirk at him. "I see you have met my lord's priests."

"An *elf* serves as a priest of the Mad God?"

"Not merely 'an elf', milord. One of the Faithful. An elf who knows the god he truly follows. Perhaps he will oversee, once they complete their rituals. Do pardon my abrupt departure earlier. Rest assured, you have my full attention now."

"Done murdering and pillaging already?" Cailean glared at him.

"The elves are dead. My men can put their heads on pikes without guidance. Rather careless of Solstice to leave them behind. Or was it intentional?"

"What do you want, Torqual?" Cailean demanded.

A metal-clad fist struck him across the face. "You're not giving orders here, Cailean. As for what I want? I want to watch you suffer."

Cailean reeled, but refused to bow. "You think you can do worse than Porephyn?" He'd faced capture and torture before.

Torqual smiled. "I'm sure of it. An interesting tidbit, not widely known. The Spears can feel pain, after a fashion. And the pain they feel, they share with their bearers." Torqual turned to someone outside Cailean's line of sight and nodded.

"*No. Stop!*" Solstice shouted in Cailean's mind.

Pain slammed into him like a lance through his chest. Cailean gasped, doubling over as far as the ropes allowed. His shoulders screamed in strain. "What did you…"

"*I* haven't done anything yet. My lord's priests, on the other hand…"

A man screamed in agony and terror. A fresh bolt of agony stabbed through Cailean. He writhed, straining against his bonds.

"It works both ways, of course," Torqual continued. "The Spear feels your pain too. Do you know what it will take to break him, Solstice?"

Anger laced with pain ran through Cailean. His lips curled back in a snarl.

"Such outrage. But really, Solstice, it's not as if Cailean

has anything to commend him. I know you don't trust him; really, why would you? He's done nothing to earn the right to wield you. He couldn't even stop Porephyn from cursing him, and nearly lost you to Ewart. He can't be bothered to understand the proper connection between Spear and bearer. He doesn't even listen until you shout. Trust Cailean?" Torqual laughed. "See what good trusting him did for his men."

Cailean's hands clenched into fists. "Trusting me did them far more good than trusting *you* ever did." He hated and feared the doubt that Torqual's taunts roused.

Torqual raised an eyebrow in mock surprise. "Oh? Lyan hasn't told you, then? Shame on him, keeping secrets from his friends."

"They're his to keep." He refused to give Torqual the satisfaction of any other answer.

"Are they? Even when they mean life or death to someone else? Truly, Lyan uses my lord's gift so poorly. You'd think he didn't appreciate it."

"The only person to benefit from a 'gift' from the Mad God is Murdo." Pain made Cailean's voice tight and strained.

"Oh, but I've found the visions most helpful indeed," Torqual countered. "A pity Lyan does not." He looked past Cailean and nodded. "I should thank that elf outside. He made the choice of a sacrifice much easier. Go ahead."

Cailean braced at those words. Pain smashed into him like a crushing boulder. He thrashed, gasping as agony drove breath from his lungs. Something in his left shoulder shifted and tore, drawing a choked scream.

The torment lasted an eternity, Solstice's pain and his own echoing each other until it finally overwhelmed him.

Cold water splashed on his face. Cailean groaned. Every muscle pulsed with pain. His head drooped, but he was being held upright. Mercifully, someone had lengthened the rope suspending his arms, letting them rest against his back. Far less mercifully, as he began to rouse from the stupor, they drew the rope up again.

His left shoulder pulsed, then screamed in pain. Cailean's vision swam, darkness dancing across his eyes.

"Stop there," Torqual said.

"You don't want the prisoner's arms drawn higher, Champion?"

"We can dislocate his shoulders later. That's sufficient for now," Torqual said.

The hands holding Cailean upright released him, and he sagged. Pain tore through his arms. He straightened as much as he could, lessening the strain slightly.

"Make sure he doesn't fall over," Torqual said.

Heavy, metal-clad footsteps moved away from Cailean. He closed his eyes and focused on just breathing and waiting for the pain to subside.

"He's talkin' to the priests, eh?" a man said from Cailean's left.

"Yeah. Guess they got more in mind for this one," answered another from his right. He sniffed. "Heating up something."

The man on the left spat. "Probably roasting themselves strips of Tou's flesh or something. Poor dead bastard."

"Nah, I don't think even Murdo's priests are cannibals."

"I dunno. The humans, probably not, but that elf. Not so sure about him. I mean, his damned name is *Blight*!"

Both fell silent when steps thumped on the floor again. Cailean raised his head and turned toward the sound. Torqual returned, followed by the human in red and black, who carried a brazier full of glowing coals.

Torqual smirked at Cailean. "I wonder if Lyan saw this in the visions my lord has given him. I do hope so. I hope it reminds him of his time in Vynzent's hands."

Cailean's jaw tightened. *Just get it over with, Torqual.*

He regretted that thought the moment searing metal pressed into his back.

The men to either side held him upright. Cailean braced for a second brand, but it never came. Sweat trickled down his face. He panted for breath.

Torqual held a mug to his lips. *I should refuse. It could be poisoned or drugged.* Cailean slowed his gasps enough to drink without choking. It tasted like watered wine, and if it was drugged, the effects did not include dulling pain.

Torqual and the priest left him again, offering no hints as to the purpose behind the single application of the hot iron—assuming that any purpose lay behind it beyond inflicting pain in unpredictable sessions.

Cailean closed his eyes. Throughout the building, he heard movement. People collecting gear, talking in low voices. Deciding what to loot and what to leave.

*They're preparing to leave. What does Torqual intend? Is he being judicious in his tortures because he intends to drag me with him? What about Solstice?* He felt the Spear's presence, but Solstice had been silent since he last roused. *"Solstice."*

Guilt.

*"Solstice. Answer me."*

*"This is my fault, Cailean. My doing. My mistakes."*

Cailean found no response. He couldn't argue the Spear's assessment, but it was far too late to undo what Solstice had done. He tried to focus. *"Torqual is leaving. If he is taking us with him, he has to move us outside these runes, or wardings, or whatever keeps your powers bound. We might have a chance to…"* To what? To fight Torqual, the Mad God's priests, and Torqual's men alone?

*"To escape,"* Solstice whispered. *"Yes."*

"What about the prisoner, Champion? You want him moved into the cage?"

Hearing the question, Cailean raised his head. A squat man spoke to Torqual, not far from him. A shiver of fear ran through Cailean. A cage could be warded, just as this spot where he knelt was.

"No need to cage him yet. The prisoner isn't coming with us. He has a different destination," Torqual answered. He turned, met Cailean's eyes, and gave him a cold smile.

Men filed out of the hall, including the pair who'd been tasked with keeping Cailean from collapsing. Without their support, he sagged, stabbing fresh, sharp pain through his back and shoulders. By the time he could spare attention for anything outside the agony, the hall was nearly empty.

Torqual still remained. "Blight."

"Yes, Champion." The bald elf strode into Cailean's line of sight.

"Once you've finished attending to matters here, cage the prisoner. If he gives you any trouble, break an arm or leg or something. That should keep him quiet for a while. We'll leave the draft horse to pull the cart. Head to Ceolvost. A ship will be waiting to take you, and him, back to your land."

Blight bowed. "Thank you, Champion."

"Give your honored astrologers my regards," Torqual said.

"Of course."

"Do you need anything else to prepare the case?"

Blight eyed Cailean. "A taste of the Spearbearer's blood."

Torqual smirked. "Take as much as you want."

"I fear he would not survive if I were to do that. I require only a taste to complete the seal." Blight drew a knife.

Cailean snarled, but struggling roused too much pain without hope of escape. He didn't know, and certainly didn't want to ask, how literally Blight meant a "taste" of his blood.

Blight opened a shallow slice on Cailean's ribs, over his heart, and let blood ooze onto the blade. He touched the point of the blade to his lips and smiled. "Yes, this will serve."

"Serve… for what?" Cailean hissed.

"The seal on Solstice," Torqual answered. "Or did you

think I would simply send Blight on his way without ensuring both you and the Spear were sufficiently contained?"

A wave of fear radiated from Solstice. Cailean shuddered.

Torqual chuckled. "I know better than to think you'd quietly accept your inevitable defeat. I'd know that even without the visions my lord's given me. But we both know, Cailean, without Solstice, you're nothing."

Cailean glared at him. "I'm going to mount your head on a pike." He forced the words through clenched teeth

"Perhaps," Torqual agreed easily. "But not until after you've learned the teachings of the Faithful, and bowed to our lord. Blight assures me that they are ready and eager to begin their lessons. Safe journeys, Cailean. I look forward to our next meeting." With a final maddening smirk, Torqual strode from the hall.

"I will never bow to Murdo," Cailean hissed after him, but the fear he felt no longer originated just from Solstice. *What does he see in these visions he boasts about so confidently? Where does Blight intend to take us? Can he truly keep Solstice sealed and restrained?*

The hall stood empty. He couldn't see Blight any longer, but he heard movement on occasion. Sounds of people outside faded into silence. Time crawled like a stinging centipede, sharp with pain and fear.

Soft steps approached him from behind. Cailean tensed. *If he intends to lock me in a cage, I won't go without a fight.*

The steps halted, then a voice whispered in his ear. "Try not to scream, Tathren. This will hurt."

He drew a startled breath. *Nylas? Is that really—how?*

Someone gripped the rope that kept his arms suspended, pulling it down slightly. Vibrations ran through the rope. Cailean winced, squeezing his eyes shut and biting his lip until he tasted blood.

The rope gave. He fell forward. Nylas caught him and eased him down to lie face-down on the floor. His hands were still bound behind his back, but after a moment, those ropes yielded as well, followed by the restraints on his legs. Cailean's eyes watered in relief. He tried to sit up, but moving his left arm sent agony lancing through his shoulder and stole his breath.

Nylas lifted him. "Can you walk?"

Cailean got his good arm over the elf's shoulder. His legs felt as unsteady as twigs. "Have to. Solstice. Have to get Solstice."

"Your man's taking care of the Spear," Nylas said, shifting his grip to support Cailean.

"My who?" *If what Solstice said was true, all my people should have gone through the portal to wherever the Spear sent them.*

"The one who nearly ran his horse into the ground to get back here after that stunt you pulled. Aikan."

Guilt, relief, and confusion struggled for dominion of his emotions. Nylas and Aikan, working together?

*"Solstice, is Aikan near you?"*

No answer.

Dread crept down his spine. *"Solstice?"*

A thin, strained answer. *"Hurry."*

Cailean gripped Nylas's shoulder. "Aikan needs help."

The elf didn't argue, nor did he ask how Cailean knew. He just growled a profanity and changed direction. Cailean gritted his teeth and pushed his legs as quickly as he could.

To one side, he saw a cart carrying a cage. The cage would fit a man, barely, for a cramped and unpleasant trip.

*How would he have kept me from calling for help? Magic? Or just stuffed my mouth with rags?*

Nylas pulled Cailean toward the far end of the hall, where a wall separated a small section from the rest of the open space. They turned the corner to find Aikan and Blight facing each other, weapons drawn, but neither making the first move to attack. Behind Blight, Solstice lay nestled in a long, slender box.

Cailean tried to call the Spear to him, but Solstice didn't

move. Jagged symbols like those that had encircled Cailean marked the box inside and out. He felt the Spear straining against them without effect.

Blight's eyes flickered away from Aikan a moment, taking in Nylas and Cailean. A thin smile played on his lips. "Ah, I see. A diversion. But which is your true goal? The Spear, or the man?"

Cailean slid his arm from Nylas's shoulder to give the elf free movement. He sagged against the partition wall, and the thin wood creaked in protest. If Aikan and Nylas distracted Blight, maybe he could reach Solstice.

Blight eyed them, but showed no alarm at the shift in numbers against him. "We need not fight," he told Nylas. "I will share my lord's rewards if you join the Faithful."

Nylas eyed him with disdain. "Not even those who succumbed to madness in Malgor Forest sank so low as to drink the blood of the fallen. Don't insult me."

"You refuse? A pity." Blight flicked his hand.

An invisible fist slammed into Cailean's chest, flinging him through the thin wall. He skidded across the floor, too breathless to cry in pain. The back wheel of the cart stopped him, sending fresh agony through his abused body and burned back.

"My lord!" Aikan spun and sprinted toward him.

*No. Solstice. Get Solstice!* He couldn't find the breath to speak.

Nylas stabbed at Blight. Blight sprang aside, fingers flickering with another spell.

*It took Lyan and Equinox to defeat the last priest of Murdo we faced.* Cailean's gaze fixed on the box that held Solstice. If he could only reach it, or someone could knock it over, free the Spear from the wards and enchantments that held it.

"My lord, do you hear me?" Aikan dropped to one knee beside Cailean and lifted him to sitting.

"Get. Solstice." Cailean gasped. *Worry about me later! Just get Solstice!*

Aikan answered with a curt nod. "Yes, my lord."

Nylas lunged at Blight again and scored a shallow cut on the other elf's arm. Aikan ran for the box. Cailean used the cart wheel to painfully drag himself upright, his gaze following Aikan with desperate hope.

Aikan made it to the box. Reached in to grab Solstice. Stiffened, and didn't move.

In Cailean's mind, Solstice strained, screaming but unable to reach the hand that hung just above it.

A burst of magic flung Nylas back through the remains of the partition wall. Blight laughed. "The seal is made with your blood, Spearbearer. It can only be pierced by the same." He walked to the unmoving Aikan. "All others will fail."

"No." The word rasped in Cailean's throat. He staggered forward, stumbled, and fell to his knees. White-hot lances of pain stabbed through his left shoulder when he tried to catch himself.

"Let them go and I won't fight you!" The words screamed from Cailean's mouth, but they weren't his own.

Blight paused, turning to eye him. The elf smiled. "I have no need to bargain with you, Solstice. You cannot fight my lord's power, nor can you protect these mortals."

He raised his knife and drove it into Aikan's heart.

Aikan's eyes opened wide. Blight ripped the blade free. Aikan sank to the floor, hands rising to his chest as if to staunch the flow of blood.

Cailean screamed in anger, grief, denial. He found his feet and staggered three steps toward Aikan. On the fourth, his leg refused to bear him, and he collapsed.

*No. No. No!*

Blight licked Aikan's blood from the knife, watching Cailean with a smirk. "Surrender, Spearbearer. Or would you rather make this journey over the corpses of more would-be protectors?"

Nylas lifted Cailean to his feet. The elf's cold eyes moved

from Aikan to Blight. "Unless you can use the Spear from here, I can't fight a priest of the Mad God alone," he warned in a low voice.

"My invitation remains open," Blight told Nylas.

"My answer hasn't changed."

"I won't offer again," Blight warned. "Refuse, and you join this one." He nudged Aikan's body with a toe. "Join me."

Cailean felt a surge of effort from Solstice, then he was pushed back within himself, aware, but unable to act. His fingers dug into Nylas's arm, and his voice hissed, "Elf."

Nylas looked to him and stiffened. "What in rot—?"

Solstice spoke softly. "You must get Cailean away from here. Take my bearer somewhere safe. Out of that elf's reach."

Nylas's eyes narrowed. "Are *you* really trusting *me* to protect Cailean?"

Cailean's mouth twisted in a thin, pained smile without humor. "Don't have much choice, do I?"

*"No. Solstice, what are you doing? I can't leave you!"* Cailean shouted.

*"You can. You will."* Solstice said. *"Aikan is dead. Lyan and the others are too far away. It's the only chance you have of escape."*

"No, you don't have much choice," Nylas said. "Fine. I'll protect him. You owe me."

Solstice grimaced. "Agreed."

Blight watched them, eyes narrow. "You have no fondness for the human Spearbearer. You sought to kill him not so long ago. Why protect him?"

Nylas met Blight's eyes. "Why? Because I'll fight alongside even a Tathren if it means spitting in the Mad God's face."

The wooden floor splintered and broke, roots bursting from the ground and whipping at Blight. Others wrapped around Aikan's body and pulled it back through the broken floor to the earth. Several grabbed for the case that held Solstice. Cailean's breath caught, and he dared hope the plants could succeed, but the moment the roots touched the case, they froze, just as Aikan had.

Blight cursed and unleashed magic at the plants assaulting him. Nylas gripped the waist of Cailean's trousers with one hand and the arm that Cailean had draped over his shoulder with the other and half carried, half dragged him from the hall.

"No," Cailean moaned. "Solstice."

"I can only get one of you out. Solstice picked you. I agreed," Nylas growled.

Cailean didn't have the strength to fight, and even his protests faded into gasps of pain. He slumped heavily against Nylas and tried to walk, though he knew his efforts were all but useless. Without support, he couldn't even stand.

Nylas dragged him outside and across the clearing. Spits of rain still fell, but the storm had passed on. The sky was growing dark, and twilight was a muted glow through the clouds.

Looking back, Cailean saw thorny brambles pushing through the mud in their wake, filling the clearing with thick walls. He didn't know if they would slow Blight for long, but any delays could only help their escape.

*Without Solstice.* Cailean's free hand grasped at empty air. His eyes stung.

Nylas carried him into the forest. All Cailean could do was keep his feet moving until finally Nylas stopped. Cailean roused from his stupor to see a horse hobbled beside a tree. Aikan's mare, Ember. She stopped her browsing of the undergrowth to watch them approach.

"Can you get on the horse, Tathren?" Nylas demanded.

Cailean blinked at him several times before the question made sense. He started to lift his free arm toward the saddle. Pain left him gasping, and his arm fell back to his side again.

Nylas growled curses under his breath. He loosed Ember

and led her to stand beside a stump. "High enough? We don't have time to waste."

Nylas helped him onto the stump. From the improvised mounting block, Cailean finally gained the saddle. The mare shifted and snorted, but settled once Cailean found his seat. He curled his fingers through her coarse mane.

"Where's Aikan?"

Nylas eyed him, as if wondering whether Cailean realized his steward was dead. "He's safe from the Champion's minion." The elf took Ember's reins and started walking. She heaved a heavy breath, but followed.

"Blight uses blood for magic," Cailean persisted, each word forced.

"I am aware of that, Tathren. The forest has your man's body and will protect it from Blight. I saw what that abomination did to the wounded human the Champion gave him." Nylas paused and collected packs from a pile on the ground. He slung two over his shoulder and hung the other four from Ember's saddle. A tangle of roots grew over the rest, hiding them from sight. Not that Cailean could see much in the night-darkened forest.

"Saw? How?"

"That building had sturdy rafters, and humans don't think to look up nearly often enough." Shouldering the packs, Nylas kept walking.

*Where are we going? Does Nylas know where the others are?* "You came with Aikan?"

"No, Tathren. I never left. When you, or the Spear, decided to send people away, you neglected to take everyone." The elf's voice was sharp.

Cailean winced. "I..."

"I saw the Champion take you down. His taunts told me enough to figure out what actually happened." Nylas fell silent. After several minutes, he spoke again. "Blight is still hunting, but he's not going too far from the clearing. I wagered he'd hesitate to leave Solstice unwatched for too long."

Cailean lifted his head. "I need Solstice."

"And *I* need an army," Nylas growled. "Or at the very least, I need the rest of my warriors."

"You know where they are?" Cailean managed. Every word scraped his raw, dry throat.

"I know where Patch is," Nylas said. "Now shut up."

Cailean closed his eyes and silently wished for relief from the pain—both that of his body and that of his soul.

2 4

—————

# KITHR

*"The greatest deeds of a man are those by which he should be*
*remembered. Let he who fell defending his home, his land, his lord, never*
*be forgotten—let his name last on forevermore."*
*~Eulogy for the Hero, unknown Tathren author*

Kithr paced. He knew he should try to sleep, but his thoughts continued to prod him toward action. He hated stopping, no matter how exhausted they all were or how secure the campsite.

The forest stood quiet, only the usual sounds of night around them. Most of Nylas's men had lost their gear, having no chance to grab it before Solstice tossed them through the darkness. The refugees rescued from Torqual had only the clothes on their backs. Kithr had told the humans they were free to leave, but none had. He supposed they didn't have anywhere else to go now, and saw the appeal to remaining with their rescuers, even if those rescuers were elves.

People slept in clumps for warmth, sharing cloaks and their few blankets. Kithr silently thanked the Tathrens for their pack horses and for carrying most of his and Lyan's gear on the animals.

Yion walked the perimeter of the camp. When he passed, Kithr said, "Your wards are just as whole as they were the last time you checked them."

Yion paused, then acknowledged Kithr with a nod. "So I assure myself, yet the need to look again remains. Much as the need to be moving does for you."

Kithr finally stopped. "Torqual is the Mad God's champion. I could have killed the mud-grubber in Cailean's keep. I *should* have killed him then. This wouldn't have happened if he was dead."

"Cailean stabbed him in the gut. Aikan sliced open his arm. We had every reason to expect Torqual to bleed out to a painful death," Yion said. "I too could have seized the opportunity to end his life. But I think it too much to hope that we would not be in similar straits had the role been given to another. And I believe it would have been given to someone, Kithr. Torqual, at least, is known to us. We may yet find that to our advantage."

Kithr made a sound of frustration. He looked into the darkness. "We shouldn't be stopping now. Torqual could be killing our people back at that clearing."

"Offering him one more target would be little help, Kithr," Yion said.

Someone darted to them. Kithr turned. "Patch?"

"The Captain is near," she said. "Coming toward us."

Kithr straightened. "Anyone with him?"

"I can't tell that. I can only sense the piece of Malgor Forest within him. But I think that if he intended to return alone, he would have done so earlier."

"Make sure Lyan's awake," Kithr told her.

Patch hurried off, returning shortly with Lyan in tow. Heavy shadows lined Lyan's face and he held his cloak wrapped tightly around himself. He'd spoken little during their forced march, and even less since saying they should make camp. If he'd slept since they stopped, it hadn't been long enough to ease his exhaustion.

*He must have known that Torqual was the Mad God's champion. Torqual himself said as much. Does this mean Lyan knew this would happen as well?*

"Lyan, should we expect trouble on Nylas's heels?" Kithr asked quietly.

Lyan shivered. "I don't know. Maybe. If there is, it's probably a construct. But not as large or strong as the one we saw before. Or there may be nothing. I don't know." He looked out into the darkness rather than meeting Kithr's gaze.

"Which is better?" Kithr asked. It seemed like no pursuit would be preferable, but he didn't trust his own judgment on the matter.

Lyan shook his head. "Both have challenges. Just… different challenges."

One of Nylas's men, Gessern, slipped from the shadows to Kithr's side. "Sir, a horse approaching. One rider, one man on foot. I think the one on foot is Captain Nylas. Didn't see anyone else near them."

"Only one with Nylas?" A chill of apprehension ran down Kithr's spine.

"Only one," Gessern confirmed. He sounded nearly as concerned as Kithr by the news.

*Aikan wouldn't leave without Cailean. But how else would Nylas have a horse? Did he steal one from Torqual? I didn't notice mounts there, but perhaps they were stabled on the other side of the hall.*

Nylas didn't attempt to conceal his approach. He climbed the single clear trail to their campsite, trailed by a weary horse bearing a slumped rider. He stopped before Kithr, Lyan, Yion, and Patch. "Good of you to wait for me," he said.

"That wasn't the withdrawal I intended, and leaving anyone behind wasn't my idea," Kithr said. "Are others following?"

"Anything following us isn't friendly." Nylas looked past Kithr and jabbed a finger toward his target. "You. Take the horse and your lord."

A muzzy Shiolto answered. "Huh? What?"

"The horse. And your lord," Nylas repeated curtly.

"You found Lord Cailean?" Shiolto asked, stepping closer.

The rider stirred, raising his head enough that Kithr confirmed he was, in fact, Cailean. Something looked wrong about his silhouette. Not just his slumped, pained stance—something important was missing.

Shiolto took the reins from Nylas. "This is Ember, Aikan's mare. Where is he? Did he send you ahead with Lord Cailean?" Even Shiolto clearly questioned the likelihood of Aikan entrusting Cailean to Nylas.

Nylas ignored the question. "Lyan. We need to talk."

"Where is Aikan, Nylas?" Kithr cut in.

"Safely out of reach of the priest of the Mad God who murdered him."

Shiolto froze, eyes wide. "Aikan? Murdered?" he whispered.

A sharp pang ran through Kithr. Shock, he was sure. Not grief. He couldn't possibly feel grief for a Tathren who had loathed every elf he met.

Lyan shuddered, closing his eyes. "And Cailean?"

"Captured and tortured," Nylas answered bluntly. "In the absence of other options, Aikan and I allied to free him. The rest of my men who the Spear left behind fell to the Champion and his men."

Shiolto and Yion lifted Cailean from the horse. Finally, Kithr identified the absence that nagged at him. He lowered his voice. "And Solstice?"

Nylas glowered. "Do you want my report in *order* or in pieces, Kithr?"

"In order," Kithr said finally.

The sound of Nylas's voice, low though it was, roused

some of the elves. Kithr didn't know what they thought, seeing only Nylas and Cailean, and none of their other missing. He could all but hear the whispered rumors begin.

Patch's gaze followed Cailean, then she turned back to Lyan. "Cousin." Her voice held a note of reproach.

"Aikan's choice, Patch," Lyan said softly. "One I wouldn't take from him."

Kithr looked from one to the other. The visions that Lyan's curse inflicted must have shown him the possibility of Aikan's death. *And what alternative was worse than that, Lyan? How did letting him go alone to his death do anything but give Torqual cause to gloat?* He glanced to Patch again. Her reproach to Lyan implied she'd also known, or suspected, what would happen, and believed that Lyan could have prevented it. *How could she know, though? She's no diviner. Gods help us, she couldn't possibly be a Seer. There's only one Seer of Eilidh Wood, and it is not Patch.*

Lyan motioned for Kithr and Nylas to follow him to a corner of camp with the illusion of privacy. Nylas scowled at both of them. "You're fortunate I didn't think either of you capable of outright betrayal and abandonment."

Kithr bristled, but he understood how things must have looked to Nylas. "Solstice evidently disagreed with the idea of retreating, and didn't want to be interrupted."

"I gathered that," Nylas said. "While I was trying to determine what, exactly, happened and why Patch was suddenly miles away, I saw Cailean's fight against the Champion."

"Torqual was one of the Tathrens who took part in freeing you from Ewart's keep," Lyan said.

Nylas nodded. "I recognized him. He taunted Cailean into attacking. I hope the Spearbearer is normally a better fighter than that, because he was an idiot there. Paid no attention to his surroundings until they actively interfered with the fight."

"Solstice was manipulating him," Lyan said.

Nylas gave him a long, hard look. "Is *that* why you aren't carrying Equinox?"

"No. Equinox must protect its shrine. And Equinox and I have a better understanding of each other than Cailean and Solstice do."

Nylas snorted. "From what I saw, that wouldn't be difficult. Torqual used those balevines to poison Cailean and take him prisoner." Nylas gazed at Lyan, eyes narrowing. "He also had some interesting things to say once Cailean roused. About Solstice and Cailean—which explained who actually was responsible for your sudden disappearance. Also, about visions."

Lyan went very still.

"You are having visions, aren't you?" Nylas pressed.

"You already heard the answer from Torqual," Lyan said tightly.

"I want to hear it from you," Nylas said.

Lyan's jaw tightened. "Yes."

"So you knew this would happen."

"No," Lyan said sharply. "I knew it *could* happen. And I knew how much worse things could be if I warned anyone. Or how much better they could have been if Solstice trusted Cailean."

"You still haven't explained where Solstice is," Kithr cut in.

Nylas scowled at him for interrupting. "Torqual had at least two priests of the Mad God there. One of them was an elf."

Lyan sucked in a sharp breath. Kithr stared at Nylas. "Impossible."

"An elf," Nylas repeated. "Torqual called him one of the 'Faithful'. His name is Blight, and he's more twisted than any Lost elf. He used sacrifices and magic strengthened with blood to craft a crate that blocks Solstice's power."

"What? *How* is that even possible?" Kithr hissed.

"The Mad God can block the Spears' powers," Lyan said. "And he can teach his followers rituals to temporarily do the same." He shivered. "Believe me—I know."

"What Blight made didn't look temporary," Nylas said. "When Aikan and I went in to free Cailean, the Spear was already in the case. Whatever wards Blight put on that case, they paralyze anything that touches it, presumably aside from Blight and Cailean. He said they were crafted with Cailean's blood, and can only be broken by the same. Aikan tried to take the Spear. Blight killed him while he stood there, unable to move."

Kithr's stomach sank. "Then Solstice is still there."

Lyan closed his eyes a moment. "And Cailean can't call the Spear back to him." He raised his head and looked at Nylas. "Torqual didn't stop you from freeing Cailean?"

"Torqual left with his men before Aikan and I made the attempt to free Cailean," Nylas said. "He and Blight had some sort of arrangement where Blight's supposed to bring one of the Spearbearers to his homeland. Torqual gave him Cailean and Solstice, and said a ship would be waiting for them in Ceolvost."

Kithr cursed softly. "Knowing Torqual, he'd have ensured Cailean wasn't able to fight, either."

"He can't stand without help and limps badly even then. Also, something's torn or out of joint in his left arm." Nylas's gaze narrowed on Lyan. "Were you aware that the Mad God's minions know how to inflict pain directly to the Spears? And that torture is felt by the Spearbearer as well?"

"I learned that not long ago," Lyan said. "Through the visions."

"Cailean learned personally. It looked agonizing."

Kithr cursed again. *Aikan dead, Cailean disarmed, Solstice sealed and imprisoned. If Torqual is trying to force us to choose between disasters, he's setting the scene for it well.* "Anything more you can tell us?"

Nylas rubbed his left arm, scowling at an oozing rivulet of liquid too thick and pale to be blood. "Torqual was bleeding pretty well after the fight, but I never saw him tend his injuries, just cleaned the blood off his armor. In fact, other than the helmet, he never removed a piece of armor. Both priests wore blood red tunics and black pants. The rest of his men didn't have any sort of uniform or cohesive unit."

Kithr glanced to Lyan. "If this priest wants Cailean, how likely would he be to chase after Nylas?"

Lyan shook his head. "Not personally. He wouldn't leave Solstice unguarded."

From elsewhere in the camp, Shiolto's voice rose. "Lord Cailean, please, lie still!"

Kithr turned. Cailean had roused to some level of awareness, and attempted to stand. Shiolto was trying to calm and dissuade him.

"Better check if his eyes are black," Nylas said.

"What?" Kithr looked at him.

"When Solstice talks through Cailean, his eyes turn black —no whites. If his eyes are black, Solstice must be close enough to reach him. The Spear can do *that* even with the wards."

Kithr rose and joined Shiolto. Cailean's eyes were wide and wild, but not black. "What's going on?" Kithr asked.

"I was trying to clean the burn on his back," Shiolto said. "He started fighting."

Shiolto hesitated to restrain his lord. Kithr knew no such compunction. He caught Cailean by the shoulders. Cailean gasped in breathless pain, and Kithr remembered what Nylas said about an injury to Cailean's arm.

"Stop fighting, Cailean. We're on the same damned side!" Kithr growled.

"No. Solstice." Cailean panted for breath, sweat beading on his skin.

"Tathren! Look at me!"

Cailean finally focused on him. Kithr crouched, holding Cailean's wrists. "Shiolto is tending your injuries. You're in our camp. Nylas brought you here. Do you understand?"

"Kithr." Cailean let out a trembling breath. "Solstice. Need. Have to…"

"We'll get Solstice back," Kithr promised.

Cailean shook his head. His hands opened and closed, grasping at the air. "Solstice hurts."

"Ash and rot." *Is that priest using Solstice to continue torturing Cailean?* Kithr looked around the camp. "Yion. Make something to dull his pain."

"At once." Yion collected one of his bags and set up a small tripod over the coals of their fire.

"Kithr, I probably don't want to know what that means, do I?" Shiolto asked. "What Lord Cailean just said."

"No, you probably don't," Kithr told him. "But you still should. Later. For now, do what you can."

Cailean didn't fight Shiolto's ministrations further, sinking back into a daze occasionally interrupted by sounds of pain. Kithr stayed close at hand.

Everyone not completely lost in exhausted sleep had woken. Low murmurs of voices hung in the background as those who had been awake longer offered sparse details to those just rousing. Kithr kept one eye on Lyan and Nylas, but whatever they discussed, if anything, they did so without open hostility.

A sentry rushed to Kithr. "Sir, something's coming!"

Kithr rose. "One of our people?" His movement drew Nylas's notice, and Kithr motioned for Nylas and Lyan to join him.

"No," the sentry said. "Not a person. It's something else."

Suspicious, Kithr followed the sentry until he could see the trail. He paused to string his bow and draw an arrow from his quiver. He wasn't surprised when Nylas and Lyan joined him, though he wished Lyan would stay further back.

A four-legged shape slinked up the path. It didn't move like an animal, nor anything else Kithr could identify. Branches and mud formed the body, though the claws and fangs looked like polished bone. Beads of golden light marked its eyes.

Seeing them, it stopped, hissed, and sat back on its haunches. The eyes fixed on Nylas, and it opened a jaw full of sharp fangs. From the depths of its throat, a hollow voice spoke. "So this was your goal. You have brought us to an impasse, it seems."

Nylas folded his arms. "I'm not returning the Spearbearer to you."

"Won't you? Very well."

Kithr frowned. The acceptance of Nylas's declaration came far too easily.

The creature continued. "Tell the Spearbearer that Solstice and I will await him in Ceolvost. If he comes without causing trouble, I will spare those whom he calls friends. If he does not, he shall make his journey over the blood and corpses of those he cares about."

Kithr set his arrow to the string and drew. Lyan put a hand on his arm. "Don't bother. Attacking the construct won't hurt him."

The creature turned back down the trail, but paused and cast a look over its shoulder. "Do warn the Spearbearer not to tarry. I am eager to return home, and if he keeps me waiting too long, I will gladly remind him again of the connection between Spear and bearer."

Kithr's arrow struck it in the shoulder, but the construct only laughed. "I will remember your face, child of Eilidh Wood. Tell the Spearbearer—Ceolvost. I will await you all there."

The creature loped down the path, shedding twigs and mud as it went. Before it reached the end of the trail, it crumbled into a broken pile of debris and bone fragments.

Kithr glared into the darkness. "Torqual is heading for the Shrine of Equinox, isn't he, Lyan? Now this priest wants us to chase him down rather than pursue Torqual."

"Do we split our forces?" Nylas asked. "A smaller group to hunt Blight, the rest to harry the Champion?"

"No." Lyan's voice left no room for argument. "We don't split up. We need Solstice. *Cailean* needs Solstice." He drew a deep breath. "As soon as Cailean can travel, we make for Ceolvost, and we bring this 'Faithful' elf to his end."

"It's about time you started giving orders like a Spearbearer," Nylas said. "To Ceolvost, then. We have a priest of the Mad God to kill."

End

# APPENDIX: GODS OF NOTE

GODS OF EILIDH WOOD:

**Soldarr:** The one male of the three gods of Eilidh Wood, Soldarr wields a battle axe in combat and is said to be a fierce warrior. In times of peace, he is lover to both Feyra and Tesseia. In the past, he has also engaged in trysts with mortal women; however, no such unions have been reported since Tesseia threatened to castrate him the next time he did so. Soldarr and the Tathren god Ahebban bear a grudge regarding Ahebban's half-elf daughter Venycia and her decision to becoming a Guardian of Equinox rather than following the wishes of her father.

**Feyra and Tesseia:** The goddesses are sisters, and both wield bows in combat. They are said to have a stronger connection to Eilidh Wood than Soldarr, understanding the forest and its whims more easily. Some Tathren priests claim that in addition to being lover to Feyra and Tesseia, Soldarr is also their brother, however, the gods vehemently deny this claim.

GODS OF TATHER:

**Ahebban, Watcher on the Walls:** Ahebban is the protector of fortresses. When a Tathren keep or stronghold is completed, the priests of Ahebban ask his blessing on it. One part of the ritual blessing calls for the god's protection on the fortress to prevent anyone outside the walls from using harmful magic against the keep or anyone inside it. He bears a fierce anger against Soldarr, and, by extension, the elves of Eilidh Wood. The bear is sacred to Ahebban. He is father of Venycia, Guardian of Equinox.

**Saiboti:** Brother to Ahebban, Saiboti is the Tathren god of warriors. He doesn't share his brother's fanatical anger against the elves of Eilidh Wood. He is known to be a god of honor, and expects those who follow him to act accordingly. The hawk is sacred to Saiboti.

**Erskine:** Erskine is the Tathren god of the fields and harvest, venerated by farmers and all who work the land. His exact feelings toward the elves of Eilidh Wood are unknown, though it's doubtful that he looks very fondly on the invaders who burned, destroyed, and looted farms and fields. The cat is sacred to Erskine.

OTHER GODS:

**Veil:** Veil is the god of divination. Said to live on the moon, Veil possesses the power to manipulate how the stars appear in the night sky. Astrologers interpret those signs to read fortunes and predict the future.

**Toirni, the Thunderer:** Toirini is the god of the weather, commonly called the Stormlord or the Thunderer. The nomads of the Apperet Plains revere him as a deity in their pantheon. He is the god they appeal to for rain. The power that Murdo has given to one of his minions, to cloud the sky, trespasses into Toirini's domain, but the Thunderer seems to be prevented from dispelling the clouds that hide the sky at night. He is father of Waldros, Guardian of Equinox.

**The Horselord:** The Horselord is the god of horses on the Apperet Plains, and primarily worshipped by the nomads there. Most depictions of him show him as a centaur.

**Nachyne, god of monsters:** Even the monsters have a deity. Nachyne rules over the monsters, including but not limited to dragons, fairies, pooka, and sirens. He's not known to care much for mortals or to any great shows of benevolence, even to his own worshipers. He tends to take the form of a dragon or a man with draconic wings, claws, and a tail.

**Cantorelle, god of roads:** Cantorelle is the patron god of travelers, and takes special interest in the protection of refugees, women, and children. He is often invoked before a journey. Cantorelle does not have temples, though sometimes travelers will build a shrine in his honor after completing a particularly difficult stretch of their journey.

The god of roads has an order of priests/defenders of the roads, called Freewardens. As the god of roads practices neutrality in national disputes, so do the Freewardens, and they are allowed to travel across any border, through any land, without being attacked or detained by the denizens of that land. Any people who they place under their protection are equally exempt. No wise person would abuse this protection, nor interfere with a Freewarden—Cantorelle is fond of his Freewardens, and angering the god of roads promises to make any future travels fraught with peril. He is father of Sirex, Guardian of Equinox.

**Jahrin, the Dreamer:** God of sleep, dreams, and nightmares, Jahrin is invoked both by those who wish restful sleep and by those who wish nightmares on others. He is said to be ever sleeping, and his waking heralds dire consequences.

# ABOUT THE AUTHOR

Sanan Kolva is a technical editor by day, and writer of epic and steampunk fantasy the rest of the time. She is the author of The Chosen of the Spears series and The Silverline Chronicles series. Her short fiction can be found in multiple anthologies.

When not writing, she can be found baking and decorating cakes, battling the forces of evil in various video games, and appeasing her feline overlords. Please drop in, leave a comment, or sign up for her newsletter at http://sanankolva.com.

If you enjoyed this book, please tell someone else who might like it, or leave a review on your preferred platform.